JANE SEXES IT UP

Jane Sexes It Up

TRUE CONFESSIONS
OF FEMINIST DESIRE

Edited by Merri Lisa Johnson

THUNDER'S MOUTH PRESS
NEW YORK

JANE SEXES IT UP
True Confessions of Feminist Desire

Published by
Thunder's Mouth Press
An Imprint of Avalon Publishing Group Inc.
245 West 17th St., 11th Floor
New York, NY 10011

AVALON
publishing group incorporated

Contents

Contents

To Mike and Cheryl Steed, who have housed me so generously. And to Reba Nell Johnson (Grandma) for saying there was nothing I could write that could make her stop loving me.

Acknowledgements

For their support and encouragement during the preparation of *Jane Sexes It Up,* I would like to thank Leslie Heywood, Susan Strehle, Kevin Sack, and Amy Blackmarr. I benefited as well from the financial support of my mother, Linda Maloney, who bought me all the vanilla lattés and queer theory my heart desired. Jane Gallop's foreword and Tony Ward's photo add an extra dimension of "sexy" to the book, and I am grateful for their contributions. The titles of sections one and two were inspired by the work of Carol Queen and the Kiss and Tell Collective, respectively. The collection as a whole drew on the energy and brazenness of many feminist writers and artists, too many to name individually. For their meticulous and heroic editorial assistance, I owe a very big thank you to Elizabeth Bickford at Four Walls Eight Windows and Joe Wilferth at the State University of West Georgia, and Kathryn Belden, for her patience and vision. Finally, the biggest thank you of all goes to the essayists included, all of whom endured a long and arduous process of writing and revision with admirable commitment and conceptual edge.

Foreword
Jane (Gallop) Sexes It Up
A Love Letter

DEAR LISA,

I read your introduction a couple of weeks ago, and it literally moved me to tears. I put my head down on my desk and sobbed with joy. The lifelong inarticulable experience of my sexuality had been articulated for the first time—by you—beautifully, elegantly, and very bravely.

As you wrote about "pussy shame," about fear, about little-girl emotions, and their place in big, strong, sexually assertive feminist women, I felt something expressed that is absolutely central to what I call my *sexity* (I find the word *sexuality* too big and proper and alienating and serious). For the first time in my forty-eight years, I felt "normal"; whereas before I had been trapped in my own personal inadequacy (expertly covered in both discourse and sexual performance by bravado, expertise, gutsiness, the performance I have learned to call "Jane Gallop"). I joined your project looking forward to the topping thrills of helping you (feeling my power and your need) but stumbled unexpectedly on your power to help me, where I felt most scared, most vulnerable, most silenced.

What I like about bringing feminism and sexuality together is that each term challenges the complacencies in the other. People who want to get rid of sexuality for the sake of their feminist politics and people who want to get rid of feminism so they can feel good about sex are choosing artificial comfort over the uneven path of conflict. I love that your book sharpens, rather than dulls, the edge between justice and desire.

I particularly liked Caitlin Fisher's wonderful memory of what girls really are like. I read it and thought about how much I had bought into the sense of girl's sexual innocence and vulnerability, even though I know better—not only because I remember my own girlhood but because every day I am amazed by the brazen power and desire that I see in my five-year-old daughter, Ruby, how she goes after pleasure and authority unabashed.

I liked Chris Daley's essay because it was modest and honest, not overblown, gave a sense of how sex is really lived, rather than the self-romanticizing overdramatizations in so many first-person accounts of "alternative" sex practices. I liked Katherine Frank's piece a lot—it's an honest, well-written, and complex look at stripping, which takes on a lot of the contradictions in feminism (especially around social class) and faces these contradictions rather than prematurely resolving them with mere wishfulness. I think Frank's way of thinking and writing is exemplary.

I admire Katinka Hooijer's bravery. She lives in Milwaukee as I do, and I've never met her, but I'd like to seek her out and tell her I admire this piece. Finally, I love Leslie Heywood's "The Importance of Being Lester." The writing is fabulous, completely compelling, and so is the concept. Leslie's piece, like Caitlin's, made me recognize something I know to be true but had not fully conceptualized before. With Caitlin's piece it was about the ambition and self-serving nature of little-girl will and pleasure; with Leslie's it's about the need to be accepted as one of the boys. If I had time I'd write an essay on what it means for Leslie's essay to be in a collection on sex. It challenges the category in a way I love.

Leslie and Caitlin are doing what you do in your "Pearl Necklace" piece—holding on to your nerve long enough to remember in public discourse what you know personally, even if it contradicts public feminist propriety. And by doing that you add to the honesty with which any of us can grapple with our bodies and our desires in this world.

I also find your pairing of man/girl in the first and third sections provocative—that's the real gendered pairing, not the logically balanced couples (man/woman, boy/girl), but the more eroticized, hypergendered man/girl. A certain puritanical feminism made both *man* and *girl* bad words, words for bad things. Both became sexier to me for it. I am drawn to what smells *man* or dangles *girl*. I am happy to see your *Jane* affirm both these elements in women's desire. It seems like a new, more expansive, more welcoming feminism—the feminisms I've been waiting for.

I want to conclude by "confessing" that in writing this foreword, I struggled with two conflicting desires—to indulge my own pleasure by writing casually, conversationally, enjoying the thrill of reading and writing about what pleases me; or to respond in a more professional role, addressing each essay equally, being a "good" academic, a "good" foreword writer, and a "good" feminist. Finally I came to see this bind as part of the very conflict between desire and politics at the center of your anthology, so that I am writing not only in my professional capacity as "Jane Gallop," lending name recognition and legitimacy, but also as *one* jane writing alongside *many* janes.

In fact, perceiving the discomfort and uncertainty of how to proceed as more than my own personal weirdness, shortcoming, or failure, considering the possibility that my experience could be widely shared, that inhabiting and speaking it might be of value—well, that is for me *the* hopeful perspective. And it is, I think, very much the wager of *Jane Sexes It Up*. If we are honest about our difficulties and contradictions, we can turn out to be . . . (what? the words coming to mind are all wrong, so I'll leave the sentence unfinished—full of possibility and capaciousness) . . .

Yours in excessive realness,

Jane Gallop

Jane Hocus, Jane Focus

An Introduction

MERRI LISA JOHNSON

> Sexuality, in all its guises, has become a kind of lightening rod for this generation's hopes and discontents (and democratic vision) in the same way that civil rights and Vietnam galvanized our generation in the 1960s.
>
> —Nan Bauer Maglin & Donna Perry,
> *"Bad Girls"/"Good Girls": Women,
> Sex & Power in the Nineties*

Generation X Does *the Sex Wars*

The world polices women—even now in this so-called postfeminist era—into silence about sex, socially constructed modesty, and self-regulating repression of behavior and fantasy. *Jane Sexes It Up*—a book of confessions and kinks—begins with this recognition of the very real limits on what a woman can say about her sexuality without putting herself in physical danger and/or social exile. Before going all out—balls to the wall, if you will—I want to acknowledge what we are up against. Each contributing essayist puts herself out there in the world, naked and exposed, not because she thinks it's safe to speak frankly

1

about sex, desire, bodies, and personal histories, but because she knows it's *not*. The fact of living in a rape culture underlines the bravery and seriousness of essays that might otherwise be taken as flippant, a-historical, privileged postfeminist play.[1] Our writing *is* play, but it is play *despite* and *in resistance to* a context of danger and prohibition, *not* a result of imagining there is none.

Young feminists in particular feel the edges of feminist history grind against the conservative cultural contexts in which our lives unfold; we live inside the contradiction of a political movement that affirms and encourages expressions of female and/or alternative sexualities, and the "real world" of workplaces, families, and communities that continue to judge women harshly for speaking of sex, much less expressing one's "deviant" acts and complex erotic imagination. Against a backdrop of half-truths and hypocrisy, this book is an action.[2] Erupting from the pressure points of women's lives, *Jane Sexes It Up* shoves propriety aside.

When I first imagined this project I thought that in writing it I would force feminism's legs apart like a rude lover, liberating her from the beige suit of political correctness. I wanted feminism to be *bad like me*. A young feminism, a sexy feminism. I found myself saying things like, "I'm not *that kind* of feminist," all sly innuendo and bedroom eyes. Early in my research, however, I discovered that *that kind of feminist* is mostly a media construct—oversimplification spiced with staged cat fights.

The spirit of *Jane Sexes It Up*, and many of its topics,

already appeared on the U.S. feminist scene more than a century ago in the form of debates between Social Purity activists (against prostitution) versus advocates of Free Love (for open marriages and other sexual experimentation), and then again two decades ago at the now infamous Barnard Conference on April 24, 1982, "The Scholar and the Feminist," where a conflict over what kinds of topics should and should not be covered turned into a long, divisive, legislative, media-mediated war over feminism's position on sex. The feminist Sex Wars that ensued got snagged once more on the seeming impasse of women fighting *for* sexual pleasure or *against* sexual danger.

Pro-sex or Anti-sex

Carole Vance's *Pleasure and Danger: Exploring Female Sexuality*, an anthology of essays from the conference, would have been our template—if we'd ever heard of it. But revolutionary ideas about sexual politics are consistently misrepresented or simply "disappeared" in most narratives of U.S. history. This face of feminism—the *smart-ass take-no-shit anarcha-orgasmic feminist persona* Gen X-ers thought we invented—is suppressed in the mainstream media. (I can only *begin* to imagine the ways corporate sponsors, women's tenuous positions as news reporters and anchors, and dominant American "family values" in the air like a toxic odorless gas converge to eclipse this unruly body of political thought.) Whatever conflicts exist within feminism, the first lesson for each generation must be about the politics of representation (which histories are handed over, which are not, and why); for it is frequently against "representations" of feminism as puritanical or anti-male or just plain crazy—not against feminism itself— that many young women posit our sexy "new" brand of bravado.

Rather than forcing ourselves on feminism, then, the *Jane* generation means to reconnect with our movement. The women who confess their messy desires in the following pages diverge purposefully from the path of "patriarchy's prodigal daughters"[3] (young women trading on *chic* renunciations of feminism) to forge a feminist sexual identity informed (not imprisoned) by the women whose writing came before us. Feminism—often addressed by young women as a strict teacher who *just needs to get laid*— is a name we want to reclaim for the intersection of *smart* and *sexy* within each of us. A theme emerges as several writers arrive via various routes at the same negotiation between feminism's most trenchant critiques of sexual politics on one hand and its devil-may-care libertinism on the other, finding fragments of desire and indignation in each direction, piecing together the usable past.

Vance's introduction to *Pleasure and Danger* bears repeating in this context, as we resist with her the loss of sexual pleasure as the "great guilty secret among feminists":

> The truth is that the rich brew of our experience contains elements of pleasure and oppression, happiness and humiliation. Rather than regard this ambiguity as confu-

4

sion or false consciousness, we should use it as a source-book to examine how women experience sexual desire, fantasy, and action.[4]

Jane Sexes It Up holds tightly to this belief that individual women's stories, narrow in scope and deep in reflection, aid in advancing the complexity of feminist social theory.

Young women define our politics in part by the second wave feminist legacy of sexual freedom—disrupting norms surrounding the body, unsettling rigid gender roles, and observing few, if any, boundaries on our speech as erotic creatures. Germaine Greer may have grown out of her "Lady, Love Your Cunt" days, but we are smack dab in the middle of ours.[5] Yet sex-positive spokeswomen, often anti-intellectual in tone, fail to give women new ways of thinking about fucking, new ways of understanding what's happening in our beds and to our bodies.

In a 1999 roundtable discussion with the bright lights of sex-positive feminism—Betty Dodson, Susie Bright, Sallie Tisdale, and Nancy Friday—*Nerve.com*, an enormously popular e-zine of "literate smut," asked, "How do you reconcile your feminism (or whatever you choose to call your convictions about sex and gender) with the more traditional feminine roles, behaviors, fantasies, positions, and exclamations that you may engage in (and perhaps even enjoy) in the bedroom?"—Susie Bright (a.k.a. Susie Sexpert, a regular columnist for *Playboy*) answers,

> What a weird question. I think you are trying to say, How can you be a feminist in the boardroom and a submissive

in the bedroom? Is that it? I don't have to "reconcile feminism," how ridiculous—I challenged feminism and demanded that it get a grip and come to terms with human sexuality. My whole written legacy is about that. I don't sit in bed with my dildo trying to rationalize anything!

Sallie Tisdale makes a similar response: "Once upon a time, I thought to be a feminist meant to eliminate all thoughts of submission. I couldn't—I didn't. I enjoy submissive postures and play sometimes—I don't see it as an issue or anything needing analysis anymore."

Seductive, this image of throwing feminism across the room like a pair of bottom-cupping panties. But as brave and brash as these women are, as alluring as their model of uncritical sexual freedom may be, their perception of sexuality "not needing analysis anymore" stems, I conjecture, from the wisdom of experience rather than widespread cultural change; in fact, they gloss over a very real conflict in many women's lives—especially those of us living far from big-city sex-positive cultures, even more so for a generation that was still in middle school in 1982 when the Barnard Conference touched off the first skirmishes over sexual correctness among second wave feminists. Crazy as it may sound, the feminists of Generation X *are* sitting in bed rationalizing our dildos.

Yet in feminist writing about sexuality, you get *either* the critique *or* the clit—not both—reproducing the mind/body split of masculinist Western philosophy that feminists fight in every imaginable arena in the world—except this one. Conversely, the sex-negative critique—what's *wrong* with fucking—has been creatively imagined and forcefully argued. Reading Andrea Dworkin unquestionably opens new ways of seeing sex, prompting a click in one's mind— marking that moment when something that has gnawed just below the surface of your consciousness, just below the level of language, emerges into plain sight.[6] Sex-positive writers have established no corresponding framework for understanding what we—as women, as feminists—*like* about sex. Or how to manage the relationship between what we like and what leaves us less enamored.

When Enough of Us Tell One Another It Is Okay

"Only women can liberate other women; only women's voices grant permission to be sexual, to be free to be anything we want, when enough of us tell one another it is okay."

—Nancy Friday, *Women on Top: How Real Life Has Changed Women's Fantasies*

The seeds of this collection, germinating long before I'd ever heard of any sex wars, lie inside a story about a girl named Bone, in her masturbation fantasies. They are not what you would call "appropriate." In them, what she wants and what she doesn't want get twisted together in startling configurations. Bone has been sexually abused by her stepfather, and she tells herself stories that turn this abuse into a scene she controls, into something erotic. Alone in bed she pulls cold metal chain links over her bare belly, a large rusted hook retrieved from a nearby river resting ominously between her legs, slippery with her body's response to the pictures in her head. She imagines her stepfather beating her—something he does often and severely—and she comes. Bone stands among the leather belts hanging down around her in Daddy Glenn's closet, feels their tough hide, breathes them in. Daddy Glenn raises welts on her legs, bubbles of water and blood form on her preteen backside. I picture this scene on my knees, forehead against the wall behind my bed, positioned over my lover's mouth.

Bone's story—*Bastard out of Carolina* by Dorothy Allison—is about more than abuse, invoking the transformative power of the erotic imagination to turn elements of an abusive environment into materials for escape: *fantasy, masturbation, orgasm*. Even this interpretation, though, is me putting a public feminist face on my messy wet response to the book. I shrink from the horror of "my abyssal self, my underworld."[7] Recognizing desire as both socially constructed and beyond social construction, Allison insists that a space must be made for women's wants—even when they are ugly, inexplicable, frightening—and I believe her. Sometimes the best thing feminism can say to a woman is, "Go easier on yourself, girlie. You don't have to make sense at every moment. You don't have to measure up to some abstract structure called *the right thing to do*."

In an essay called "Public Silence, Private Terror," Allison directly addresses this theme so powerfully dramatized in her fiction, calling for an honest look at "how we all actually live out our sexuality." She holds out her naked hand, taking some of the lonesomeness out of her admission that "we are all hungry for the power of desire and we are all terribly afraid." In feminism, "[t]he myth prevails," she concludes with dismay, "that 'good girls'—even modern, enlightened, liberal or radical varieties—don't really have such desires."[8] Despite my expectation that a number of feminists will join mainstream culture in condemning the desires confessed in these pages, *Jane Sexes It Up* presses forward sex-positive in a culture that demonizes sexuality, and sex-radical in a political movement that has been known to choose moral high grounds over low gutteral sounds. We press forward with this improper feminism in the spirit of Bone, the fictionalized but familiar girl-child inside us all who combats the abuse heaped on her body with stories of her own desire.

Jane Leaving Blue Rind Behind

A man steps up to the podium and introduces today's speaker: Catherine I. Eisenhower, who will be reading from her poetry dissertation, *See Jane*. Cathy is in her late twenties, a few years ahead of me in graduate school. I like her blunt bangs and cat-eye glasses. She looks like someone I'd like to know, but somehow we've never spoken. I watch her smooth command of the room—unassuming, unafraid—and feel an almost gravitational pull drawing me up tall in my seat. As she begins to read, I realize I have a crush on her.

Cathy reads her abstract and then her poems. When she gets to the one that will someday lend its title to this book, "Jane Sexes It Up," the room suddenly darkens into shades of blue—like dawn, like Salomé, the stripper I would work with years later, when at the height of the night shift's delerium, Doug the DJ would shine a shaft of blue onto Salomé's body and smoke would rise from a vent in the floor. When she danced, the strip club stood still—customers froze midgesture as they reached to pay for a drink, bartenders stopped midpour, an arc of liquor suspended above an empty shot glass, and me—my mouth hanging inadvertently open. That's how it was with Cathy when she introduced this poem with the offhand remark, "It's about masturbation." Nonchalant. Bold. Fucking hot. The whole room—desks, table, chalkboard—skidded sideways, three wheels in the air. Cathy's very third wave feminist assumption of independent female sexuality as a valid part of the public sphere sifted through my consciousness for years. The poem—not just the poem but its public reading— came to represent for me a certain sexual daring.

The figure of *Jane sexing it up* as I am using it here embodies a specific form of feminist writing that weds resistance with joy to create a sexuality that pleases and a world we can live with. *Jane*—this co-mingling of playfulness and effrontery—is Cathy when she introduced her poem about masturbation to the gatekeepers of her profession without flinching, and *Jane* is me admiring Cathy and her poem. *Jane* is the prepubescent girl I once was, masturbating in the basement shower long after the water ran cold, and *Jane* is her shame when daddy banged on the bathroom door with a bellow. *Jane* is, finally, the dialog between that doubtful sexual naif still crouching inside many grown women and the mature self-ownership and sexually confident women we aspire to be.

Jane is the conflict.

And the glee.

Jane Sexes It Up
by Catherine I. Eisenhower

Jane in her
blue skirt, Jane
in her prime
supple time,
Jane sifting,
Jane drifting,
Jane striding over
linoleum
like a legend.

She's hungry as a widow.
She yawns like
a lake.
She cuts her hair
on a broken chair
in the front yard, no
grass, no rain, air
dry as a tooth.

Jane in the
Chevy, Jane
leaving blue rind
behind.
Jane hocus,
Jane focus,
Jane sliding over
vinyl split
like a ripe fruit.

1

Fuck You
& Your Untouchable Face

Third Wave Feminism &
the Problem of Romance

MERRI LISA JOHNSON

SITTING IN THE TUB with my boyfriend in our
Marriott Hotel room, I rub my steamy face with wet hands
and try to decompress from the presentation. A mere
twenty minutes ago I shared a panel at a women's studies
conference with two other women writing for *Jane Sexes It
Up*. The positive response from our audience thrilled me,
but soon adrenaline drops away and exhilaration turns to
exhaustion, mildly manic euphoria winds down to vague
uncertainty. We—he and I—are talking about feminism.
Specifically, he is reflecting on his presence as one of only
two men we saw at the conference. Feminism, as a movement for social equality, he concedes, has noble goals, but

how viable can a movement be when its audience is so limited? Aren't you sort of preaching to the choir? We sit facing each other in the hot water, exchanging perplexed half
smiles. My lower back aches as I arch away from the cold
faucet behind me.

The Troubled Heart of Heterosexuality

I cringe as I write that word, *boyfriend*, in this context—
"[t]he qualifier 'heterosexual' is, at best, an embarrassing
adjunct to 'feminist'; at worst, it seems a contradiction in
terms."[1] Feminists are strong, independent women.
Boyfriends are people whose class rings you wear around
your neck—er, on a chain around your neck. Feminists
don't have boyfriends—do they?

Well. Feminists certainly don't talk about our boyfriends, except in bars late at night over drinks. Only in
these dark, liminal, off-the-record spaces do the sordid
details of our personal lives emerge—the obsessions and,
less frequently, the orgasms. We don't mention any of this
the next day as we pass each other in the hallways of our
professional lives.

Growing up with feminism like an eccentric aunt always
reminding us how smart we are, how we can do anything,
be anyone, the women of my generation hesitate to own up
to the romantic binds we find ourselves in, the emotional
entanglements that compromise our principles as we shut-
tle back and forth between *feminist* and *girlfriend*, *scholar*
and *sex partner*. For if feminism is right, and we *can* do

anything, be anyone, it follows logically that the obstacles we face must reflect personal failures, individual shortcomings in the face of unlimited feminist possibility.

For this reason, one of the hardest things for me to do *as a feminist* is admit that in relationships I willingly, or at least automatically, live within the man's emotional weather—quiet when he's withdrawn, ready to talk, fuck, go dancing, anything, *anything* he wants. I am infinitely flexible.

Except when I'm not.

You know what I'm talking about—those late-night screaming matches in the kitchen, throwing your favorite crystal goblet into the sink with a splintering crash, all the myriad ways suppressed anger, resentment, and human indignance eventually and inevitably march forth.

This portrait suggests that the twenty- and thirtysomething women of today inhabit a transitional period in U.S. history, with deferential femininity from the not-so-distant past layered beneath (not simply replaced by) hard won career-related advances toward equality. Women's rights have been part of pop culture lingo all our lives. All this apparent progress makes it hard to turn to my eccentric Aunt Feminism and say, "I'm still having some pretty big problems." Or, "I know I don't *have* to be the second most important person in a romantic relationship, but somehow I keep finding myself there anyway." (Why *do* I always choose the faucet end of the tub when my boyfriend and I go for a soak?)

The intellectual tools of feminism train women to see

through blockbuster movies like *Jerry Maguire* and to critique the enormous film industry perpetuating a myth of romantic love as *the* purpose of life. For savvy readers of media culture, an ironic distance from such scripts comes second nature. My dad taught me this lesson when I was three.

But—and here's the important part—when Jerry (played by Tom Cruise) finally comes to his senses and beseeches his precious, pouty, young wife to take him back, surrounded by a living room full of bitter divorced women, he utters three words that floor us: "You complete me."

Ohgodjesus—I could live on that for the rest of my life.

The longing for a man to make each of us feel *necessary* surrounds young women, is sedimented stubbornly in our most fundamental emotional fibers. (Now that I think about it, Tom Cruise may be personally responsible for a significant portion of Gen-X feminist angst; his brand of sexy—all ego and tenderness—has been thwarting the reconciliation of fantasy with feminism since I was, what, thirteen?) The contradictions of romance and feminism form the very curl and thread of our cultural DNA. Perhaps this explains the appeal of punk folk rocker Ani Difranco, whose lyrics are like the broken glass I sliced my palms with in eighth grade—sharp, dirty, and just a little dangerous. We like her bravado in the face of certain pain, her willingness to let the contagion of emotion spill "out of me, on to you." She pinpoints over and over again the precise place where fairy tale meets dark forest, the anguish of love never more intense than when just out of reach:

> You look like a photograph of yourself
> taken from far far away, and I don't know what to do
> and I don't know what to say, but
> *Fuck you* and your untouchable face.
> *Fuck you* for existing in the first place.[2]

I wish you could hear how concert halls go wild at these lines, wish you could see young women crying alone in their cars after a bad date or, worse, a good one. What is it that Ani captures so well here, what source engenders the exhilaration of this particular "Fuck You"? This gnashing of teeth, this rending of garments, this long bottled anger at, at—what?

The college-educated class may be hip to the exploitation of women's bodies—as sex objects, cheap labor, incubators—and most of us girls know something about *becoming the man we wanted to marry*, how women *can and should complete ourselves*. Yet somewhere between knowing and living, the ground gapes open and we all fall down.

Wanting Him Anyhow

I spent the last four years trying to convince a particular man to marry me. ("Think what you will! Shock, shock!")[3] You could say we broke up in August of 2000, you could even say we broke up over the marriage *issue*, but the truer thing to say is that our relationship modulated from marriage track to something less well defined but infinitely more pleasant.

I met this man at a time when he was turning decidedly

away from marriage, during the emotionally intense period between unofficial separation and legal divorce—not, most experts would say, the best time for forging new relationships, and he would have agreed. I, on the other hand, having been divorced for several years, and having recently extracted myself from a terribly mismatched couplehood formed in the desperate wake of my own divorce, was ready for my second husband, and he was going to be *it*.

Long story short, we fell madly in love despite all the odds and reveled in our passion for a long time and from very long distances. We rendezvoused in Vegas and Buenos Aires. I hung an old poster on my bedroom wall from a play called *Love Rides the Rails* to commemorate our unconventional affair and dedicated myself to becoming the *new* New Woman—independent, unpossessive, self-sufficient, supportive.[4] I would learn to love lightly, in May Sarton's phrase,[5] to be passionate without being desperate.

And indeed I did develop a more mature sense of self and of relationships through the interlocking processes of wooing him and getting over my need to be wooed, but the bottom line is, I also wanted him to marry me. To prove I was good enough. To win the prize, be the bride. Ever since my disastrous first run for beauty queen in sixth grade, I had longed deeply and stoically for the trophy and the glory. He wouldn't give me either.

And in my quiet reflective moments, I didn't want him to.

But something about the machinery of the relationship, with all the weight of heterosexual history bearing down on me, usurped my best feminist intentions, pressing my desires for companionship into cookie-cutter shapes—hard edged, straight, inflexible—and I ended up channeling some chick from the fifties, complete with hope chest and china pattern. Worse, I became a Whitney Houston song: "Hold me. Marry me. Love me forever and make me feel safe." Pitching idea after idea—"Marriage doesn't have to be *that way*. It can be whatever we (read: you) want"—I debated and finagled, strung long threads of philosophy, drew his attention to relevant movie plots.

Me: Don't you love me enough to make me your wife?

Him: I love you *too much* to make you something *that small*.

Me: You're right, you're right, I know you're right.

I stalked around my house like a cat making a fat tail, thinking *this is crazy!* Women have *way* more to lose than men by getting married. If anyone should be holding back, I huffed, it should be *me*. I knew about (and believed) feminist critiques of marriage, and truth be told, I *wasn't* sure I could revise it to please us both. All that notwithstanding, I wanted to marry him anyway. Part of me still does.

There is no clear moral to this story.

In the time since we "broke up," I have liked myself better, liked him better, and liked us better (on the occasional phone call or email message). I don't know how long something like this, without a name or any rules, can be sustained before it collapses into the available paths of *exes* or *getting back together*, but it feels like there's a clue or seed of relationship revolution in the dynamics passing between us now. Outside the prison house of our capital *R* Relationship, we are free to go about the business of enjoying each other once more. Now that I've given up the project of convincing him to marry me, I have less to lose by admitting in public that I don't know how to be a girlfriend or wife and maintain that space between us, that connection without clutching.

I can own up to the noteworthy fact that I've never felt as relaxed in a room with a man as I feel right now—alone after midnight, drinking coffee, and working at my computer. Solitude gets sexier and sexier the more I relax into it—like an herbal tea bath—let myself steep.

Feminism and the New Courtship

When a man says, "I'm no good at relationships. I have been alone for so long, perhaps I was meant to always be alone!" or "You'll probably come to hate me, deep down I'm a real asshole," take him at his word and run like the wind!

—Cassandra O'Keefe, "Girlfriend, Listen Up,"
The BUST Guide to the New Girl Order

I am thumbing through my copy of *Bitch: In Praise of Difficult Women*, by Gen-X author Elizabeth Wurtzel, and a star in the margin of the following passage catches my eye:

I think feminism has really taken us to the point where we cannot possibly discuss who does the dishes or who folds the laundry one more time. I don't give a shit. It's all the emotional figuring, the tallying of who is more in pursuit of whom this week, and how do we keep the romance alive, and am I being a nag, and are you tired of me darling—it's all this obsessive, circular, insomnia-driven dread that is still mostly women's work, and it's fatiguing as hell.[6]

Wurtzel basically says Fuck That. My stomach turns over when I read the lightly penciled question I wrote in awe and admiration a mere three years ago: "Will this be me at thirty?" At the time, I couldn't imagine saying Fuck That to the women's work of maintaining a love relationship. I would have done anything in exchange for traditional couplehood. This was, maybe still is, the weak spot in my practice of feminism, and I'm not the only one. "Helping a man get his 'head' together seems to have become the respectable post-feminist replacement for making him a cup of tea."[7] (This therapy culture terminology, let's be clear, probably means something less altruistic than supporting a man's growth as a human being and more like wrangling a marriage proposal out of him—a dubious cause for both parties.) Now nearing twenty-nine, I join Wurtzel in admitting I'm tired of that way of being in love, and I'd like to find some other way.

Whereas women now constitute a significant presence in the American workplace (though there's still more to be done on that front), we've come nowhere close to such an advance within the heterosexual couple (or without it, since single womanhood remains maligned as unorthodox). Feminist critic John Stoltenberg, author of *Refusing to Be a Man: Essays on Sex and Justice*, points over our often clouded heads at the structure of gender inequality curving across the sky like a benign arrangement of stars. Against the "common sense" notion that relationships are about "give and take" (one of those handy pocket-size credos people rarely examine before repeating), Stoltenberg writes, "The actual reality beneath 'give and take' may be quite different: for her, swallowed pride and self-effacing forgiveness; from him, punishing emotional withdrawal and egomaniacal defensiveness."[8] Stoltenberg's purpose is not to deride men, but to say that conventional masculinity poses a conflict between men's gender identity and their moral sense of right and wrong, and that upon making this realization, men can begin contributing to the antisexist work of reformulating the terms of romance. In such a world, perhaps communicating with one's lover would no longer be, as Wurtzel phrases it, quite so "fatiguing as hell."

The problem of women not being able to talk to men about or from the perspective of feminism spoils our best relationships. I've read tons of material on the work feminists have done to sustain dialogues between white women and women of color, between lesbians and straight women, between sex workers and antiporn legislators. But there's no body of work on sustaining feminist dialogue between women and men. And we're out here floundering—longing for feminism, making do with the Dixie Chicks. Men and women who have grown up with feminism *want* to be different from previous generations; we *want* to treat each other equally and with respect. But we don't know how.

This confusion is met all too often with the socially irresponsible Prozac feminism one finds in publications like *Cosmopolitan*, what cultural critic bell hooks calls "lifestyle feminism"—feminism women can claim "without fundamentally challenging and changing themselves or the culture."[9] Worn on the arm like a faux Fendi bag, this feminism goes with everything. An article written by Karen Lehrman in 1995, "Feminism and the New Courtship," illustrates this feel-good feminism and its pitfalls.[10] As with many feminists' work, I find myself agreeing in places with Lehrman, vehemently disagreeing in others, and unable to follow her logic at all in still others. She begins:

> I was brought up to like sex. Not by my parents, surely; the subject never made it past clinical descriptions. Somehow, though, enough feminist zeitgeist penetrated suburban Philadelphia during the seventies to convince me that not only was I allowed to like sex as much as a man, but I was also supposed to act as though I did.

Lehrman argues that by giving women the right to fuck, feminism makes her feel kind of funny realizing she prefers flowers first. And while feminism may have freed women to fuck, the fuck—and "the role of the fuck in controlling women"[11]—has in many ways stayed the same. Of equal importance, the virgin/whore divide still organizes most men's (and many women's) brains. Hence the persistence of modesty and shame closing like parentheses around supposedly liberated sex lives. Almost inadvertently, Lehrman reveals the weak link of feminism for this generation: how we can't seem to bring it into our relationships, admitting "there are still women who have, for example, Ph.D.'s in nuclear physics and who turn into naive, adoring little girls whenever they're in the company of men." This passage empties the political content of an important third wave concept, fetishizing contradiction for its own sake, not moving toward social change or personal growth. "It's horribly schizophrenic," she sighs. "At work, we're bulldozers, fearlessly asserting our opinions and ordering about our underlings. But socially, we hesitate, allowing men to make the first (and often the second and third) move. It's often more comfortable and fun this way. Is that so wrong?"[12] I guess I'd be oversimplifying things if I just answered "Yes."

Lehrman rightly points out the collisions of liberated ideas with real-life situations, but then seems to lose her train of thought, and instead of imagining new ways of being in relationships, she hearkens to some idealized past when men were polite, and women treasured. She makes trenchant critiques of heterosexual romance:

> My female friends complain that in addition to having trouble finding a man who's discovered his emotions, it's nearly impossible to find one who is secure enough to support them in their own career. (I sometimes think there's an inverse relationship between a man's professed desire to do good in the world and his ability to have an egalitar-

ian relationship.) A few friends have resigned themselves to finding men who at least don't mock their goals.

But she follows these valid complaints with opiates like "maybe the most important thing we've discovered is that some things are not going to change—and that we wouldn't want them to anyway." The glaring non sequiturs of Lehrman's painful observations and popcorn light conclusions only make sense in the context of her self-identified position within a "transitional generation" of "feminism's guinea pigs."

Perhaps we are witnessing the newest incarnation of the "problem that has no name." Betty Friedan's code for housewife malaise in the 1950s hints at the emotional distress Gen-X feminists feel, a product of being caught between phases of social change, lodged between the idea of liberation and its incomplete execution.[13]

The Dirty Little Secret of a Generation

Oprah has called it a silent epidemic. The women of America are flocking to Chicago to reveal a terrible secret from behind closed bedroom doors. They have little or no desire for sexual intercourse. There's no ignoring it anymore: *women don't want it*. The camera pans the crowd, cutting from one face to another; hair swings side to side in sync as guest after guest admits that yes, she too feels sex is a chore, something to avoid, a service, a nuisance. It's just *gone*, they exhale, wide-eyed and glassy, observing from the sidelines the dip and swell of their own sex drive. Oprah has put her finger on it once again—the pink nubby pulse of the nation (or lack thereof). Yet, as is frustratingly common to the show, she slides along the surface of the problem, then veers into various ruts of conventional wisdom. Her guru of the day chalks it up to women's internalized sense of themselves as mommies rather than hotties, avoiding all the truly interesting, complex questions like why can't mommies *be* hotties, or what could the *men* in the audience be doing to make sex more physically pleasurable to these women? Perhaps the epidemic is not that women don't want sex, but that women don't want sex *as we know it*.

Conversely, what sex-positive culture leaves unresolved is how to be a woman who loves sex, even likes it *mean* now and then, but still feels enmeshed in inequality in heterosexual couplehood to the extent that she can't or won't say what she wants out of erotic encounters, in which case the heterosexual bedroom remains locked, a private arena of tense physical exchanges and inarticulate desire. Concern about a male lover's ego combines with one's own insecurities to produce muted pleasures. Quietly, secretly, we search for the right tone of voice, struggle against the undertow of misogyny in our bodies and culture, knowing of no register for "discussions" initiated by women other than bitching, nagging, complaining, whining. "It's the dirty little secret of a generation," Peggy Orenstein confides, "young women . . . feel an entitlement to sexual pleasure on which they can't convince themselves to act."[14]

The following email is my own dirty little secret. In

exposing it here, I am outing myself as one of those women who hold Ph.D.'s in nuclear physics (actually mine's in literature, but you get my meaning) who turn into adoring little girls in the presence of the men we so long to be loved by. This is me, meek and knock-kneed, walking the tightrope between a feminist rhetoric of equality and a feminine appeal for male benevolence. Listen for the halting speech of my competing needs and allegiances.

July 23, 2000. 8:56 P.M. (E.S.T.)

Subject: Sex—Doing It & Doing It Well[15]

Dear K____,

I am reading the book I mentioned to you a while back, *When the Earth Moves: Women and Orgasm* by Mikaya Heart, skimming it really, sexpert that I sometimes take myself to be. I don't immediately count myself among the book's audience of women who need to be prodded to overcome their inculcated shame over sexuality. I'm not uncomfortable with sex. Or am I? I made myself slow down and reread a section titled "Asserting Ourselves," a subject I initially assumed fell below my level of sexual sophistication. Heart writes,

> "[A]t some point in your lifetime you need to take charge and make sex into a form of play where you make the rules and call the shots. . . . [I]f you never say, 'Okay this is what I want,' then the relationship can never grow. . . . [D]ecide what it is you really want and negotiate with your partner from there."[16]

I took it for granted that I know my "rules," my pleasures, that I know how to get off. So why do I cringe when

I think of "real" sex—the nitty-gritty of opening my legs and feeling a body push inside me? Why do I turn off so completely to sex when I'm having it regularly?

One of the pitfalls of not living together (or anywhere near each other) is that we don't have the luxury of time to explore each other's sexuality honestly or to confront our own. I guess I come across as more sexually sure of what I want or don't want, or expect or whatever. A ball-breaker. Emasculating. The truth is I am so vulnerable and afraid and totally lost. I'm twenty-seven years old and I never got a chance to become sexual outside the pressures to perform—for my man, for my ego. (Does anyone?) One woman in the book says her husband has been impotent for twenty years and that he makes love like a woman, with fingers and tongue. I caught myself thinking *how wonderful*. Then—pause—why wonderful? What a strange thought for a (primarily) heterosexual girl like myself.

Fingers and tongue. Before you say anything, let me clarify: I'm not suggesting I just want to be eaten out all the time and never fuck or suck anyone off or do anything for anyone but myself. It's not selfishness I'm speaking from. Fingers and tongue sound good to me because they mean *slowing things down* from the first erotic charge that passes between us to slamming penetration. (The "uh, uh, uh" disguising impact as passion.) How do I ask for something different without facing your disappointment, feelings of being rebuffed, controlled, dismissed, chided (I'm searching for words because this story is newborn, wet with membranes I don't want to tear). I hear you challenging me, "Why is it always about what *you* want or don't want?" And me thinking, "Why isn't it *ever*?" Something's clearly wrong if we *both* feel ripped off by this sex thing.

Let me jump into some painful truths. When I think about making love with you, I feel nervous. Literally—my chest is tight right now with that feeling I get when I realize something's wrong and needs to be talked about, but I don't know how or what the result will be. I feel nervous because I don't know how to talk about having sex with you without either hurting your feelings by exerting my own sexual will (to say no, or more, or let's do *this* instead of *this*) or subordinating my own feelings in order to have sex that looks great from the outside but still feels off, a little, to me. (This is all sounding much worse than I mean for it to. I love fucking you. I love when you want to kiss me passionately, pull me up hard against you, your tongue blurring lines with mine. I'm so grateful, honestly, that you want to fuck me.)

You like foreplay where we talk to each other from across the room, getting off on each other's minds, but I want to get close to you, face to face. You have such a beautiful face. I want a lover's entitlement to be closer to it than people in everyday conversations. I want to smell your neck and make you grimace from the expert hand job you're going to teach me to give you. I want to feel as electric as fifteen year olds. To go into sex not knowing what I will find there. And not expecting you to know, either. We pretend we know what we're doing, but are we really just following examples from *Top Gun* and Jenna Jameson pornos? (How to phrase this so my personal sexual growth doesn't feel like an assault on your sexual abilities? I consider you a great lover. I wouldn't feel I could talk through this if you weren't.)

Please know that I'm *not* suddenly turning into a *make-love-to-me-don't-fuck-me girl*—god forbid! I'm earnestly trying to imagine what would feel good to my body, instead of living with what sex has pretty much always been for me: an effort to withstand gracefully a little more than I can take at every stage—fingers before my cunt unfolds, penis chafing *the dry vestibule of my vagina*.[17]

"Rules, rules, rules. You have too many *rules*! You *want* too much, *think* too much, *fuck it all up* with expectations so high no man could fail to fail. With you."

Who am I hearing here? Is this my inner critic? Is it you? Is it "the relationship" talking? Despite the language Heart uses, I'm actually looking for a moving away from rules into rulelessness. Instead of the rule being, for instance, "Fuck, and if you're not ready, grit your teeth until your body catches up," I'd like to find out how I like to fuck in the same way one discovers a preference for cotton pima sheets—by paying attention to sensuous pleasure.

The sex we had in New York before we ever had "intercourse" was the best sex of my life. I felt like—and this may sound self-centered or one-sided, but I don't think it has to be—you were showing me things about my body that I could never learn alone. You were mapping the cave of my cunt with your fingers, hand spread inside me, pushing my edges, making me expand into new shapes. (I *still* don't know what all you were doing down there!) It reminded me of the college guy whose dorm room I visited a few times in high school; he didn't want to fuck because that would be cheating on his girlfriend, so instead he decided to teach me how my pussy worked. Looking back, I realize he pressured me to have a kind of orgasm I couldn't have (lots of overstimulation on the G-spot) because he thought I ought to be able to come the same way as his girlfriend, and I was too inexperienced to know pussies are like fingerprints (no two alike). Those sessions with Trace made sex into a learning environment. You and I recaptured that feeling in our first two months of dating, but once we crossed the intercourse border, the erotic build-up—that sense of having all the time in the world and just wanting to turn each other on—went away. Orgasm came at the expense of pleasure, if that makes any sense.

Penetration feels uncomfortable physically, even with lots of lubrication (Astroglide is *not* the answer), without building up to it by kissing and pressing, fingers skimming over skin (not just the "private" places) making me long for your hand between my legs by grazing the backs of my calves instead, gradually advancing to finger insertions, one, two, maybe three, before the penis (this part—permitting my body time to open itself voluntarily—I figured out only recently during my first gynecological exam with a midwife). I don't know what to say if this sounds like too much of an ordeal for regular sex sessions. I mean, I'm reading this sex therapy book, thinking it's good to discover and articulate my physical desires, but at the same time, I fear you'll hear my description as narrow rules and a me-first sexuality, like I'm saying *this is my playhouse, learn the rules or stay out!* Then again, if it isn't *my* playhouse, whose is it?

I just believe so totally in our physical partnership, I want to do it justice by overcoming inhibitions to speak these things, to draw attention to the awkward, the uncomfortable, the uncertain, to face it all head-on, trusting that we have each other's best interest at heart. I want us to be like Carol and Robert (without fucking you in the ass).[18] I feel it's worth the discomfort of breaking through the screen between me and every man I fuck, worth learn-

31

ing how to talk, since I hope to be fucking you well into old age.

I look back over this message, though, and hate like hell this pleading posture, how the fear runs so deep—of abandonment, of defensiveness, of turning you off. All I ask is that we acknowledge my pussy doesn't open like a god-damned Broadway show as soon as our eyes meet from across the room. It's true, sex in this way would be a time commitment. What is it that makes us reluctant to make that commitment? I'm guilty of it, too, avoiding masturbation for months because I dread the long afternoon it requires—strange, I didn't used to dread desire.

I'm not looking for an argument, by the way, or even a debate. Instead I invite you to come out of the hard shell of masculinity for a moment and be vulnerable with me. I'm not going to be an acquiescent (post)adolescent girl my whole life. And I know you wouldn't want that, so please be careful how you react to what I see as a key transitional moment in our relationship toward becoming each other's soul mates.

Love,
Lis

I'm disheartened when I reread this letter, written just last summer, uncomfortable with its hyperconciliatory tone; my self-in-relation pales against the blood-red derring-do of *Jane Sexes It Up*. I don't recognize myself. And yet that's not true—because I eat, sleep, and breathe this conflict, bear it in the marrow and joints of my body, like the scoliosis that keeps me from standing completely straight.

Andrea Dworkin confronts this emotional push and pull

of sex: "Intercourse is frequently how we hold on: fuck me."[19] I challenge any Dworkin critic to deny the fact of this dynamic in many women's lives, resorting to acrobatic sexual feats to feed otherwise unattended emotional needs, an ineffectual smear of dark lipstick across the face of little girl fears.

John Stoltenberg (Dworkin's student and lover) tells us, "Men [and, in this generation, women] learn from sex films how to have the kind of sex that is observable from without, not necessarily experienceable from within. 'Showable' and 'performable' sex is not particularly conducive to communicating what is going on emotionally between two people in sex."[20] Jessica Baumgardner's Gen-X directed "Dysfunction Junction, What's Your Function?" ventures a sociological reading regarding the "problem" of sex:

> According to a study published in the *Journal of the American Medical Association*, more than forty percent of women have "sexual problems." . . . Almost half of all women, they suggest, have a physiological disorder that requires medication—a bleak diagnosis, to be sure, and one that seems a little simplistic to me, like prescribing Valium to the legions of depressed housewives in the sixties.[21]

She points to "social, economic and cultural factors" that may adversely affect women's sexuality, perceiving much sexual dissatisfaction as the product of adolescent "sheepishness about telling [her] lovers what was wrong, or right." I would pause to consider certain areas she brushes past a little too quickly: the medical establishment's economic investment in pathologizing women's lack of physical pleasure, as well as the American cultural persistence of taboos precluding communication about female orgasm, despite a proliferation of sex-positive information in the forms of books, videos, catalogs, broadway shows.

For instance, why *do* one's teeth sometimes tingle, as Baumgardner describes, from receiving heavy G-spot stimulation? And what is *up* with only being able "to climax with a partner after hours of eyeball-squeezing concentration with cunnilingus"? And finally, why the *fuck* had I never heard a single other person mention these shared experiences until stumbling across Baumgardner's essay in the December 2000 issue of the edgy, sexually thematized, online literary journal *Nerve.com*? I realize I'm flirting here with that angry feminist tone we third wavers so want to avoid, a dangerous rhetorical decision since I'm no longer housed comfortably within heterosexual couplehood where my critiques might be kept soft and doughy.[22] But you know what? Anorgasmia—my own and others'—makes me mad.

Date Rape at the Redneck Riviera

There is an awful poverty here, in this time and place: of language, of words that express real states of being; of search, of questions; of meaning, of emotional empathy; of imagination. And so, we are inarticulate about sex, even though we talk about it all the time. . . .[23]

—Andrea Dworkin, *Intercourse*

I have told some people that I was date raped in Panama City Beach, Florida. Big deal. Who hasn't been. What I haven't told anyone is the whole story. How he was soooo cute. How I was soooo lonely. I never said how we kissed all sexy and sour, tasting each other like tropical drinks. I never said there was romance, fantasy, *this*:

It was April of 1994 when my roommate and I loaded the trunk of her Celica with beer bought in bulk at Sam's. We were on our way to the spring break capital of the world. My acrylic nails were painted toxic orange, hair streaked platinum halfway to my ass, push-up bra bikini packed and ready for action. When we reached the beach, heads turned. Music thudded: "Lemme ride that donkey, donkey; lemme ride that donkey, donkey."

Girls grinding pelvises in an R-rated version of the hoola hoop lined the stage for a bikini contest. I wanted to be them. I wanted to be up there with them—brave, self-confident, provocative—I wanted to bathe in waves of applause. The next day I drank rum runners until the emcee called for today's contestants, and, slightly more blonde than awkward, I placed third. I never felt so sexy in my life.

That night my friend and I went out to celebrate. We danced, we drank, and most of all we scanned the beautiful boys. One in particular caught my eye. I recognized him, a very popular guy whose attention I'd never quite managed to merit at campus parties. In the democratic spirit of booze and special occasions, he finally looked my way. We walked down the beach, night air raising the hair on my arms, waves sloshing in and out like they do in romance novels. We came up on an overturned sailboat—the perfect make-out spot, a great story for my girlfriends.

His hand was under my shirt, in my pants. I liked it. He leaned me backwards against the boat, its spine crunching against mine, and started to unbutton his pants. I called time out—I mean, I wasn't going to fuck him for Christ's sake. He wanted to have sex and I said no. (So far so good.) He went down on me. I let him. And I liked it—what's not to like? (Here's where everything loses focus. I can hear the voices: "Ohhh, well if you let him go down on you—what'd you expect?" And the voices make sense to me, except . . . not quite.) With one hand he held my wrists together over my head, my hips pinned under his. With the other hand he got his pants down and his dick in me. I thought: *this is how it happens. This is how boys hold girls down.* I had never been able to picture the strength and coordination required for rape; my experiences of sex so far had shown me only fumbling and awkwardness. Yet here he was, penetrating me swiftly, head and face pressed privately into my shoulder, retreating into darkness and shadows and orgasm. No, I didn't scream, didn't kick. I said no and struggled with my legs, but I was too embarrassed to draw attention from passers-by further up the beach, and a little afraid, too, of turning his drunk violent. He finished and we did up our pants. My hair was soaked with sea spray; rivulets of salt burned my eyes. We walked back to the club in silence, sobered.

"That was alright with you—wasn't it?" (Preparing his defense for the potential lawsuit already, I imagined.)

"Doesn't matter now, does it?" I said, sullen and distant.

When I got back to the college town where I lived I heard he'd been accused of rape by two other girls that year, but he "got off." Well, it wasn't like I'd been pulled into an alley by a stranger or beaten in the face with a fist. There was no gun, no knife. No pregnancy, no STD. I was fine. Ultimately, I figured a quick fuck would be easier to bear than the wrath of a sexually frustrated frat boy on a week-long bender, but his act of penetration was utterly against my will. Call it what you will, but there is no way around that fact. No words for how thin the line is between desire and domination. How much is alright for me to want? There is a cultural logic, unspoken but implacable, that if I want some (oral sex), I better want all (a dick in me). That's how I lost my virginity, after all, in another scene that could be loosely categorized as date rape—trusting the older guy I had such a crush on to stop at "everything, but" penetration as he pledged, feeling somehow unentitled to point out that he had reneged on the deal when I felt him slide inside.

One of the co-authors of *Manifesta*, a recently released overview of third wave feminist activism, tells a similar story:

> When I was a junior, and already a pretty well-known radical feminist on campus, I had a close, kinda foxy male friend who had "feelings for me" and with whom I flirted.

One night he came into my room all drunk and got on top of me. He said, "You wanted this," and the thing was, I didn't want that—him on top of me, trying to scare me, possibly fucking me. But I did want him wanting me in less freaky circumstances.[24]

These narratives have no name in feminism or mainstream culture that doesn't distort the conflict by conflating it with rape or dismissing it as bad decision making. Like the *Manifesta* authors, I'd like feminism to "help articulate what happened to [us] when it's not clear whether [we] had a choice."[25] We need words for the middle grounds of subtle coercion where our libidinal drive is used against us, words for that adolescent place of fingers and tongues and exploration where so much female sexuality could thrive but, once one "goes all the way," is more often frustrated or misused.

Fucking, Fighting—Is It All the Same?

It has been a sticking point in feminist theory for many years, the way pleasure and power interlace like legs between passionate lovers—hard to make sense of how a woman could write about her own date rape(s), assert the inadequacy of mainstream approaches to female sexuality, then turn right around and say she used to hope she'd get raped on the way to the mailbox in fifth grade so she could have sex and not get in trouble for it.

My doubts about feminism as a mode of analysis reveal themselves most irresolutely in moments like these, when my feelings or experiences conflict with what I think a feminist *should* feel, when I respond *as a feminist*—flattening out the nuances of life and love according to this false icon of the cultural imagination. ("Go get something pierced," Aunt Feminism shoos me from her room.)

I am scanning a shelf of movies in a small video store. My boyfriend is three rows over, scouting our evening's entertainment. He likes my taste in movies, so we never fight over what to rent, but sometimes he makes suggestions. We stand shoulder to shoulder at right angles, covering ground and kind of flirting silently with each other. He points to a box and asks me if I've seen it. No. He asks if I want to. No. The movie is *Fight Club*. Oh god, I think to myself, another *In the Company of Men*, I can't bear it. He doesn't argue.

Months later, I am restlessly flipping channels and pause on a grainy scene with two men seated in the emergency row of an airplane trading remarks about the anonymity of travelling alone. Good dialogue. I watch for a few minutes, then flip to the TV Guide channel only to discover I am watching *Fight Club*. I am surprised, then dismayed—my quick dismissal (as a feminist) had been way off. I turn back to the movie channel and put the remote down. For two hours I am riveted to my seat, fixed on every scene.

The plot revolves around Jack, a guy in his late twenties or early thirties who feels increasingly unfulfilled by the world of material success, represented by his Horchow Collection condominium decor and, more powerfully, by his morally bankrupt and gruesome job. He works for "a very popular" car company, going to the scene of accidents caused by faulty machinery to assess formulaically whether to recall the model and fix the problem in the car's build or to risk the sum of insurance claims likely to be filed if they leave the flawed vehicles on the road.

Jack soon meets the (anti)hero of the story (played by Brad Pitt), Tyler Durden—a poster boy for Gen X (anti) values like untethered freedom, Jacksonian masculinity, and the familiar Huck Finn resistance to being civilized by women—and basically falls in love. The two join forces and withdraw from mainstream society to build an underground counterculture for the waves and waves of men like them, numbed by life in corporate America, seeking some kind of real contact with their fellow man. Not touchy-feely contact, though, more like beating the fuck out of each other. In a typical "fight club" meeting, no pansy-ass protective gear gets in the way of their good clean fun, just rock solid knuckles hitting rock solid jaw bone and nose. Blood slings from face and mouth, marking the floors on which these men pin and fraternally brutalize their partners, and they all get *way* off on it. (So, I confess, do I.) Watching *Fight Club*, my pulse comes faster, adrenaline kicks in— and not the Horatio Alger blood-pumping "heart" of the theme song to *Rocky*, either, something darker, un-American, decadent.

Like Greek gods, the members not only perform Olympian feats, they eroticize the male body, ripped and bare-chested, lock limbs and hold tight, returning to work the next morning with love licks imprinted like forget-menots on cheek bone, jaw, and chin. In fact the noises of these underground street fights, held in basements below bars and condemned buildings, sound very much like sex, each thrustlike blow landing with a grunt, bodies ripe with sweat and dirt. In the words of a popular song by Sublime (whose lyrics typically prefer dogs, pot, and male company to romance or women), "Fucking, fighting—it's all the same."[26]

In *Fight Club*, this blurred line repeats itself in the heterosexual bedroom. Sex scenes are shot from the kitchen below, plaster knocked loose from the ceiling. Fucking is a house falling down. As the sounds of sex echo the athletic, barbaric brawls beneath the city, the audience is pressed to consider the Dworkian equation—sex is violence—in all its strangely seductive dimensions. We see Marla, the girlfriend, falling off beds repeatedly in a stupor of sex and cigarette smoke and sometimes a little vodka. Tyler/Pitt catches roommate Jack listening outside the door and offers crudely to let him "finish her off." Wearing only the plastic yellow dishwashing glove on one hand, Tyler engages our most primal erotic fantasies, later characterizing his encounter with Marla as "sport fucking" rather than love. His memory of her words, "I haven't been fucked like that since grade school," leaves him shivering in mock disgust the following morning.

Literalize the analogy, fucking-is-fighting, and the film's disturbing implications emerge from the fray like a blood-smeared face. One might see in it an inadvertent allusion to the slaughter-fuck of a final scene in the 1972 film *Looking for Mr. Goodbar* or, similarly, to the Jack the Ripper narratives popularized in London periodicals at the end of the nineteenth century—parallel examples of textual backlash against women's sexual liberation, produced at politically charged moments in feminist history.[27] The familiar connection of sex and violence provokes in me two responses: there's the proper feminist critique (violence is bad, connecting sex and death devalues the erotic, condones and fetishizes the brutalized female body) and then there's my real response.

The one where I want someone to fuck the shit out of me.

"Fuck me like you're killing something!" I once cried out in the midst of a particularly raucous love making session. (And yes, it can still be called love making when it's loud and rough, just like fucking can be tender and sweet.)

Interpreting the correspondence between sex scenes and fight scenes in terms of violence against women seems off—a facile response to the movie's overarching theme of corporate culture as a form of indentured service. Is feminism helping me see the movie more clearly, then, or is it a lady wearing a fancy hat in the row ahead of me in a theater?

"People know more about the messiness and variety of sex," queer theorist Micheal Warner urges, "than they allow themselves to admit in public."[28] Warner's analysis of safer sex campaigns sheds light on my erotic response to *Fight Club*, and, by extension, my rejection of "sex-negative" feminism as an incomplete representation of sexuality: "Most efforts to encourage us to take care of ourselves through safer sex also encouraged us to pretend that we were never abject, or that our only desire was to be proper and good."[29] Being a proper and good feminist in this case means believing women always want what's best for us. We don't. Like Warner says, "We all have contradictory desires: to be safe and at risk; to be responsible and to fuck the law; to know what we're doing and to forget ourselves."[30]

In this light, feminists who want to be fucked hard, held down, thrown against walls and pressed into them cannot be explained away by the simple charge of false consciousness (the idea that we eroticize the conditions of our own oppression). To the contrary, it is our feminist consciousness that makes *Fight Club* and the violent masculinity it depicts sexy. As feminists, we've learned to critique this gender role, we know there's something wrong with it, it has been removed to the space of transgression, that which we are not supposed to want. As Carol Queen observes of her own circuitous erotic paths, "Being dominated by a woman was one thing. . . . Submission to a man was *really* perverse."[31] Only here, within this multilayered mapping of feminist desire—from false consciousness (enjoying the movie), to second wave feminist consciousness (criticizing or rejecting the movie), to a postmodern, parodic, third wave feminist consciousness (getting off on the movie)—do we even begin to approach the complexity of sexual politics in the current historical moment.

Any theory of feminist desire must acknowledge the impact of the time period, kilnlike, in which that yearning is fired. We are the first generation to grow up in a culture where feminism influences national policy making, yet continues to be vilified, judged unnecessary, pronounced dead at regular intervals. Feminism, along with family and church, falls within a range of establishment values for this generation. This is not to say that Generation X believes the hype about feminism being over and done with, or that we would ever want it to be; rather, feminism exists in us in *both* forms: resistance to authority, and the authority we resist; permission to explore our sexuality, and the sexual limits we transgress.

For this reason, arguments that come down unambiguously on one side or the other in debates over sex and power are only half alive to us, alienating and outdated. Lesbian separatists may fascinate and provoke us in the classroom, but they are hard to take home. Like the Social Purity feminists of the nineteenth century, these social critics put sexual correctness above the lived messiness of most people's sex lives, fucking for a cause. In her essay, "How Orgasm Politics Has Hijacked the Women's Movement," Sheila Jeffreys writes:

> Dee Graham's wonderful 1994 book *Loving to Survive* looks at female heterosexuality and femininity as symptoms of what she calls societal Stockholm Syndrome. In classic Stockholm Syndrome, hostages bond with their captors in terror and develop submissive cooperation in

order to survive. Handbooks for those who might be taken hostage, such as I was once given when working in a prison, describe survival tactics that resemble the advice offered in women's magazines for how to win men. . . . Stockholm Syndrome develops among those who fear for their lives but are dependent upon their captors. If the captor shows any kindness, however small, a hostage is likely to bond even to the point of protecting the captor from harm and entirely adopting his point of view on the world.[32]

Andrea Dworkin describes penetration in a similarly extreme mode of critique:

Being owned and being fucked are or have been virtually synonymous experiences in the lives of women. He owns you; he fucks you. The fucking conveys the quality of the ownership: he owns you inside out. The fucking conveys the passion of his dominance: it requires access to every hidden inch. . . . Women live inside this reality of being owned and being fucked: are sensate inside it; the body learning to respond to what male dominance offers as touch, as sex, as love . . . and being erotically owned by a man who takes you and fucks you is a physically charged and meaningful affirmation of womanhood or femininity or being desired.[33]

. . .

What intercourse *is* for women and what it *does* to women's identity, privacy, self-respect, self-determination, and integrity are forbidden questions; and yet how can a radical or any woman who wants freedom not ask precisely these questions? The quality of the sensation or the need for a man or the desire for love: these are not answers to questions of freedom; they are diversions into complicity and ignorance.[34]

Despite their frequently dismissive tone towards sex-positive feminists, I find the work of Dworkin and Jeffreys to be incredibly bold and insightful. They are bad-asses, and brilliant social analysts. But they don't say much about what to do in the face of their crippling critiques, what to do besides turning off heterosexuality completely or turning away from feminism into quiet complicity. These are not adequate choices.

We must begin to imagine a heterosexuality without heterosexism, but separating the two can be difficult, as Caroline Ramazanoglu has argued:

> We do not need to see all men as personally oppressive, but what is urgently needed is a sense of how difficult it is for both men and women, day in day out, to counter social pressures in transforming heterosexuality. . . . Men have much less reason to struggle and go on struggling than women. This can leave feminist heterosexuals fighting lonely battles in the kitchen, over childcare, in bed and about money.[35]

Sick of fighting, a majority of heterosexual couples nevertheless embrace the idea currently circulating in pop culture that war is the natural state of relations between the sexes. John Gray is getting rich off this best-selling stereotypical tripe. His spots on the *Oprah Winfrey* show are part of a larger pattern in which host and guests guide viewers to accommodate personal and cultural circumstances rather than to change them.

Despite Ms. Winfrey's espoused efforts to liberate women from the myths of romantic love, her show relentlessly instructs women to change *themselves* rather than *the system*. The manipulative notion that women's dissatisfaction comes primarily from within puts the burden on the individual to solve the "problem" of her relationship rather than approaching the structures of heterosexuality, marriage, and intercourse as human projects—flawed and pliable.[36] "Tell It Like It Is" Phil, for instance, forcefully reframes familial conflicts and couplehood, but neither he nor Oprah *ever* questions the institutions themselves (although Oprah's personal decision not to marry her long-term live-in partner, models a subtle feminist resistance watched daily by women around the world). A better approach to improving the dynamics of couplehood—a third wave feminist approach—would consider how women and men might collaboratively shift the terms of heterosexual partnership, popularizing the thus far primarily academic point that there are, in Lynne Segal's words, "many 'heterosexualities.'"[37] But as long as women remain "remarkably good at subordinating their own active needs,"[38] the system will shimmy along.

Queering Heterosexuality

Instead of guilt-tripping heterosexual women, feminists would do better to enlist them in the "queering" of traditional understandings of gender and sexuality.

—Lynne Segal,
Straight Sex: Rethinking the Politics of Pleasure

In "How I became a Queer Heterosexual," Clyde Smith explains this hybrid self-identification as the result of his "desire for a world of multiple possibilities." Located in a collection of essays called *Straight with a Twist*, Smith's essay is part of a volume dedicated to creating a more capacious heterosexuality, a vision that differs markedly from the Mars and Venus debacle rocking the nation. The queer community entertains wider possibilities for rearranging romance, and thus may appeal to the men and women of Generation X more than traditional notions of romance or feminist rejections of it. Carol Queen, one of the leading lights of sex-positive feminism and queer theory, flips normative sexuality on its head when she remarks, "I don't see myself engaging in heterosexual relationships even when my lover is a man."[39] We are looking for, in Eve Sedgwick's words, "a completely different principle of affiliation," one "[n]ot structured around blood and law."[40]

Queering heterosexuality, or exploring the possibility of many heterosexualities, seems like our last best hope for finding companionship that doesn't cost us our separate lives or limit us to existing models of togetherness, and for discovering an eroticism organic to the human body, experienceable from within rather than merely performable from without. A queer heterosexuality might be comprised of some or all of the following elements:

- less restrictive gender roles, allowing for feminine masculinities and masculine femininities

- nonreproductive sexuality, justified by pleasure alone

- recognition of pleasure as a fundamental human need, not an expendable luxury

- heterosexuality as one relationship configuration among many, not the norm

- the nuclear family as one relationship configuration among many, not the norm

- sex as play rather than work, pleasure rather than obligation (doing one's "business")

- total body integrity for both partners, clarity regarding who has access to whose body and when, how that access gets granted or denied

- noncoital eroticism, fucking with *and* without penetration, nonpenis-centered sex[41]

This list is only a preliminary sketch, less manifesta than first gesture toward further dialogue. If these sorts of values were brought into the feminist heterosexual bedroom, perhaps we would see genuine improvement in women's sex lives, rather than the red herring of "politically correct sex." Queering heterosexuality, it seems to me, would mean estranging ourselves from the "givens" of sex, love, romance, and partnership in order to perceive the current order of things as a social construction, not a law of god or nature.

Apart from lesbian separatist analyses of heterosexuality as a form of political hostage, and antisex critiques of penetration as violence against the female body—neither of which do I mean to caricature or wholly dismiss—the third wave feminism I am trying to imagine and live focuses on the margin between A.) *institutionalized heterosexuality* (heterosexuality as we know it, through marriage and hallmark and movies and the television show *Friends,* etc.) and B.) the as yet unarticulated *possibility* of women and men as social, political, economic, and sexual *allies*—a focus, in other words, on the margin between how things *are* and how they *could be*. For now, I have taken a break from being a girlfriend and aspiring wife until I learn how to inhabit that role and still maintain my self in some recognizable form.

So. Is it impossible to have romance and feminism too?

Do boyfriends and politics automatically cancel each other out?

Okay, yes, they often do, but—and here's the earnestly hopeful face of third wave feminism—surely to goodness they don't have to. Surely there is a place for men in the lives of feminists, not just in the bathtub after paper presentations, but side by side, shaping the philosophies and practical endeavors of human *relationship.*

Part One
Real Live Nude Girls

I feel most powerful in dresses.
　　　—Lisa Ortiz, "Dresses for My Round Brown Body"

2

The Sexual Girl Within

Breaking the Feminist Silence on Desiring Girlhoods

CAITLIN FISHER

> One of the many, many, many scriptures imposed on me
> once I got big, was: 'It is your duty to ignore mean boys and
> their games.' . . . [N]ow that I was big, even if I tattled . . . no
> one listened or cared. If I retaliated, I got in trouble, lost
> jobs, made enemies. Oh how I sometimes longed for those
> days on the playground when kicking a boy's ass was a
> mundane occurrence in any given school week.
> —Inga Muscio, *Cunt: A Declaration of Independence*

I BEG MY MOTHER to let Sabrina stay over, like always. We're ten years old and she is my best friend. At night, Sabrina and I make a tent from our bedding. We have a flashlight, which I hold, and she strokes my hair with both hands. We take off our clothes, slowly, still under the covers, passing flashlight from hand to hand, giggling; examine each other in its harsh beams and soft shadows.

"Turn off the flashlight. *Turn it off.*"

Sabrina rolls on top of me, perched on her elbows.

"You are NOT going to believe this," she says.

"What?"

"Butterfly kisses."

Sabrina always has good ideas. I wonder silently where she gets them. I feel jealous, worried, a little nervous, excited. I move the hair from her face and try to find her lips in the dark. I kiss her quickly—

"Like this?"

"No. Like this"

And Sabrina *knows* how to butterfly kiss. She flutters her eyelashes against the side of my face, my shoulders, across my chest. She turns on the flashlight.

"Turn it OFF!"

She butterflies across my stomach ("If you laugh, I'll kill you!") and between my legs. She takes her time. She's a butterfly expert. *Shhh.* We don't want anyone to come in. I never even knew she *had* eyelashes before now. I count in my head so I don't make a sound. Sabrina winds a path across me and through me with eyelashes and small lips. I count up to 809 before she stops. Sometimes even now at night, alone, I begin to count—809, 810 . . . And she's there.

███

As I enter my thirties, I find it difficult to claim a theoretical space for the girlhood I remember as sexually empowered and erotically complicated in ways that the feminism I grew up with didn't help to explain. I went to grade school in the seventies. Female protagonists in the textbooks, equal ice time (sort of), told I could be anything (even, in my case, a space detective), and, yes, teachers sometimes still said things like "can I have two strong boys help me with the apparatus?" but I would roll my eyes and put up my hand because, well, she was hopeless if she thought Gavin with his thin arms could do a better job than the girls, who were taller, stronger, and at least knew how the apparatus *worked*. The playgrounds I inhabited were female-run spaces, my memories filled with sexual, laughing girls. Girls were powerful. Girls were cruel. Girls were good kissers. Boys, on the other hand, were timid, lacked imagination. When they kissed, they could never make up a story and whisper it to you; their tongues were too rigid, and they'd push saliva into your mouth. No, the slow, practiced, hours-long kissing with girls was so much better. Girls were expert-everything. This isn't everyone's story, of course, but I'm not the only one whose girlhood is populated by great sexual experimenters. Risk takers; kissing girl gangs.

Why do so few feminists talk about this girlhood I remember? And what do those of us with these girlhood memories carry into our feminist adulthood?

There are lots of feminist narratives about girls told through powerful fictional and autobiographical works, through the disciplines of sociology and developmental psychology, and in the interdisciplinary space of women's studies. But few public narratives have been generated by feminism about sexually desiring girls. Why do they play such a small part in the stories we tell ourselves as feminists? And what might be the consequences of the feminist theories we are building? Does the wealth of material focusing on sexual disempowerment and vulnerability block our vision of positive, or just different, experiences? As if the very gesture of writing down the words sexualizes them, changes them, touches them inappropriately. Feminists consistently tease ambition out of girls, but not desire.

When I say "girl," who do you picture? What fantasies do you have of girlhood? Who do you see when I write, "She desires . . ."? Is it ever a child? And the hand, there, on her small thigh—is it always large, male, frightening? What happens if we allow that sometimes—just some-times—it's another small hand, sometimes another girl-hand, desiring, tentative, fierce, exploring.

And what do we call her if she spreads her legs a little wider?

As a white woman in women's studies I have not only noticed that desiring girlhoods are mostly absent from fem-inist books and conversations, but I also became acutely aware of the racist and classist exceptions. Some girls did fall outside of the dominant narrative. Sometimes we read about teen pregnancy—girls of color who got abortions, white girls who kept their babies. Some texts allowed that sexual license or girl-girl violence happened, yes, but only in certain working-class or immigrant neighborhoods and, significantly, only after puberty. Feminist theory thus pre-served the middle-class white girl as icon—the tabula rasa of white feminism—a desexualized, written-on girl.

One compelling narrative feminism weaves about girls is our subtle exclusion, the assumptions and stereotypes about gender at work from infancy. This is a story of how girls are segregated from boys. Girls are taught that they're less capable, and girls carry all this in their bodies and spirits. Our girlhoods remain desexualized, except within the vocabulary of abuse. The familiar feminist coming-of-age story begins with a "golden age" of asexual tomboy girlhood (that we can and do talk about), nothing much *good* happens until you find feminism. This has promoted directly or indirectly silence in women about active and pleasurable girlhood sexualities.

Lyn Mikel Brown writes in her preface to *Raising Their Voices: The Politics of Girls' Anger* that, in part, the book is a reaction to the public response generated by her earlier text, *Meeting at the Crossroads: Women's Psychology and Girls' Development*, co-authored with Carol Gilligan. *Meeting at the Crossroads* is a feminist developmental study of girls at a private school in Ohio. The study revealed that schools shortchanged girls in ways that resulted in a loss of self-esteem. Brown writes that she "continued to hear . . . primarily about the psychological trouble white girls were in," noting that few people responded to the ways *Meeting at the Crossroads* was also centrally about how girls resist conventional notions of (particularly white) femininity.

The Sexual Girl Within?

Many feminist accounts of childhood urge us to retrieve what has been stolen or lost to women on the way to adulthood. The story of the girl child emerging as adult feminist is told often by developmental psychologists, and in some versions, the arrow of time moves backward into the past as well as forward. Emily Hancock's *The Girl Within*, for example, makes a claim for a "primary childhood identity" that adult women can "unearth from beneath the rubble" of the conventions weighing her down in adult womanhood. Crucially for Hancock, this more "authentic" self, "the girl within," is an earlier self to which adult women can return and draw strength. My own intervention into feminist narratives of girlhood departs in significant ways from Hancock's "girl within." The "sexual girl within" I'm looking for is not an "authentic sexual self" found within us all, retrieved from a time before we were broken and revealed through the methods of developmental psychology. Rather, I am interested in the production and erasure of the sexual girl within feminist discourse. I am pressing for room within feminism to recognize the perhaps uncommon but by no means nonexistent idea and practice of sexual pleasure during girlhood. Within feminism we must find the room for stories by and about a diverse group of girls with varied preadolescent sexual experiences.

After girls hit puberty, feminism has a great deal more to say about sexuality (appearing only now, as if by magic), especially the mechanisms designed to control it: double standards, low self-esteem, weight obsession, compulsive heterosexuality, and no education regarding the sensuous body. Society does not dare girls to take control, to assert themselves. Feminism made sense of my postpubescent life in powerful ways. But I want to ask, gently, doesn't anyone remember the kissing?

███

At ten, Sabrina is one of the greatest sexual experimenters I have ever met. We play Get Smart and Agent 99; we play naked *Little House on the Prairie*. We smuggle *Playboy* into the linen cupboard, a space just large enough for two girls eating Lick-a-Maid to sit.

"Close your eyes," Sabrina says. "Now, put your finger on the page. There! Open your eyes. Would you do it?"

"Do what?"

"What's in the picture."

"No way . . . but maybe this."

My linen cupboard has a big door and a bottom filled with blankets. It smells like Yardley soaps too good to use. Sabrina runs her Lick-a-Maid stick over my lips and flips the page.

███

I search the women's studies list archives and find a folder labeled "girls and feminism." It confirms my suspicions about the limited place of girlhood in feminist theory. I find requests for materials on young girls and body image, story books recommended as good, safe places to start integrating feminism in preteen girls' daily lives.

Suggested activity: "What would it be like to be a boy for a day?" As if!

I don't think I'm misreading the question as one that implicitly urges girls to name the privileges of boys. As if no one would ever *choose* being a girl. What would it be like to be a boy for a day back in grade school, back on those playgrounds I remember? What about the now hard-to-imagine moment when girls enjoy physical advantages over boys? What about the cruelty that can come with power—even little-girl power?

At age ten, I am with Tracey and a few girls we've never met before. The boy we are chasing is on foot, but we have bicycles and soon we've blocked his escape route. He retreats to his bike. Wary. Two . . . Three . . . He's off. I watch him . . . his thin calf, the back of that flying bicycle, his wild, scared eye, as he turns. Our girl eyes look in one direction. We are giddy, in pursuit. When we see the flutter and swallow in that boy's face, the left foot slipping from the pedal, his skidding, the unforced error, we are a burst of electricity. We hold back, not wanting to catch him just yet, moving on our bikes, with his fear. And the weird thing is, we're silent. I think back and the only sound I heard for the duration of the pursuit was tires on gravel and the boy's thin wheeze up front.

Boys don't frighten any of us. I know this fact, although I don't know any of the girls' names. I've never seen these girls before, but I know that at all our different schools the girls are smarter and bigger and choose gangs and friends first and grab boys and kiss them and keep them corralled for the whole of recess. It's always been like this. At ten we press our girl bodies against them and our tongues into them. And yes, we scratch—why not?—we scratch and pull hair because all's fair and even if the boys turn, catch us in their small hands, and, running, push us, momentum, not them, sending us to the ground, they can't hold us. Other boys might come running to look but never in time because boys don't have weight, don't have the substance to keep us on the gravel, and by the time a crowd arrives our hands like hammers have forced the boys to release; our legs, strong, thick-kneed dangerous have twisted them underneath us, and sometimes they are crying out by the time other defeated boys arrive. This is what I come to know as I ride: like bees, we girls are reading each other's minds.

Pursue. Slowly, in unison, not speaking, we encircle and stop this boy, and we make him take down his pants. We pull away his bicycle and the sandpit is huge and there are no adults anywhere in the world. And one girl kicks sand, and then we are all kicking, kicking wildly. I can't even remember seeing what we were doing, just breathing and tearing and pulsing—together. As the sand clears, he's crumbling, sobbing, and we seem suddenly so much bigger than he is, lying there, a shell-less thing, his penis coated with gravel. *He wasn't supposed to be so small.*

He turns his head and presses his face right into the dirt. Lets out a scream. Muffled. Crazy. Two—three—four—five.

Then we're running, scattered, scared of what we've done. I taste blood in my mouth as I get back on my bike.

We're off like bees but not before we take his clothes. I'm sorry, we say, silent, it's only to slow you down.

I never see those girls again. Heading back to Tracey's, I worry what her mother will say to us so flushed, tingling, panting into the garage, clutching a small boy's shirt. But her mother is sleeping—again—and Tracey and I go upstairs, take off our own shirts. It seems hours since I spoke. Tracey pulls the bottom drawer right out of her dresser and in duet I place the shirt to the very back. She closes the door, and I put my fingers on her warm chest to slow her heart, and she presses her lips against mine, sealing secrets. Her body is beauty-marked, her hair falling thin across a lazy olive eye. I swallow hard. I would say something spell breaking, but I can't feel what running boys feel, only this wave of girls.

I revisit that feeling often—the feeling of our girl bodies being so much more substantial than those of boys, of seeing our bodies as less vulnerable. What do those of us with these memories of girlhood power carry into our feminism? The dominant image of boys I have to this day is one of boys afraid of us. Peripheral. Vulnerable. Girls taking boys behind the skate shack to French kiss. Girls as horrid. Girls as powerful. Girls as allies.

■

It didn't last. How could it? As silent as feminists had been about my girlhood, they were on the money in their explorations of female adolescence in North America. Like a case study out of Mary Pipher's *Reviving Ophelia*, by the time I was in grade seven, we girls had transformed. Even Sabrina. Even Tracey. Small, well mannered, every time Derek or Mark or Angelo would say "hello baby" we'd stop and say "hello."

"Hey what's up pussy?"

Stop, turn. "Nothing much Angelo." Two, three. We don't want to be mean or actively disliked.

"I'm talking to *you*!!!!" That gets us every time. Not just one, but all of us. We turn singly and in groups, and Derek or Mark or Angelo takes a girl hand and places it on his crotch. Squeezes. The others girls leave, and if you laugh, you get to go too.

Feminism told me, don't wait for a prince, and I still think we must rescue ourselves. But there's more to the story, I discover, in writing about my girlhood. I remember, so I'm telling you: I was no sleeping beauty. I was awake all along.

Weren't there dangers?

"Yes, of course," I say. Then, a little softer, "but let's not forget the kissing that came before."

I am drawing on my feminist training to read official public discourses of girlhood sexuality critically against my own private narratives of experience in order to widen it to applicability. When people ask, "Can it ever be different," it was feminism that taught me the value (for girls and for feminism) of answering, "For me, it *was*."

3   *Sex Cuts*

BECKY MCLAUGHLIN

ONE SOFT SEPTEMBER day, I took to the road—north on the New York State Thruway in my Toyota station wagon. I drove with the window down, my left elbow relaxing on its metal perch, fragrant, balmy air circulating through the car. Traffic was light, so my job as driver required minimal concentration. Earlier in the week, I had passed my comprehensive exams (appropriately referred to as the "orals"—I had swallowed a good deal of material and coughed it up again). Now I would begin serious work on my dissertation; I felt myself moving smoothly through the ranks of my chosen career. Recently divorced and in a new relationship, I was re-evaluating long held and at times crippling notions about sexuality and desire. I felt powerful and alive, invincible in my new-found freedom and— dare I say it?—*womanliness*. (I had seen myself previously as androgynous, sexually neutral, so to be able to declare myself a *woman* and, better yet, a *desiring* woman, a *sexual* woman, constituted a major breakthrough. I felt good enough to bellow like a rutting deer.)

I steered my car into the middle lane where I came abreast of a pick-up truck—that most manly of vehicles, reminiscent of the farming community where I grew up— commanded by a driver about my age who glanced over as I passed him. Almost by accident our eyes met, and in that momentary look a surge of sexual energy passed between us. As my car drifted ahead, I playfully considered signaling him to pull off the road. I did no such thing, of course, completing the pass in the usual driverly fashion and reveling privately in my voluptuous fantasy of roadside sex.

Directly on the heels of these thoughts, though, stepping on them as it were, came a feeling of terror so dramatic that, at first opportunity, I swerved off the thruway down an unfamiliar exit ramp, veered into the parking lot of a defunct gas station, and brought the car to an abrupt standstill. By this time my legs were shaking so much I could hardly work the brake and clutch; my hands shook, too, and a sudden coating of sweat loosened my grip on the wheel; my heart pounded in my ears; my breath came in short gasps nearing hyperventilation. My head felt sloshy, like a ship at sea during a storm—all the furniture shifting to one side and threatening to tip overboard. If I had stayed on the road one second longer, I felt certain I would have lost control of the car and plunged head-on into an embankment to an early death. Although grateful to be alive, my terror from the episode (its suddenness and inexplicability) kept me from returning to the thruway. Instead, I wormed my way through a maze of city streets until I reached my destination (late, of course). I recognized the event as a panic attack, though ten years had passed since my last one. The earlier attack took place under very painful circumstances, so I couldn't imagine why the panic returned after so long, and why *now*, when I felt so incomparably *good*.

Several years later, I have come to understand that my panic attacks re-emerged and ultimately mushroomed into a full-blown driving phobia precisely *because* I was feeling so good. If I were an analyst, I'd say my neurotic engine runs on deprivation and punishment. Driving, a source of "lawful" or "sanctioned" pleasure, unexpectedly became equated with "unlawful" or "unsanctioned" sex. Something in me was startled by this exploratory "road trip" through a wider sexual landscape. Something in me wanted the trip aborted, wanted me off the new thruway, wanted me, that is, not to go through with it (illicit sex? womanhood? the guiltless euphoric moment? choosing my own direction and speedily propelling myself there?). Prior to that day, whenever I set out in the car, especially on the highway or the open road, I felt as if new and fascinating sights waited around every bend, each exit an exotic promise, even as I whizzed by. My body manifested this pleasurable tension as a sort of precoital fullness, my senses swollen with expectation. After the panic attack, the open road triggered insurmountable horror. Only the orderly intersections with their four-way stop signs and clearly legible traffic lights, the reassuring perpendicular and parallel lines, the twenty-five to thirty miles per hour speed limit—i.e., only what I could find within the city "limits"—felt safe.

In this essay, I am trying to write my way back into a more expansive public space, to find words for a body brimful of warring desires and self-policing reflexes. Like a path through narrow and twisting city streets, my stories meander, wander in one direction for a while, and then another, looking for the self I mean to be, experimenting with novice navigational skills, recognizing my own (speed) limits, but driving on.

Spillage

Theatrics: an overly dramatic presentation. *Histrionics*: an excess of emotion. Both words imply a surplus, something too much, and both words are often used to describe, indeed to criticize, women's behavior. Even little girls are accused of excess. Consider this parable: at breakfast one morning, a little girl filled her bowl so full of cereal that the bowl overflowed and excess cereal spilled on the table. When her mother exclaimed, "That's too much! Put some back," the little girl replied, "Too much is how much I want." Unlike the just-right bowl of porridge that

68

Goldilocks chooses in the children's story of the three bears, a bowl of porridge neither too hot nor too cold, this little girl's "just right" is not representative of the golden mean of socialization; instead, her desire demands an excess or surplus. In traditional psychological theory, the unconscious spills over the limits of the conscious or the confines of the bowl and, according to conventional gender roles, some of us respond by putting some back, and some of us do not. Artists let themselves spill out of bounds. If John Coltrane had "put some back," he could never have made the saxophone moan, honk, and shout in the radically innovative way he did. If Skip James had "put some back," he could never have played Delta Blues on slide guitar and sung in that eerie falsetto, the effect of which is not unlike the high lonesome sound of bluegrass musician Bill Monroe, another artist who refused to "put some back." If William Carlos Williams had "put some back," he could never have made a little red wheelbarrow a cornerstone of modern poetry. Men are not often asked to give up their excesses. Excess is, in fact, their birthright. In the case of the little girl and her spilled cereal, while she maintains in the face of parental law some small access to excess pleasure, the effects of this access will no doubt be labeled "theatrics" or "histrionics" when she grows older.[1] Girls are supposed to grow out of this entitlement to pleasure—to learn to play nice, share, to actively not want.

Hélène Cixous has argued that the repression of the unconscious, particularly the female unconscious, is the foundation of Western ideology. A politically activist female text would be, in her view, completely free of cultural strictures. But is such a text possible? And, if so, what would it look like? Maybe it would resemble what Roland Barthes calls a "text of bliss"—unsettling our assumptions about the world around us. There's not much of a place in public life for such an exploratory approach to writing and knowlege. We're taught to expound, to know ahead of time where we are going. The conjunction of feminism and psychoanalysis has, however, created a space in which to give up control, a space in which not knowing is not only acceptable but necessary. In fact, the nicely decorated package of our neuroses must be unwrapped, opened up, its contents allowed to spill out if we are to access knowledge and/as real enjoyment.

The idea of spillage in all its permutations— [ME *spillen* [OE *spillan*, to destroy, squander, akin to MHG *spillen*, to split [IE base **(s)p(h)el-*, to split, split off] SPALL, L *spolium*] 1 to allow or cause, esp. unintentionally or accidentally, to run, fall or flow from a container, usually so as to result in loss or waste [Who *spilled* the milk?] 2 to shed (blood) 3 *a*) to empty the wind from (a sail) *b*) to lessen the pressure of (wind) on a sail 4 to scatter at random from a receptacle or container 5 [Colloq.] to let (something secret) become known; divulge 6 [Colloq.] to cause or allow (a rider, load, etc.) to fall off; throw off 7 [Obs.] *a*) to kill *b*) to destroy or ruin *c*) to squander; waste—marks an important sexual motif in my writing.[2] Having spent far too long trying to get off on "not enough," my writing is one place where "too much" is how much I want, and I find that "too much" here, at the intersection of autobiography, feminism, and desire.

Rupture(d)

It would be wrong for me to say I had a perfect childhood until I encountered my first English teacher, but I think I can safely say I had never been publicly ridiculed by an adult before. I was at the age when the pain and frustration of sounding out words had begun to abate and the enormous store of pleasure in language was slowly dawning on me. As a child, I would not have known that Leda Gorham (whose patronymic I will always understand as G-O-R-E-'E-M) was an angry, repressed woman, but her black plastic glasses, pursed lips, and tweed suits worn with an air of indignation at the hot, sultry climate of the Belgian Congo, where my family then lived, should have suggested something sadly awry.[3] As a kind of antidote to what I perceived as her rigidity, I literally cut my way out of bounds and scissored into her visual field.

In the midst of my coming to language, Leda assigned a book report. What a pleasure to be asked to read something and then tell about it, I thought as I assembled my materials. After drafting the report in the luscious curvaceous letters of a newly learned cursive hand, I made a costly aesthetic judgment: I decided that the one-dimensional, smooth, white plane of paper with wriggling black marks imprisoned flatly on its surface could be rendered more animate by cutting out each sentence, carefully moving the scissor blades around the loops of my l's and the tear-drops of my y's. When I finished cutting, I stacked the sentences in the proper order and tied a ribbon around them to maintain the integrity of the essay form. Too bad I had not yet heard of controlled accident or discontinuous writing or John Cage or William Burroughs because, for this seemingly unprecedented "experimental" piece, I was reprimanded harshly in front of my classmates. In fact, Mrs. Gore-'em told me I should be ashamed of myself. I connected shame with sexual "misconduct," so when this teacher—this authority figure, this person-who-is-supposed-to-know—used the word in relation to my book report, sex and writing became linked in my mind as mirror expressions of unruly, unwelcome desire.

In the years following her indictment, I struggled with two opposing impulses: to please and to provoke. The question, "What does the Other desire?" alternated in my mind with its evil underside, "Who gives a shit?" Leda's angry ejaculation became one of the anchoring points of my dual identity as dutiful and devious, shapeless and ill-defined until she "cut" into me with her words. Our exchange revealed the capacity of language to be a double-edged sword, both wounding and redressing the wound. Words are, in fact, homeopathic, "curing like by like," poison by poison.[4] In goring or puncturing me, Leda ruptured my childish, one-dimensional, smooth, white plane of "selfhood," or what psychoanalysis calls *the subject*. What it has taken me nearly thirty years to understand is that the path I have carved for myself originated in this interaction, beginning with an act of rending, rupturing, or goring a textual body (i.e., cutting up my book report), to which Leda responded by rending, rupturing, or goring me with a reprimand ("You ought to be ashamed of yourself!"), and culminating with my becoming a "Gorham" (i.e., an English teacher). And as I write this paper, I realize I am repeating the offense first committed on that book report, cutting up the body of this text, revisiting the original traumatic moment from the other side of shame.

Cuts

PERVERSION

I was prepubescent but conscious of myself as a sexual being by the time my parents agreed to leave the United States and work for the Presbyterian Mission Board. The year was 1965, and Zaire was in trouble. Although the country had gained independence in 1960 and instituted a plan for decolonization, all was not proceeding as hoped. A wave of rebellions had broken out by the end of 1963, and the Abdoula government was in collapse by June of the following year. Because of the mass exodus of Belgian functionaries and army personnel, mission organizations stepped in to help maintain continuity in basic services such as health care, education, and communication. My father, a crop duster in southeastern Arkansas and member of the First Presbyterian Church, was called upon by one such organization to take part in an emergency program for training Congolese airplane pilots and mechanics. At age twenty-nine, my father flew out of the cotton fields of the Mississippi River delta and into the villages of tropical Africa, taking his wife and three daughters with him. Our family had answered a call from a church agency, a call to serve, to be servants. Yet we looked and acted very much like the Belgian oppressors of this "dark continent," with our stucco houses, our cooks, gardeners, and maids, our cars, our white faces. In serving the Congolese, I wonder now, did we truly submit to them through our spiritual service? Or did we collude in their domination by appointing ourselves their "educators"? Was it Christian service and succor that we offered? Or Christian dogmatism and coercion? Were we martyrs? Masochists? Masqueraders? What, precisely, was the nature of this relationship? Could it have been that we and our fellow missionaries occupied a perverse relationship with the Congolese, using our African brothers and sisters as the fetish that covered a tear in the fabric of the church?[5] And I wonder, too, if the ambivalence that must have permeated our lived relationships between "missionary" and "native" spills over, for me, into sexual relations, establishing an expanded notion of the tame form of copulation known as the "missionary position"?

VIOLATION

I'm pedaling down a broad, dusty avenue on my bike. A ridiculously blonde, obscenely curvaceous Barbie doll lounges in the wire basket attached to the handle bars. No matter how much the hot African sun beats down on her, she never tans—unlike the little girl who owns her. I'm taking Barbie to a white playmate's house when, suddenly, a young Congolese boy steps in front of my bike and grabs the handle bars. I'm forced to stop, and as I stand straddling the bike, my heart racing, the boy picks up the Barbie and wrenches her long, shapely legs apart. Then, when he sees the look of horror on my face, he laughs and tosses her back into the basket, face down, hair and limbs askew. He lets me ride away, untouched, but strands of pain and violation are already threading through my erotic imagination.

MASOCHISM

Summer 1966. A swimming pool in Léopoldville, later called Kinshasa. The central characters in this foggy scene drawn from memory are five teenage boys, all Belgians. The oldest one smoked a cigarette. With luxurious raven hair, eyes hidden behind dark sunglasses, and black bikini briefs molded to his pelvis, he stood out like a movie star. He was seventeen, let's say, and I was six. I remember him because he was the leader and, by far, the most self-assured. But I also remember the youngest boy, the victim, also beautiful, almost girl-like in long blonde curls and soft white skin. Play turned haphazardly to violence, like wind to tornado, between the two boys, responding, perhaps, to the strange energy of almost-naked bodies enclosed together in a small, wet space. The four older boys dunked the youngest member of the group. If he had laughed off the first immersion, his companions would have stopped, I imagine, but as soon as they saw his fear, they made the dunking a sort of game or rite of initiation. They pushed him under and he came up choking, begging them to stop. Down he would go again, to the bottom of the pool, only to reappear momentarily, blonde curls dripping chlorinated water, his frightened young face twisted in agony. The other boys laughed as he clawed for the surface and gasped for air. Maybe the oldest boy watched from the side, smoking his cigarette and directing the proceedings. As I looked on from the protective arms of my mother and her friend June Eiseman, I was at once horrified and delighted to think how easily it could have been me at the mercy of the teasing laced with sexual threat. Finally, the boy's cries were too much for June. She walked over to the side of the pool and in a stern voice, with her very best French, yelled at the boys to stop. The maternal voice carried weight; the boys dragged their victim out of the water and laid him on the side of the pool, legs cut and bleeding from having scraped across the rough concrete bottom. Perhaps this scene at the pool was my first encounter with what Jean Clavreul refers to as "the perverse couple," for there was something oddly erotic about the handsome Belgian boy smoking a cigarette and directing torture in an alluringly detached manner and the beautiful younger boy lying bloody and spent on the side of the pool.[6]

Sex Cuts

SADISM

This time it's a playground in Léopoldville. I'm on the merry-go-round with an assortment of kids. No adults are close at hand, but there's another young Belgian boy, somewhat older than the rest of us, who gallantly pushes the merry-go-round and makes it spin very fast. Suddenly, he loses his footing in the circular rut, which is muddy and heavily footprinted, and he falls beneath the wheel. Because the wheel is low to the ground, he is trapped there and dragged for several revolutions as we ineffectively try to brake the madly spinning top. Finally, a stray adult appears, pulls the boy from beneath the machine, and lays him on the grass. I am fascinated by the boy's sandals, leather, and the dirt and blood on his wounded legs and arms.

VOYEURISM

Back home in Luluabourg, my parents are sick. Bill Threlkell (do my young ears hear ill?/thrill?/kill?) is called in. He is a missionary doctor and friend of my parents. I peek into the bedroom and see my parents naked, sheets covering their lower bodies. And there's Bill Threlkell! What's he doing in there? I feel shame for (ashamed of?) my parents, but I know something serious must be going on because both Mother and Daddy look white and abject, exposed and vulnerable. Their backs are bowed and their heads hang down in defeat. Later, I hear something about meningitis and a spinal tap. I don't understand completely, but I form an impression that the doctor has stuck a long needle, or a long needlelike tube, into their spines. What I began to know then and know with certainty now is that in any sexual relationship, there are *always* three.

BONDAGE

We're on the way to school with our Scottish neighbor, Gavin Scoogal, and their cook. On this morning, we've taken the back road, which feels like the back of the world. Halfway to school on this untraveled road, the cook runs into a friend of his, a member of the army or the police force. (Disciplinarian figures all look alike to me: frightening in their shiny black boots, sunglasses, and berets.) The army man speaks Chaluba to the cook. They look at us and share a knowing laugh. The army man takes our childish, fragile wrists and holds them in one of his big hands. Our hands look very white against his brown palm, like spilled manioch flour. He pulls out handcuffs as if to lock us up. When he sees fear on our faces, he laughs again and squeezes our wrists more tightly. I think he will never let us go, that we are doomed to something unspeakably horrible. Gavin kicks and flails with all the windmilling strength of his seven-year-old body. One small kick lands on the army man's shin, and he laughs a third time from his great height. Gavin's struggle excites our captor, but a fellow officer approaches and he lets us go. As the cook walks us the rest of the distance to school, he tells us we were lucky this

78

time but we will certainly be bound and taken away next time. The whole world takes on a sinister aspect as he continues to chuckle and mutter, "Next time."

FETISHISM

I recently bought a pair of plastic handcuffs, wrapped them in tinfoil and decorated the silver package with a strip of black lace and a spiked, ruby-colored bow. "Should I open it now?" he asks, fingering the cruel red bow and wincing. "No, not yet," I say, wanting to prolong the mystery or, perhaps more accurately, delay the drama I had not thought through to its end. Later he asks again. "Okay," I answer, giddy with fear and excitement. I don't know how he'll respond to so perversely suggestive a gift. "Put them on me," he says. Because they are meant for children, they barely close around his adult wrists, but I force them on and snap them shut. "Now what?" he asks. "I don't know," I say, suddenly afraid of the power the handcuffs give me. He sits silent for a moment, tumescent, awaiting my next move. I make none. I have retreated into a hysterical numbness. "Take them off," he says, knowing I am choking on my own desire; the game is over before it has begun. I insert the plastic key into the lock and try to turn it, but it jams. His wrists begin to throb, he tells me, impatient to have the handcuffs off. I turn the key this way and that, and suddenly it breaks in half, the stem still in the lock, the impotent hilt in my hand. Fortunately, there is a second key. This one breaks, too, but not before releasing the spring that opens the cuffs. For days now the handcuffs have lain on the kitchen table as a reminder of unfinished business. "Next time," I say to myself. "Next time."

SUTURE

When Lawrence Ferlinghetti compares the poet to an acrobat who is "[c]onstantly risking absurdity / and death / whenever he performs / above the heads / of his audience / . . . / balancing on eyebeams / above a sea of faces[,]" he accurately describes my experience reading the previous autobiographical material above at a very important conference in my profession.[7] In the moments following my "confession" of perversion, I wondered whether I'd made an absurd mistake, a deadly miscalculation, whether I'd just spent twenty minutes "performing entrechets / and sleight-of-foot tricks / and other high theatrics" amounting to nothing more than self-indulgence, hysterics, excess.[8] I determined not to think of my performance in terms of success or failure, triumph or humiliation, but as spillage, messy and necessary. In the days that followed, I received in fragments the feedback withheld during the presentation itself.

A number of people approached me—significantly, in bathrooms or bars, places associated with spillage—to say how fascinated they had been by my performance. Yet during the session itself, there seemed a certain discomfort with the content of my paper, palpable in the audience's tense silence. Perhaps they sensed the connection between writing and sex that pulsed in each part of my paper on some wordless level of energy passing between us. Jacques Lacan describes this sublimation of desire in a particularly striking passage: "In other words— for the moment, I am not fucking, I am talking to you. Well! I can have exactly the same satisfaction as if I were fucking. That's what [sublimation] means. Indeed, it raises the question of whether in fact I am not fucking at this moment."[9] Perhaps witnessing the confessional nature of my filmic "cuts" placed my audience and me in the position of sexual partners, satisfying ourselves through sublimation but feeling a little embarrassed in the aftermath—as two strangers might who have leapt into bed together and are forced to confront each other in the unforgiving light of morning. Or perhaps my performance was akin to a public striptease, an exhibitionist's desire to expose that "other" body—the body of the unconscious— and an invitation to the audience to act as voyeurs.

Why was I compelled to repeat an act that ended in trauma? That is, why did I risk "cutting up" with an audience chockful of Leda Gorhams, an audience who might assess my performance as shameful? Did some part of me want to be publicly reprimanded or humiliated? Did I achieve, through repetition, a perverse pleasure akin to masochism? (The masochist ought to be understood not as passive agent but as one in charge of stage directions: do this to me, hurt me in this particular way, one who flouts the law from within.) If I needed to be liberated from the hegemony of the Other's desire (in my case, Leda Gorham and the professional discourse she represents), then perhaps I was trying, like the little girl in the anecdote, to dump more cereal into my bowl than is allowed, shaking the box with such fury, in fact, that its contents scattered all over the room. Perhaps this was my version of the "talking cure," or "chimney sweeping" as Anna O. dubbed it, a desperate effort to take control of memories that had lain, unexamined, in the dark far too long.

If storytelling is "always a way of searching for one's origin, speaking one's conflicts with the Law," then it is an important personal and political act, but, I think, an (un)feminist one.[10] "(Un)feminist"—because I have yet to decide the ramifications of admitting that one might want (at least in one's imagination) to be treated like an errant Barbie doll. That one might like being victimized by a group of scantily clad Belgian boys. That one might get a libidinal charge out of gazing at a wounded body. That one might enjoy reading passages from Georges Bataille's *Story of an Eye* like this one:

> [O]ne day when we were in a car tooling along at top speed, we crashed into a cyclist, an apparently very young and very pretty girl. Her head was almost totally ripped off by the wheels. For a long time, we were parked a few yards beyond without getting out, fully absorbed in the sight of the corpse. The horror and despair at so much bloody flesh, nauseating in part, and in part very beautiful, was fairly equivalent to our usual impression upon seeing one another.[11]

I say "(un)feminist" because the truth of feminist desire is that—as excess, as "too much," as more than what women are "allowed"—it lives in the pulsation of pleasure, fleeting, not to be sorted out. It is always in midleap. Unresolved. And yet it drives on.

NAUSEA

Civilization makes women hysterical. Our genitals disgust us. We are especially repulsed by the smells and liquids that spill from them, the life and death muck of us. Like the skin on the surface of milk in Julia Kristeva's *Powers of Horror*, the viscosity of sperm or vaginal secretions (life-giving or life-supporting substances) seem almost more than we can bear. If we touch or taste them, we gag, our stomach lurches. The same goes for excrement. This restriction of the body stops up women's writing. The hysteric censors herself, self-edits, until nothing comes out anymore. Or if something does come out, it is small and hard, barely worth the effort of expulsion. The answer to this constipation of consciousness? The couch—the feminist psychoanalytical couch, to be specific. What makes psychoanalysis liberating is not necessarily being cured of our neuroses but accepting them as our own and taking responsibility for them: "Enjoying our symptom," Slavoj Zizek says. The point of analysis is to get the hysteric to speak, to get her to give up a turd or two, for it is through language that she constitutes her desire.

I speak of the hysteric in the third person, as if she is some distant and troubled other, but I am really speaking of myself. My own verbal constipation illustrates the very height of my hysteria: when I was a sophomore in college, I lived off campus with three other young women. At that time, there was a long list of words I could not, would not utter, words that simply could not be housed in my mouth. Yes, I could fart in private (even I recognized that to avoid doing so might end in explosion or rupture), but to *say* the word was impossible. In fact, saying it held more shame for me than doing it. I had never even written the word. When my housemates got wind of this linguistic difficulty, they immediately set out to cure me by a tactic you might call desublimation. One night when I returned from class, the entire house was decorated with the word *fart*, and the pièce de résistance, drawn on the bathroom mirror using a bar of soap, was a visual image of a woman's buttocks expelling a thundercloud of flatulence. While laughter may be the best medicine, it did not cure me. But the ease with which my housemates, who were no more or less ladylike than I, handled the word *fart* suggested my problem could no longer be written off as southern gentility or proper feminine prudery.

Symptom

VOICE

As I moved from childhood into adolescence, I was immensely pleased with my voice. And, perhaps to the chagrin of my family, I often roamed about the house glee-fully whinnying, bellowing, whistling, and singing at the top of my growing lungs. Whether the sounds emitting from this young mouth gratified others was entirely beside the point. It simply felt *good* to fill the throat with vibration and have it wobble on to the airwaves and enter my ear. Repetitious, ludicrous ditties would be interrupted by sudden leonine roars and raucous laughter. How could such a slender girl—dainty hands and feet and mouth—make so much noise and take such obvious satisfaction in crude sound and vulgar mirth?

SOUND

"Hey, hey good lookin'! Wha-whatcha gotta cookin'? How's abouta cookin' up somethin' good with me-e-e-e? How's abouta cookin' up somethin' good with me-e!" Draw out the final *e* and then laugh like a hyena. Launch immediately into the next tune: "She wore blue velvet . . ." Don't remember the rest of the song but indulge in the first four words. Work the *velvet*. Let a couple of tears slide down your face. Then burst into laughter and a few lines from *Midnight Cowboy*.

Too wrenching—how about some lighter fare?

"You can take Salem out of the country, but . . . you can't take the country out of Salem!" Repeat several times. No call to giggle. Just come down hard on the but and pause before swinging into the punchline.

Next a little Johnny Mathis:

"Just an empty tube of toothpaste and a half-filled cup of coffee: Odds and ends of a beautiful love affair . . . " Feel the vowels on *odds and ends*. Make the *s*'s sound like *z*'s. Go up on the *of* and down on the *a*. Get giddy at the words *love affair*.

Swing into something snappy, the impatience building, the urge to stamp and roar and bite and tear coming on strong: "Oh, the B-I-B-L-E, yes, that's the book for me. I stand on the *Word*, yes, the *Word of God*, the B-I-B-L-E!"

Roar. Bellow.

TONGUE

Phil Plunkett started with three strikes already against him. He was fat, nearsighted, and nerdy—he played the trombone in the junior high school marching band. But he also had the hutzpah to announce to me soon after he joined the First Presbyterian Church at the corner of Maple and Seventh Streets that he could speak in tongues.

"How do you do it?" I inquired.

"It just comes out," he said. "Simple as that."

"What does it sound like?"

"I can't describe it, but I could demonstrate if you like," he said, lowering his voice and looking furtively at the elders gathering in the fellowship hall for coffee. "Only certain people have the gift, you know," he continued, as if to convince me of his authenticity. "And they can do it anytime they choose. Turn it on and off like a faucet."

Then Mr. Berry, who owned a grocery store and sang in the choir, was pinching our ears and handing us yellow boxes of Chiclets. He didn't seem to realize that we were

86

too old for the magic-ear trick. Once Mr. Berry was out of earshot, Phil said, "But if we're going to do it, we'd have to do it somewhere private. It takes concentration." I frowned, uncertain about accompanying the fat trombone player out of view of the adults, but Presbyterians did not allow such exotics in the sanctuary. Those padded pews were for people who stood and sat when told and sang without zeal in one uniform voice. In the end, curiosity got the better of me.

"Come on," he said, "We can do it in the rec room. There's no one in there." Although Phil did his best to add drama by closing his eyes and pressing his hands together before speaking, his tongue sounded oddly familiar. Arabic perhaps?

"I thought you were supposed to be filled with the Holy Spirit when you spoke in tongues," I said when he paused to see whether I wanted to hear more. "How can you control the Holy Spirit?" Phil did not have an answer for this, but if he could have come up with one, his next move would have been to ask me out. The thought sickened me, but I couldn't stop imagining his pale, wet lips hungrily tugging at mine, his slack, plump body pressed urgently against me, his thick tongue lodged in my mouth. . . .

SONG

The heavy, oak drawing-room doors are closed; only the comforting sound of murmuring voices can be heard. Soon, however, a new sound issues from the two-inch crack between closed doors. I walk casually by and peer in, but I do not watch for long. Foreign, unfamiliar words come from my mother's mouth. Gutteral, gurgling, glottal. As if her vocal chords are drowning in honey and she's calling for help. Is she choking? Singing? What then?

Her mouth looks as if it will never close, as if her jaw has been jammed open so this strange tongue can channel freely through her inert body. I turn away from the door and go as far from the drawing room as possible. I no longer feel like whinnying, bellowing, singing, or roaring—ever. All I do is whistle, my lips pressed firmly together. Nothing can get in, and only the smallest stream of air can get out. From then on, my pleasure will be small, carefully contained. Even in the privacy of my own bedroom I cannot bring myself to open my mouth, fearing the tortured, ecstatic oral emission my mother seemed to enjoy will come uncontrollably out of me.

At camp, when it's time to sing around the campfire, I momentarily forget my uneasiness and join the song. When I feel joy and emotion well up, I stop in horror. I mouth a few words but do not engage the grain of voice created by loosening and tightening my throat. I watch the others, their eyes gleaming with pleasure, mouths open in oblivious, unself-conscious harmony, with new-found contempt.

SEX

When I become an adult and begin to experiment with sex, I often see a look of ecstasy in a lover's eyes as I hear him make the same strange, gutteral noises from the family drawing room of my childhood. I break off relations soon after with inexplicable haste, disgusted by this show of pleasure/pain, fearing that my own face, if I could see it, must also twist and emote. Later, I find a man who understands my grave disdain for intense shows of emotion and bodily sensation. As the years go by, however, he breaks the pact by becoming tender and passionate, by desiring me, the dark and hidden parts of my physical self. This, above all else, I cannot bear. I could stay with him as long as the love remained an abstraction, a purely aesthetic concept. But when it threatens to become concrete—when it is marked in the softness of a thigh, the coarseness of tongue and curve of hip—I grow sick and go as far from the drawing room of desire as possible.

THROAT

My mother knows about self-help. Her latest kick is what she calls NLP, or Neuro-Linguistic Programming. I don't like the sound of it, but because it is important to her, I try to be open-minded. One morning, she and my sister Bonny ask me to join them for an NLP session. Reluctant and nervous, I do. I am asked to introduce myself using my first name and a two-word phrase that sums up the problem I want to work on. As I shake hands with Mother and Bonny, I introduce myself as "Becky Lacks Courage"—and feel ridiculous.

"Where does the cowardice affect you, in what part of your body?" Mother asks.

"The throat," I answer after a moment's thought.

"What sound does cowardice make?"

"A strangled, choked, inarticulate gurgle."

"Can you demonstrate it for us?"

I open my mouth but no clear sound comes out, just creaking like a rusty hinge. An occasional frustrated sigh, followed by a "well . . ." that trails off into silence. An "uhm" of delay. An intake of breath that seems to signal the start of speech but winds up exhaled, stale from long storage. Lips open with promise and snap shut in obstinance.

"What would you like to replace your cowardice with?" Mother asks.

"A fearless, intrepid joy," I answer.

"And where would that be located?"

"In my chest and throat."

"What is the sound of fearless, intrepid joy?"

"A roar or bellow," I answer, feeling sheepish.

"Roar for us, Becky," Mother says.

I want to roar, to bellow, to make joyful noises, but I am afraid. It takes me several minutes, several trial roars to really let go and do it—to let my lungs expand and contract as the air rushes out of my body into the room, filling it almost to the point of bursting with sound.

It feels good.

It feels very good to roar.

4

I Learned from the Best

My Mother Was a High-Femme Whore

PAULA AUSTIN

> Using femininity as an economic tool is a means of exposing its constructedness and reconfiguring its meanings.
>
> —Eva Pendleton, "Love for Sale"

I CANNOT TALK ABOUT sex without talking about being a lesbian femme who enjoys topping, without talking about being African-Caribbean, without talking about growing up a Black working-class woman from a formerly colonized country, without talking about living as a feminist and literacy activist, without talking about my mother. And I do want to talk about my mother—because she taught me everything I know.

My mother always talked very openly about sex. Sometimes, I think, too openly. I remember her catching me masturbating one night, flinging back the bedspread to uncover my hand between my legs, playing with the few

hairs growing there, one finger deeper inside. After exposing my bare body to the night air, my mother proceeded to
tell me that "it" (whatever I was doing) was natural. Mixed
messages, huh?

Let me tell you about my mother. My mother taught me
many things, some of which passed between us without
words, shaping my gestures, threading through the fibers
of my flesh. My mother's childhood left her wounded. Yet
she was a woman men desired, who gave birth to many
children, four of them alive, others not. She moved thousands of miles away from her home, to a different continent, a different culture, to work and work and *work*. She
left her four children, all girls, back home with their grandmother and father until she could come back for them. My
mother taught me to work hard, be hard, to fight mean, to
fear love—and to question it. She taught me the meanings
of *honor* and *retribution* and *fear*, and pain that goes way
back. She taught me what she could, what she knew. Desire
and sex and sensuality. How to flirt and be coy, demure.
How to be femme, a high diva, how to dress well, acces-
sorize, show off my cleavage. How to be looked at, how to
be invisible and afraid. How to survive, stay alive.

For my mother, Ena, sex was work. She grew up in colonial British Guiana, South America, in the thirties. She
lived in rural Bartica, where people were poor and Black
and struggling to feed their children. My grandmother
took in clothes from rich white people seven days a week.
Stood long hours at the washer board and basin, and then
later at the ironing board. My grandfather left his family

when my mother was ten. She scrubbed floors to help her mother. She took care of her sister's child. And she became a prostitute.

Ena's idea of strength lay in the power of her sexuality: looking good and getting what you need. On her limited budget, she was always clean, well-groomed, sexy. Heaving breasts, round wide hips, hugged by a long-line brassiere and girdle. Her hair wound up on top of her head, pressed, and singing with hair grease. She knew how to get "things"—money, kerosene to light the lamps, food for her children. This was her work, to survive and keep her girls alive while her husband supported his other family across town. In sex work, she found a reason to feel accomplished, adequate, of use to her family. She found a means to control her life, her body.

My mother married my father, or at least the man purported to be my father, when she was twenty-one; he was twice her age, and she was not a virgin. My mother always had many lovers. The man who had been supporting her until her marriage often came to the house and drank with her husband. Many men coveted her, and she used their desire to her advantage at a time, in a country, when dark-skinned poor women had few opportunities. Colonialism, imperialism, and racism invested shades of black with economic significance; light-skinned women were more likely to enjoy lives of leisure, leaving dark-skinned women as the workers, thick headed and service bound. My mother says she never had the brains for school. Her formal education ended at sixth grade, but she's been studying all her life, an accomplished master of cultivating sexual power in the face of tremendous odds.

My mother is ailing now, and her ability to get "dolled up" as she calls it, is limited. Still, the vision of her getting dressed is in my mind's eye each time I "doll up" for a date with a beautiful butch woman.

■

I once told my lover, a butch lesbian college professor (out and cute as she can be), there is something indescribably amazing about making love to her. Something that almost takes my breath away. And the truth is, though I would never tell her this, I've had this feeling before, making love to other women. The act of touching another woman's body, watching the pleasure on her face, hearing her moan, feeling her body moving to my strong rhythm, is for me a true moment of feminism, of womanism.

Sex. I caress the curves of her body, this woman beneath me. Her legs long, her arms outstretched, face to the side, eyes closed, mouth open. I want to devour her, every inch of her into me, me into her; my lips find every crevice. I want to have her whole breast in my mouth; I want to stay, my face between her legs, forever. I slide my fingers inside, her back arches.

I watch her: short hair, full lips. She doesn't like to be pegged as butch, lumped into a category so simply, but she is. I mean she must be, for me to be making love to her right now. Not that I haven't admired, given long lingering looks to beautiful femme women, their curves, breasts, high heels, tight asses in tight pants, but I have not wanted to devour them in this way. I look longingly in admiration, appreciation, not lust. Who can explain attraction?

Today I am all dolled up going to the airport for the Professor's arrival. She is coming to visit me, *me,* I say, really feeling it. Purple is the color of the day—high heel sandals, silk shirt tight around my large breasts, nipples erect, glittery green necklace, cowry shells, a hint of cleavage and the tattoo of Nefertiti on my left breast, body glitter, my hair piled on top of my head, eyes lined with deep purple. Is it too much? I catch my reflection in the floor-length windows on the way to the terminals and like what I see. I feel my ass sway like my mother's, my calves flexed in high heels, the jostle of my breasts, my hair flying back, and in my wake the smell of sweet, sweet body oil. Men turn to look as I rush by. I smile knowing I will soon be kissing a woman in this airport.

███

In 1984 I was a junior in high school, in love with my best friend Jennifer, and beginning to entertain thoughts of my strength as a woman, but not yet as a lesbian. This was the year Susan Brownmiller's *Femininity* came out. A little over two years passed before I read it and discovered Brownmiller's discussion of femininity took for granted women's heterosexuality, focusing, for instance, on competition between women for men's attention. Brownmiller says, "feminine armor is never metal or muscle but, paradoxically, an exaggeration of physical vulnerability that is reassuring (unthreatening) to men."[1] Sandra Bartky, too, writes of femininity in ways I don't find useful. Her ideas about "normative femininity" and the "disciplinary practices" of makeup, high heels, and skin care do not sound the depths of femme femininities.[2] When she compares the feminine woman to "a schoolchild or prisoner," she does not account for my mother, and the real constraints on what a woman can be and do for herself when she is poor and of color.

Considering my mother as a sex worker puts a frame around her femininity that separates it from traditional self-subordinating womanhood. Many femmes share a history of sex work. "We have the attitude to pull [sex work] off," writes Amber Hollibaugh.[3] Men looked at my mother when she walked down the street, and she never looked down or away.

Like Joan Nestle, I want to say of my mother, she was "both a sexual victim, and a sexual adventurer."[4] The stories my mother told me, of an outrageous girl washing her naked self on the back steps in the twilight, of a young woman starting a new life for herself and her children in a new country and a different culture at the age of forty-two, of a woman whose empowerment knew many bounds, but who did what she had to for her children to survive, a woman who somehow, in the midst of her own internalized oppression, transferred racial and gender pride to her daughters—these are the stories that I keep alive and recount as evidence of a strength that runs through me and all the women in my family. I have respectful awe for my mother's deep passion and true sexuality, and her strength to address and even transform the limitations of her situation.

Like race, gender, and sexual orientation, femme and feminist are interwoven in me, shaping how I see things. This acceptance of my femininity—and my mother's—is in direct conflict with the lesbian feminism of the 1970s, which rejected both butch and femme as a "heterosexist imitation of the oppressive gender roles of patriarchy."[5] Even though I came out in the 1990s, after Judith Butler's *Gender Trouble* (where she establishes the difference between biological sex and socially constructed gender, asserting that gender can be a political and erotic performance), a large community of lesbians, young and old, primarily middle class and white, still subscribed to separatist philosophies of the early women's movement, and I felt constrained by this community. In their eyes, I saw parts of my mother's story fall away, and with them, parts of myself.

▬

I watch my mother from the bed. She has already taken her whore's bath, the art of cleaning all the right places with Jean Naté and a paper towel. My sister and I took whore's baths too. Freshening up, my mother called it. She takes out each clip from her hair and rings of long pressed black hair unravel down her head. She brushes it back hard, pins it up and to the side. Then she twists the back in a French roll and brushes a little bang behind her ear, securing it with a clip. She pulls on control-top panty hose over her shapely thighs and ass. I always envied my mother's ass—wanted my ass to look like hers—large, but round and firm, so dresses fell over it just right. Over her hose, she pulls on her girdle and then fastens her long line brassiere. Sometimes she asks me to help. Then she sits at the side of a small bedside table facing toward me on the bed. I watch her do her makeup in front of the two-sided mirror, one regular, one magnified. She dabs foundation from the bottle into her hand and smears it evenly across and around her face. She uses concealer around her eyes and covers it with powder. Then the eyeliner, black, above and below her eyes, accented with eyeshadow and mascara. Lastly, she lines her lips, using some shade of burgundy on them. She finishes dressing—shoes and pocketbook always matching, the smell of expensive perfume in the air. Her dresser, lined with perfume bottles and jewelry boxes, created in me an appreciation for pretty woman things. The way she adorned and washed her body was a way to honor it. And it was also her armor—the shield that brought her strength and power. She was modeling this unsubdued womanhood for me—not knowingly, but modeling nonetheless.

One of the many things I was punished for as a young girl was wearing makeup on the sly. I would wait until my mother was out of the room at bedtime and sneak the eyeliner from the makeup drawer, hiding it under my bed in the room I shared with my sister and mother. The next morning I would pretend to look for my shoes, slip the eye-liner into my pocket, and sneak it out of the house. Somewhere between the apartment door and the building door five flights down, I hurriedly applied the makeup, lining my eyes from a blue pencil and combing on black mascara. Never delicate enough, rough, heavy-handed, but once I stepped out from that apartment building—out onto Ocean Avenue in Flatbush, Brooklyn, where I was a poor Black girl living in someone else's home in an all-white neighborhood, where my family was seen as the help—I walked to the bus stop with my head high and without flinching. Femininity would be my armor too.

When I was growing up, I wore what my mother called "rags." I admired my mother's discipline of always being put together, groomed carefully, her attention to detail and style, but I didn't take after her yet. One late-spring afternoon, I was walking home from school and unexpectedly met my mother coming toward me from the opposite direction. Under her measuring gaze, I became aware of my appearance, as if she were a mirror moving toward me, showing me to myself. I wore Day-Glo orange socks (remember those?) and little black boots, a pair of faded orange pants tailored to midcalf, white T-shirt and gray cotton vest, and my hair, in carefully arranged disarray, completed the picture.

I also became aware of my mother's body, different from mine, her way of moving through space. She had a sexy gait. I don't remember exactly how she walked, I've lost that part of her; her knees are "bad" now, and even with a cane she struggles to get around. But in this memory, she walks toward me in a blue-and-white floral polyester dress that hugs her breasts and hips. Her strong calves like carved wood, adorned smartly in black pumps. Hair coifed atop her head, black pocketbook hanging from her arm. She walks steadily in my direction, inspecting me from head to toe.

■

I often wonder whether my mother ever enjoyed sex. I want to think she did, but I don't know. There is a secret story my mother has told me. It is the secret story of Norma Anthony who lived next door. I am told that Norma wanted my mother to give me to her when I was born, that she held me longingly. After I told my mother I am a lesbian, I learned more about Norma. How Norma was also "that kind of woman." How everyone in town knew it. How Norma seduced my married mother repeatedly, and, the story goes, when my mother wanted to break off the affair, Norma hung my mother's bra out on the porch to send a message to the town that she'd had this woman.

Here is how I imagine the scene:

They were friends. (My mother doesn't like to admit that because she says Norma had a bad reputation.) And they must have spent a lot of time together. They would drink Mauby together, maybe sorrel, adding sugar and smiling at each other. They'd sit by the window and quietly gossip about people passing by. Maybe they would go to market together, my mother spending the money Mr. Austin and her other lovers had given to her to support us girls. They would walk home together, or ride their bikes, or get a ride from some nice man my mother knew. It was so hot, the sun would beat down on their heads and by the time they got home, Norma would invite my mother in for a cool glass of ginger beer and my mother would go. And this is probably how it had gone on for a while. A courting of sorts. 'Cause my mother, I know, was a flirt. Attention paid to her was all it cost to get a playful touch from her, a batted eye, a shyness hinting at a deep, loud, full passion. So one day, after the laughter, the walking, and the hot sun, Norma must have leaned across the table and kissed my mother's lipstick-painted lips. (And I know it was Norma who leaned in, because my mother is very strict with her femme-ness.) Norma touched her neck, traced her fingers down to my mother's breast. I imagine my mother closed her eyes, too caught up in the heat to stop her. Too caught up and needy to care that it was a woman who had laid her down and undressed her.

This is the story I have created about my mother's passion. Maybe I see it this way because I need to understand the connection between my mother and my lesbianism. Norma, who once wanted my mother to give me to her, playing butch to my mother's femme, is one way to express this connection. I allow myself to linger in this story about their affair, to make things up. I imagine this woman-woman encounter as my mother's only experience with sex that entailed love and passion and orgasm. I imagine Norma caressing my mother's tired feet, Ena with her eyes closed, all her attention focused on just feeling it. I imagine this experience with Norma defines my mother's sexuality because where else but with another large Guyanese Black woman like herself could she learn to care for every inch of her body with the tender excess of a lover. I imagine this experience as completely unlike any other, with her many male lovers who coveted her for their pleasure alone—and gave her none.

Maybe I lie. Or maybe what I learn later is another part of the truth. The story of Norma as the town crazy woman. Norma who ran into the street naked, who was taken away and given shock treatments. The story of a woman who worked for the telephone company as an operator, who listened in on people's conversations and informed wives when their husbands were cheating. A woman who got fired from her job, rumored to be a lesbian, a woman who lived alone. This is a woman my mother knew only because she did Norma's hair. A woman who "liked my mother *in that way* and wanted to show [her] that part." (My mother's words about Norma.) Norma, who then began to "scandal" my mother's name. A woman eventually sent to the United States for psychiatric evaluation, who can never leave Guyana again except to visit because of her tainted medical record.[6] Crazy woman. Lesbian. This is a very old story.

Flirting? Mmm, yes. I remember hearing my mother on the phone, or watching her with company. She flirted with everyone, speaking in sultry tones, placating men and asking questions like a little girl, giggling, sighing, eyes wide and suggestive. Did the men and women on the receiving end of her powers know what she was doing? Did they allow themselves to be manipulated, or was it beyond their control?

███

I am on my way back from the beach. Long cotton dress, slits up the side, flip-flop high heels, hair in large curly pom-pom atop my head. I am with a friend, somewhere between Durham and Wilmington, North Carolina. I am a northerner with all kinds of frightening stereotypes about the south, and they come out my pores like sweat when I find myself stranded on the side of the road at twilight. We trudge across the highway to what looks like a road toward town. We end up, somehow, at a bus repair shop up on the overpass. A man with a deep drawl meets us in the shop. My friend is concerned about her baseball cap and butch appearance. I am concerned about being Black. I tell him that we have broken down and ask to use the phone. My friend nods, smiles, stands idly by. A woman emerges from the recesses of the garage. The man directs me to the phone. I call triple-A and tell them I have a flat tire. I say, "I can't seem to get those screwy things off, you know, they hold the tire on?" The tone of my voice is equal parts distress and silliness. I shift my weight from hip to hip, smile at the greasy man as I wait for them to dispatch a truck. My friend does not speak.

When the tow truck arrives, we squeeze into the front seat. I'm pushed up close to the white man in the driver's seat, and I take a deep breath of stale air, years of spilled cokes and cigarette butts. We drive ten miles back to the highway. To keep this good old boy from taking too much notice of the Black woman and her boyish white companion in his truck, I chatter on. I say we couldn't get the darn screwy things off, you know, the things that hold the tire on. "Lug nuts," he chuckles. "Is that what they call them?" I giggle. "I just don't know a thing about tires." Giggle. My friend's leg is pressed up against mine, she mostly stares out the window. When we arrive at my stranded car, the tow truck driver takes out a large jack and begins to hoist my car in the air. "Man size," I say. I move around him, flitting. Trying to be of use but not really. My friend watches him work. I'm aware of the playacting I'm doing, feeling powerful in my convincing show of girliness, enough girl to overcome the racial prejudice bred in his bones. He is responding to my femininity. I can tell it comforts him. I look the part, like my mama taught me.

Brownmiller is right about femininity reassuring men of their rightful dominance. But she misses the power in it, for me and for my mother. She misses the art, the craft, the resistance at its core. She misses how looking like a proper woman can provide cover for far deeper survivals. Joan Nestle describes something like what I'm talking about:

"There is a need to reflect the colonizer's image back at him yet at the same time to keep alive what is a deep part of one's culture, even if it is misunderstood by the oppressor, who omnipotently thinks he knows what he is seeing."[7] For me and my mother, femme performance has provided both a safe disguise and secret nourishment.

5

Cutting, Craving,
& the Self I Was Saving

JENNIFER LUTZENBERGER

> Like revolutionaries working to change the lot of colonized people globally, it is necessary for feminist activists to stress that the ability to see and describe one's own reality is a significant step in the long process of self-recovery, but it is only a beginning.
>
> —bell hooks,
> *Feminist Theory: From Margin to Center*

A FEMINISM OF DESIRE would fit me, I think, like a corset. Instead of wondering why I'm corseted in the first place, and whether others have to wear a corset, or what the corset means, or how I might remove it, I could instead focus on the intensity of sensation afforded by the constraint, becoming increasingly aware of the boundaries of my own body. A feminism of desire would hold me together, prop me up, cinch me in between thick pieces of social fabric, my gross-grain ribbons pulled taut. With it, I could get a better sense of where I begin and end, what I am up against and what is beyond my ability to change as a single body in the world.

In my early twenties, I lived with a man who abused me. After I left, I began training in the martial arts. I thought it would be smart to become physically stronger and learn techniques of self-defense. I expected to learn these techniques "consciously" (I would purposefully think a new way in a dangerous situation), but instead I found I was training my body to have different instinctive reactions (I learned a new set of movements and reactions *underneath* my thinking; I taught my body to make something else happen in response to a stimulus, such as a hand flying at my face, without engaging my "conscious" mind at all). I assumed martial arts would be like weight training, in that I would be building muscles or increasing flexibility to allow my body to take more of the same, to find my limits again and again, and to keep surpassing them. Learning karate has not, for me, been a dedication as much as a reconfiguration; my job is not so much to remember the movements but instead to repeat them until they grow into me, become part of me.

At my dojo, my teacher asks advanced students to teach the beginning students the first, most basic movements, those on which all else depends. These sets of movements (katas) were learned so long ago, sometimes it's hard for advanced students to remember the basic motions and not add things learned in subsequent years. It's so easy to mis-remember the ways we've come to learn something, to embellish, but remembering precisely is so necessary for the task of relearning something with other people; in this way, what one learns can be shared and not isolated in individual psyches. There is a *growing together* that this kind of learning process makes possible. I want to highlight this space of growing together as a site for third wave feminist political action.

This essay presents a story of intimate trauma as a way to understand the intricate relationship between "inner" desire and "outer" practice. I put these words in quotation marks because, though I think we often feel a distinction between our selves and our actions, I don't think it's useful for us to hold these two as distinct, nor to give one (desire) a special, interior, location. At the same time, our experiences often demand we enforce such a split to keep us going, to make us feel safe and whole (so that, for example, we feel our "inner" self is safe from or untouched by different sorts of actions or relations we are forced to perform or engage "externally"). We—all of us—respond to the desires dictated by our roles and expectations, our personal and cultural histories, the media, the limitations of the buildings in which we live, the movements our bodies must make to achieve highest efficiency. While it may be the case that these responses are "hardwired" within our personalities, our brain chemicals, and/or our learned and chosen desires, how we make sense of them for ourselves and others, and how we use this understanding to choose a course of action at a later time, is not "hardwired" in the same way. That a feminism of desire would fit me like a corset, in other words, does not mean the only way to speak to my desire is either to bind me up tighter (so the corset continues to command my attention in newer, sexier ways) or teach me the oppressive history of corseted women (so I can refuse or deny my desire based on new enlightenment). If I want a new desire—if I want to take on my desire as a feminist project to be created with others—it is not enough to understand what I desire. It is not enough to continue to practice my desire noticing all the ways I play against the "expected" script. Nor is it enough to refuse what calls to me, to pretend my desire goes away if I stop acting on it. To take up desire as a feminist project is to take up *desiring feminists*, with all our complex urges and contradictory behaviors, to go through the katas of political action as beginners together, to create a new, shared ground from which to take an otherwise impossible step.

When I was younger, I loved a man who gave me advanced lessons in turning myself inside out, a history lived throughout the house, in the dents and blood stains (some visible to others; most visible only to me, as I willfully remembered them) on the walls, the bathtub rim, the steam radiator, my scalp. While I was working to love him "despite," I taught myself a nice trick; I would keep my mind sharp and away from him by planning to cut myself. I would let myself drift off into the details—what I'd cut with, and where, and how deep—whether I'd make a pattern only I would understand, whether I wanted to leave a scar or have it heal completely, and then how nicely I'd treat it afterwards to make it feel better, how carefully I'd bandage it, keep it clear of water and dirt. I could always elaborate with enough details to distract myself from whatever he was saying or doing, and later, once he was out of the room, I would cut myself according to plan. I loved it. I loved everything about it. I loved how it felt not only to cut myself, but to watch myself doing it, to watch and feel at the same time. I especially liked cutting my forearms, hands, and fingers, which meant for a little while I didn't wash dishes or do laundry; otherwise the cuts would reopen and I'd bleed all over his food and clothes. These passive-aggressive scenes made for too much blood, when joined with all the marks of me he'd embedded into the structure of the apartment (which I refused to clean up, often encouraging them instead into permanent stains), for him to live in comfort and thus afforded me a limited but very real sense of power. I now recognize self-cutting as a coping strategy.

When I was being abused, I hid the evidence from my friends and family. This was not very hard. In my community (middle-class, white, college-town progressive), being discovered as abused would have meant a particular sort of invasion of my privacy, which I was not prepared to handle. I grew up abuse free (my parents did not believe it was okay to spank, believed it was barely okay to yell at children, not to mention all the other great unmentionables of child abuse—if they ever heard a story of such abuse, their response was to declare it beyond belief, to declare they *just couldn't comprehend it*). With that lucky accident of birth came a whole set of expectations, including, for instance, that I would seek out the same sort of benevolence in boyfriends and, eventually, a husband. I knew nobody would support me in my relationship if they knew I was getting hit. They wouldn't be able to understand why I didn't want to leave, why I wanted to work things out. Not that I enjoyed being abused—I didn't—but I thought I had it under control. I had figured out the pattern of that relationship and how to stay in it, how to keep everyone unaware of what was going on and take secret care of myself. I had, after all, discovered a way to turn at least the pain I inflicted on my own body into pleasure, which made me feel deeply and privately powerful.

Most of the literature available on self-mutilation (also called self-cutting or self-harm) focuses on bringing this disorder into the antiseptic light of respectable medical attention. Armando R. Favazza, in his seminal text on social responses to self-cutting, explains the resistance he encountered when discussing the issue:

> Laypersons with whom I discussed self-mutilation invariably thought it to be a grotesque act. In talking with hospital staff on psychiatric and surgical wards, I was impressed by the anger, awe, and even fear that self-mutilative patients seem to elicit among caretakers. It is as if the presence of a self-mutilator threatens the sense of mental and physical integrity of those around him or her.[1]

Other texts on self-cutting begin at this same point: the revulsion felt by cutters and noncutters alike toward cutting. Why, these authors wonder, would people deliberately harm themselves, especially given the fact that a majority of self-abusers report some form of physical, sexual, and/or emotional abuse in their past?[2] Given that self-abuse is typically conducted in secret, at least in its more treatable forms, texts on self-abuse are not often written by people active in the practice. They are typically written by people in recovery from self-abuse, or taken from reports on cases in recovery by therapists, or they are written with the goal of helping the still-closeted self-abusers by care providers or other interested people. Firsthand literary accounts of self-abusers uninterested in "recovery" are rare. Only in the world of art do authors consider self-abuse outside the safe and pervasive language of addiction, disclosure, and recovery to provide imaginative accounts of why desire sometimes turns out so "different."[3]

The psychotherapeutic and recovery-oriented nature of secondhand accounts is not especially useful for my purposes; I neither wish to disclose and/or categorize my story as pathology, nor am I trying to "reach out" to other cutters. Rather, I am interested in descriptions provided by case studies and firsthand accounts of self-mutilation because I believe cutting is a perverse site of self-care, a coping strategy, and thus warrants attention from feminist theorists of desire. This requires some explanation, as I think I'm not using the word *perverse* in the accepted psychological manner.

To my mind, perversion is one response to a world split into opposites; our bodies, options, ability to see others, to make decisions, to want something—all this is divided into two, and one of the two is considered normal, correct, valued. The other is there for contrast: the not-normal, incorrect, without value. Feminism works against this way of seeing the world, especially as it relates to gender dichotomies (feminism reveals and challenges the "common" association of men with the rational, universally "human," public domain and women with the irrational, particular, domestic sphere, for example). These dichotomies are not natural or true; they are the way we come to understand difference, how we negotiate territory and understand boundaries. Everything conspires to convince us that these divisions are simply *the way things are*; not only do we learn there are no other options or ways to understand ourselves and others, we learn that it is pointless to think about and fight these divisions, since they are at once natural ("just" the way we think about the world) and symbolic (we equate men with rationality, but this doesn't mean all actual, individual men are rational or all women are irrational). Accepting this view of things is expected; not accepting it is perverse, a refusal to believe all that is set up for you to believe, sometimes when there isn't a clear or well-developed alternative.

Perversity, to my mind, is not merely to go against the grain, to do the "other" thing, but to do so in relative isolation, according to one's own compulsions and attractions, with no real goal other than intensifying pleasure. A perverse desire goes against not only what society might make of you, it often goes against what *you* would make of you, if you had more *control* over the circumstances of your choices. Perversity is about wanting something that goes against my own purposes—it's me getting in my own way—reminding me I am not entirely self-made. At the same time, my perversity keeps me afloat in a sea of contradictory demands, roles, and regulations. What I want sets me apart, and I like that feeling. I relish expressing what is strange and overwhelming in the space of my wanting—how it forces me apart from friends and family, an unsettling presence among people with "regular" desires.

And this difference keeps me seeking delight in disturbing quarters, keeps me moving, keeps me from finding a comfortable home. The less exciting part is that it keeps me stuck inside my own unsettled self. I know that I don't want most of what I see before me, but that doesn't mean I know what I *do* want. Perversity does not hold an object before me as a way to keep me working toward a goal—rather, it holds my desire open like a question and forces me to refuse or resist all definitive answers. This refusal, however, doesn't leave much solid ground on which to stand.

When I was being abused, I remember my most vivid desire was to be left alone. I didn't want to move from my house, or even from my room; I didn't want to leave my relationship, nor did I especially want to participate in it; I didn't want to spend time with my friends, my family; didn't want to cultivate social connections; I wanted to be alone. My life experiences led me to believe that to be alone, a woman needed to be living with a man in some form of intimate partnership. (I certainly knew women who lived together, but they didn't seem to me to have any time "alone"—their situation seemed to me the same as living with sisters, which for me had always meant a lack of privacy, rather than living like "adults," which was what I wanted.) I had not yet learned the many ways people might live together distinctly unlike a "traditional" heterosexual nuclear family. When the abuse got worse, I became even more ferocious about my privacy, not out of shame, but to protect the little control I still felt over my life and the world around me. It may not have been much, but I felt extremely reluctant to give it up; the options around me were not, to my mind, better or less fraught. I remained aware of the contradictions within which I lived—staying in a relationship because I wanted to be alone; cutting myself to draw my attention away from other pain—but what I wanted (to be left alone) lagged behind what was available to give me comfort (cutting; protecting time alone and the secret that would take that away). I felt "being alone" as a kind of goal (I thought someday I'd leave him), but the things it would take to get there (telling someone what was happening so they could help me get away; finding a place to live; getting "on" with my life) did not, at least for a time, compel me nearly as much as all the things I was doing to permit myself to stay.[4]

I like to torture myself when I remember this story by saying "and I would have stayed forever, if I hadn't been found out." I don't remember if that's true, or how much I helped others discover what was happening to me. Surely there had been other, earlier moments where people noticed something was wrong and confronted me, and in each of these moments I must have diverted their attention from the situation; then there must have come a day when I didn't do that anymore, and everything changed. Sometimes I like to remember I was "rescued," but I don't think that's true either, or if true, it's not what I want to remember anymore. The memory of my perverse responses to abuse is no longer useful for me if I want to build a new becoming for myself.

But sometimes, I can't help it. Even now, when moving through the world gets to be *too much*, and my mind swarms with decisions I've made or haven't made, I fill my bathtub, slide inside, close my eyes, and pretend I am cutting my wrists open, very carefully, along the vein. I imagine my blood mixing with the bath water, coloring my submerged body red, marking what's below from what remains above the surface.

Will it hurt, I wonder, to put my wrists underwater, like it hurts when you get accidental cuts wet?

Would it throb?

And for how long? I can easily spend a long, luxurious hour imagining the details of cutting myself and bleeding to death, my insides mixing with tub water while I lie in the slow space of holding myself open. This meditative fantasy of harm and release calms me almost as well as cutting myself once did. It's a guilty pleasure, but a pleasure nonetheless.[5]

Here is the thing: I know all about relations of power, positions of privilege, constructions of identity, the dissemination of differences, but *knowing* something does not translate into *doing* something, or even *wanting* to do something. I knew I had to leave; I wasn't ready to leave; I made something inside that contradiction that made it possible for me to leave and to stay, both at the same time, without having to stop questioning or noticing all the things going wrong. I could sit perfectly well inside the contradiction, in other words, without having either to resolve or deny it. I could play games with this contradiction, turn it around, use it to my advantage, make one thing into another thing, and I didn't have to move anywhere or change anything.

I magnified and restructured the violence, turned it against my own skin and flesh, took it into myself; I encompassed it. In fact, being perverse taught me an important truth about the violence of my own desire: that there is no relationship beyond or safe from violence, not even my relationship with myself. And I have become attached to this violence, sexualized it, and continue to love it as part of my personal independence and control even as I recognize its place in a destructive social structure of unbroken binaries.

I always understood the relationship between being abused and cutting myself. I never thought I deserved or liked being abused; I never thought the abuse was okay. I just didn't want to leave, not yet. Had cutting no longer worked, I could have invented infinite varieties of things to do inside my head to make myself feel better. But I am beginning to question what good this mental play does me. When I act perversely, I'm doing something despite what power would make of me, within yet in excess of power. I'm not letting the contradiction close down or resolve itself prematurely, or lie to me, or coerce me into doing something I'm not ready to do, or let me believe that I can't do anything at all. But taking pleasure from pain doesn't really make the pain stop, nor does it make sense of pain in the first place.

I did other things to care for myself besides cutting, but it has taken time for me to recognize them. The cutting always struck me as active—positive, decisive, agentic—I was aware of feeling something, doing something, making something, when I cut myself. I was less aware of the other narratives I made of my abuse—blood, broken things, dents—in(to) the apartment. I alone cleaned the apartment, and since I refused to clean up the evidence of abuse, he and I had to live around and among it, inside it, until the marks either went away on their own or became something we pretended not to see. At some point, there was just too much blood and broken-up shit for me to live there anymore. I couldn't stop seeing it—the story of abuse. That was when I knew it was time to move on. It wasn't that I woke up one morning and felt I'd had my fill, exactly, but more like my home, which I once loved and refused to leave for so long, stopped looking like home to me and started looking like a place of torture. At some point, I could no longer see all the nice things I'd sewed and placed and worked so hard to make beautiful; instead, I perceived my home as a weapon to be used against me, paying attention to what was made of glass and metal, how many places there were to lock me in or shut me up, how thick the walls were, how far away the nearest neighbors, how small and terrifying to be inside that apartment with him, how exhausting it all was.

I said before that perversity came naturally to me; it relates to the value I place on being alone, the American individualist. I grew up equating adulthood and independence; I believed learning how to live should be done in relative isolation, by trial and error, the frontier way. These values come from many different and sometimes conflicting sources—growing up middle-class, female, and Catholic, generations removed from my immigrant language and history, believing I deserve and will inherit my share of the American Dream, the "good" life. I was taught to put myself first, every man for herself, sort of a semiconscious social Darwinism. At the same time, I was schooled in particular forms of dependence, most notably, economic and social dependence on men. Like many women, I wanted all the things a man could give me; also like many women, I wanted to be left alone. This is the awkward dance of white, middle-class feminist womanhood—reaching confidently for what I want and at the same time curbing the enormity of my desire before it ever emerges into the light of day, moving with agility between self-expression and self-denial; like many women, I never learned how to do the dance well or right.

While researching self-abuse for this essay, I encountered a surprising number of writers who describe cutting, burning, or otherwise abusing themselves in ways that reach beyond pleasure into self-constitution. In account after account, people assert that damaging their skin paradoxically allowed them to feel they could hold themselves together. Many self-abusers report feeling as though they are falling apart, being subsumed by an uncontrollable chaos, or are unable to distinguish their own boundaries in some other way.

> During the experience of a phenomenon known as depersonalization, persons may retain a grip on reality yet feel that something strange is happening to their sense of self. To terminate this frightening and numbing feeling they may deliberately slice open their skin. At first glance this act may seem paradoxical since skin cutting might be thought to open a portal through which the inner self and outer world might flow into each other. In fact, a very different process occurs. The cutting causes blood to appear and stimulates nerve endings in the skin. When this occurs, cutters first are able to verify that they are alive, and then are able to focus attention on their skin border and perceive the limits of their bodies. The efficacy of this process is startling; skin cutting almost always terminates episodes of depersonalization.[6]

That cutting and other forms of self-abuse tend to be enacted in secret, on easily damaged and inconspicuous parts of the body, and with a high degree of ritualistic precision, further suggests a relation between self-abuse and self-care: specifically, the construction and maintenance of a complete, unfragmented self. In my own experience, cutting created an opportunity for self-control and self-care in the face of untenable contradiction. Cutting held me together because it expressed physically what I was experiencing emotionally, and communicated this experience to me in a way I otherwise would not have been able to recognize. When I look at my scars now, I see my almost limitless capacity for magnifying pain as a way of taking charge of my body's sensations and circumstances, transforming pain into pleasure and thereby staying in a destructive environment rather than transforming or abandoning that place.

The trope of "writing the body," common in contemporary feminist theory, generally refers to abstract correspondences between words and ideas of femininity as fluid, cyclical, associative. In cutting, I see a more concrete example of this intellectual concept. I inscribed the story of my relationship with an abusive man into myself, into my arms, along with the story of my resistance to the abuse, my deep-down awareness that I would not stay there forever, placing these two things together in the undeniable bond of blood and scar tissue.

I've always carried shame about sharing the story of my abusive boyfriend with other people—not because it's strange and embarrassing, but because it's common as shit, boring, nothing here worth looking at or discussing. Every time I see a made-for-television movie, go to a Take Back the Night march, or overhear women speaking in hushed tones about what might be happening to their girlfriend, I hear my stupid, average, boring story, and it makes me want to stop speaking, maybe never to speak again. The only part of my story that ever stood out to me as powerful, positive, or worth considering was the perverse part, the cutting.

Recently, however, I've become equally intrigued with the way I left marks in my apartment, enacting a very different kind of response to violence, and a very different form of self-care, than the response motivated by my primary, self-oriented, and inward desire. I think leaving marks on the walls and throughout my apartment had less to do with self-control, less to do with making myself feel whole and complete, and more to do with communicating with others. Instead of keeping the violence inside myself, I made the violence of my home external, made myself able to see the situation for what it was, and allowed myself the opportunity to refuse not just what the violence would make of me (as I did when cutting), but also to refuse the violence itself. It took telling my story to other people to make this part visible and valuable.

Understanding my perverse desire as active and resistant has been a necessary step in overcoming the shame of my experiences, providing one way I've learned to see myself as more than what my abuser would have made of me and what society would have made of my abuse (a victim, a battered woman). I was never that woman. I was *always* doing something other than what I was supposed to be doing. But my perverse desire has been so compelling to me, so sexy in comparison to mainstream cultural representations of domestic abuse, with their oversimplifications of right and wrong, victim and victimizer, staying and leaving. I liked this sexy part of my story enough that all the other ways I resisted were hard to remember or recognize. Those "other" forms of resistance occurred outside the way I viewed myself at the time.

So while I see perversity as a way to turn further inward, to protect one's sense of self, which is resistant and valuable to individual women in certain phases of coming-to-consciousness, I recognize and assert that this perversion as a strategy of social criticism and transformation is limited. But having noted this limit, and the necessity for coalition in feminism, which likely would mean bracketing one's individual desires, I would end these reflections by affirming the in-between spaces where women hang suspended—between knowing and wanting, staying and leaving, complicity and resistance. Perversity is the measure of freedom for women inside various states of coercion; it's whatever way a woman is able to move back and forth within the limits of one's current self and current desire, to feel (returning to my earlier metaphor of the corset) the external limits of one's self against whalebone and fabric.

I am indebted to the Methodologies for Resistant Negotiation Working Group, not only for the dialogues and workshops within which these ideas were multiply voiced and nurtured, but also for support throughout the process of my writing this essay. The members of the working group are Jackie Anderson, Mildred Beltre, Chris Cavanaugh, Nahum Chandler, Manuel Chávez, Jane Drexler, Laura DuMond Kerr, Tabor Fisher, Michael Hames-Garcia, Easa Gonzales,

Cutting, Craving, & the Self I Was Saving

Mauro Graciano, Sarah Hoagland, Steve Jee, Crista Lebens, Anne Leighton, Maria Lugones, Ernesto Martinez, Elizabeth Morrison, Rafa Mutis, Joe Navarro, Joshua Price, Lisa Reynolds, Rick Santos, Sarah Towne, and Rudiah Primariantari. I would also like to thank Lisa Johnson for her editorial comments and support.

6   *Of the Flesh Fancy*

Spanking & the Single Girl

CHRIS DALEY

> My response [to my Critical Inner Feminist] sounds a bit
> like a Zen koan: Erotic thrill is powerful, and empowering,
> even if the source of the thrill is the illusion that one is help-
> less.
>
> —Carol Queen, "Over a Knee, Willingly:
> Personal Reflections on Being Spanked"

SPANKING CHIC dominates the marketplace these
days. Barnes & Noble stocks up for Valentine's Day with
Patricia Payne's *Sex Tips from a Dominatrix*. Inept partners bungle with hairbrushes on *Ally McBeal*. Vodka ped-
dlers shackle their bottles for that Absolut Sadist look. At
S & M supper clubs, it's duck for dinner and discipline for
dessert. Spanking is hip, and—as with 1970s porno chic,
where "nice" couples flocked to see *Deep Throat*—middle-
class American consumers are eating it up. Lisa Palac aptly
commands, "Degrade me when I ask you to."[1] Spank-me
feminism is on the rise, and as a feminist with a fetish for a
slap on the ass, I'm here to support women in their dal-

liances with discipline. I trust women to make healthy decisions and believe we are at our most extraordinary when free to express our most complicated desires. We have the ability to transform practices developed in patriarchal cultures into turn-ons, sexing up what would have otherwise tied us down.

Snap

Like any proper fetish, the spanking started long before actual sexual intercourse. I was never, ever spanked as a child. I was never even grounded. I was the angelic daughter, every parent's dream. So when my first boyfriend at sixteen laid me over his bony knee and spanked me, something snapped. We weren't having sex and never did, but he was the first boy to touch my bare breast, the first to awaken clitoral tinglings I mistook for an urge to urinate, and the first to introduce his palm to my buttocks. He never spanked me while undressed, rather through the tight Jordache jeans I wore with panache.

The fact that we didn't "do it" emphasizes the performative quality at the center of spanking's charm. It was a sort of game. He experimented with punk rock makeup, and I chased a ball around a field with a big stick while wearing a short skirt. When I pretended to stumble on to his knees, we were not replaying the traditional gender roles some feminists might perceive in spanking; rather, our game straddled the divided worlds of adult and child.

The dynamics of erotic power differ according to the age of participants; as adolescents, spanker and spankee are, in my case at least, engaging in a process of sexual maturation together, with "us" on one side and "them" (the adults who would prohibit our activity) on the other. One might even say sadomasochism is a central dynamic of growing up, pubescent bodies dangling awkwardly in the middle space between dependence and autonomy. Like erotic domination, adolescent rebellion "embod[ies] the desire for both independence and recognition."[2] For adults, however, erotic domination is enmeshed in already existing power dynamics of gender inequality both in and out of the bedroom. In this world, spanking has some serious baggage.

Yet we were still free to enjoy the blissful obliviousness of childhood. At a tender sixteen, my drummer boy and I loved one another, independent of pop psychology pressures. We were equals: equally inexperienced, equally naive, equally curious, and equally randy. What we played at was a freedom with each other's bodies that, until then, we knew only adults were allowed. He was terribly excited to be touching my body, and I was terribly excited to be having my body touched by him. I occasionally took the liberty to touch him as well, and it felt good.

Eventually we broke up. He left me for an exgirlfriend who won him back by carving his initials in her stomach with a razor. Our spanking sessions paled in comparison, and we went on to lose our respective virginities to others.

I would pause here, though, over the image of this young

woman bringing a blade against her tender abdominal flesh, branding herself with the name of an ex-boyfriend. The real violence of self-mutilation and the simulated violence of erotic spanking may seem part of the same patriarchal power structure that leads women to despise our bodies and identities, but I draw an important distinction between the two, between *permanence* and *pretense*, *masochism* and *playful masquerade*. Before making room for spanking within feminism, I want to acknowledge the systemic domination of women worldwide via cultural regulations on the female body; I recognize that this system produces bodily effects that "cannot always be undone."[3] Here, precisely, lies the difference between self-cutting and spanking: one can be undone. Cutting one's skin creates tangible and permanent scars; the theatrics of spanking don't even necessarily redden buttocks, if both parties so desire. Further, the roles assumed during the performance do not generally extend beyond the bedroom into "real life." When I indulge my craving, I return triumphantly to the rest of my life feeling invigorated, sexy, and free. I am a woman who knows what she wants and how to get it—*good*. When my high school sweetheart and I finished our "homework," our bodies remained intact and sixteen with acne, curfews, and limitless sexual curiosity. There were no scars, inside or out.

The exploratory quality of this precoital world disappeared once I started having "real" sex, so I didn't think much of spanking over the next few years. Like necking in cars, steamy windows, and heavy petting's unconsummated high, spanking fell by the wayside. In all honesty, I didn't miss it. It was not yet central to my sexual repertoire, rather a specific act with a specific partner, a fond memory. Some experiences linger, though, in the pages of a body's scrapbook, returned to again and again as the moments and gestures that shape erotic personality. Sadly, adults often bury these marvelous adolescent discoveries of subtle sexual play out of fear, holding back the twists and turns of one's particular kink. We limit physical gratification without even knowing, deferring automatically to the culturally preferred genital-focused fuck.

Crackle

After a prolonged period of abstinence from spanking, a Hollywood native with a green convertible reignited the fantasy full force. I shouldn't not have been surprised (but was nonetheless) when he literally brought my inclination out of the closet. In the midst of a vigorous romp, he bounded from the bed, opened his closet door, and removed a disturbingly titillating object. I knew his exgirlfriend trained horses, so I thought it might be a souvenir from their relationship. He told me to get on all fours and applied the miniature horse whip gently to my flanks. A brief sting mellowed quickly into a pleasant burn—not painful, just present—and as it faded, a second snap of the whip focused my attention on a new spot.

Afterwards, I had serious second thoughts. Was I the same person as before? Was I still a feminist? What did I do with the fact that there was little of the patriarch in this particular man? What if I wanted to go back for seconds— was I "deformed"?[4] At the time, I did not have language for my ambivalence. I just thought, *What have I done?*

I turned to books and ended up in a section surprisingly titled "Women's Studies" instead of "Shame on You, Little Girl." I fingered the spines, pulling promising titles from the shelf and making a pile at a nearby table. I took in the growing stack, astonished, I blinked: so many smart women addressed the subject. I thumbed through the pages, plumbing their dark notions of sadomasochistic behavior. Here's what some of the experts had to say:

> If any form of sexuality has a prima facie claim to be regarded as politically incorrect, it would surely be sado-masochism. I define sadomasochism as any sexual prac-tice that involves the eroticization of relations of domina-tion and submission.
>
> —Sandra Lee Bartky

> Masochism is a search for recognition of the self by an other who alone is powerful enough to bestow this recog-nition.
>
> —Jessica Benjamin

> We must note first of all that attributing an erotic value to pain does not at all imply behavior marked by passive sub-mission.
>
> —Simone de Beauvoir

> [Sadomasochism is a] drama or ritual. . . . The partici-pants are enhancing their sexual pleasure, not damaging or imprisoning one another. A sadomasochist is well aware

that a role adopted during a scene is not appropriate during other interactions and that a fantasy role is not the sum total of her being.

—Pat Califia

Probably none of us is free of sadomasochistic feelings; no doubt the hostility sadomasochists inspire is in large part horror at being directly confronted with fantasies most of us choose to repress, or to express only indirectly.

—Ellen Willis

In the face of conflicting perspectives, I began to distinguish between various *sadomasochisms*, led by my own desire for discipline, which feels less like passive submission than active surrender, an act of choice and self-knowledge.

After our break-up and the corresponding termination of my access to his sex toys, I promptly visited the Pleasure Chest and bought myself a cat o' nine tails. I should interject a note on terminology here, as I object to the word *whip* with its synonyms of *flog* and *thrash* that belie violence alien to my spanking experiences. (While I recognize the existence of a sadomasochism that hinges on hurting or being hurt in a permanent way, for me, that's not what it's about. I am the S & M version of a Sunday driver.) For those unfamiliar with the device, the cat o' nine tails is a whiplike item with a six-inch leather-wrapped handle attached to approximately nine thin pieces of leather. The most common color is black, but the Good Vibrations catalog offers an assertive red version. The top of the handle often sports a small ring for hanging the tails privately in a secure location or displaying as part of an S&M decor. Mine hangs from a pair of handcuffs clasped conveniently around a bed post.

After my re-initiation to spanking and my introduction to spanking accessories, I started asking men I dated (however briefly) to indulge me. They always complied, but with a half-heartedness that dampened the fantasy—it didn't do it for them. In *Come Hither: A Commonsense Guide to Kinky Sex*, Dr. Gloria G. Brame admits, "I won't lie: Being kinky and single can be tough on the ego." When I want a spanking, I don't have the privilege of turning to my husband and suggesting we try something "different." My requests cannot be couched in a semirespectable rhetoric of "spicing things up." I often must make a bold move early in a relationship and 'fess up. I can only speak of very narrow circles—mostly white, urban, middle-class, overeducated, aspiringly "politically correct" heterosexuals somewhere between twenty-five and forty—but what I see is deep ambivalence among the men in my dating pool, tripping along the fine line between subordinating their sexual partners and boring them. We are all grasping for a new romantic ideal, hoping "[t]here is heterosexuality outside of heterosexism," but not knowing for sure.[5]

This postfeminist dilemma over power relations in the bedroom elucidates the appeal of spanking. Role-playing offers a way to escape the burdens of gender inequality. Sex partners can try on different erotic selves, and playing with these roles—even playing with traditional gender roles—

can mean the difference between sex*y* power and sex*ist* power. When I whisper a breathy "Spank me," I am able for a moment to step outside a world where I fight tooth and nail to climb the ladder of success as fast and skillfully as any man, and I give my partner a taste of power over me he'll never experience in any other realm of the relationship. Because feminism equipped me to cultivate equality in relationships with men, I can flirt with the no-no of submission without reinforcing double standards or inviting sexual exploitation.

Pop

One night, during the third visit of a six-month long-distance relationship, I let several glasses of vodka stir up trouble in the darker corners of my mind. A comment I no longer remember led to my inebriated conviction that I was a bad girl in need of reprimand. In previous spanking sessions, I never played up its punitive potential, but I wanted to this time, even though (or more likely because) the reality of my life contradicts this dynamic relentlessly. To the chagrin of my inner slut, I'm just not a very bad girl in real life.[6] In fact, I'm almost too good, and that may be at the root of my fetish for discipline, bringing to light the short-skirted infidel inside of me, letting her out for a night or three. Teaching underprivileged urban students, pushing drinks at a second job to subsidize lousy adjunct rates, committed to my friends, an ardent feminist and strict monogamist—there is something about being so good all the time that makes me tired. Working hard, taking responsibility for all my actions, aspiring always to selflessness in the service of social change—being good drains the sexual energy right out of me. But nights when the booze, the boy, and the bad girl banter converge, I become a self-indulgent little brat just cruisin' for a bruisin'. I understand Lisa Palac's pragmatic viewpoint on this matter: "[i]f the world were a different place, a happy rainbow place filled with total peace and harmony, maybe then I would come all the time from thinking about making love in a field of daisies," but this is not that world and all is not total peace and harmony.[7] I can't even remember the last time I came across a field of daisies, literally or figuratively. During the next few months of this newest relationship, we incorporated spanking into our sex life regularly, sometimes as *Titanic*-style orchestrated performances, sometimes as a pleasant sharp surprise.

A slap on the ass hovers at the edge of masochism—a frightening prospect to feminists and conservatives alike—transgressing the saccharine borders of the unspeakable. In a world where child services can be called in for a smack on the backside when your six-year-old tells you to fuck off in the cereal aisle, spanking suffers from a bad reputation. The oversimplification of spanking as abuse by any definition burdens the sexual single girl with yet another stigma to combat, another no-no. How can you ask someone to spank you and still expect him to respect you in the morning? In a culture where domestic abuse is at once publicly disavowed and privately tolerated, erotic spanking breaks open

our hypocrisy. The slippage in our minds between spanking women and beating them lumps two very different
physical experiences together, obscuring the difference
between women's desires and systemic misogyny; to clarify
this difference, one must begin by prising apart the twisted
logic of an abuser—she made me hit her, she pushed me to
it, she was asking for it, she wants it—from the very different
logic of a feminist spanking, which, rather than eroticizing
already existing violent tendencies towards women, is more
about developing a whole-body eroticism. A sultry spanking refuses to divide the body artificially into private/sexual
parts and public/nonsexual parts.

Not too long ago, I met my spanking match, and it's as if
after years of trying to jam a square peg into that round
hole, one day it just fit. He assumes the role of dominating
top with breathtaking mastery in bed despite being decidedly untoppish in real life, a delightful combination. Our
role-playing unfolds in an environment suited to my every
sensual desire; he surrounds me with pillows and pretty
talk before snapping into a belt-wielding sexual force. Like
many mild sadomasochists, "I need a certain feeling of love
or appreciation built in to my top's authority. I need to feel
s/he's proud of my submission and my response, that s/he
delights in having me over his or her lap just as I delight in
being held captive there."[8] The reciprocity present in most
fantasy means consciously identifying with the Other as
another version of yourself. Of particular importance to
this sense of S&M as reciprocal is the phenomenon known
as "topping from the bottom." When the spankee initiates

and commands the sexual play, the lines between top and bottom, between wielding and submitting to power, blur.

So with this spank-me feminism in mind, I urge single girls everywhere to keep looking until they find the person that will let them speak, act, and perform the needs and fancies of their dreams. As feminist pornographer Nina Hartley points out, "Women are denied pleasure because pleasure is very, very powerful, very, very potent. You're no longer at the mercy of men when you understand that. It lets you see clearly and it makes you more powerful, makes you confident in your sexuality." I want a feminism that taps into this power and frees every woman to be as unconventional as she wants to be. Surely I'm not the only well-adjusted young woman looking for a little discipline in her life.

7 *The Feminist Wife?*

Notes from a Political "Engagement"

PATRICIA PAYETTE

> Can one be within the framework of a marriage?
> —May Sarton, *Journal of a Solitude*

THE SUMMER AFTER I graduated from college, my high school friend Heather married her college sweetheart, Jeff. When it came time for the single women to circle together to compete for the bride's bouquet, my friend Vonda and I obediently joined the small cluster of women. As Heather's bouquet flew toward us, I discretely ducked out of its path. I don't remember who caught the bouquet but I do remember my distinct feeling at that moment: I was twenty-one years old, a newly minted college graduate contemplating my career choices and a whole new life. The last thing I had on my mind was becoming the next bride.

Ten years later, in 1998, I am the bride-to-be, living with

my fiancé, struggling with a new set of feelings about getting married. There would be no bouquet tossing at my reception. In recent years, I became embarrassed when single women herded together at a reception to compete for the bouquet, as if getting "lucky" enough to be the next bride was all they had on their minds. I began to hide out in the bathroom during the event and felt relieved whenever a bride decided to forgo this tradition.

During the nine months I spent as a fiancée, I documented my emotional journey to the altar in a computer journal I simply named "engaged." Reading over the journal a year after my engagement, I see now that while I was writing, I was actively "engaged" in a process of sorting through the meaning of marriage and the significance of wedding traditions. I experienced waves of varying emotions—excitement, astonishment, chagrin, ambivalence, confidence—as a self-proclaimed feminist about to engage in one of the most traditional feminine rites of all.

My story as an independent, feminist woman who also desired to be married, and struggled with that desire, is not an uncommon one. Stacey D'Erasmo, writing in the *New York Times Magazine*, observes the abundance of contemporary tales tracing the single woman's search for a husband, as evidenced by the television shows *Sex and the City* and *Ally McBeal* and the fiction bestsellers *Bridget Jones's Diary* and *The Girls' Guide to Hunting and Fishing*. D'Erasmo writes: "In nearly every medium, the marital quest of the fashionable, sexually well-traveled, thirty-something woman has become so popular as to seem

like the dominant narrative of life on earth right now."
Noting the "melodrama" and "misadventure" that follow
these single heroines as they pursue a husband, D'Erasmo
believes these narratives prove that feminism is "over" and
has "failed."[1] Her reasoning suggests that yearning for
marriage is not only incompatible with feminist beliefs, the
fact that the desire exists proves feminism is dead. My
experience proves feminism isn't dead; it's merely under-
going a transformation at the hands of young women like
myself who are refusing to submit to outmoded paradigms
that tell us what we should and shouldn't desire for ourselves. The abundance of contemporary narratives about
outspoken single women questing for satisfying personal
and professional lives is a testament to our determination
to speak truthfully about our generation's unique needs
and desires. Hundreds of women like myself are struggling
with age-old prejudices in order to reinvent the meaning of
single life and the matrimonial urge.

The second wave adage "A woman without a man is like
a fish without a bicycle" doesn't serve women or men in
coming to terms with the thorny issues surrounding equality, mutuality, and marriage in this nation and historical
moment. Portraying women as either domesticated victims
of male patriarchy or angry, man-hating feminists doesn't
permit the nuances of real women's lives to come into clear
view, just as the assumption that single women who long to
be married must be "unfeminist" obscures a more complete picture of contemporary women's psyches. I endorse
a new approach to the marriage bond that undermines the

power dynamics of male-female relationships in which we must choose between being master or slave, as Jessica Benjamin describes relationships in *The Bonds of Love: Psychoanalysis, Feminism and the Problems of Domination.* Benjamin concludes that the only way to avoid becoming trapped in a dualism of our relationships is to embrace the paradox "posed by our simultaneous need for recognition and independence," to sit comfortably with the desire to be both autonomous and to be connected.[2]

I grew into feminism as I grew up. Like many third wave feminists who grew up in the 1970s and 1980s, I was raised in a familial atmosphere of feminist ideals nurtured by my mother and my aunts. I learned a great deal from my female relatives through the example they set in their lives. My mother worked part-time during part of my growing up years, first as a dental hygienist when my brother and sister and I were very young, and then later, when we reached school age, she earned an M.A. in education and was a lab instructor in anatomy and physiology at the college in the small town where we lived. She was the first woman elected to the water board in that town and later was active in the League of Women Voters. My mother's scope of activities and interests has always ranged outside the home.

Even my mother's mother has been a dynamic role model for me, for she was, and is, a lively, active, and witty grandmother who treated me and my siblings to solo vacations with her to special places. While growing up, I learned as well that men could be feminists when my father, an auto dealer, supported women's equality in his traditionally male-dominated field by hiring women managers and even promoting a woman to general manager of his dealership. For the past twenty years, his dealership has sponsored a free workshop called "Women's Day" to help women become more comfortable buying and maintaining their cars.

My mother's eldest sister, Pat, is a nun whose extensive travels, business savvy, and spirited sense of humor forever nullified in my mind the stereotype of a nun as passively church bound. My Aunt Maddie also became a nun and garnered much attention by speaking out on behalf of feminism. Maddie eventually left the convent, got married, and retained her last name, had a baby, and started a successful career as a social worker and therapist, all the while remaining active in feminist causes. One summer my Aunt Molly, an activist and lawyer, arrived at our home during a trip cross-country by way of motorcycle. Throughout my childhood, Molly encouraged my interest in books and writing, and when she carved out special time for us to spend together, she talked to me as her peer and was comfortable and open about her sexual orientation, bringing her female partners to family events. My youngest aunt, Terry, also talked to me honestly and openly about sexuality, and lived for several years with her boyfriend before marrying him. She, too, kept her own last name.

In fifth grade, I questioned the gym teacher, Mr. Lando, about why he chose only boys to serve as team captains. Although I don't remember his response, I do remember that after I challenged him, he sent me to the office to fetch his coffee. Later, in high school, I got better results when I gently corrected my civics teacher—"congressperson"— aloud in class. He thanked me and corrected himself. Shortly after that, he and his wife began hiring me to babysit for their daughter.

As a preteen, I spent a great deal of time reading and writing stories and plays. My younger sister Maggie, interested in horses and talented in art, also picked up some sewing and cooking skills from my mother, but I was not interested in acquiring those skills and my parents never pushed me to learn them. These events did not seem unusually significant to me at the time, but I now understand Maggie and I were granted "permission" to be the kind of girls we wanted to be.

Nevertheless, I became self-conscious of those moments in life when the values of feminism appeared to be at odds with my own desires and impulses. During my undergraduate years at the University of Michigan, I was thrilled to find like-minded feminists among my peers, both men and women. Although we sometimes dressed and acted the part of "feminine" women and "masculine" men, we were acutely aware of our social conditioning as gendered subjects and often mocked our conformist impulses with sarcastic humor. If I broke a nail, I expressed displeasure and made fun of my reaction at the same time. We acted upon our sexual freedoms, but sometimes felt bound by ancient dating rituals and found prefeminist sexual assumptions hard to shake. Even though we knew we could make our own rules, my girlfriends and I wondered what it *meant* if we slept with a man on the first or second date.

In *Third Wave Agenda: Being Feminist, Doing Feminism*, Leslie Heywood and Jennifer Drake describe the third wave movement as "feminisms" that grew out of the social context of the late 1970s through the late 1980s: "Because our lives have been shaped by struggles between various feminisms as well as by cultural backlash against feminism and activism, we argue that contradiction—or what looks like contradiction, if one doesn't shift one's point of view—marks the desires and strategies of third wave feminists."[3] The second wave generation of the 1960s frequently constructed the freedoms of feminism in opposition to the social strictures of femininity, but I have consistently sought balance between what I saw as the feminine and feminist sides of myself, precisely because I do not see them as contradictory.

Although "third wavers" hold strong to the belief that men are not the enemy, we take a cautious stance toward the twenty-something wedding mania as witnessed in pop culture portrayals of young women like Monica on the popular sitcom *Friends*. During my college years, and throughout my twenties, I savored a sense of emotional and financial independence that grew over the years. Time enough later for marriage, I told myself as I became absorbed by getting my M.A. and cultivated a strong connection to friends, family, and various community activities. I never eliminated the possibility of meeting Mr. Right during those dating years, but the search for a marriageable man didn't dominate my life. My single friends and I discovered that a happy and successful life didn't require a husband, or even a boyfriend.

This attitude toward marriage is commonplace among the third wave generation. Journalists and sociologists are sitting up and taking notice of the growing number of women staying single longer, and the abundance of "never married" women and their stereotype-shattering lives. In a 1996 issue of *Psychology Today*,[4] Anatasia Toufexis dispels the popular assumptions about "never-married" women as "unloved, unwanted, unhealthy" by citing the numerous healthy, happy, successful single women buying houses, running companies, and having children on their own. I read Toufexis' article the year I turned thirty, and I identified with her "single woman as heroine of her own life" thesis, yet I also found myself more and more longing to be in a committed relationship.

Gradually, the freedoms that I had cherished in my twenties began to lose their charm, not because I felt incomplete without a man, but because I finally felt ready to take on a serious, loving, committed relationship with a man. I witnessed the settled homes and shared happiness that many of my peers, including my younger sister, had found with a mate, and I felt increasingly impatient with my charmingly noncommittal boyfriends, yet I still resented the frequent, worrisome questioning from my parents and others regarding my persistent single status. Why did they find that topic so much more pressing than the promising academic career in English literature I recently embarked upon? What happened to my feminist parents who raised me to cherish independence, but now pestered me about settling down with one of my male friends? Although I didn't perceive myself as one of the "never marrieds" for whom Toufexis advocates, I strongly related to her assertion that single women "have been staging a quiet revolution, battling social prejudice, family expectations, and their own apprehensions to set a new standard for what it means to be successful, fulfilled, and content women."[5] The article helped me realize, for the first time, that a lot of my worries stemmed from internalizing the "social prejudice" and "family expectations" Toufexis names. Regardless of their intellectual commitment to women's independence, my parents had no personal experience to help them imagine what it was like to be a "never-married" thirtysomething adult with a fulfilling life. Marrying in their early twenties and then turning their attention immediately to raising children, they had no idea what life was like for a woman in my situation. I mailed them a copy of Toufexis' article. They seemed relieved.

I met my future husband, Ed, just as I was preparing to turn thirty-one. I was enjoying an intellectually active and socially engaging life, and on top of that, I often felt gratitude for the peaceful solitude of living alone and experienced relief when the occasional "socially free" weekend rolled around. But as happy and busy as my life felt, it also felt as if a piece of the puzzle, in the form of a loving partner, was missing. I wondered why it mattered to me that I was not attracting, or was not attracted to, the "right man."

Was I merely brainwashed by my society's assumption that successful, single women just aren't successful enough unless they have a man to come home to? Was my mental preparation for a future with children (as a single mother, if necessary) just evidence that I was buying into the "biological clock" cliché? Meeting and dating Ed, just as I was preparing to turn thirty-one, nudged these questions out of my mind, as I started paying attention to the present moment; later these questions would come into sharp relief when our relationship grew more serious.

I met Ed during a group bowling outing with some mutual friends and was immediately attracted to his quiet, self-possessed air and his shy, sly sense of humor. Shortly after, I emailed an invitation to have coffee with me. By making the first move in approaching Ed, a pattern emerged that would shape our future as a couple. I became the extroverted, forward-looking force in the relationship, complete with my own set of plans, worries, and restless energy. In contrast, Ed was the introverted, even-keeled, and contemplative one, consistently flexible and amenable in the face of my constant state of enthusiastic organizing. Getting to know each other was an important lesson in identifying and giving up our assumptions of how men and women can relate. I discovered that Ed, like most of my male peers, many of whom were raised by second wave feminist mothers and aunts, shared a commitment to overturning the conventions of gender norms for the benefit of both sexes.

Spring 1997, Ed and I are spending every weekend

together as we get to know each other. One Saturday afternoon, we are quietly sharing the love seat in his bedroom, academic books open in front of us. We've been dating for three months and I am thrilled to have found a lively intellectual partner whose interests encompass gender roles and women's history. As two doctoral students with similar liberal politics and social views, we were in complete intellectual agreement that women and men ought to be equal partners in a relationship. However, on this day I am thinking about marriage, specifically, I want to find out his reaction to my determination to retain my last name (or at least take on a hyphenated surname) after I marry. Somehow, I bring up the topic of marriage. "I know lots of women who kept their last names after getting married, including two of my aunts," I say and try to sound as casual as possible, afraid I might scare him off. Ed is still half-focused on the book in front of him, but nods and agrees, "Well, yes, all women should have the right to make that choice." While I am relieved to hear this, I feel disappointed that he isn't more passionate about the issue. I secretly hoped he would profess his desire that, no question, his future wife would keep her name. The conversation continues, and although I do not remember all the details, I do recall that we conclude our talk by tentatively agreeing that marriage is a definite goal, sooner rather than later, in each of our lives. "I'm impressed," I say to him that day. "We're talking about marriage and you're not screaming and running from the room." Ed smiles. I was never able to reach this kind of comfortable conversation about marriage with any other man I've dated. Much later, while planning our wedding, I declare my intention to keep my last name after marriage. I anticipate the subtle disapproval I will feel from some family members, friends, random store clerks, and even Ed, but it never materializes.

Despite my rational commitment to equality in a marriage partnership, I find that sometimes old stereotypes die hard for me. A year after our conversation on the love seat, our relationship is now serious. Our couplehood feels comfortably established as we discuss our plans for careers and a family. On the way home from the video store one night, I acknowledge my ambition to land a high-profile academic position, wondering exactly how this fits in with his picture of our future together. Ed admits that he, for one, would be happy with a less prestigious teaching position at a community college. When I point out that our different career paths might dictate that he will spend more time taking care of children and household obligations, he agrees. I am surprised at my relief—why am I clinging to old stereotypes that assume a man will resent his wife for being on a more ambitious career track? Is part of me uncomfortable with this imagined scenario, and had I been projecting this onto Ed?

According to a survey by Prudential Securities, women still hesitate to take the main bread winning role in the family. Only 34 percent of men felt it would be problematic if their wives earned more money on the job than they did, whereas 53 percent of the women said they thought this scenario would create a problem.[6] Clearly, I was one of those women who still needed to shed my assumptions about the undesirability of ambitious women. I had unconsciously held on to some anxieties about how far I could move outside a traditional partnership and still be acceptable.

Six months into our relationship, Ed and I take our first vacation together. We are driving down a busy thoroughfare in my hometown of Louisville, Kentucky. "Look! We have to stop," I say excitedly after spying a large outdoor clearance sale at the housewares store I am particularly fond of. I insist that we attend the sale and then spend the next twenty minutes piling into Ed's arms my bargains: a set of placemats, some wine glasses, a variety of cooking utensils. Ed is clearly amused at my enthusiasm and half-jokingly exclaims: "I see that all those books I read about the 'cult of womanhood' are wrong! It isn't socialization! Women do have a natural urge to be domestic after all!" While I laugh along with him, I feel a pang of apprehension—has Ed uncovered my secret weakness for decorating and dinner parties? Can I enjoy being both a party hostess and an ardent feminist? I understand more clearly in hindsight. Asserting one's social and sexual rights need not conflict with acquiring a well-stocked kitchen. The clearance sale provoked both of us to unearth certain gendered assumptions, like enlightened women aren't supposed to care about attractive dining room suites. Buying housewares with Ed on that summer day was a test of my ability to be true to myself, to be a fully realized feminist who knows a good bargain on table linens when she sees it and isn't afraid to admit it.

As the first anniversary of our relationship arrives, Ed and I begin talking about moving in together later that year. Yet I start wondering: are things "too" comfortable between us, too settled? Other days I'm wondering how we will overcome our personality differences. Over the phone I voice my concern to my sister: "Is he truly the one for me, or have I just wanted him to be Mr. Right so badly that I've chosen to overlook certain problems?" She directs me to trust in the process of sharing my fears and concerns with Ed honestly and openly. Ed and I begin to discuss our differences more directly, including my desire to get engaged and his need for more time. We examine and study our personalities and disparate preferences and attempt to find the meaning of it all: how do we really know if this is a marriage-worthy relationship?

In between itemizing those things that draw us to each other, we spill our daily frustrations and our larger fears. Rather than *fixing* these frustrations and fears, we simply give ourselves and each other permission to experience them, to find solutions or eventually accept them as part of our relationship. By openly talking about our doubts rather than neatly solving them, we learn to see there can be two ways to approach the same task—socializing at a party, writing a dissertation, or parking the car—and we can each learn to value the other's style without invalidating our own. I learn about patience and understanding by noticing the gentle and humorous ways in which Ed challenges my control-freak tendencies. He begins to see the practical sense behind my organized approaches to handling money and time. In retrospect, I see the answer to the riddle—"is this the right person for me?"—is revealed in the process of attempting to solve it.

Later that year, Ed and I prepare to rent a house together. Our decision provokes a great deal of anxiety in my parents. I am taken aback at their disapproval—after all, Ed and I are adults in our thirties. My sister translated my mother's concerns as the old cliché: "Why should he buy the cow when he is getting the milk for free?" In other words, Ed would have all the benefits of a marriage— including a convenient sex partner—without actually having to marry me. I pause and consider the truth of this. This assumption on their part skews our relationship, painting me as the commitment-crazy woman and him as the commitmentphobic, sex-crazy man. What about the fact that I would also be enjoying the benefits of living with my partner, including sex? Not to mention the fact that we'd still be having sex even if we weren't living together.

My parents' concerns about my life were genuine to them and arose out of love and concern for my future happiness. However, I needed to recognize that those fears were theirs and not mine. "Straying from tradition makes many people very anxious," observes Marcelle Clements in *The Improvised Woman: Single Women Reinventing Single Life.*[7] Clements explains that a "social reorganization" is slowly changing prevailing attitudes about those who couple and uncouple in a variety of ways: "where once there was a wall between the fortress of the married and the wilderness of the unmarried, there is now only a thin, permeable membrane."[8] Clements asserts that this "membrane" makes possible a range of choices for women who move "from one state to the other" as it serves their interests and desires—marrying, remarrying, cohabitating, or deciding to "pause between relationships for a month or a year or for a decade."[9] Clements clarifies the extent to which marriage is no longer a "given" for women, but just one life choice among many. Neither is it the only socially acceptable option available for those who wish to be in a committed relationship.

Although staying single is a viable choice for more and more women, it's still not a completely comfortable choice. "[S]ingle women," Elizabeth Wurtzel declares "are not societally sanctioned in their singleness." She adds, "No matter what clever tricks feminism has come up with, it has not quite succeeded at truly legitimizing an unmarried woman as an autonomous being, as a person in a chosen living arrangement and not as someone whose life is in abeyance."[10] The nagging worries and insecurities on my thirtieth birthday surely betray my failure, despite long-held feminist leanings, to overcome the feeling that my life was "in abeyance" until I married. Paradoxically, moving in with Ed was both a declaration of my social autonomy and one step closer to marriage.

After a month of living together, and twenty months into the relationship, Ed produces a diamond ring over a special dinner in our rented duplex and asks me to marry him. The scene certainly sounds traditional, but we did not arrive at this point through a conventional courtship. I had voiced my readiness for marriage about six months earlier and was dismayed when he needed more time. I tried to relax because the last thing I wanted to do was pressure him to marry me before he was ready. On good days I appreciated the slow, thorough consideration he gave to life decisions. His proposal was not about a man inviting a woman to be his helpmate; it was about Ed making himself ready for couplehood, the mutual engagement we had been working toward together.

I soon catch myself staring at the winking diamond on my finger. Owning such a beautiful piece of jewelry to wear every day makes me feel suddenly grown up and responsible. I experience a swell of happiness and an undercurrent of dread at my pride of owning this diamond ring. I see myself at twenty-five, declaring indignantly that I would never wear an engagement ring because it signifies a man's "claim" on a woman and proof of his "worth" to support her. And yet, I am shocked to note how much I want a ring. It doesn't have to be a diamond, or even a rare gem, but I want a ring. I mull over my "forbidden" desire and wonder, am I caving in to social conditioning? Certainly our commitment would be just as strong without it. As my relationship with Ed deepens, so does my understanding of why a piece of jewelry can hold such emotional weight. It is tangible evidence of our new status, a symbol of permanence and commitment. Earlier that year, Ed's maternal grandmother had passed away and left him with enough money to pay off one student loan and still buy a diamond ring. She always supported our relationship, and we feel that she would have loved to know we invested her money in a future family heirloom. Still, those first days after our engagement mark the beginning of my quiet doubts over "selling out" to the seemingly superficial trappings of a traditional, hetero-sexual union. There was no denying the pure pleasure I took in the diamond engagement ring, or the embarrass-ment that sometimes shadowed that pleasure.

Two women I know, both doctoral students and recently married, congratulate me and then add ruefully: "You know, you won't get *anything* done on your dissertation before the wedding." I feel slightly panicky, for they had tapped my secret fear: my wedding would suddenly take over my life, which was up to now focused on completing my degree. I worry about becoming one of those women who gets a ring on her finger and suddenly talks of nothing but tulle and place settings.

I am determined that wedding planning will not inter-fere with my dissertation progress or my teaching assist-antship. Ed and I decide on the location and date of the wedding, and after that I allow myself to complete one or two wedding tasks in a small chunk of time each week. While both Ed and I are increasingly excited about the July 3 wedding weekend, I feel contempt for the bridal maga-zines that build this day up as the "most important day of my life" and the day on which I need to be "my most beau-tiful." As if living a happy life on my own and supporting myself and then working toward my Ph.D. were mere side trips toward the most important journey—down the aisle into the arms of a man! While many people warn me about the stressors of dealing with family and fiancé during the wedding planning, I am unprepared to meet the stress of confronting my own mixed feelings about each piece of the process, feeling dreamy and at the same time indignant.

A month after our engagement, my Aunt Terry and Uncle Pat host an engagement party for us. We are honored by this gesture, for they had witnessed our courtship from the very first months and had gone out of their way to make Ed feel a part of the family. This is an important event because it brings our parents and extended family members together for the first time. It is the start of a new life in which we are extending a new branch of our family trees. Our relationship suddenly feels "official," for at the party there is a toast in our honor; cards and gifts shower upon us. It is a wonderful outpouring of love, and it makes us feel very special. Afterward, it strikes me that the party represented a social sanctioning of our togetherness, a public recognition of our private connections. In my journal I write:

> The most profound change is not in our relationship, although it has deepened and settled in a wonderful way. The big change is how people view us, and even what I call Ed has a certain cachet, "fiancé."

People see our relationship as more significant. We garner a measure of respect, of "coupledom," that wasn't there when we were "just" dating.

Before my engagement, I never truly appreciated the purely social construction of marriage. I now witness the "thin, permeable membrane" that Clements says separates those couples who are married and those who are not, and I see the social hierarchies in place.[11] Two people could live together for years, buy a house, raise children, be active in their community, yet never be viewed, from some perspectives, as fully "mated." Only marriage, regardless of its day to day quality completes the relationship. Our union was being celebrated by our family and friends, and we were touched by their support and approval, but it was also a source of wonder for me. What had we really accomplished that was worthy of this fuss, other than just living our lives together?

After the engagement party, many wedding decisions await us. I consider whether or not to walk down the aisle on the arm of my father. I am aware that this tradition is rooted in patriarchal social traditions in which the bride is symbolically "transferred" from one man's possession to another. Yet when I picture that moment in our ceremony, I want to walk down the aisle and share this transition in my life with my dad. Whatever it may once have meant, for me it represents a father-daughter bond I cherish. When the event actually occurs, it is an extremely emotional moment and I feel thankful to feel his love and support for me and my relationship with Ed.

Weddings have a long history to overcome of containing women's sexuality and denying our selfhood, but the meaning of this ritual is changing—is being changed by— the evolving needs and desires of women primarily.

While I was busy fretting over my many options as a

future bride, what was Ed doing? "There are no groom's magazines," writes historian Mark Caldwell.

> Wedding plans belong to the bride, who governs the epic splurge accompanying the marriage. From a feminist perspective, this is ambiguous. It could be seen as a delusive ploy, in which a spending spree blinds the bride to the inherent inferiority of her position and her impending loss of independence. It might, on the other hand, just as easily betoken a coming of age, an affirmation of her power in the relationship, and a symbolic righting of an otherwise endemic inequality between men and women.[12]

In January, I write in my engagement journal:

> I feel like I've been handling the burden of the wedding planning and keeping up the house. I tend to let it build and then express my frustration to Ed when I'm about to crack, usually on the verge of tears. Last week it happened with the wedding and my frustration at having to negotiate so many details and so many family members. He got on the phone that day, and started calling for the honeymoon tickets and menus for the rehearsal dinner. Yesterday he spent two hours helping me clean the house, when he would rather be working on his dissertation.

Yet we have agreed to share these duties—it's not like he is doing me some great favor by helping.

My "type A" tendencies to plan, make lists, and take on too much responsibility prevented me from getting in touch with my feelings earlier on and sharing more of the work with Ed. His "type B" relaxed, spontaneous, procrastinating personality allowed him to stay on the periphery of the planning as long as I seemed happy with all I was doing. I faced my reluctance to share most duties for fear of them being done "incorrectly." Ed was there, ready and willing, when I asked him to help out, or when we agreed on what he needed to do, but we still needed to learn how to decide upon and negotiate large and small tasks in a way that suited both of us. I had to let go of control so a trusting partnership could develop.

The tensions over sharing the wedding planning mirrored similar issues concerning our living arrangements. Even before moving in together, I initiated discussions about household chores and my desire to share them equally. Ed was in wholehearted agreement with me, and as is my style, I suggested we set up regular routines in advance. As we discussed it, the easiest thing appeared to be to share the cleaning. Since I wanted to learn to be a better cook, I volunteered to do the majority of the dinners, and Ed expressed a preference for doing the dishes. He was willing to take out the trash, and I volunteered to manage the household recycling duties, so that was that. After we moved in, without any discussion, Ed began to do the outdoor-related tasks and I took on the bulk of the laundry work. Immediately, I had qualms about this division of housework, for it was almost completely split down traditional gender lines. We were both doing regular work around the house, yet the jobs we had each chosen to do felt preprogrammed by gender roles. Just by equity principles alone, shouldn't we be sharing all the jobs?

The Feminist Wife?

I felt some relief when I read bell hooks's reflections on this topic in *Wounds of Passion: A Writing Life*:

> I decide that the issue is not sameness, that equality cannot be measured this way. That we all have to map our journeys according to our own desires. If I hate taking out the garbage and don't want to, and he does not mind, then that can be his chore even though it has always been defined as the male chore (at least in our family). And in our case I hate to do the shopping so he does. I love to clean so I do most (not all) of the cleaning. So we begin with equality in that we both have the skills to do the same chores, then we break them down according to desire making sure that everything balances out in the end.[13]

This passage allowed me to rethink my own assumptions about chores. There was nothing *wrong* with what we had devised. I was enjoying the cooking and I preferred to be in charge of the laundry and Ed preferred doing the dishes and taking out the trash. As far as equality with regards to skills, I knew we could work on that. Ed could show me how to use the power drill and I could teach him how to cook for two. Additionally, during this period, I came to agree with hooks's assertion that we each must "map our own journeys according to our own desires." In other words, my feminist beliefs evolved and I became more comfortable with my role as a politically conscious bride-to-be.

As spring passes and early summer arrives, the wedding details double and Ed and I spend more and more time on preparations. I also spend more time on my dissertation, attempting to get the first chapter done and approved before the wedding. I am determined to focus on academic work—and not exclusively to the wedding—which I had accomplished in the first seven months of the engagement. With the arrival of May and the end of the semester, I turn in the next-to-final draft of my chapter and allow myself to enjoy the last two months of wedding planning. I spend some time at home with my mother working on wedding banners for the church, and Ed and I prepare and mail out all 175 invitations. Meanwhile, I finish my dissertation chapter on time and I no longer worry that I'm a woman whose life revolves only around her wedding day.

Dozens of wedding details swirl around us that spring, and I am disturbed by how frequently the wedding day is framed as a day of closure—when the bride "seals the deal"—rather than a day that begins a new chapter for the couple. Ed and I agreed early on that getting married could not be our central relationship goal; that kind of thinking would erroneously make the wedding seem "proof" of our compatibility. We needed to see it as just one point, a special and unique point, on a longer continuum that represents our ongoing commitment and growth together. I knew this to be the truth of any marriage, but I still found myself half-anticipating the romantic atmosphere of "happily ever after" that would settle around us magically as we arrived hand in hand at the reception. Would things really be different—or feel different for us—starting on that day? Would the contours of our everyday world begin to smooth themselves out naturally?

My engagement journal allowed me to express both my frustrations and my insights:

> Ed is not perfect, but neither am I. Loving someone is so much about coming to terms with the imperfect person that they are (he forgot to give me a phone message until late and I got mad about that, but it just as easily could have been me who forgot) and coming to terms with the imperfections in myself. We will work out a system for us and a balance to our personalities, our styles, our needs. That is part of what this trip to the altar is doing for us. Forgive, trust, and love. They all go together. I'm still learning that.

The secret to relationship success is knowing there is no such thing as a soul mate, no perfect person fated for each of us to marry. Our relationship will always be a work in progress, a set of challenges for us as individuals and as a couple. First we must give up the fantasy images we unconsciously attach to our mates and accept them as their own people—flawed, human—instead of trying to believe we were perfect for each other. Learning to be vulnerable, to be patient, to be wrong, and to be willing to change—it wouldn't be easy.

When our wedding finally arrives, I savor each moment: getting ready with my closest girlfriends and female family members, walking down the aisle with my dad with tears in our eyes, carefully and lovingly delivering each word in my vows to Ed, and as a couple, dancing, kissing, hugging our way through the reception with our nearest and dearest. For a woman who felt a great deal of anxiety over the engagement months and the wedding ceremony, I feel no fear about my transition into wifehood.

Who decided that successful, smart, and savvy women are weak and "unliberated" if they desire a mate? Our feminist foremothers didn't fight for our right to seek fulfillment only by living life solo, but to be free—to feel liberated—to make meaningful personal choices: a career, or a mate, or children, or all three at once. Can a feminist be a wife? In order to answer yes, the trick is to stop considering a wife as one who must obey certain rules, take on expected duties, or measure up to particular standards. We need to stop seeing *wife* as primarily a service role. Instead, we need to let our attitudes, personalities, and lifestyles expand the definition of what a *wife* can be. Marriage is not a sign of the failed feminist, it's the healthy recognition that a loving partner can make a sweet life sweeter. The key to a "feminist engagement" is to be truly engaged with one's own developing sense of marriage, gender roles, and personal desires.

Postscript—January 2001

It's been a year and half since Ed and I married. Being a married couple has not magically transformed our relationship or our lives as individuals—for better or for worse. The most notable shifts in our relationship took place during that first year of living together and planning our wedding as we hashed out the details of our shared life: juggling expenses and bills, keeping the house clean, setting a comfortable rhythm for weekends. My concerns about how to be both a feminist and a wife are pushed to the back of my mind amid the flurry of tasks and minutiae of everyday life. Ideally, I wanted a marriage in which Ed and I would sometimes "trade off" those traditionally gendered tasks in order to strike a balance of equality around the house. At the same time, I wanted us both to be able to embrace those interests and concerns that make us who we are, regardless of whether they seem conventional or not. Achieving a comfortable balance is easier said than done.

What I've discovered is that it is much easier to just be ourselves—for me to do the lion's share of the cooking because I enjoy it and for Ed to attend to the automobile maintenance because he has more experience in that area. Additionally, I've continued to be the one taking the driver's seat, initiating plans and goals for us, and Ed is continually flexible and agreeable to these efforts. We work as a team, and if I want a game plan it is up to me to pull out the calendar or clipboard. It's true that this makes me uncomfortable sometimes, for it doesn't live up to my feminist ideals, but life runs much more smoothly when we play to our strengths and don't try to be something we are not. Or is this just what I tell myself when I am feeling too lazy to move outside of my relationship comfort zone? After all, it would be very practical for me to know how to use the jumper cables in case my car breaks down—it's not simply a feminist move.

Initiating healthy change and growing as a person—and a couple—takes energy and commitment. Most days, I have to admit, I don't have a lot of energy and focus to spare. So right now I settle for appreciating the little moments that assure me we are growing as individuals and as a couple: when Ed encourages me to spend time alone with my friends, when I take the time to deepen my relationship with his family members, when we reach for each other's hand during a movie.

So, if we maintain love and trust in our relationship, does it really matter who takes out the garbage? I am reconsidering this question since my daughter Molly was born last month. I want her to grow up in a household where her parents share the chores, the decisions, the child-rearing duties. Yet raising Molly in the feminist spirit in which I was raised means that Ed and I must freely be ourselves and encourage her to develop her own unique identity. I know that when it comes to being true to the feminist spirit, rigid politics and policies do not need to dictate the details of one's personal life. At the same time, it is important that we—as a family—make conscious choices that allow our actions to reflect our larger principles and beliefs. This tension can be productive and informative if we allow it to be.

Right now, however, I am focused on learning to be a mother to Molly without rendering my former life unrecognizable. Just as the women in my family demonstrated to me the many ways a woman's life can be meaningful, I want to model for Molly one way in which a woman can choose to be a wife, a mother, a scholar, and a feminist. I want her to know that these roles are optional and the boundaries between and around these loaded terms are fluid and flexible. I wish for her to become her own person, to name her desires and concerns, and perhaps claim her place in the flow from one wave of feminism to the next.

Part Two
Super Feminist Porno Stars

I felt unbearably gorgeous, when suddenly I realized that my clit was glowing. I mean, like silver neon lights in Las Vegas, my pussy was beaming artificial light all over this very delicate and elegant fête.

—Ntozake Shange,
Liliane: Resurrection of the Daughter

8 *Stripping, Starving, & the Politics of Ambiguous Pleasure*

KATHERINE FRANK

I T ' S GETTING LATE in the day and the pool area at the strip club where I work is clearing out. I am dancing on the pool stage, a one-foot-wide, raised, tile runway between the pool and the hot tub. The space limitation and the fact that I am wearing five-inch heels on a slick surface mean that my dance moves are very restrained. On the pool stage dancers walk up and down making eye contact with the men until they approach the stage. Then we move very slowly in front of them for a moment or two and they slip money in our garters. Many men, a surprising number of men, have never seen a nude girl outside in the daylight. Before I started working this job, I had never seen a nude girl outside in the daylight either. In fact, I hadn't ever been nude outside like this myself.

Daylight is unforgiving compared to the stage lighting inside the club, and dancers develop a number of strategies to perfect their appearances. You can't miss a stray hair on an ankle or thigh. Pubic hair must be carefully tended— you cannot be completely clean shaven and must, for legal purposes, have at least an inch of trimmed fuzz in the front, but most of the women remove the rest. Razor burn looks awful, so we rub deodorant on our bikini lines to make the nasty red bumps recede. Bruises and veins show up mercilessly, as do scars. Makeup can cover them inside, but out here, unless you are endlessly vigilant, the makeup will streak or be just a shade away from your natural skin color. The sun gets hot working poolside and if you sweat while dancing the makeup will run. Within a week of starting here, I learned from the other dancers which brands of studio makeup were most durable. Eye makeup also needs to be perfect—too dark and you look ridiculous by the pool. Even though we wear sunglasses, we take them on and off during our set because men like to look at our eyes. Sunglasses can't be too tight, then, or you get those red marks on the side of your nose. Chipped toe nail polish, gray hairs, and fine lines around the eyes—every detail must be tended diligently.

I find a definite satisfaction in working the pool. By the time I set foot on that stage, I have checked every inch of my body in the mirror in the dressing room and in natural light. I have rubbed oil on my skin so that it glistens in the sun and I have painstakingly covered every blemish. I wear long diamond earrings that sparkle, a matching necklace, and thin belly chain. Sometimes I put blue and pink glitter on my skin—it gives me this Little Mermaid look that works well. White high heels make my legs look long and tan, not to mention the untold hours I spend working out and lying in a coffinlike tanning bed. This is as close to "perfect" as I get. Even now, of course, there are many things I can't stand about my body. But the customers don't see those because I control where they look. And for a little while, I impersonate Malibu Barbie, in my very own life-size Barbie dream setting.

Tonight the men tip me quickly. They know I will lose the bikini as soon as I collect ten dollars in my garter. Then they can sit back and watch. Before the first song ends I have removed my top. An older man approaches the stage and I dance for him for a few seconds. "Turn around," he demands, and I do. "How much more to get you naked?" he asks as the song ends.

"Five dollars," I say, laughing to myself. Naked? No. I am a performer, as fully clothed as anyone here, even without my bikini, if only through my painstaking ministrations to the "costume" of my bare body. He folds a five-dollar bill lengthwise and deposits it behind the white sequined elastic decorating my midthigh. I rest a hand on his shoulder for balance and pull my bikini bottoms off. Some of the girls have bottoms that snap away, real stripper gear, but men like it when I have to stumble a little to take off my bathing suit. Then I don't look too professional, too slick.

Right now, I wobble a bit for effect. I stand back up, smile shyly, and toss my bottoms onto a lounge chair. He slips a few more dollars in my garter and returns to his seat.

I have two more songs before my set is over. The men are still watching, but I begin to drift off. The folded money against my leg alternately bites my skin and caresses it like rough fabric. I have already made enough money this shift to stop counting, and I am aware of it moving with me. I smell it, the thick smoky smell of men in bars. Money always smells like its traders. I can also smell my body, all the familiar smells I collect from a day of dancing—oils and lotions and liquor and skin. The final song is by Roxy Music, a sad, echoey eighties song I often request. I smile to myself and toss my sunglasses onto the lounge chair, remembering the countless times I have listened to this song, the endless emotions that have accompanied it.

The sun is setting over the high fence that surrounds the pool area. The last rays fall on my skin, reaching around the sides of my body with a pleasant warmth. My back, my butt, are cool and I am aware of the movement of my hair on my skin. I feel sorry for the men and the waitresses who have their clothes on, who are not allowed to take them off. Only I am allowed to take my clothes off in public, and only here.

As I walk the tile runway, I feel the steam rising from the hot tub on my left leg and the cool vacancy of the air over the pool on my right leg. My chest faces the sun. I tilt, forced by my high heels, but it feels good right now, as if I am sucking the last of that warmth into me, into my deepest lungs. A feeling of rich solitude comes over me. The sky is orange and salmon, large brush strokes of color. Instead of city streets on the other side of the fence, I imagine hills, wild animals, water. I take the careful steps of a deer, quiet and ready. A light breeze lifts the hair off my face, zips between my legs and under my arms. I feel a curious heaviness from the earrings; the delicate chain around my waist moves as I lift my arms and stroke them through the air. My feet feel weighted down by my stilettos, yet the rest of me is rising, lengthening. The sun is setting fast. I roll my head, tossing my hair around to feel it on my breasts. For me. The light wind blows it back behind me and it plays on my body. I am hot and cold, left and right, up and down, front and back. I am a circle of sensation. I am at the end of the runway and I stand still for a moment. The light is fading and a plane leaves tracks in the distance. For a second or two I am naked, completely open, outside in the twilight.

As if from far away, the DJ's voice calls me back to the moment. I realize my audience is behind me, my set over. As I turn around, I see folded money on the walkway, blowing back and forth like fall leaves. A dollar bill floats serenely in the hot tub, drifting through the steam.

Growing Up "Girl"

I remember playing as a little girl, standing in my basement in front of a giant, heavy mirror—cold but excited, draped in an adult-size lacey slip, too much jewelry, a soft yarn shawl over my shoulders. I moved back and forth in front of the mirror like a fashion model, pretending to be Nicolette Sheridan from the television show *Paper Doll*s as my sister and best friend shifted from foot to foot in high heels that were several sizes too big, waiting for their turn. I remember sitting in the bathroom watching my mother get ready for an evening out—thrilled by how she lined her eyes, excited when she taught me how to apply decals to my nails. Femininity held so many possibilities for theatrics and pure fun. All play and adornment, ritual and wordless bonding.

During adolescence, this world of exploratory femininity narrowed. By the time I entered college as an undergraduate at the University of Michigan in the late 1980s, I was both a radical feminist and a struggling anorexic. I agreed with, and found comfort in, feminist theorists such as Susan Brownmiller, Rosalind Coward, and Naomi Wolf who argued that beauty practices and standards, including thinness, were oppressive, debilitating, and distracting, as well as part of a systematic oppression of women. At the same time, I felt bound to my disciplinary practices—dieting, exercise, makeup, body hair removal, etc.—and guilty about my desire to retain them in the face of this critique. There was nothing playful about my beauty routines anymore—they had, if anything, become deadly serious. It was not until I entered graduate school and started working in strip clubs that I personally came to *experience* femininity as a performance again (something I already knew intellectually and could remember, vaguely, from my childhood play), and to distance myself from it enough to use it strategically in ways that were impossible for me during my earlier battle with an eating disorder.[1]

Yet what exactly did it mean politically when I took pleasure in the disciplinary beauty practices necessary for my job in the strip clubs? Was this pleasure related in some way to the pleasure I once took in starving my body? To what extent did I challenge this disciplinary space of T&A when I danced to what I called my "eighties queer set"— something that gave me a great deal of campy pleasure— when my actions were read unproblematically as "straight" by the customers? Or when I managed to earn a great deal of money from a single customer—something that also gave me a great deal of pleasure (a job well done; my Midwestern work ethic kicking in), not to mention incredible feelings of self-efficacy—by agreeing with everything he said and performing a submissive femininity through my conversation and demeanor? And how can I reconcile my desire to appear in a particular feminine way (along with the pleasure I take in these performances) with the social and political realities of the modern world: knowing that other young women are starving themselves in pursuit of beauty and thinness, knowing that impoverished women most likely sewed the lace on my lingerie, knowing the money I spend on makeup and beauty treatments supports large, socially irresponsible corporations and could probably feed small villages in underdeveloped countries?

The idea of femininity as performance or masquerade has a long, rich history.[2] In this essay, I limit my observations to the process of *developing an awareness* of gender as performance (my own developing awareness, along with the developing awareness of some of my customers, other stripper-writers, and, ultimately, the general American public) and the usefulness of this awareness for feminist politics.

Here's the Science Part, Girls, So Listen Closely

In *Fantasies of Femininity: Reframing the Boundaries of Sex* Jane Ussher draws on a series of interviews with women about sexuality and gender to outline several different positions women take in relation to femininity: being girl, doing girl, rejecting girl, or subverting girl. "Girl" refers to "that archetypal fantasy of perfect femininity we see framed within the boundaries of heterosexual sexuality and romance."[3] The woman who wants to *be* girl, in Ussher's analysis, is one who suspends disbelief in the rituals of romance (and the rigid gendered roles that accompany it) and accepts as natural the proposed differences between men and women.[4] Traditional femininity, however, is a mythic ideal and therefore represents a difficult and ambiguous position to occupy. Women who *do* girl, on the other hand, recognize the "fragility of the facade of femininity" and position themselves in control of their performances, perhaps even enjoying them. Part of the pleasure here, Ussher notes, is "the ability to shift between appearing to be girl and ridiculing the very performance of femininity."[5] This kind of savvy appeals strongly to many young feminists.

Women who resist girl, in Ussher's analysis, ignore or deride "the necessity for body discipline, the inevitability of the adoption of the mask of beauty, and the adoption of coquettish feminine wiles," despite the ensuing risk of condemnation or even physical danger.[6] And finally, women who *subvert* femininity "knowingly play with gender as a performance, twisting, imitating, and parodying traditional scripts of femininity (or indeed masculinity) in a very public, polished display."[7] Ussher invokes the "lipstick lesbian" as an example of subversion, as well as Madonna's controversial photo-essay, *Sex*.[8]

Ussher's analysis provides an interesting starting place for my own inquiry into the pleasures, uses, and limits of performing femininity as a feminist act. Some dancers in the clubs where I worked saw their performances simply as an extension of their "natural" and traditional scripts, in which they ardently believed. However, as stripping requires the transgression of female virtue (making public what is properly kept private), this disobedience and the inevitable stigma of dancing cancels out the option simply to *be* girl. In general, then, stripping involves a conscious, creative, and sometimes pleasurable kind of reflexive masquerade, a form of doing and sometimes subverting "girl." In the dressing rooms and while shopping for costumes and props, strippers continually mediate images of "sexiness" through constructions of work personae in response to each other and the many images that surround us in pornography and popular culture. Dancers create various forms of "sexy" not as truths but as *strategies* and *tactics*. Together we learn and perfect tricks of the "gender trade": some of which, like the application of stage makeup on one's genitals, were specific to dancing; others, like ways to boost a male ego or feign interest in a heterosexual interaction, are applicable in a wide variety of settings, revealing a consistent element of performance in personal relationships between men and women.

Dancers often draw on standard cultural fantasies in their self-presentations and fashionings. Some women design their approach to customers based on the "bimbo" stereotype—bubbly, giggly, and lighthearted. Some presented themselves as the "girl next door"—students, friends, even possible lovers (in fantasy). Others took the position of "bad girl"—dressing in black and leather, swearing and talking dirty, promising dominance or adventure. Still others, like myself, switched approaches depending on mood ("I don't have the energy to be a bimbo tonight") as well as the type of customer and what the other women were doing that night. In one city where I worked, the "Catholic schoolgirl" look was particularly popular, and the dancers laughed and rated each other in terms of who could look the most innocent or naughty, the most virginal. We talked about which secondhand clothing stores to comb for authentic schoolgirl uniforms, where you could buy those little white ankle socks with ruffles, what kinds of earrings schoolgirls wore nowadays.

The rewards and costs of tactical femininity in strip

clubs were clear to me at once, in the tangible forms of cash and contusions. As I sat on my bed the morning after my first shift, bags of frozen peas draped over my knees ("works better than ice," the house mom told me) to reduce the swelling from dance after dance on hard wooden tables, I sorted my money excitedly into stacks: hundreds, twenties, tens, fives, ones. For the first time in my life, I could measure my income in inches.

On some nights, when the club seemed too noisy and too crowded, when the dancers seemed larger than life and customers looked like lost clones of one another, I experienced a more discordant relationship with this space of erotic consumerism. Hence, my *Ode to Baudrillard*—a set of songs that clearly linked my work as a stripper, in my mind, with social observation and critique. I opened with White Zombie's "More Human Than Human." Baudrillard writes about people, places, and things that have lost their histories (if they ever had them) and about representations or copies that have become more real and appealing than the originals—indeed, originals no longer exist. White Zombie's song about replicants, specifically, the synthetic humans from the film *Blade Runner*, reminds me of Baudrillard's work. From the stage I looked out on a sea of bodies—most women naked, all the men clothed; some figures moving, some still; all washed in flashing, burning lights—and I would think about the idea of symbols that don't stand for anything, about hyper-reality. I watched the dancers with an overwhelming sense of the interchangeability of female bodies—*the erotics of simulacra*—my eyes following them as they paraded up and down the stages and through the audience: Marilyn Monroe was often there, Pamela Anderson, the geisha and dominatrix, the sexy secretary or nurse. (You had to get on the floor early if you wanted to be a dominatrix—the costume wouldn't make money for more than one or two dancers a night— but of course there was always room for another Marilyn.)

These replications do not, however, conform perfectly to ideal types or fantasies, and this space between reproducing traditional images of sexiness and producing new "readings" of these images intrigues me. Dancers take up particular images and change them, personalize them. In strip clubs, as in other venues of the sex industry, excitement can be generated by creative juxtapositions or transgressions of the audience's expectations. In one club, for example, I knew a bodybuilder who called herself "Ronnie." Wearing a man's watch and appearing more muscular than the other dancers (and many of the customers) she was the very picture of gender ambiguity when she aggressively took the stage and stripped to a thong. Imperfections, or differences, sometimes draw customers as magnetically as the airbrushed images in elite men's porn mags. Vicki Funari notes, though the sex industry "promises variety to its customers," it is a variety with limits: "you won't find any three-hundred-pound women or postmenopausal women dancing." Nevertheless, she learned on the job (as did I) that men host a greater variety of tastes than she once believed, and as a result she overcame her own anxieties about having "abundant" body hair.[9] Funari's self-acceptance reveals the possibility that stripping—far from being simply an individual manipulation of sexy images—is a social process of testing and exploiting the boundaries of gender and appearance.

Even though I've retired from dancing, little jars of body glitter, dark smoky eyeshadows, and red lipsticks still line my bathroom cabinets. As an expert at "doing girl," I no longer feel *required* to use makeup, style my hair, or lower my head and gaze up at men through curled lashes—in sharp contrast to my self-presentation during the years of my eating disorder, when even my closest friends never saw me without these feminine accoutrements. Through dancing, I developed a *feminist ethos of femininity* that allows me to use the skills of performing gender to produce specific effects that differ according to context and my purposes there. I can "do" traditional fantasies to make mad cash in the clubs; I can also get up the next morning, pull my hair into a ponytail, and head to the supermarket without makeup. Perhaps it is the ability to move among these and other options for womanhood that measures contemporary Western women's feelings of freedom (or lack thereof).

Queering the Strip Club[10]

I make my way across the crowded floor and ask Todd, the DJ, to play "Smalltown Boy" by Bronski Beat, "How Soon is Now?" by the Smiths, and "Cuts You Up" by Peter Murphy—my "queer set"—songs I originally heard in gay bars as a teen. Euro-fag music, people called it then. Hearing these songs now in this heterosexual strip club amuses me—like seeing frat boys spell out the Village People's "YMCA" with their vigilantly heterosexual bodies at sports events. History dissolves. "Smalltown Boy" suddenly stars a straight young man making his way through a first year at college (a.k.a the thirteenth year of high school), "YMCA" becomes just another aerobic dance song with exaggerated arm movements for people with no rhythm.

"No one wants to hear those songs," Todd warns, "especially on a Saturday night. How about classic rock?" I offer him twenty dollars from my garter, which he folds and slips into his pocket, shaking his head. "Okay," he says, "as long as this makes you money." I smile, knowing it doesn't. What it does do, though, is help me get through Saturday night—bachelor party night—the most difficult night of the week for me. Bachelor night is the night when all the anachronisms come out—the double standard, the virgin/whore split, militant heterosexuality. My customers rarely surprise me on Saturday nights, though other nights repeatedly challenge my beliefs about who uses the sex industry and why. I would never even work Saturday nights if they weren't required, but since they are, I have a few glasses of wine and make the best of it.

I stand just out of sight behind the main stage curtain as the dancer before me finishes her set. Classic rock, an old song by Aerosmith. I do some quick stretches to loosen up and check the knot on my long wrap skirt; if I've tied it too tight I'll be unable to remove it smoothly on stage. The music ends, the lights change, and Peter announces me over the loudspeaker. The first few haunting notes of the song set the tone while the other dancer gathers up her clothes. Then I take the stage with a smile. As I move toward the center, I scope the crowd, subtly noticing where dollars have already been placed on the padded edges of the stage. I position myself over the floorlights, turn to face the mirrors, and Peter flicks the strobe lights on.

My queer set is an ode to my high school friend Dave, the first gay man I ever loved, who taught me how to do my hair and makeup when we were still teenagers. He could always "do girl" better than I, and I think of him often when I'm getting ready backstage. Before our first night out to the clubs in Detroit, he stripped the pink yarn bow out of my hair, talked me into buying red lipstick, and lectured on the appeal of long, tight, black skirts. Dave also loved Bronski Beat, the Smiths, and Bauhaus—wondering aloud to me what that meant the summer before he went to college and decided to come out. How funny, I thought at the time, that liking a song could *mean* something about who you are. When we went dancing together, I learned to close my eyes, spin around, and disappear into the music, wishing I had the whole dance floor to myself. In the strip club, I do.

A few customers mouth the words of the song, singing along with Jimmy Sommerville without registering the words. I watch the group of men to my right, sitting closer to each other than they will ever get to a dancer in this club. The bachelor shifts uncomfortably in his seat. His friends keep folding dollars and setting them in front of him, beckoning to me. "Embarrass him! Get him!" One guy hands me a five-dollar bill. "Will you bounce up and down so that your breasts hit his face?" he asks. This is a favorite move of many bachelor parties—the dancer kneels down, leans over, puts her hands on the bachelor's shoulders, and bounces up and down. I point to my A-cups, shrug my shoulders, and move on down the stage, filling my G-string with folded bills.

Going to strip clubs for bachelor parties is part of a heterosexual mythology of desire and its limits. Such groups embark on a sanctioned male activity (visiting a club alone, looking hungrily for emotional companionship, on the other hand, is not sanctioned and can be experienced as shameful). My job, in part, is to ease the customers through what Eve Sedgwick calls a "coercive double bind" in a culture that refuses to recognize the continuum of possible emotional bonds between men. My nakedness, and the men's desire for me (real or performed), serves as material through which they can "fuck" each other: the "man's man" can be as slobbery and affectionate with his pal as he wants, as long as he remains in the presence of the hetero-safety I embody, reassuring and validating him.

Two young men sit next to each other at the end of the stage. As I move slowly in front of them, I notice that they train their grateful eyes on me without looking at each other. I untie my long black velvet skirt to reveal a neon pink velvet T-bar and flap the skirt gently so glitter dusts the rail. In this place of supposed sexual abandon, here sit these men, rigid, frozen. There is no public space in this culture for them to move freely as I am doing now. In my fantasy of the perfect strip club, I writhe before them and they lean toward each other and kiss. I imagine their hands in each other's short, preppy hair; I, in my glitter and velvet, am the catalyst for their polymorphous desire. I long for places where classifications and identities melt away, where desire is no longer fixed toward an object but is emergent. Even in this place of seemingly immobile categories—where women get naked and men do not—things are constantly in flux. "I'm a lesbian trapped in a man's body," a businessman tells me as he laughs and looks around at his companions to see if they get the joke. "It must be fun to be up there being desired," a young guy says, "I wish I could try it." "I've told you things I've never told my wife," a regular says. "I think I'm actually bisexual," an older man confesses after four martinis and a glass of champagne.

"This is mostly for my friends," the bachelor whispers to me, feigning uncontrollable desire for the sake of his friends.

"I know," I say.

Talking 'Bout Those Bad Girls: Excess, Satire, Disobedience, Reclamation

In an article examining the "excessive femininity" of Mary Kay beauty consultants, Catherine Waggoner argues that consultants disrupt patriarchal codes of femininity even as they seem to conform to them because their performances are marked by an "aesthetics of excess." Their exaggerations, Waggoner writes, "illuminate the performative nature of the code of femininity, suggesting that womanliness is a mask that can be worn or removed rather than a natural essence of women."[11] Strippers also use an "aesthetics of excess" in constructing their work performances, employing signs of beauty and wealth to construct their work identities. Everything is overdone: necklines plunge, hemlines rise. Makeup is exaggerated. Costumes are extravagantly accessorized: wigs, elbow-length gloves, garters, stockings, feather boas, six-inch stilettos, pearls, rhinestones, and sequins. Dresses of velvet, silk, nylon, leather, and transparent netting, brightly colored, even neon. An increasing number of dancers become quite literally larger than life through breast augmentation. As surgically enhanced breasts increasingly become the ultimate accessories, the idea of the "natural" female body is itself destabilized with repercussions extending far beyond the strip club walls.

When I first started working as a stripper, I often sleep-danced, standing up on my bed in the middle of the night, pulling up my nightgown and then letting it slip from my shoulders, the freedom of forbidden movement surprising me even in my dreams. Later, dancing in nightclubs with my girlfriends, I had to learn to censor my movements anew. Prancing, tossing my hair, and sensuously caressing my torso and breasts—movements I originally adopted for an audience but which had since become mine, part of the music and the dancing—were recontextualized as reckless provocation of the male libido (hard to forget Jody Foster's fateful dance in *The Accused*). The strip club, in many ways, is a safe place to disobey.

In "Love for Sale: Queering Heterosexuality," academic, feminist, and sex worker Eva Pendleton argues that regardless of the sexual self-identity of the performer, sex work always involves a *performance* of heterosexuality.[12] Comparing the ideological and political conditions of sex workers to those of drag performers, she writes:

> Much of what sex workers do can be described in terms of mimetic play, an overt assumption of the feminine role in order to exploit it. When sex workers perform femininity, we purposefully engage in an endless repetition of heteronormative gender codes for economic gain. Using femininity as an economic tool is a means of exposing its constructedness and reconfiguring its meanings.[13]

Pendleton argues that sex workers "fuck with heteronormativity" from within the sex industry—a potentially transformative political move.

One night, I shared a side stage with a woman named Mel who refused to dance for the patrons during our set—instead, she insisted we watch Kitty's performance on the main stage ("Kitty is so fine—she's the main reason I work here," Mel said). Safely out of sight of the DJ who would have chastised us for not performing, we ignored the men at our stage and watched Kitty twirl around in her floor length gown and boa. She winked at us and blew a kiss. Mel, in turn, flashed her breasts and struck a pin-up pose—shoulders back, head tilted and throat exposed, one knee bent—for Kitty. Not only was Mel claiming public space to express her own desires (with an audience of angry men, no less), but she was going a step further, thwarting the primacy of male desire in a heterosexual institution. Though many men would like to believe that the dancers are "not just doing it for the money," at least the money usually guarantees a dancer's attention. Unable to compel her performance with either desire or cash, the customers in this case became outsiders—the performances passing between Kitty and Mel were not for them.

In "Femfire: A Theory in Drag," philosopher Jacqueline Zita imagines a transcendental female figure, "able to place the conventional signifiers of femininity on her skin without harm, mean consequence, or violent abuse." "No one really owns the signs of femininity," Zita argues, even though these signs are abused in reality and embedded in a host of pre-existing social relations and inequalities.[14] Nevertheless, it is possible to reclaim them.

Isn't it?

The Limits of Performance

My experiences as an anorexic make me cautious of the extent to which performances of dominant standards can be put forth as subversive in and of themselves. Anorexia, while in some ways a conformity to cultural ideals of thinness and an adaptation to a climate in which women's bodies are objectified, can simultaneously be seen or experienced as mocking those ideals and representations. For certain cultural theorists, the body of the anorexic and her symptoms constitute a kind of unconscious feminist protest, "involving anger at the limitations of the traditional female role, rejection of the values associated with it, and fierce rebellion" against the expected trajectory of women's lives.[15] Yet as Susan Bordo notes, the anorexic's protest is "not embraced as a conscious politics—nor, indeed, does it reflect any social or political understanding at all."[16] In fact, she warns, the fixation on staying thin becomes so all-encompassing that it actually precludes the emergence of political understanding. The anorexic may be resisting conventional womanhood (large breasts, round hips, menstruation), as well as her sexualization by others, but she is also slowly dying. Bordo recognizes the limitations of anorexia as a form of resistance or subversion, and argues that a concern for female body praxis should have a central place in modern feminism. She writes: "I view our bodies as a site of struggle, where we must work to keep our daily practices in the service of resistance to gender domination, not in the service of docility and gender normalization."[17]

With anorexia, however, may come the same feelings of accomplishment, power, and control that many women talk about when they discuss "doing girl." Starving may be experienced as a successful tactic for negotiating cultural ideals of femininity. Despite the physical dangers of anorexia and its financial and emotional drain, there were also many things I enjoyed about my disorder that made it difficult for me to give up. I enjoyed the discipline, the intensity of my focus, my success at literalizing an ideal (a job well done, that Midwestern work ethic kicking in again). I enjoyed the heightened sense of awareness that hunger brought with it. I enjoyed the way that my body fascinated people (*Look at her arms! Your legs look like they might break if you walk on them!*). As I lay in bed at night, measuring the protrusion of my hip bones with my index finger and feeling excited when it sunk to the second knuckle with no effort, my body felt like my own. Anorexia was once primarily limited to young women of the upper and middle classes, and thinness remains a sign of affluence and status. I knew this, and for me, anorexia thus also worked as a means of class climbing, the desire to take on the status of positions I believed were otherwise unavailable to me. When I finally did let go of my rites and rituals around food, I mourned them. At the same time, however, the physical dangers of anorexia, the despair that accompanies the inevitable failures (nights when the hip bones do not feel so pronounced), and the solipsism that ensues when one's single purpose in life is to grow smaller and lighter certainly undermine a conscious and effective feminist politics.

Performing femininity as part of a job in a strip club does not have the immediate physical ramifications of anorexia; in fact it widens the opportunities available to many women through financial empowerment. Though stripping is a form of class plunging (ruining your reputation, performing physical labor, etc.), I have yet to earn as much money doing white-collar work. Thus, without rejecting the idea that self-consciously performing femininity can be empowering at a personal level and a potentially resistant or even subversive political move, and without overlooking the ways women revise the existing scripts of femininity, I would be remiss in overlooking class and race differences among women and how these different relations to power determine who can afford to play with femininity—and who can't.

Whoring is High Class Work: Femininity as Cultural Capital

As I walk into the dressing room after one of my early sets, I see two naked women standing next to the row of lockers, looking down at an open suitcase overflowing with lingerie, makeup, and high-heeled shoes. Saturday afternoon, the day when managers hold auditions, brings a steady stream of applicants today. So far, no one has been hired. These two women look out of place. Not just their body types, but their posture, hairstyles, the way they packed their supplies. One woman is black, with a deep scar on her leg and a large mole on her buttock. The other is pale, possibly white, and is overweight in comparison to the rest of the dancers in the room. She has a Playboy bunny tattooed on her shoulder. With a feeling of embarrassment, I notice that neither of them has shaved her bikini line very neatly. I wonder if I should tell them that the management might count this against them, but I say nothing.

"I hope she has some Dermablend for that tattoo," a dancer named Molly whispers to me as I take my place at the mirror. "And that scar." The women dig through the clothes in their suitcase—transparent slips, some worn-looking strappy thongs, cheap rhinestone-studded bikinis. She turns to Jasmine, the only other black dancer in the dressing room, and asks, "Can I wear this for the audition?" With a quick glance at the faded bikinis, Jasmine, wearing a form-fitting pinstriped suit with stilettos and pearls, returns to the mirror to finish lining her lips. "No," she says, with distaste. "You have to wear a gown or a suit, and nothing sheer."

"A gown?" the pale woman asks. "We don't have a gown."

"We've been traveling for a long time," the black woman says. "We'd like to get this job and stay here for awhile. I've heard this is the best club in town." She holds an opaque turquoise slip up to her body and looks at it in the mirror. The pale woman watches her. "This will have to work," she says.

"They sell gowns in the boutique," Molly tells them as she walks out of the dressing room for her set.

"Can I borrow a dress?" the black woman asks Jasmine.

"None of my dresses will fit you," Jasmine says. "I have them custom tailored."

The two women look at each other. They turn away from the mirror and do not ask anyone else for help. "We'll both wear the slip," the pale woman says. "You go first, then come back in here, and I'll put it on." They begin to put on their makeup, sharing Maybelline eye shadows out of the suitcase. I see Tiffany make a face in the mirror—she only uses M.A.C. makeup and would never consider sharing. I pull off my long white gloves and begin to go through my own makeup box, looking for a lipstick.

"I really want this job," the black woman says, pulling on the slip.

"What are the rules here?" the pale woman asks me. "Can you do floor shows?"

Tiffany laughs, then looks disgusted.

"No," I say. "They are very strict here."

"You can't lie down on the floor and spread your legs at all?" the other woman asks.

"You can't touch the floor with anything but your hands or feet," I say.

The pale woman sifts through the suitcase and pulls out a bottle of perfume. She sprays it on her legs, working her way up her body. I recognize the scent at once as Primo, an imitation designer brand I wore in high school before I could afford to buy original scents. Tiffany grabs the sequined dress hanging from her chair and moves to the back of the dressing room to put it on. Feeling guilty, I also move away so the cheap scent won't get on my clothes. I leave the dressing room and Jasmine follows me into the club.

"Redneck enough for you?" she asks with a laugh. "Someone should tell them they'll never get the job. And even if they did, there isn't enough money for *two* black women here."

Social class clearly enables and limits one's ability to "do" gender convincingly. In *Formations of Class and Gender: Becoming Respectable*, an ethnographic study of working-class British women, sociologist Beverly Skeggs discusses the notion of "respectability" as it informs class and gender distinctions among women. "The discourses of femininity and masculinity," she writes, "can be used as cultural resources," carrying different amounts of symbolic capital in different contexts.[18] More "legitimate" performances carry more privilege. Historically the most respectable form of femininity (and thus the most legitimate), she argues, was that of white, middle-class women; this was, however, also "the most passive and dependent of femininities." Both black and white working-class women, on the other hand, were sexualized and coded as paradoxically both "healthy, hardy and robust" (rather than physically frail) and as a potential "source of infection and disease." "Femininity," Skeggs writes, "was always something which did not designate them precisely."[19] Working-class women and black women, then, cannot "play" with gender as freely as white middle-class women. Any deviation will be seen as *failing* at femininity, rather than revising or reshaping it.

As these representations persist today, working-class women may make "investments in the forms of femininity to which they have access" in an attempt to avoid being positioned as vulgar or sexual.[20] Skillfully manipulating the signs of femininity through appearance and conduct is one way working-class women can "cut their losses" and

attain a degree of financial security; these "are not mas-
querades employed to generate distance (that was already
guaranteed) but tactical deployments of forms of femininity
which protected their investments and gained cultural
approval and validations."[21] The goal of feminine performances, then, was to pass, not to protest. Hierarchies within
the industry reflect this stratification of social class:

> Just as we are born with access to different amounts of eco-
> nomic, social, cultural and symbolic capital we are also born
> with a physical body which may or may not fit into the sign sys-
> tems which define what it is to be attractive. Physical attrac-
> tiveness may work as a form of capital (corporeal capital) but as
> [Pierre] Bourdieu notes, this is often a form of class privilege.[22]

The more upscale the strip club believes itself to be, the
more dancers are chosen for their conformity to traditional
gender stereotypes of demeanor, comportment, conversa-
tional style, and appearance. The images of class sold by
the club are constituted in part by the manner and appearance of the dancers (though of course the club's atmosphere and furnishings are also carefully cultivated).
Particular working-class signs can be used to exclude
women from the more upscale clubs through policies
against tattoos, piercings, weight, shape, excessive makeup
or hair spray, ways of speaking and moving. Large scars or
bad teeth, often corrected by women with the economic
resources to do so, are generally permitted only at the lowest tier clubs. Some middle-class women who seek transgression through sex work find their "bad girl" space

undermined in the upscale clubs when asked to reproduce middle-class femininity through rules against drinking beer, smoking, swearing, dancing in a sexually aggressive manner, wearing certain kinds of outfits, or even directly asking customers to buy private dances. Yet the women who enjoy the most options in choosing where they work, what kinds of services they will perform, and when to retire from the sex industry are usually those who are able and willing to conform to middle-class standards.

The issue of respectability depends heavily on context. The general public views stripping as a working-class job, a professional dead end (it certainly isn't something to put on one's resumé). The phrase "high-class whore" is often used ironically to point out *there is no such thing*. Dancers may make distinctions between themselves and others using the notion of respectability: behavioral virtue ("I don't do lap dances"), the venue where they work (an "upscale" club versus a "dive"), and appearance ("she looks trashy—this is a classy club!"). At the same time, however, any woman who chooses to display her nude or seminude body for money will be viewed in certain circles as "trash."

Significantly, the signs of femininity critiqued most severely by feminists in the 1980s were the least expensive, therefore most available to working-class women, and associated with sex workers: makeup, hair styling products, hair removal, long painted fingernails, and high heels, for example. They are the signs most likely to be interpreted by others as excessively sexual if not used correctly. At the same time, many middle-class feminist academics still abide by the rules of respectable femininity: "classy" or stylish "feminine" clothes, professional haircuts (with no need for styling products), minimalist manicures (it is okay to spend money, but the nails cannot be too long and the polish should be clear), respectable heterosexual marriage, and "proper" mothering (which of course changes during different time periods). These signs are less likely to generate critical whispers at a Women's Studies conference than heavy kohl liner and a cheap pair of fishnet stockings. Although that may be because these signs are sexualized, it is also important to remember that "sexualization" itself has a classed dimension.

Dancers' freedom to choose their clients can be severely limited by financial concerns; spending an evening with a man who talks down to you, bores, repulses, or angers you, is sometimes what it takes to pay the rent. You may groan within when he asks you to change into something white or wear a lighter color of lipstick, but if you want to make fat stacks, you do it—with a smile. A dancer who is too outspoken, too "feminist," or too political, for example, may find that she must adjust her behavior to be more in line with male expectations if she wants to remain competitive for financial gains. In an economic system where women face unequal job opportunities, sex work is one way young women can get ahead (maybe even enjoy themselves in the process). A feminist politics of stripping, if one can exist, needs to be aware that the power of beauty remains deeply intertwined with class, age, and race hierarchies, and as a result, what is playful to one woman may be painful or impossible for another.[23]

In the Eye of the Beholder

Over the last several years, I have interviewed many male customers in strip clubs about gender, sexuality, relationships, and politics. For the most part, I find they hold very normative views about gender roles. Though customers typically appreciate a wider vision of female beauty than *Playboy* suggests, they still retain unrealistic expectations of what women's bodies should look like: "I wish my wife's breasts were as perky as yours," "My girlfriend is too heavy to be attractive anymore," etc. They tend not to see the work that goes into our performances—the makeup, the lighting, our stage personalities. Many of them also believe every existing myth about sex workers and every line they ever heard from a dancer: "I'm an exhibitionist, I don't do this for the money" or "You aren't like other men." Performances are thus taken as sociological data.

Given this distorting lens, what is the effect of my double-agent approach to womanhood on the men who gaze up at me? The hard truth is that I cannot predict or prescribe how my performances will be interpreted: while a woman "who knowingly dresses herself in the fetishistic garb of stilettos, stockings, and suspenders may claim she is making a postfeminist statement about her ability to *choose* to masquerade as sex object," a man may still see her as sex object.[24] His interpretation does not cancel out her experience of agency, but the power of men to appropriate and redefine my own performances sobers me. If I am consciously performing a role, yet it is taken as truth—the truth about "women," the truth about "whores," the truth about "me"—is anything really transformed or subverted when I dance?[25]

I have had to come to terms with the fact that, in general, male customers make very different meanings out of our interactions than I do. My performance of bad girl sexuality in the club hardly strikes most men as transgressive—after all, what would you expect from a *whore*? I fit neatly into their already existing categories of women as good or bad, virgins or sluts. Their investments in heterosexual masculinity reinforce this willful blindness to the theatrics and economics underlying dancers' performances of desire. I did occasionally meet politically progressive men interested in seeing the boundaries of gender reframed, who wished women were more comfortable with their bodies, or longed to take up the position of the "sex object" themselves for a change, resenting the double standard of sexual behavior. Customers expressed feelings of vulnerability in their relationships with women (and with men) both inside and outside the sex industry, and were by no means out simply to "dominate" women, yet these exceptions cannot erase or absolve the enormous privilege and power men exercise in these clubs.

As many of the male customers of strip clubs are married or involved in monogamous relationships with other women, our transactions surrounding femininity are triangular, often involving a woman "at home." Because many men are taught to devalue and even despise the aging female body with its "stretch marks, varicose veins, sagging breasts, and cellulite-marked legs,"[26] a feminist politics of stripping also needs to be sensitive to the fact that the sex industry as it now exists reinforces male privilege and entitlement to the detriment of women's practical and emotional investments in their nonstripper bodies. My performance in the strip club, then, reinforces certain stereotypes, ideals, and privileges even as it destabilizes and challenges others. As I discipline and adorn my body, then ritually disrobe in front of an audience for money, I obey and disobey norms of femininity, sometimes at intervals, sometimes simultaneously.

The enduring question, for which I have no answer, is this: *Who owns the signs of femininity?* Those of us who employ those signs in daily practice for pleasure, for security, as part of our jobs? Men? Women? Institutions like marriage that reward us for their proper deployment? Is it the corporations profiting from our dependence on their products? The plastic surgeons who performed cosmetic surgeries on 2.1 million Americans last year?

Anyone?

No one?

Conclusion

I look back at the poolside dance narrative at the beginning of this essay and see that it could be viewed as a simple "body as resistance" narrative. I experience my body as being both inside and outside of the control of the club managers, the customers, cultural representations, even myself. I am other than my gender performances and my work. Whether or not this is somehow "true" does not seem as important a question to me as what I choose to *do* with this particular interpretation, how I use it to make meaning and decisions. For me, dancing tells the story of my second coming-of-age. If my first coming-of-age was becoming an adult, this has been the more satisfying transition into sensing myself as a sexual agent who can ask for what she wants, explore what she wants, questioning assumptions about what this might be. Stripping initiated and embodied this feminist coming-of-age, not because sex work is somehow itself an *intrinsically* feminist act, but because the meanings I attached to my specific experiences there, in contrast with my prestripping socialization as a good girl, represented a departure from following someone else's script of sexuality. The feminism, then, is not in the stripping, per se, but in the stories I tell about stripping. Consequently, stripping is feminist to the extent that a community exists to hear my story and understand the sense I make of it.

In an interesting cultural trend, it turns out that many sex workers are telling their stories these days, and while this genre feeds a parasitic media appetite for titillation, these stories also intend to transform feminist politics. In *Whores and Other Feminists*, Jill Nagle points out a number of openly identified sex workers "speaking as feminists about feminism." The contributors to the volume, she notes, "reflect a particular historical moment in U.S. culture and particular conditions, largely white and/or middle class, that afford the opportunity to forge feminisms directly from sex worker experience."[27] My own experiences of pleasure in dancing are of course related to these same conditions—my upbringing, education, social class, and race, my own particular skills and interests, and my relationships. My story, which centers the white middle-class female dancer, can only gesture towards dancers of color, working-class dancers, or uneducated dancers in the margins, but perhaps it contributes to the cultural work of making a space for sex worker stories and stories of other women impacted by the sex industry.

The same goes for anorexia's cultural narrative. I wonder about the potential of first-person stories to underline gendered appearance and behavior as tactical maneuvers to deconstruct normative gender ideologies. Could restrictive eating be taken up consciously as a feminist statement about freedom from traditional gender expectations and from unwanted sexualization? Might the pleasure in modifying one's body through weight loss in some way be expressed as a conscious politics? Perhaps rechanneled from its self-destructive form of refusal into, for instance, an empowering ecofeminist statement against the meat industry, processed foods, and corporate control over plant genetics?

I am reminded of a dinner I once attended at a professional conference. Although it was a mixed crowd, I ended up sitting at a table with eight female academics from various disciplines. After we ordered our dinners, one of the women casually asked me when I became a vegetarian. Feeling bold, I answered with a laugh, "When I was in college I was an anorexic and cut out everything but lettuce. I've been adding things back in for years, but haven't yet gotten around to meat." A moment of silence followed. Then: "I was bulimic in college," another woman said. "It's taken me a long time to be able to keep a meal down. And to think I just now ordered pasta!" "I was bulimic, *too*." "I was anorexic." "I was a compulsive exerciser, and would run five miles every time I ate an apple." "I don't think there was a name for what I was—I just know that it consumed my life." And so, buttering our bread and drinking our wine, we began to talk about the complexity of our experiences. We talked about hiding our secret from friends and relatives, about our attempts at recovery, about our successes, about how we sometimes missed the control and euphoria of the early days. We talked about our work and how our struggles with gendered bodies influenced our chosen areas of specialization. We talked about how rarely we talked about these things, especially over dinner with strangers.

Feminist critics have argued that personal experience narratives risk reproducing rather than contesting given ideological systems. Confessing pleasure, then, may or may not be political in and of itself, and performance may or may not be transformative, depending on all kinds of factors. Yet certain *interpretations* of pleasurable experiences can, especially when formed within a community of "confessors," be useful for feminist politics. When stripping is an "inside joke,"[28] for example, when it becomes involved in a relationship between the jokers, it turns into a shared and therefore powerful counternarrative. In this public realm, personal experiences of pleasure and feelings of resistance wield political force. When we talk about our own "tactical deployments of femininity," we make personal stories available for others to draw on individually and collectively for developing feminist consciousness and movement. We open spaces of resistance within the heteronormative culture of the strip club and elsewhere. Perceived this way, the work of reframing the boundaries of feminist desire is not merely the narcissism of what has been called the me generation of feminism, but rather a way to build politics on the material of life, a long-held feminist value.

9   *Co-Ed Call Girls*

The Whore Stigma Is Alive &

Well in Madison, Wisconsin

KIRSTEN PULLEN

I WISH I LIVED in a world where I felt free to express my sexuality publicly, to fully identify with sex radicals, a world where I felt free to work as a whore if I chose. Theoretically, that world exists. Carol Queen speaks for many when she maintains "that it should be everyone's right to do sex work."[1] I, too, support that right, but despite prostitution's benefits of economic and personal freedom, whoring is often a limited and limiting career choice for young women. In subtle ways, the whore stigma continues to restrict all women's behavior and self-presentation. Prostitutes' rights activist Priscilla Alexander argues that women are kept from "freely exploring, experiencing, and naming their own sexuality lest they be called whore."[2] Maintaining rigid boundaries between *women* and *whores* thus polices the acceptable forms of female display in the contemporary United States.

I interviewed about a dozen sex workers in Madison, Wisconsin,[3] and came to believe that despite small enclaves of sex worker feminisms in certain progressive communities, these women struggle intensely with their (often conflicted) identities as fantasy females available for sex on demand and as normal, everyday women. On one hand, none of the women expressed guilt or shame over being paid to have sex with strangers. On the other hand, most of them hid their sex work from friends and family. Prostitution for these college and college-age women constitutes a contradictory practice, offering adventure, community, and financial rewards while demanding they keep this activity secreted away. This consistent refusal to openly characterize their work as prostitution is the point on which the rest of my analysis turns. The escorts' silence about prostitution convinces me of the deep and largely unexamined fear of the whore stigma that rules women's lives even now, at the beginning of the twenty-first century, despite popular cultural declarations of postfeminist freedom for all. Sadly, the utopia of affirmative attitudes toward sex work that Carol Queen calls for does not exist in any generalizable way.

Women's silence on sexuality, whether whores or non-whores, creates a public facade of conformity and safety, but in private, acknowledgements of sexuality are more forthcoming, varied, and confident. With my friends, family, and lovers, for instance, I talk about sex a lot, and I have long believed that sex is never bad. With each other and with me, the Madison call girls I interviewed spoke freely about their experiences with sex work. But moving this discussion from the private to the public is something those call girls feared, and something I believe they have good reason to resist. When I delivered a version of this essay at an academic conference, focusing on the rhetorical strategies Madison sex workers used to avoid calling themselves whores, I was accused by an audience member (and prostitutes' rights activist) of being the very force that made the girls ashamed of their work. It was my fault as an outsider and potentially deprecating judge, she argued, that the girls didn't identify themselves as prostitutes. While I recognize the ways research can be skewed by the researcher's bias, and while I even acknowledge that my own fear of the whore stigma may have colored the interview process, I nevertheless assert that something besides me was operating on these women, leading them to duck the word *whore* in describing their work. The Madison escorts in my study are part-time sex workers who primarily identify themselves as students at the same university where I conducted my research. They aren't activists, and many of them don't identify as feminists. Like me, they know they don't have the social power to flaunt their whore status without serious repercussions on both self-image and public reputation.

Third wave feminism has attempted to frame a pro-sex

position that accounts for the variety of women's sexual experiences, including whoring, in order to move away from repudiations of sex work and heterosexuality in general, encapsulated by Andrea Dworkin's statement that "[t]he metaphysics of male sexual domination is that all women are whores."[4] Wendy Chapkis' *Live Sex Acts: Women Performing Erotic Labor* is a key third wave text on sex work. According to Chapkis, "sex radical" feminism (associated with queer and otherwise pro-sex feminists such as Pat Califia, Susie Bright, Tracy Quan, and Carol Queen) presents sexual relations as a "terrain of struggle."[5] Patriarchal power relations between men and women crash head-on into sex workers' efforts to subvert and co-opt those power relations. In theory, my position resembles Chapkis', but I am unwilling to ignore what happens to these liberatory ideas in real-world practices. It's one thing to take the name of sex radical feminist. It's something else entirely to self-identify as a whore. Though third wave feminist theories offer a welcome intellectual escape from the oppressive whore stigma, they do not acknowledge the extreme difficulty of excavating the internalized moral division between good and bad girls.

The narratives that emerge from my interviews suggest that some women working as prostitutes are caught between the sexual autonomy and financial independence sex work offers, and the stigma attached to whoring, experiencing a degree of newfound freedom but in a necessarily covert form. Madison sex workers deal with the contradictions of their experience by treating prostitution as a performance.[6] As Carol Leigh (a.k.a. the Scarlot Harlot) declares, whores "need status as actresses!"[7]—a rallying cry to legitimate sex work, acknowledge the necessary performative skills of the job, and erase the whore stigma. Equating whoring with acting permits these young women to understand and reconcile traditional concepts of femininity with their activities as working prostitutes. In fact, my main argument is that these co-ed call girls use "acting" or "performance theory" intuitively as a way to cope with their multiple roles of womanhood and to mitigate the personally damaging effects of the whore stigma. Legitimizing sex work as a skilled performance allows these women to maintain self-respect while employed in a demonized (and criminalized) industry.

Between September and November 1996 I interviewed thirteen sex industry workers—five escort agency owners and eight escorts.[8] These sex workers' narratives were clearly performances, enacted for me as an interviewer/audience and deployed to install a barrier between what they thought of as their real lives and their work as escorts. First, they performed normalcy for me, never naming themselves prostitutes or characterizing their work as prostitution. They were "escorts" and "strippers," not whores or call girls. They went on "dates" and "appointments," not calls. They saw "clients" and "guys," not tricks or johns. Second, they performed for their clients, playing the role of sexually insatiable girl-for-hire. These performances confine *bad girl* to a small part of a sex worker's reality, allowing the *good girl* to remain intact beneath an artificial character, a provisional role.

Thinking about prostitution as a performance introduces a new context for feminist discussions of sex work
that might move the subject beyond its current impasse of
prostitutes' rights versus critiques of the profession's
inherent sexism, two "opposing" views that share much in
spirit and intentions. Sociologist Erving Goffman is well
known for his work on the social roles people adopt in
order to convince others of their competence, trustworthiness, and character. For Goffman, self-presentation operates by dividing oneself into front and back space. Goffman
defines *front* as the visible aspects of an individual's performance available for interpretation by the audience.[9]
The *back* (corresponding to the theatrical backstage) is private space, "where the impression fostered by the performance is knowingly contradicted as a matter of
course."[10] As private space, the back is rarely accessible by
audience members. All of the sex workers I interviewed
presented a front of banality, meeting me in their offices,
homes, at local bars, restaurants, and shopping malls. I
called them at home, and they called me. I likewise presented the front of hip, sexy, feminist researcher, meeting
them whenever and wherever they asked and empathizing
about the pressures of going to school, holding down a job,
and juggling multiple relationships. I intended to establish
a common ground through these mutually constructed
"fronts" so each of us could feel safe from being judged
negatively based on our otherwise glaring differences—
namely social class, sometimes race, and of course profession. And, like them, I tried to keep my "back" hidden;

feigning comfort and trust when they shocked or scared me, or when I thought they were exaggerating and lying.

Confronting this contradiction remains difficult and painful. I know, in hindsight, how much my fear of the whore stigma shaped the distance that remained always between me and my research subjects. Afraid of identifying too closely or too personally with the sex workers I interviewed, I imagine I may have given off a vibe of judgment despite my conscious intention to "connect" with them. The possibility of appearing naive or hopelessly straight-and-narrow laced my interactions with self-consciousness and sometimes fear. I felt especially vulnerable during my conversations with agency managers because they smoothly turned the tables on me by speaking as if they were interviewing me for a job, rather than me interviewing them for a research project. My critical academic distance, then, was constantly called into question. When they offered me jobs, it was all too easy to imagine accepting, the money and adventure all too tempting. Yet I did turn down their offers. I never wanted my mother to experience bailing me out of jail, never wanted to watch the face of a future lover darken as I confessed my dalliances with hooking, never wanted to risk a job to it. Ultimately I cannot reconcile my theoretical belief that all women have the right to be whores with my fear that I might someday be judged as one. This very real and prominent feminist conflict is part of the reason why sex workers translate their field into more acceptable professional terminology.

▬

I met Kevin one sunny October afternoon in his downtown Madison office. He was about thirty-five, white, and beginning to bald—attractive in an aging frat boy way, like many of the men in suburban Wisconsin. Kevin began the conversation by describing his contract system and the security it provides.

"I tell the girls that the contract protects both them and the guy. This way, nobody can be arrested. And if they don't want to have sex with the guy, or there's something they don't want to do, all they have to do is refer to the contract. The guy's not paying for sex, he's paying for their time only."

I asked Kevin if the girls usually had sex on their dates. "Well," he leaned in, "they're not paying for sex. But that's what they expect. And 99 percent of the time, that's what happens." The contracts are a key component in framing prostitution as a performance, and the official, legal framework of the contract mitigates the whore stigma for everyone involved. For the owners, the contracts establish them as legitimate businessmen and women. For the escorts and clients, the contracts remove the taint of prostitution. These contracts list a series of propositions that clients and escorts accept and initial at the beginning of each transaction. By accepting the contract, clients and escorts proclaim that no acts of prostitution would occur—even though, according to Kevin, "99 percent of the time" it (or something closely resembling it) does. Instead, whatever happens becomes, through this contractual sleight of hand, mutually consenting sex between two equally desiring parties. Prostitution is illegal, but sex isn't. In a shared reconstruction of reality, the clients and escorts consider the contract a document that legalizes any activity that takes place: there is, by definition, no possibility of prostitution and thus no whore stigma attached to their intercourse.

During our interview, Kevin regaled me with stories of his own work as an escort. He had "about ten" regular (female) clients who paid him three thousand dollars for a night of romance. Kevin boasted of having been instructed in the arts of love by an experienced, older, Japanese woman while serving with the Navy SEALS in Japan. As a rule, I generally believed what my interviewing subjects told me—that is, I didn't assume that when they told me they started work to earn extra money they were *really* sexually abused, drug addicted, misguided young women—but there were times when their statements contradicted each other, especially about money. Kevin's employees shifted around how much money they made a week or per date, and the number of dates they went on each week. I imagine a hard look at their cash intake would have drawn out the whore stigma in too-bold ink. Kevin's estimates of how much money his employees made contrasted sharply with the extravagant figures he quoted from his own work as an escort, undermining his credibility significantly. According to his math, he would have pulled in thirty times as much as they. Unlikely, I'd say—even if he were taught by a geisha. So why might Kevin have exaggerated? Partly, he was just bragging to impress a girl, or more accurately, a smart girl, a college chick. And partly it was a sales pitch, pure and simple, to convince me to work for him by highlighting the lucrative rewards of prostitution. Like all the agency owners I interviewed, he offered me a job. He was especially impressed by my conversation skills (I'm not a theater major for nothing) and my bra size: "What are you, a C–D cup?" When I confirmed my "talents" as 36D, he told me I could go to work that afternoon. He also offered, as a starting bonus perhaps to show me his impressive (if widely shared) vibrator collection—available to all his employees for work or pleasure.

I enjoyed Kevin, and I trusted him, despite his manipulation of our interview's dynamics and certain "facts" of his trade. He seemed harmless, reminding me of other men I know. I didn't feel the same way about Darrell and Dwayne, the African American managers of Private Entertainment. I went to their house on a side street at 10 P.M. on a Thursday night, clutching tightly to my notebook and the promise extracted from a girlfriend that she'd call the police if I weren't home by midnight. The two co-owners ushered me into a room with a long couch and two folding chairs. I didn't want to look too official, or too scared, so I sat on the couch. Darrell offered me a joint and a beer and sat down beside me. Dwayne offered me a job and sat on my other side. I declined all offers and chain-smoked Pall-Malls instead. I was afraid of these men. They embodied so closely the stereotypical white fears of black men and prostitution, and I felt the racism of a white girl raised in small-town Iowa join somewhere deep inside me with the whore stigma common to most Americans. Though I like to think I'm hip to these twin forces of oppression—a card-carrying member of the *multicultural feminist resistance*—I distinctly felt the pressure of multiple biases and media hype well up and spill past my lips in the form of manic conversation about hip-hop.

This particular evening of field research brought home to me very intimately what it feels like to be a whore in a culture that criminalizes prostitution—what it feels like to be positioned as human refuse, interchangeable, disposable. Throughout the interview, a steady stream of men entered the apartment without knocking, went into the kitchen, and left. Most said hello to me, and no one seemed surprised to see a nervous girl sitting on the sofa. Darrell started by assuring me that his agency had the "guaranteed best-looking" girls in Madison, flattering me and distinguishing himself in one smooth gesture. I asked him if the escorts had sex with their clients. He answered with a quick and adamant "no."

> We're an escort service. The girls come in, do a strip, give the guy a full-body massage, and then leave. They never have sex. See, we have a contract. The guy signs a piece of paper saying he knows he isn't going to have sex with the girl. Prostitution is illegal in Wisconsin. But soliciting for tips isn't. So the girl can say I'll do this if you tip me, and it's completely legal.

> (Q) What do they do for tips?

Oh, anything they want to. But they don't have sex. See, I tell them, don't whack them off for less than fifty dollars, don't blow them for less than seventy-five dollars, and don't fuck them for less than one hundred dollars. It's their body, you know, and nobody's fucking me unless I get paid really well, you know, and unless they use a condom.

(Q)   So they do have sex.

No. They don't have sex, unless they get tipped $100 at least. Or that's what I tell them. I don't know, maybe some of them have sex for less, I don't care, it's their business. But if it was me, I wouldn't fuck anybody for less than $100.

Of all the conversations I had in the course of this research, this one stands out for its extreme twists in logic to redefine "sex" and maintain a space where their work remains legal and dignified. Like Kevin, these men relied on contracts to separate their business from prostitution. Of course, Darrell and Dwayne know on some level that sex is sex, regardless of the price or terms of negotiation, but they refused to refer to their service as prostitution, or to themselves as pimps, in order to produce a sort of "play" or "drama" where the rules of reality are suspended and they can "act" as if their work is legitimate and their "characters" morally and socially correct. These sorts of mental back flips are not new to the black community, which has historically participated in two cultures at once—the "white" culture where they "perform" blackness as subservient and docile, and the "black" culture where they satirize white culture and the black characters it requires. There's no telling what Darrell and Dwayne had to say to each other about me and their work once I'd gone. Despite, or perhaps because of, the prevailing media stereotype of black men as aggressive pimps—perpetuated by the media in texts like the recent HBO documentary "Pimps Up, Hos Down"—Darrell and Dwayne avoided the whore stigma as carefully as anyone, maybe more carefully, since they had more at stake in any confrontation with the police.

While I was in their apartment, Darrell and Dwayne introduced me to Cheri, their top booker, who had just come from an appointment. I asked if she'd mind describing it (sex or no sex, how one negotiates the tip scale, etc.). Instead, she talked about what she did "generally":

> Usually, the guy is really excited before I even get there. I hand him the contract, and while he looks it over, I get out my massage oil and put on some music. I start oiling them up, telling them they're sexy, and that I'm wet and stuff, and then I tell them to jack off. I keep talking to them, telling them that they're doing a good job, and that I like their cock. Then I tell them to come on my tits. When they do, I clean up and leave. They almost always tip me, and they almost always call back.

Cheri was gorgeous, with dark blond hair and deep green eyes. She had on great leather boots and a crisp white blouse. She was a student at Edgewood College, a small, Catholic, private college in Madison. I never determined for certain whether Cheri had sex on her calls, or solicited for tips, or what, but I can believe her clients called her back. I would have. I can also believe that no one ever called her a whore; she was too classy, beautiful, and self-assured to match the stigmatic stereotype.

Sitting in Darrell and Dwayne's house, though, I thought about what would happen if police officers rang the doorbell. They were smoking dope, we were talking about prostitution (whoring by any other name remains the same), and I'm pretty sure the guy in the kitchen was dealing drugs. Cheri seemed to think I was a new recruit, and in fact Darrell and Dwayne talked more about what would happen if I went to work for them than their business in general, still hard selling me as a potential new whore. The men visiting the kitchen probably assumed I was an employee as well, or at least interested in a job. I imagined trying to explain to the arresting officers that I was just here doing research. That I was a good girl, well within the letter of the law. I'd flash my student ID, Cheri would flash hers, and no one would believe me. Why should they? Sitting on the couch, officially employed in the business or not, I was implicated as a whore. By inhabiting this marginal cultural space, even as a visitor, I gave up my good girl privileges temporarily. I could be prosecuted with the lot of them—mishandled, verbally abused, finger-printed, the whole whore package. I felt comfortable being related to a working whore by people in the business; there was no social hierarchy, no judgment, no disdain. Like most call girls I met, I felt okay being classified as a whore, as long as no one outside called me one. And since no cops came by, I didn't have to face the reality of my fears that night, but the slippery slope between whore researcher and whore remains close at hand.

My meeting with Meshella, the third agency owner I talked to, took this zone of discomfort into a public space—the local mall—and my nerves were further jangled. At nineteen, Meshella was the youngest agency owner and the only African American escort I met. As we walked through the mall, she spoke freely and unselfconsciously (easily audible to suburban passers-by) about her agency, Luxuries, which had been open only two weeks.

> See, we're an escort business. I work myself. We do a little strip tease, shake our titties, tell the guy about all the kinky stuff we've done—not really done, you know, just stuff to get him excited. And I tell the girls that if they want to, the guy can, you know, lick them and stuff, finger them. That way they're not having sex with them. It's something the guy is doing. But girls don't fuck. If anybody tells you we fuck, they're a goddamned liar. The cops are going to be watching us for awhile, and until the heat is off, we don't fuck nobody.

Meshella and her escorts performed, then, not only for their clients and for me, but also for the local police. She staged her "play" with law enforcement in mind as a key audience. Meshella's explicit focus on the criminality of prostitution echoes a major concern in the prostitutes' rights movement. Many activists, such as Margo St. James, argue that the prohibition of prostitution "serves to subjugate women" by adding legal penalties to the social penalties of the whore stigma.[11] For Meshella, this was the real threat of the whore stigma—the material threat to her freedom. Where race, class, and fucking intersect, limits abound in the form of laws, jail cells, probation, and general disregard. In Meshella's logic, once the police accepted Luxuries as a legitimate business, she and her employees would be free to fuck whomever whenever they want. In this case, prostitution only takes place if police name it and intervene; otherwise, it's just business as usual.

Meshella and I walked through the mall to J.C. Penney's where she confronted a clerk who had spread rumors about Luxuries and slept with a client as a Luxuries employee. Their argument escalated to a screaming match threatening violence. When an older female clerk came over and asked what was going on, Meshella screamed at her as well. She walked away and called security. The rent-a-cop escorted Meshella and me right back out of J.C. Penney's, and the older woman shepherded the clerk to the back. Though Meshella promised to get in touch with me again and introduce me to her other employees, I never heard from her again. The "good girl" in me, the part conditioned to behave in a "classy" manner at all times, especially in public, still stings from being ejected from the department store. My "interview" with Meshella seriously challenged the boundaries I set up between myself and my interview subjects. In my previous conversations with agency owners, I tried to remain a privileged yet detached outsider gathering information and anecdotes about Madison's sex work industry. That's the scary part about the whore stigma—how it spreads from body to body, how it sucks you in, implicating us all. Secure in my identity as a white, middle-class, academic feminist, I merely slummed in the world of sex work, yet it wouldn't take much—guilt by association—to lose that privilege in the eyes of the law. Walk a mile in whore's shoes and you'll feel it the next day—in the hamstrings and the hot flush of shame.

I developed a particularly close relationship with Lesley, an eighteen-year-old college dropout, who treated me kind of like an older sister, asking advice about work and personal matters. In return, I worried about Lesley more than the other girls I interviewed. She seemed naive, putting herself repeatedly in what struck me as unsafe or self-destructive situations. Like many women, she had a hard time saying no, wanting to please the people around her, and she was easily swayed by the compliments and affection clients offered. Lesley told me about her first call—a double, two escorts and a client, with her coworker Carrie.

> After an hour, after he done it with both of us, he wanted to come again so I told him I'd give him a hand job. He just looked so grateful, and told me I was really beautiful. That's the best part about this job. They tell you they love you and you're gorgeous.

Lesley, as much as any of her clients, believed in the illusion of romance, producing a degree of affection and desire beyond what is necessary for the prostitution exchange. I joined her for a lingerie shopping trip to Victoria's Secret and helped pick out a teddy for her next date with Doug, a regular. I asked if he made a specific request. "No," she fingered the red satin strap of an expensive lace negligee. "I just want to look sexy for him." Buying specific clothes for Doug—not unlike buying a garter belt for a boyfriend's birthday—manifests Lesley's need to model their relationship on the nonstigmatic romantic model, denying the taint of money and overt male control.

Most of the Exploits escorts got emotional support and erotic pleasure from one special client. Carrie had a lengthy relationship with Paul. They had amazing sex, ordered pizza, and drank wine, listening to disco albums. She saw him at least once a week, often for several hours. Carrie didn't charge Paul for the extra time and in fact gave him her beeper number so he could contact her directly to bypass the agency's fee; she charged the bargain price of $100 instead of $150. Carrie's relationship with Paul blurred the boundaries of the typical whore/john exchange, pointing to a spectrum of dynamics each "trick" might evoke:

> I know Paul wants me to just be his girlfriend, and I some-
> times want to date him too. And since I'm not seeing any-
> one right now, it's like I *am* his girlfriend. We talk about
> school, what I'm studying, his job, our families, every-
> thing. But when I borrowed money from him for my
> tuition last semester, I paid him back in cash. He wanted
> me to just see him three times for free. I couldn't do it. It
> was too weird. If I'd seen him for free it would have been

like we were dating, and I couldn't ask him for money the next time. But I *need* him as a client, cause it's really steady money, so I had to see three other guys and pay him back out of that.

By focusing on positive experiences, like eating pizza, buying lingerie, and genuinely liking certain guys, the girls can tell themselves (and me) that prostitution isn't particularly different than any other heterosexual relationship. And in many ways, it isn't.

Setting up an alternate persona functions to give the whore stigma the slip as well. Escorts perform a specific identity distinctly different from their "real" selves at work. When on a date, they use clothing, makeup, and behavior to create a hyper-feminine, hyper-sexual fantasy for their customers (and for themselves). The first time I saw Kristeen, she wore the average college girl attire of sweater and jeans. Next time we met at a local bar after she finished a call. Here she wore a tight leather skirt with a slit that meant business, white lace, thigh-high stockings, black, high-heeled pumps, and a white silk blouse, topped off with expertly applied cosmetics. I complimented her appearance, and she talked a little about the image she tries to create:

> The guy is paying you $150 an hour, and you better look sexy. Plus, I just saw this guy in a hotel, and I have to walk through the lobby and look like I belong there, not like I'm there to do business. So I think a lot about what I wear, trying to look sexy and not trashy. I have bought a lot of clothes that I almost never wear unless I'm going on a "date."

In her everyday analysis, it is clear that she recognizes the connection between sexual self-presentation, economic worth, and entitlement to admittance in certain high-class public spaces, but she stops far short of critical insight, moving unselfconsciously within the limits of her profession, set by the patriarchy in general and enforced by the various men she—all of us—encounters, everyday.

As adept as Kristeen is at role switching, she did not discuss her actions in those terms. Other call girls named this experience explicitly as performance. For example, Alex spoke of her background in amateur theater:

> I did acting in high school, and I've done some improv. That's what this is. You go in and pretend to be someone else. You kind of make the scene up as you go along, and I like to get really creative, telling the guy some wild stories, and trying to get him to play along.

Similar to role-playing in "normal" heterosexual couples, this translation of prostitution into theatric performance permits the actors to move beyond personal and cultural sexual limits. Call girls reframe sex work as a temporary role in a mutually constructed artificial space "free" of external and internal restraint. "Hooker" becomes a look, something to put on and take off at will, separating their "true identity" from the work—a core self remains relatively safe from the whore stigma.

Each of these co-ed call girls acknowledges the difficulty of maintaining boundaries between work and their "normal" lives. Hardly surprising—their frantic schedules fit appointments between boyfriends, classes, parties, and homework. As a result, performing both normalcy and hyper-sexuality in a single afternoon, they often find that emotional confusion erupts frequently. Amanda made this point about her "calls":

> They take a long time. I have to take a shower beforehand, get all dressed up, and then go. I usually take a shower with the guy, and have sex with him in the shower. They really like that. Then I have to take a shower when I get home. It's kind of a pain trying to explain why I have wet hair all the time.

For Ashlee, another of Kevin's employees, the pressures of prostitution became unmanageable. I met her the first day I interviewed Kevin, when she returned from a call to drop off her money. At first she told me she liked her work and triumphantly showed me the $145 she had just made. But as we continued to talk, her confusion and despair surfaced. Peppered with nervous giggles, Ashlee told me that her phone had been turned off, and, in fact, that she had started working for Kevin out of pure financial need (rather than a sex-positive feminist expression of prostitution as valid work). She began to sob:

> Sometimes when I'm with my boyfriend, I just want to kill him. I look at him, and I feel like I'm doing all this stuff for him, and he's doing nothing for me. I never come with him. I never come when I'm working. I only come when I'm by myself. Maybe there's something wrong with me.

Ashlee reached a crisis point in terms of her sexual identity and desire, a conflict that was accelerated by immersion in the heterosexual economies of sex work and "romantic love." Once sex was revealed as a job, the illusions of childhood about intimacy dissolved and she started to question her sex life with her boyfriend, becoming angry, frustrated, and sad. A few weeks later, Ashlee stopped working at Exploits in order to spend more time with her boyfriend and try to have a baby. I was relieved that she quit, but less glad for her alternative "choice," which represents the narrow range of options available to working-class women looking for economic stability and emotional intimacy. By attempting to re-embody traditional notions of femininity, Ashlee sought to blot out her past as a prostitute with the revered role of motherhood.

Though none of the other escorts I interviewed expressed as much anger and confusion as Ashlee, they did report that sex work changed their ideas about sexuality and identity for the worse. Carrie voices a common sense of performance anxiety in the bedroom:

> I have trouble sometimes having one night stands. I start thinking about how to turn him on, I want him to like me, and so I do stuff I've done at work. It can get confusing, because I sometimes can't tell if I'm having a good time, or just pretending.

Carrie's words express the same confusion my friends and I feel. I know very few women who haven't faked an orgasm, and in a world where women are considered frigid and hung up if they don't enjoy sex, I imagine many of us have exaggerated our enthusiasm at one point or another.

How much of a difference is there between "having a good time" and "just pretending"—can anyone really tell?

Third wave activist Rebecca Walker, in an essay called "Lusting for Freedom," claims that the "pleasure and the confidence" that sex gave her carried over into her everyday life, teaching her to raise her hands in class and cherish female friendships while acknowledging that there are "forces that subvert girls' access to freeing and empowering sex."[12] The whore stigma is one of those forces. The reality for me, for Madison sex workers, and for many women is that we're trying to fulfill our sexual desires while remaining good girls in the eyes of the world.

For this reason, I prefer to perceive myself as an actor in the same play as the call girls I met, rather than an audience member, inertly observing the actions on stage, or a script writer, shaping their responses to me by setting the terms of our discussion ahead of time. Yet it's hard to write about hookers and not feel like a pimp. When I make a narrative from the lives and words of Kevin, Meshella, Alex, and Carrie, and when I present my research at conferences and in books like this one, I'm pimping their stories for academic legitimacy—there's no escaping that fact. The truth is, I get a certain amount of respect for going to pimps' houses in the middle of the night and hanging out with local escorts. When I tell these stories to amuse cocktail party guests or achieve academic status, I am redrawing the boundaries between me and the sex workers, separating my experience from theirs, reassuring myself of my safety and respectability even as I fundamentally believe that prostitution should be decriminalized and that in many important ways my situation as a woman resembles theirs. It can feel like fun and games at first to get in touch with one's inner whore, but when she ceases to perform as an actor in a play, when the reality of her role reveals itself to be not a mask, not something one can remove backstage, we young women are often left trembling and alone, mute with stage fright.

The Plain-Clothes Whore

Agency, Marginalization, & the
Unmarked Prostitute Body

KARI KESLER

PROSTITUTES OFTEN speak of being present in
body and absent in mind during the sexual acts that constitute their work, effecting a mind/body split to deal more
effectively with the experience at hand. I often worked
through a night, looked back, and wondered exactly what
happened. This is not to say I experienced a blackout or
even blocked distasteful moments. I was plainly aware of
what transpired, yet it was somehow not my knowledge,
but secondhand or scripted, like that strange sensation of
returning to one's home airport from another country: The
other country is present in the mind, your memories are
clear, yet the story stars you-as-character rather than you-

231

as-person. In telling and retelling yourself the scrambled story of your adventures abroad, after a while the memory takes on a new shape, a polished narrative, cropped and framed like a postcard. Soon, you can no longer place yourself inside your experience in any meaningful way. During the nine months I worked most actively as a prostitute, I often felt dissociated from my experiences, which belonged to that other country of the night world. Many times I told myself I should be keeping a journal. I reasoned that it would both document my experiences for future analysis and help me process the disorienting work as I went along. Instead, my writing self felt blank as the lifeless page in front of me. What to write? Heidi Fleiss I am not. The raw details of prostitution were not the part of my job that compelled me most. What else? Descriptions of the men? The madam I worked for? Having to ask directions to a trick's house at the 7-11? There were in fact many interesting stories to record, but none were really about *me*.

Outing oneself as a prostitute comes, for many, from a similar motivation to out oneself as a homosexual. Claiming this identity expands the notion of who is/was/can be a prostitute, serving to lessen the stigma attached to prostitution. This is not my goal in this essay. This is in fact, the issue I ask you to look beyond, in order to break out of the existing terms of discussion set primarily by nonprostitutes, those who wonder "what kind of woman" could be a prostitute. Instead, I make the prostitute-as-knower central, despite (or perhaps because of) the conceptual flexibility this perspective requires of my non-prostitute readers. I choose to foreground the desires and conflicts of the prostitute (in this case, me) and to subordinate questions and concerns held by those whose work is more clearly affirmed by the dominant culture. I will not allay your concerns about my welfare or the moral fabric of society or explain the possibility of my being in your world. You may be tempted to see me through your current view of prostitution, but I will not devote this essay to reminding you *I am not that woman,* because I am not seeking a space within your reality.

It is true that I struggle with a deep ambivalence toward prostitution. Do I think it was an inherently good or bad experience? And what would constitute "good" or "bad" in this scenario? Who decides? What was my motivation? Does my discomfort arise from prostitution itself, or from the stigma attached to prostitution? Can prostitution be experienced in the U.S. apart from the whore stigma? My answers shift and change from day to day, depending not only on what I am thinking at the moment, but which moment I choose to consider. The whore *intelligentsia* confirms ambivalence at the core of *sex worker feminisms*. Annie Sprinkle—self-proclaimed slut and goddess—admits,

> I did feel used and really treated like shit, really taken advantage of. There were times when I was in total power. There were times when I received a lot. There were times when it was wonderful. I got in it for the money. But I also got in because I needed to be touched. I wanted the attention. I wanted the status. There are so many reasons. The problem is that everyone is always trying to simplify it.[1]

The "everyone" Sprinkle discusses includes feminists and nonfeminists, people who simplify prostitution into *either* victimization *or* empowerment. Prostitutes work the spectrum in between.

I was not forced or coerced into this work by monetary concerns or a lack of opportunities. I attended college and held a respectable day job. I did not dislike my work as a prostitute—often feeling powerful, sometimes only tired, and more than occasionally annoyed. Prostitution's dailiness, its mundane repetitiousness, is often overlooked in favor of exotic representations or conversion narratives— only the glamour or gutter makes news it seems. The constant recreation of self proved physically and mentally exhausting for me. For every client, I take the performance from the top, as if each moment were new, generated from our particular chemistry instead of an eternal return to the same moment, the same words, the same manufactured "reality" I churn out like piecework on an assembly line. My likes, dislikes, background—all creative interpretations of the truth: "This is my first time doing this; I love this job because I get to have sex all the time; I was raised on the West Coast/East Coast/Midwest; yes, I really came." On some level the men must know we are playing a game with each other and with reality, but we tacitly agree not to spoil the fun by admitting to it out loud.

And all the people with whom I interact during the course of an evening must join in this game of mutually reconstructed reality—airbrushed, soft, and whore free. The hotel clerk who rings me up to visit my "uncle," the chatty cab driver whose battery of friendly questions trail off as he gets too close to a truth neither of us wishes to permit in the social space between us—these daily occurrences form the foundation of my experiences as a prostitute. Not horrific, nor exotic. So, not being able to write during this time did not come from having trouble coping with tragic circumstances, nor out of a sense of shame about myself or my work. Surely my writing block came in part from this collective cultural agreement not to talk about prostitution, not to allow it into the "normal" lexicon of casual conversation. Trying to journal the whoring experience would have meant overcoming the deep schism between dominant representations of sex work as either degrading or titillating and the everyday reality of prostitution as far more similar to most "regular" jobs than non-prostitutes generally want to admit. Unable to tell a different story about prostitution and unwilling to repeat the expected stories, I found myself unable to write at all.

The moments I remember most clearly often involve this tension between socially constructed expectations of prostitution and the decidedly less shiny reality. My undercover work—as the plain-clothes whore—entertained me; I wondered if people could tell I was a working girl. At the 7-11, dressed in jeans and a sweatshirt, buying condoms and asking for directions to a house I could not seem to locate, I wondered what the clerk and customers saw. Most people think they can spot a prostitute by her dress alone. The men I saw often requested that I dress casually, for exactly this reason, to keep their neighbors from knowing they consorted with whores. The slutty clothes often associated with prostitutes actually only characterize the subset of streetwalkers. But, even in my casual clothes, I remained alert to other people's glances, vigilant in evaluating potential sources of danger or exposure. I felt transparent, afraid something in my manner would reveal my illicit purpose, or that I would slip and say something inappropriate.

In one vivid memory, I am making a phone call to the woman I worked for from a pay phone in the parking garage of a downtown hotel. I was working with another woman that night, and my madam asked if we wanted to go on another call. Without thinking, I turned to my friend and asked her. She said yes, but looked sharply at me. Aware of her silent rebuke, I noticed a man further away in the garage listening to us. I was embarrassed and ashamed, not because the man knew we were prostitutes, but because I placed myself and another woman in danger through a careless mistake, and showed myself to be naive, clumsy at inhabiting two realities at once. In the moment of that phone call, I had forgotten who I was supposed to be in the space of the garage and compromised my friend's self-presentation, leaving us vulnerable to harassment and violence, even arrest. This fear of exposing myself during these in-between moments—not fully in my role as prostitute, not fully free of it—reminded me constantly that whoring meant trespassing in dangerous territory. My success and my sanity depended on navigating this murky region, switching roles swiftly and smoothly.

The stigma attached to prostitution makes it difficult to

immerse oneself fully, even when one chooses the role relatively free of coercion. My ambivalence now arises from a similar reluctance. Constructing a positive standpoint on prostitution means standing on the thin line between choice and coercion, roughing out a space for individual decisions within a field of options limited by a sexually disciplinary culture. I resist the perception of prostitutes as necessarily lacking in agency (the ability to act on the world around you). Agency exists on many levels and is not static. The circumstances of prostitute women vary by background and work experience. Working for an escort agency or on one's own as a call girl gives many women a higher degree of control within their lives than other kinds of work, providing a flexible schedule, financial rewards, and freedom to service or deny individual customers. Within the dynamics of heterosexuality, as well, many prostitutes experience a higher sense of equality and control than in personal relationships with male lovers and husbands.

The question I wrestle with is whether agency within prostitution is by definition still a form of oppression for women. I could easily get mired down in this question. But even while I turn these theoretical problems over in my mind, I feel strongly that this agency is not mere delusion. Like heterosexuality in general, prostitution represents a "hard bargain," a process of negotiation, like courtship rituals and marriage, for access to the female body between two socially and economically unequal parties.[2] The superstructure of patriarchal culture continues to produce this uneven playing field between men and women, but within that uneven field, women make affirmative and relatively liberatory choices. A feminism that disrespects this compromised agency is impractical and exclusionary.

The limits of agency, for me, took the form of an inability to speak my reality—to loved ones, or to anyone while in public, and even on a certain level to myself. As a prostitute, I occupied a space that I could speak of only to a select few. I lived with a constant fear that I could be exposed at any time, aware at every moment of risking my day job, my apartment, my schooling, my lack of a criminal record, and the respect of my family. Is it any wonder that I could not keep a journal? The act of claiming a political identity as a prostitute conflicts with the everyday reality of whoring, which depends on hiding signs of prostitution from everyone around me. It was important not to become too comfortable in my role as a prostitute when not actually engaged in it. This comfort, an overconfidence of sorts, led me to forget what could and could not be said, and placed me in danger. Yet distancing myself from the role for reasons of safety and social decorum conflicted with my need to feel comfortable with myself and my job when actively engaged as a prostitute. Eventually I learned to turn these safeguards of comfort and discomfort on and off. The movement between these two stances toward prostitution (hiding it and excelling at it) might have become reflex after a period of time, except for the occasional unsporting gatekeepers in swanky hotel lobbies. I hold only a tenuous grip on my alternating roles because I rely on other people—the cab driver, convenience store employee, concierge, or whomever—to feign ignorance. Together we maintain the illusion of a whore-free America as a "cover" for illicit desires and deviant identities, invoking a dramaturgical ploy in which everyone follows the same imaginary script. When I entered a high-rise apartment building at 2:00 A.M., regardless of what I wore, whoring showed through like blaring white panty lines. I still had to ask the door-person to ring me up to the apartment. When I left the building exactly one hour later, we all knew what had happened. Sometimes, men asked me to arrive with a pizza in hand, or, earlier in the night, with a notebook like a scrubbed-face student. I would ask a cab driver to come back in one hour to pick me up, and as I reapplied lipstick and counted money in the backseat, we both knew the nature of my business, but we politely refrained from acknowledging it. I was dropped off, rung up, given directions, sometimes with a smile, sometimes a look of disgust, often just cool indifference. It's all in a night's work, for myself and for them. The scene required our tacit agreement to facilitate whoring but respect the whore stigma with our silence. Breaking this careful silence, on either of our parts, would leave us adrift in unscripted social interaction.

I am left, finally, with one thought. My agency as a prostitute was circumscribed and contingent but nevertheless valuable and real. I was powerful within my role as prostitute insofar as I got fully and comfortably into character, and I was powerful in other areas of my life insofar as I disengaged with my prostitute self. It seems to me now that what I lacked then was not anything so simple as self-esteem or moral education or any other condescending talk-show variety of solution. I did not yet know that life sometimes means maintaining many separate realities, adhering to the customs of each, for your own comfort and the comfort of others. Comfort and discomfort can be seen as needles on a compass, indicating when one is safely within the appropriate reality of the moment and when one veers dangerously off path. My imagined need to reconcile my two worlds—whore and not-whore—kept me from processing my knowledge of either one. If I had understood, while working as a prostitute, that one's selves do not always fit seamlessly together—that, in fact, the patriarchal Western form of logic that requires resolution of conflicting roles, fragmented selfhood, unseemly parts, need not control my tongue or mind—perhaps I could have written more at the time.[3] Even now I have trouble getting the words out. Finally, I maintain that as a prostitute I made choices and acted on the world around me, but I do not claim to have maintained this agency or autonomy in every situation. The stigma attached to prostitution functions not only to provide non-prostitutes with a way of disavowing the prostitute presence (in the world and in themselves); the stigma also prevents prostitute women from examining their own experiential knowledge and expressing it as a valid basis for feminist theory and social transformation.

Autobiography of a Flea

Scrutiny & the Female Porn Scholar

LISA Z. SIGEL

For the last ten years, while working first on my dissertation and then on the book version, I've often provoked strange looks, uncomfortable silences, and finally the question. I'm a historian; I research porn. What people want to know is how does pornography make me feel, or more to the point, does it turn me on? The leap from my study of sex to the study of me studying sex seems automatic and reflexive. After ducking it for a decade, I've decided to confront this question by writing my own autobiography as a flea. Being a flea would be a real step up for me. After all, I am a historian. But in the real *Autobiography of a Flea* (1885), a minor pornographic work of the nineteenth century, the flea is not the lowest of the low. That place is reserved for deviant girls. For the purpose of this essay, I, a mere girl of a scholar, intend to be the flea.

The *Autobiography of a Flea*, like many pornographic works of the time period, criticizes Catholicism, sexual hypocrisy, and ignorance. The book is narrated by a flea who latches onto a beautiful young girl named Bella. Priests, seeing Bella's voluptuous nature and ignorance, seduce her. Once corrupted from the womb outward, Bella pulls in her friend Julia to be likewise corrupted. Corruption spreads like disease. The text inverts Catholic values, turns them inside out; celibacy becomes deviance, innocence thinly covers the lechery underneath, and the bystanders—the flea and those reading from the flea's narration—enjoy the vantage point of voyeurs who can relish at the same time they condemn.

The *Autobiography* allows readers to explore deviance in two ways. The reader can follow the path of Bella, the young beauty, as the priests seduce and corrupt her. Or the reader can follow the path of the flea who, in commenting on Julia's fall from grace, voices a community's outrage at the transgression of its agreed upon boundaries. The deviant is not just the person who performs specific aberrant acts, the deviant is also the person through whom society communicates its beliefs and disciplines behavior into either normative or deviant categories through punishment, torture, ridicule, shame, exclusion, and voyeurism. These performances allow the "good" people of society to discuss, relish, pity, reconstruct, and narrate the deviant from a position outside.

In the *Autobiography*, the flea focuses the imagination of
the reader on carnal copulation. Narrating from outside the
activity, he can simultaneously enjoy and condemn, enliven
and constrain, watch and exclude, all within an apparently
moral framework. Yet the act of telling the story of deviance
blurs with the deviant acts themselves, producing pleasure
only thinly veiled as a lesson in conduct. In the final scene,
the flea describes the orgy that precedes Julia and Bella
becoming nuns. The flea states:

> The superior also had now the opportunity of indulging
> his antiphysical states; and not even the recently deflow-
> ered and delicate Julia escaped the ordeal of his assault.
> She had to submit, and with indescribable and hideous
> emotions of pleasure, he showered his viscid semen into
> her bowel.
>
> The cries of those who discharged, the hard breathing
> of those labouring in the sensual act, the shaking and
> groaning of the furniture, the half-uttered, half-suppressed
> conversation of the lookers on, all tended to magnify the
> libidinous monstrosity of the scene, and to deepen and
> render more revolting the details of this ecclesiastic pan-
> demonium.
>
> Oppressed with these ideas, and disgusted beyond
> measure, I fled.[1]

The reader can watch the flea watch the onlookers watch
the ravishment of Julia. The magnification of the gaze separates those who watch and then flee (flea?) from those
who get left in the libidinous monstrosity—titillating,
revolting, and oppressed both by the action and the

description of the action. The flea hops away, leaving Bella with a priest lodged in her bowels; her story ends while, he, a mere flea, innocently moves on.

In the *Autobiography*, the reader—through the flea's narration—encounters the image of woman as easily seduced and assaulted by men's desires. Bella and Julia, because of their natures and circumstances, become the sites of sexuality. The priests, the onlookers, and the flea consume Bella and Julia. While Bella and Julia have the capacity to act in their own interests, ultimately their only action is submission. Both women, girls really, are deviants whose bodies provide titillation laced with moral lessons. Even as they submit to the bodies and the will of the priests, they submit to the prurience and moralism of the flea.

For the purpose of this essay try to consider me as the flea, although I'll keep the moralism to a minimum. As a historian, I can show you how British pornography changes over the course of the nineteenth century, how it reflects and contributes to changing gender, class, and other distributions of power. As important as my analytical work on sexuality and its relation to the culture, though, is the fact that I'm female. My culture—multilayered because of my position as student and teacher, female and intellectual—is primarily one of marginality with a threat of deviance; marginal for I stand at the bottom of many hierarchies of power. I don't *have* position; I *am* positioned.

When I put myself as the flea, I mean to read not only the performance of deviation in nineteenth-century texts, but also the performance of deviation in the social construction of Lisa Z. Sigel, scholar of pornography. People assume that because I study pornography I am deviant; then they discipline me in much the same way as the voice of authority disciplines girls in the texts I read. By putting myself as the flea (rather than as the girl), I am placing myself outside of this process to explore how discipline keeps everyone in her place.

That deviance is implicit in pornography strikes me as a curious position to take. Pornography is commonly understood as sexual material intended to arouse for the primary purpose of masturbation. Regardless of the fact that humans are complex creatures who don't always respond to stimuli in predictable or consistent ways; regardless of the fact that sexualized objects from bananas to underwear exist around us all the time without turning us on; regardless of the fact that arousal and masturbation are (sometimes) no longer considered deviant, the purposefully arousing nature of pornography marks it as deviant. However, if we don't masturbate when reading it, pornography, like a Grecian urn, is also an artifact that tells us a lot about the culture from which it comes. Sexuality, like pottery, changes over time and across cultures, and its representation reflects broader changes in the dynamics of power and vulnerability. My job is to expose the complex interaction between erotic fantasy and political reality. Then, as now, ideas about sexuality valued some people and devalued others. Over the nineteenth century, Britain became the world economic and political power. Its economic strength allowed it to be the overt agent for change in much of the world—from the opening of China through the conquest of India to the divvying up of Africa. The continuation of slavery in the American South owes a great deal to the British desire for cotton for her mills, tobacco for her pipes, and indigo for her fabrics. Britain not only consumed and exported cotton; she also consumed and exported fantasies, imagined erotoscapes in which hierarchies of class, gender, and sexual access were reproduced. The fantasies of sexual dominion underlay Britain's practical dominion; they contributed to science, governance, class relations, language, politics, and family; they created patterns of thought that real people negotiated in order to live their lives. Just as the *Autobiography of a Flea* built on allegations of sexual deviance in the Catholic Church and allowed the British reader to enjoy and condemn Catholic (and catholic) sexuality, other works of pornography popularized distinctive views of racist/race-based eroticism. Works like *The Memoirs of Dolly Morton* (1896) offered the British reader a sexualized account of slavery, the underground railroad, and the American Civil War. Thus, the trade in cotton produced fantasies as well clothes. *The Lustful Turk* (1828), in which European women are captured, sold, and sodomized by the Dey of Algiers, reinforced the prevalent view of the Ottoman Turk as the supposed "sick man" of Europe. Real social relations became the background for fictional sexual relations, the two realms bouncing off each other into perpetuity.

In each story, the stock character of a young girl (like Bella) functions as a main site for working out ideas of sexuality. In each case, the young girl waits to be seduced. One final example, *Sweet Seventeen: the True Story of a Daughter's Awful Whipping and its Delightful if Direful Consequences* (1910), will highlight the dual position of women as incapable of thought but quite ready for deeds, not unlike the bind I often find myself in as a female scholar of pornography. In *Sweet Seventeen*, women rely upon men to liberate their most deeply held desires, the ones they simply cannot face. But in doing so, they realize the very childlike nature that precludes them from having a voice to begin with. In *Sweet Seventeen*, the father, Mr. Sandcross, realizes his lech for his daughter, Fanny. In spite of supplying her with pornographic novels and taking her to obscene plays to raise her passions, he can find no way to approach her beyond the occasional caress and kiss. One night, his lack of progress so frustrates him that he begins to beat and then caress her. Although she desists, calling him and his desires "loathsome," the beating raises her sexual longings. The scene culminates in penile/vaginal intercourse playing heavily on their oppositions: "One fierce lunge and [her hymen] gave way, as Sandcross felt every inch of his huge fatherly organ nipped by the sore, excoriated lips of his daughter's virgin cleft."[2] After intercourse, he tucks her into bed as if she were "his tiny little baby girlie" and she returns to a state of apparent purity: "As her nervous system gradually reverted to its normal state of quietude, so the babyish look returned to her violet eyes, and her face was as full of innocence as heretofore."[3] The more they have sex, the younger she becomes.

The younger she becomes, the more desirable she is to the father. Though she hadn't understood her own desires, luckily the father—by pursuing his own longings—helped her realize the embedded sexuality of her body. The two carry on a long-term sexual relationship. Eventually the mother discovers their relationship and dies of shock, leaving the two to assume a state of marriage. The issues of age, blood, and social class that dominate this tale echo those found in more respectable literature, and certainly offer fertile ground for transgression in this piece of pornography.

The text builds upon a structural tension within the culture—the taboo of incest—which it accentuates to create excitement. Social institutions (like family) that provided a set of boundaries for sexuality in real life, a disciplinary framework, translated into sexual titillation in pornographic texts. Incest had become savory as a fantasy precisely because the Victorian world put ever more emphasis on the family.

Furthermore, the readership of the text was comprised of just the type of men that Mr. Sandcross personified. Rich, white men controlled the production and consumption of the texts at the same time that their textual doubles controlled desire in the texts.[4] The particularities of pornographic distribution in the nineteenth century, including the rarity, cost, and limited distribution, lead one to believe that pornography reached only wealthy white men. However, the reach of the pornographic imagination went much further. Pornography, in creating a racialist sexuality where colored bodies were set against white bodies, defined a world of sexual accessibility for those reading it. The ability to imagine, organize, and overlay people's bodies and their sexualities with dirt, deviance, pleasures, and dangers informed the sexual caste system, which meant that the powerless were treated as empty canvasses for the powerful. In both Britain and America, then and now, documentation is supposed to be a one-way process. The strong communicate about the weak. Women, children, and otherwise powerless categories of people became the object of rich men's understandings of sexuality through the voyeuristic devices in pornography. Challenges to pornography centered on the problems of women and children and the powerless seeing representations of themselves as sex objects, vulgarly used by propertied white men's erotic imaginations. A judge presiding over a case that featured nude pictures stated: "If you had found such things in a private house perhaps they would not be regarded as obscene. But [at] an exhibition for boys and girls they clearly are."[5] From Anthony Comstock to Lord Campbell, legislators' concern over the effects on women and the young have long fueled attempts to get rid of pornography, preventing them from seeing it in the name of "protection."[6]

The one-way process of communication continues. There's a lot of discussion about the growing evils of pornography, but very little documentation of it. Without a historical record for comparison, people can (and do) make blanket statements about pornography getting worse, they can (and do) raise sex panics, and they can (and do) legislate and incriminate on the basis of sexuality. Joan Hoff connects the lack of historical studies on pornography with the proliferation of policies against pornography. Hoff points out that while both the Meese Commission (1986) and the Johnson Commission (1970) acknowledged the need for histories of pornography, neither commission would sponsor the work. Instead, both recommended broad policy changes based on fictive, historical projections. Hoff argues that detailed histories of pornography would interfere with the political agenda of social control.[7] In the wake of Mapplethorpe, advocating social control rather than encouraging study has only intensified. (Try applying for grants to study pornography if you don't believe me.)

Young, female scholars looking at sexuality disrupt the political agenda of social control by inverting the one-way process of communication. We look at how those with power position the powerless and part of that work includes looking at the way we are configured. Pornography, then, is not a Grecian urn. (Unless, of course, the urn is pornographic.) The nature of pornography and the power relations implicit in it remain so potent that even the study of it—rather than any actual deviant action—can be corrupting. (Didn't Fanny's father introduce her to sexuality by giving her pornography?) I am precisely the person who couldn't look at the pornography in the nineteenth century and I am the person who gets disciplined for doing so in the twentieth. I am deviant as a scholar, as a woman, and as a (relatively) young person. I get disciplined in just the ways that Bella in the *Autobiography* got disciplined— through a process of voyeurism and the invocation of conventional morality.

The historical issues about which I'm concerned become lost in morally heated debates over free speech versus antipornography, positions made even more rigid as they intersect with feminist theory/history. The antipornography efforts spearheaded by Catherine MacKinnon and Andrea Dworkin claim that pornography teaches men how to treat women like objects. Pornography, in this view, is fundamentally about the degradation and subjugation of women. If women are to be free, then men must cease oppressing women through pornography by making pornographers accountable for the harm they inflict.

The anticensorship efforts of Pat Califia, Nadine Strossen, and Wendy McElroy, on the other hand, counterargue that free expression about sexuality is central to women's continued battle for equality. From this perspective, the censorship of pornography will create a paucity of sexual alternatives for women and will ultimately be used to censor women's voices. Feminist progress toward a woman's rights to her own body and its desires will be swept aside in the attempt to purify men's desires. As Nadine Strossen explains, "Women's rights are far more endangered by censoring sexual images than they are by the images themselves. Women do not need the government's protection from words and pictures. We *do* need, rather, to protect ourselves from any governmental infringement upon our freedom and autonomy, even—indeed, especial-

ly—when it is allegedly 'for our own good.'"[8] The two positions are at such loggerheads that there's little room left to
negotiate between them. Or as Pat Califia has put it, she'll
admit that pro- and anticensorship feminists are all working
toward the same goals "when pigs fly."[9]

I find myself pulled back into these issues regardless of
my research agenda. After presenting a paper about how
men wrote their own bodies in truncated and dirty ways, I
was called to the carpet for not confronting the misogyny of
pornographic language. (True, but irrelevant to my point.)
A paper on the construction of whiteness in pornography
was reduced by one audience member to "hearing rape stories." (She couldn't hear that these were race stories as
well.) I've been told that I ignore the feminist issues implicit in pornography (by not focusing on misogyny) or worse,
that I ultimately take an antiporn feminist party line (by discussing power inequalities and objectification). As feminists we've been so busy wrestling with pornographic
images of ourselves—affirming, denouncing, refining, reinventing—that there's little room for other types of work, yet
the work of establishing a body of feminist history ranges so
far beyond whether I stand *for* or *against* porn that I am
almost dumbfounded by such ludicrous constraints on the
conversation. The philosophical Ping-Pong match insists I
take a side in an ever-devolving argument of which I want
little part. Porn happens. My feminist work is to conduct
critical inquiries into the phenomenon as part of a much
larger system of representation and the powerful inequalities within a given culture at a given time.

Catherine MacKinnon begins her book *Only Words* with an ahistorical incongruity that positions women on one side or other of this polarized debate (and an odd use of the second person):

> Imagine for hundreds of years your most formative traumas, your daily suffering and pain, the abuse you live through, the terror you live with, are unspeakable—not the basis of literature. You grow up with your father holding you down and covering your mouth so that another man can make a horrible searing pain between your legs. When you are older, your husband ties you to the bed and drips hot wax on your nipples and brings in other men to watch and makes you smile through it. Your doctor will not give you the drugs he has addicted you to unless you suck his penis.[10]

This slip into second person seems more than just a narrative ploy. MacKinnon implies I, the reader, should imagine myself treated in this way. I should imagine myself held down, tied up, sucking off doctors, dripping with melted wax. Isn't that the same process that pornography deploys? As I read the quote, the use of the second person insists that I—Lisa Z. Sigel, studier of pornography—live the "hundreds of years" of sucking off that are overlaid with voyeurism and moral lessons. No longer the flea; I am reduced to Bella.

I'm not the first to recognize the demeaning silence required of women in pornographic culture. MacKinnon's feminism, as represented in the passage above, works very much like pornography in this respect, manipulating and violating my readerly body, drowning out my story, as a feminist historian, with hers. Kate Ellis, Barbara O'Dare, and Abbey Tallmer argue that "we live in a culture where sexual speech and behavior for women is still severely restricted at an informal level. Thus much of the debate about pornography has served as a way for women to talk about sex, and about sexual variation, explicitly and publicly for the first time."[11] MacKinnon seems not to recognize the ways her own argument implicates her as part of the cultural disciplining of women's bodies, which she herself protects: "You learn that speech is not what you say but what your abusers do to you. Your relationship to speech is like shouting at a movie. Somebody stop that man, you scream."[12] But what if I want to think about the movie rather than stop it? What if I want to interrogate the orgasm?

The fact of the matter is pornography doesn't have to be conceived as language with its dick in my mouth. It doesn't have to stand in for my words. The conversation around porn calls out for restructuring (or was that my voice I heard?).

■

When I was in London for a number of months doing research I met an interesting man who told me he didn't want to get involved romantically with me because he had a girlfriend in California. We agreed to that. We talked, went to a movie, drank coffee. He propositioned me and I said, "No." And I said, "No." And I said, "No." He then told me that he only wanted to sleep with me because of my research. He thought I would be adventurous in bed. I had to say "no" quite a number of times because at some level he couldn't believe I was inaccessible as a sexual partner. As a woman who studied sexuality, I was assumed to be sexually accessible and sexually voracious. He also meant to insult me. The sum of my worth as a sexual partner came from my "adventurousness" predicated upon my intellectual leanings. I had teased him as a woman because of my studies and he could retaliate by denigrating my worth with an "only." According to him, as a woman I did not deserve attention; my value came "only" from my supposed deviant sexuality. I received a cultural disciplining through this man who cast me as Bella when I wanted to be the flea.

Normative discipline works as the flip side of deviant discipline. Women are sexualized and accessible *or* they are protected from sexuality, as I discovered when I tried to return from a research trip to England. In preparation for the trip I had contacted Customs to find out exactly what was illegal. (I'm the type who always gets her bags searched so I figured some preemptive planning was in order.) According to them, there are two main categories of representation that are illegal: child porn and bestiality. Behind the practice of search, seizure, and arrest for child porn is the theory that children should not be sexual objects for adults. Representations of sexualized children encourage adults to sexualize children and provide lasting testimony to the children's shame in which adults continue to take pleasure. The belief that the state should protect the weak (children) from harm by the strong (adults) is implicit in its stance toward child pornography. However, the definitions of child porn remain remarkably fuzzy. Is literary child porn illegal or does it have to be pictures? What if the images are drawn rather than photographed? If the photographs were taken of an adolescent when the age of consent was twelve, rather than eighteen, the current age of adulthood?

Bestial pornography remains even less clear. When considered at all, bestiality is generally seen as degrading toward the humans involved and not the animals. Instead of protecting animals (the weak), restrictions against bestial pornography protect humans (the strong) from thinking about such acts. (Perhaps because we haven't yet decided whether animals are sentient, we cannot assess the extent of their harm.) Because the theory is muddled, the practice is even more so. Does a photograph of a naked girl kissing a cat constitute bestiality? How about a stuffed dog held against a woman's genitals in a simulation of cunnilingus? The permutations on these bizarre questions become quite relevant when one hopes to avoid arrest in a busy airport.

I informed Customs when I would arrive and an agent met me as I exited the plane. The Customs agent, who seemed like a nice person at first glance, asked, "What does your mother think? Isn't she ashamed of what you're doing?" The agent hadn't even seen my research materials and couldn't know if they were deviant according to the legal definition of restricted materials. Child pornography and bestiality aside, the problem was that I *had* pornography, that I *looked* at pornography, and that I *thought* about pornography. I broke a boundary—went against *customs*. I thought about bad things. In a disciplinary response, the customs agent positioned me as child, referring to my mother and placing me under the protective umbrella of family and state. I found myself once again inside the materials, identified as one who needs protection from porn rather than one who studies it from a point outside.

Under the current terms of discussion, I can only be outraged by pornography or abused by it. I can only be the woman in the texts or the one who throws stones at the woman in the texts. People curious about my research slip unselfconsciously into questioning me. The assumption that I am open to questions is implicit. They can learn about my feelings and my sexuality by standing outside enjoying the deviant and normative playing on the surface of my body. They can enjoy and condemn, often in the same sentence, without having to think about the implications of their actions. Regardless of these inappropriate encounters, however, I am not a child. I am not looking to be seduced or protected. So if you're wondering if pornography turns me on—

I am not the object of study, so it's none of your business.

On the Medicinal
Purposes of Porn

KATINKA HOOIJER

> Cheap soap.
> Raunchy porn.
> Tight jeans.
> A deep throbbing kiss.
> Overzealous masturbation.
> Erotic expectation.
> Fleshy anticipation.

WE'VE ALL experienced it—a burning vulva. The key is to differentiate. Become aware of all the sensations your sweet lips are capable of—all the gradations between that good burning feeling brought on by a naughty thought and that holy-fuck-it-feels-like-someone-doused-my-pussy-with-Tabasco-sauce *bad* burning feeling.

When I first experienced my burning vulva, it was great, like "Ooo, wow, what was that?" It was probably my first erection (orgasm would be an exaggeration) spurred by a *Playboy* bunny, an image of a perfectly tanned blond naked woman bent over a stationary bicycle by a Burt Reynolds look-alike, her perky butt pointing straight up for all to enjoy.

All I asked for Christmas that year was a long blond wig.

We were six years old, my girlfriend and I, sneaking repeatedly into her dad's bedroom to pull out that same issue. The stationary bicycle sequence came through for us every time. (Don't try to tell me I was brainwashed by the dominant patriarchy to think I was aroused. At six years old I couldn't even spell patriarchy let alone be tricked into orgasming from it.)

After that, pussy pleasure was pretty much all downhill, except for that sporadic someone who could actually locate my clit. Eventually thwarted pleasure gave way to eating good food and watching bad porn because my vulva started to burn in a far more disquieting way, and not just when a penis was in the vicinity. It burned unexpectedly and inconveniently. It burned at school. It burned at the grocery store. It burned at the bar. It burned when I ate ice cream. It burned when I drove my car. It burned when I had sex—and that part really sucked.

First diagnosis: Too rigorous sex. Wow. There's actually a chronic condition caused by having hard-core intercourse. Well, I wasn't that big of a porn queen. Medical advice: try more foreplay. Try lubrication. I followed all the rules: lots of K-Y jelly, soft gentle entry, minimal friction. No luck.

Second Diagnosis: Latex allergy. Medical advice: try not using condoms. That's fucking twisted in this day and age.

So the boy got checked out, was pronounced clean, and we went ahead, bareback. I sent him into cum heaven, but I got shot into burning vulva hell.

Third Diagnosis: Seminal fluid allergy. That's fucking hilarious. Talk about not being compatible with someone! "Honey, I'm allergic to your sperm." Medical advice: abstinence for three weeks to break the pain cycle. Then try sex with condoms. THREE WEEKS! I'm in my prime here, my early twenties, it's the middle of a summer romance. . . .

Fourth Diagnosis: "Your burning vulva, well, it's all in your head. Are you sure you've never been abused or raped? I can't find any physical symptoms of your pain, so it must be psychological."

Fifth, Sixth, Seventh Diagnosis: Strains of vaginal bacterias that for some reason do not grow on the culture. Translation: We have no idea what it is but we'll just say it's a bacteria and give you an antibiotic and hope the symptoms go away. I spent eight months on antibiotics. I had yeast infections in between each dose because the antibiotics flushed all the good bacteria out of my system and fucked up my "vaginal environment." I ended up with a compromised immune system.

Three weeks of abstinence turned into three years. My vulva burned non-fucking-stop. I dropped out of school because I couldn't sit in class. I had to keep a water bottle next to the toilet to rinse after a piss because I couldn't stand the agony of wiping. I couldn't use tampons so my mom made me panty liners out of cotton diapers. When my menstrual blood started feeling like battery acid I had to take hormones continuously so I wouldn't get my period anymore. I stopped wearing pants. Stopped wearing underwear. What a slut, hey?

My doctors were as frustrated as I was but not nearly as horny. I had shitloads of tests. No STDs. No bacterial infections. No raging yeast infections. Wear condoms, don't wear condoms, change detergent, throw away enticing polyester panties, try really unsexy cotton underwear, go off the pill, put steroids in your vagina, rub hormone cream on your vulva. Nothing eased my inflamed labia. At last a specialist enlightened me. Instead of asking me to regress into my childhood subconscious to identify the horny bastard who supposedly molested me, this doctor inquired about my sexual activity. "Was intercourse always painful for you?" Finally a doctor who distinguished between intercourse and sex. Was intercourse always painful? I guess I wasn't sure. I mean I never remember having completely pain free or totally comfortable penetration, ever. Pleasure. Pain. It's a fine line. Pain can be a way to rate (or a minor consequence of) a good fuck—you can still feel it the next day. Most men assume you are moaning because you can't get enough of that man-rod of theirs, not that you are withstanding various degrees of pain. So what kind of idiot would endure this type of vaginal abuse? Come on, we've all been conditioned to see sex as a means to an end: for some it's an explosive orgasm, for others fertilization. And well, besides all that, sometimes the pleasure of making someone else feel good can be very powerful in itself.

Final diagnosis: *Burning Vulva Syndrome!!!* I am not shitting you. How patronizing to name an incurable chronic disease with no known cause after the primary symptom. It's almost funny. Can you imagine . . . "Um, I can't come to class because my *burning vulva syndrome* is acting up— I can bring a doctor's excuse" or "My doctor told me not to wear panties because I have this condition, *burning vulva syndrome*; yes, I've read the dress code in the employee hand book, but . . ."

I researched the shit out of this disease. After three years and seven different doctors I needed to know what was so rare about my condition. What makes it seem rare is that most cases go un/misdiagnosed for years. So the statistics are really off. Initially women are very reluctant to report symptoms due to embarrassment or fear of cancer as an underlying disorder. Also there are all kinds of social stigmas attached to having a burning vulva. The formula goes something like this:

> lots of sex = lots of partners = high risk = STD = pelvic inflammatory disease = penny whore

In actuality, anybody can get a burning vulva—sleazy porn queen or virginal sitcom mom—but try telling that to a guy on your first date.

The medical term for what I have is *vulvodynia*. It's described as a syndrome of unexplained vulvar pain, psychological disability, and sexual dysfunction. The intensity of pain varies according to subtype but is commonly described as burning, stinging, irritation, or rawness. The pain can be mild to disabling, which can prevent most daily activities like sitting, wearing pants or hosiery, or using toilet paper. Sexual intercourse is not an option for most women with this condition. Not only can you not have intercourse, you can't even wear the enticing clothes that invite such lusty encounters—like synthetic disco pants or hot pink tights (I'm not one to go naked under a mini skirt . . .). What a misogynist disease.

I spent the third year on all kinds of experimental therapies, but I was too far gone. Maybe if that specialist had caught this earlier . . . Maybe if I hadn't been misdiagnosed for three years (that's the average—three years and five doctors before women get the proper diagnosis and treatment) . . . Maybe. My doctor described my condition as a neurological disorder in which the nerves in my vulva fire constantly, causing a burning sensation. I had biopsies done, leaving stitches in my inner labia. I took steroids for a year to bring the inflammation down. Nothing worked. After four years I decided to have part of my vulva surgically removed. Penile penetration was pie in the sky—I just wanted to use toilet paper again. Mmmmm.

It's pretty weird having part of your vulva cut off. In fact it's gross. For two weeks I didn't walk much and sat around with a bag of frozen corn between my legs. My vagina looked like a bad accident: bruising, swelling, stitches. At least it's too moist in there for scabs to form. Two months after my partial vulvectomy, the doctors said I should be able to get laid, so using toilet paper and tampons seemed within reach.

For some reason I got worse after the surgery.

It turns out the pharmacist at Walgreens made a mistake entering my prescription in the computer. So eight months before the surgery and two months afterwards, I was on the wrong medication. Oops. The results of the surgery weren't bad enough to make mad cash in the porn/freak industry but not good enough to sit on anyone's dick. What a rip. Maybe I wouldn't have had to have part of my genitals removed if I'd been on the right meds, if that pharmacist hadn't fucked up, but no doctor would say for sure, no expert medical witness dared a definite answer in the face of the elusive Burning Vulva Syndrome.

I tried to sue Walgreens, but pussy pain and suffering are subjective, and not being able to have sexual intercourse for those ten months, well, the lawyers made sex look like a form of recreation or luxury, not a normal human need. They didn't even consider the psycho-social effects since I wasn't seeing a therapist. Pissed off, bitter, horny, and unsatisfied, I was really sweating this pussy disorder. You never realize how much a girl defines herself by her penetrability until your pussy lips shut down the show. The fact that I didn't see a therapist is no measure of the mental anguish caused by this condition and my medical mistreatment.

Six years after my vulva took over every aspect of my life I am finally engaging in sex—I mean penetrating activities. (It's weird how most straight people define sex. Oral sex isn't really sex, heavy petting isn't sex, anal sex isn't even considered sex—in some Latin countries you can put your dick in some chick's ass twenty-four/seven and as long as you don't slip and go through the front door she's still considered a virgin. Reality check: sex is pure penetration and culminates with male ejaculation, as in, he gets off, sprays her walls.) Sometimes intercourse is still uncomfortable, even hurts (so good), but sometimes it's mind blowing. The fact that it's even remotely possible and sometimes pain free astounds me. Although my surgeon guaranteed a cosmetically acceptable entrance he warned some men might feel a difference. Those soft hugging folds between the inner labia and the vagina no longer offer that succulent seal of approval, but most people don't notice.

At least I still have my clit.

Women often experience physical disorders, especially surrounding sexuality, as reductions of our femininity. And feminism (in the cultural feminist guise of pussy worship as well as the pro-sex feminist celebration of fucking) just confuses the issue. Affection versus orgasm, female desire versus male lust, emotional attachment versus raw physicality, erotica versus pornography, virgin versus whore, pain versus pleasure. I haven't found much solace in feminism's impractical theories and universal sexual norms.

It was porn that saved me.

Is Porn Bad Medicine?

The first time I used porn to deal with vulvodynia was completely unintentional. I was in the right place at the right time for this gorgeous accident—back in the day, way before doctors and meds, back when I thought my burning box was due to my well-endowed Italian stallion boyfriend. A roommate of his was raving over a hilarious porno he scored. I watched the video because I didn't want to be a prude, and found myself, quite by surprise, disgustingly aroused, while the guys rolled on the floor in tears. The video featured a series of dreams, placing its viewers not only inside the starring girl's bedroom, but inside her head. The ones that most strongly affected me involved self-induced pussy pleasing, the big "M"—which until then had never really occurred to me. Second wave feminists might be surprised at the ongoing miseducation of young girls about their bodies, but the fact is Nancy Friday's concept of the "mental cliterodectomy" still applies far too widely in the U.S.

In one scene, we join Suzie Homemaker in the kitchen

making Cream of Wheat and cooing "Oooh, I just loooove Cream of Wheat, it's soooo warm and creamy." The camera zooms in on the Cream of Wheat box and *Bam!* A guy appears inside a life-size box like one of those dirty singing telegrams, and of course he comes equipped, big dick sticking out in the most unsanitary way. He eats from his bowl of steaming cereal, wooing Suzie with his southern porno drawl, "*I'll* warm you up inside!" Indeed he does, but more compellingly, she warms herself as well, getting herself off by hand while she sucks and fucks him. Hot cereal fetishes notwithstanding, scenes like this one set the stage for my own public solo-sex adventures. Masturbation—*duh*. Why didn't I think of that before? Orgasms are always available—close at hand—at school, the gym, or the old stand-by, at home. I can actually say with certainty that the Cream of Wheat scene is directly responsible for teaching me to flick my clit while sucking dick to build and insure fulfillment of my voluminous orgasmic potential. If you want the job done right . . .

Another scene featured an anal fuck-o-rama, poor girl slamming up and down on some stud's lap. Ouch. And yuck. Like most folks, my gag reflex has been carefully conditioned over the years to reject connecting sex with my rectum. The nervously twittering frat boy line—this is an exit-only ramp—springs to mind, but with the handy-dandy tool of feminist analysis I have learned to think twice about knee-jerk reactions. Porno chick is clearly enjoying herself, and her vulva sits safely above the fray. Although few people admit it in casual conversation, we've all had our share of pleasurable bowel movements, so why not at least consider the possibility of this alternative fuck hole? I won't say anal sex caught on with the fury and delight of masturbation, but I keep it filed in my porno Rolodex. The accidental porn-watcher—that's me. I learned that afternoon not to discount cheap thrills and experimentation.

———

Amsterdam is a good place for open minds. My parents were born and raised there, and as a kid I spent summers with relatives and grew to adore this sexy city overseas. In the heat of vulvodynia hell I attended the University of Amsterdam, working on a certificate in sexuality studies (of course). I became interested in studying the specific constraints of my medical condition (and ways around them), so I proposed a research project investigating how women with vulvodynia maintain their sexuality during illness episodes. I guess my personal connection to the topic was a dead giveaway; when I presented it to a roomful of professors and fellow students, I broke down in hysterics. Crying during scholarly presentations doesn't make for professional success, even in the most progressive institutions. So most nights I acted as my own research subject, discovering ways of maintaining my sexuality with pot, wine, and cheap late-night porn. I didn't even have to rent it because in Amsterdam, porn *is* late-night TV. High, drunk, and satiated with cookies, I took in the cheesy seventies porn as icing on the cake, masturbating to my heart's content on my aunt's black leather couch. On more venturesome nights, I wandered the red-light district with a girl I met at school. She and her boyfriend joined me on jaunts to live sex shows where men and women would fuck so close to you, you could smell it. And then there are the Amsterdam strip clubs, where women walk up and down the bar, allowing patrons to lick them and stick all kinds of things in every imaginable orifice. I realized from visiting— and digging the shit out of—this scene that sex doesn't have to be so emotionally laden, so private, or so serious.

After watching girls shoot Ping-Pong balls out their asses at boys drinking Heineken at the bar, peep shows in the U.S. didn't intimidate me at all, except for the illogical fear of being seen by someone you know. I went with a boyfriend to seem less perverted. We both hid our genuine desires by treating our trip like a silly gag, as if watching strippers (like watching porn) were merely "funny," rather than a valid form of sexual gratification. We "othered" the rest of the customers, positioning ourselves outside their erotic economy as observers of the depraved. The porn-filled aisles profering sexual toys, magazines, and videos enclosed us in the netherworld of sex for sale. Mammoth tits and perfectly shaved pink porno pussies graced packages and covers, filling me with a roiling combination of envy, disgust, and fascination. We joked our way to a long hallway of doors— Masturbation Central—the peep show booths!

We stepped inside one, carefully making sure not to touch the walls, lined in red vinyl like the booths in U.S. Mexican restaurants. I could sense semen all around me, despite the establishment's efforts to keep ecstasy tidy—a box of store-brand tissues and a small half-filled trash can in the corner. The far wall was made of a huge piece of Plexiglas with a twelve-inch television behind it. Along the side of the screen, through the Plexiglas, poked four worn out buttons with a title next to each.

We could choose from "Lurid Plumber" where a house-wife delights in receiving her buck-naked plumber who arrives in nothing but a tool belt; then there's "The Farmer's Daughter," wherein a girl "accidentally" spills oats on her pussy and is pleased to have them eaten off by an enthusiastically hungry horse; and then, my favorite, "Dr. Jackoff and Mr. Hump," a tale far scarier than the predecessor it parodies. The screen flicked off before we got to the fourth button—"White Women Who Crave Huge Black Cock"—because our dollar's worth of time had run out. We didn't insert more coins; it just seemed too pathetic, some-how beyond "funny," for us to pay more than a buck. Turns out I don't like porn in public. Porn, in my sex life, is personal—a medium of intimacy between me and my pussy.

Prude or Porn Queen? Something In-Between?

Porn. It became an obsession—the topic of my thesis, catalyst for my girls' group, Feminists for Fornication, and most recently an underlying issue in my dissertation research. I posited porn as liberating because I could get horny and get off without relying on anyone. And I don't even have to get lockjaw giving some guy a blowjob afterwards! Porn makes me sexually independent, which is a big deal to me in the aftermath of being at odds with my pussy for so long, and utterly dependent on the medical establishment to define my illness experience. Through monthly progress reports, experimental therapies, even the simple act of naming the condition, I relied on doctors and researchers for hope, relief, and answers. Sexually explicit material offered an arena where I took control of my pussy. Being able to access erotic pleasure through visual images gave me a way to say, "Fuck you, Vulva, I can have fun without you *or* the boys."

I still couldn't withstand vaginal penetration, and porn filled this gap so to speak, representing the very type of sex I could never indulge in: fast, raw, purely physical. And yeah, it was usually mainstream (male-oriented) stuff, but the romance and plot development of "female-oriented" porn (a.k.a. erotica) was about as nasty as a Sunday school lesson. I'm not bashing porn made for and by chicks, I know it works for some of us, but not for me, not so far at least. I'm not going to pretend there is no moral conflict between mainstream porn and my feminist values. Some of the stuff I get turned on by is downright raunchy, even offensive. But not when I'm through with it. I am a real-live example of how "[p]ornography is not 'just' consumed, but is used, worked on, elaborated, remembered, fantasized about by its subject."[1] The third wave position on porn highlights and celebrates this active female audience stance:

> We must recognize that women actively consume mainstream porn—resisting, twisting, and sometimes subverting it. Mass culture does not simply victimize women, and

anybody that claims that it does belittles the vast majority of women, whose desires, fantasies, and subjectivities are irretrievably bound up in it.[2]

So I admit I consume some pretty sexist stuff, but in using it to negotiate my body's needs and limitations, I make porn feminist.

Catherine MacKinnon is hard-core antiporn and says women like me are "merely denying the 'unspeakable humiliation' of having been 'cajoled, pressured, tricked, blackmailed, or outright forced into sex.'" Then she throws down the gauntlet: "If pornography is part of your sexuality, then you have no right to your sexuality."[3]

For me, porn is literally medicinal. Sex-positive author Sallie Tisdale turns away from MacKinnon and her ilk for reasons that resonate clearly with me: "That branch of feminism tells me my very thoughts are bad. Pornography tells me the opposite: that *none* of my thoughts are bad, that anything goes."[4] In this sense, porn *is* feminism.

The Prudes

If there is anything that antiporn feminists abhor it is pussy pain, but the solution of giving up dick did not "do it" for me. Their victim stance provided no useful tools for enduring a burning vulva episode. Heterosexuality, in the form of penile penetration, constitutes violence (physical intrusion, the force of pushing oneself inside another) against women. "A saber penetrating a vagina is a weapon," writes Andrea Dworkin, and what would for normal women be obvious exaggeration describes exactly what intercourse felt like for me.[5] The only violence, though, was the injustice of not being *able* to fuck. Penetration would have seemed like winning first prize in a naked spelling bee, because like it or not, heterosexuality revolves around penetration. Why? The answer is simple: *straight men want to stick their dicks in you.* I endure the discomfort for the same reasons other women do: because I want to get something out of the deal. Maybe tonight he'll go down on me, or I'll at least stimulate myself to clitoral orgasm while he thrusts in and out from behind. Fantasies of rape cloud my head because rape is supposed to hurt, so my psychic discord of wanting to fuck and hurting from fucking is sort of resolved. Plus our egos tell us we can hold out longer than any pocket pussy and not dry out either. There's nothing quite like the post ejaculate compliment; the "ohmygod" effect is great for the psyche even if hard on the pussy. It's a familiar balancing act, even though feminists rarely talk about it as part of our daily lives: giving pleasure and demanding pleasure. Bad sex. Painful sex. Unwanted sex. Fact is, in a couplehood, you can't get it on only when *you* want it. This is the compromise of intimacy. Say no too many times and sexual frustration infiltrates other areas of the relationship.

Why do we submit repeatedly to unwanted intercourse?
Why do we bump and grind till we're raw?
You tell me.

The Porn Queens

Pro-sex feminists promote bad-girl sex, the kind without love and commitment with or without partners, definitely *with* porn, the kind that guarantees no strings attached grrrl powered orgasms. Fuck me. No, I'll fuck you. Fuck it, I'll fuck myself. Ellen Willis writes of porn use as a form of defiance: "a woman who enjoys pornography (even if it means enjoying a rape fantasy) is in a sense a rebel, insisting on an aspect of her sexuality that has been defined as a male preserve."[6] And further, "It is precisely sex as an aggressive, unladylike activity, an expression of violent and unpretty emotion, an exercise of erotic power, and a specifically genital experience that has been taboo for women."[7] Unladylike—I love it!

But dream on.

The reality of a broken pussy is that you need to trust somebody enough to tell them you can't have a lot of friction, that you need a lot of foreplay to relax your pelvic muscles or else he might not even be able to get in, that it needs to go nice and slow with a soft and gentle entry ("Oh, you want me to make love to you not fuck you. . . ."), that you need to go through a bottle of lube, ("Oh no you make me wet, honest, I just have this condition and I need to be really wet or else I might have a flare-up afterwards." "Flare-up? Whaddya got?") How's that for a mood changer? Or worse, having to ask for it from behind, you know, doggy style, because he's got one of those curved penises I absolutely cannot take from a missionary position because of all the scar tissue on my vulva, and isn't that romantic on those occasions when I want to be oh so demure. I tried casual sex, and still do after long periods of celibacy, to see if I miraculously healed during my abstinence. Sometimes in these encounters I tell men I can't have intercourse, but we could do other "fun stuff" to stimulate ourselves (read: blowjob). Some thought I had AIDS, but I didn't care. And don't think I don't know the blowjob thing sounds demeaning. I admit I was never fulfilled on these one-way one-night stands, but they alleviated my feelings of sexual inadequacy, at least for a while. I got a rise out of being able to send someone on an orgasmic trip. But this deal soon bored me. Even though I could theoretically still enjoy receiving oral sex, I didn't trust anyone near my hot box. Then I took a break from fucking to regroup. My first failure as a pro-sex feminist: when my practice doesn't live up to my theory. Sometimes you dames make me feel, well, kind of well behaved.

With the men I love, denying penetration felt like denying us both the ultimate form of intimacy (can feminism *please* do something to redefine intimacy without either celebrating or demonizing penetration?). Long story short: after a half year sabbatical, I returned to fucking with penetration, at least occasionally, as a symbol of my true looove. They really dug my born-again virgin feel. What's new about women compromising their pleasure to get someone else off? From free meals to saving relationships to just feeling generous, women do it all the time. Sex should be consensual and loving, but "consent" is a sticky issue when you're in love and your pussy hurts. Vulvodynia drew out the question operating silently at the heart of most heterosexual relationships: what's more important—his desire (and my desire to fulfill his desire) or my physical comfort (and, on a good day, pleasure). Maintaining self-respect as a heterosexual woman sounds like it should go without saying, but in my own attempts to subordinate my discomfort and satiate his desire, I recognize an exaggerated version of something quite common in this sense of sex as a choice between him or me. This time I eroticized the pain.

Now what kind of feminist was I?

Pro-sex feminism doesn't explain what to do when you want to fuck for reasons other than mutual pleasure. Lynne Segal is right on in her critique of feminist sex research for focusing on physical pleasure, an angle she says disowns "a woman's complex emotional life" by reducing sexuality to a woman's "biological potential for orgasms, and her right to have them."[8] I extend this critique to pro-sex feminist rhetoric—with its separation of emotional from physical, affection from orgasm, and self/woman-oriented sex from other/male-oriented sex—as if no reciprocity passes between these. Give me a feminism that allows for my "complex emotional life" *and* the appeal of slamming intercourse it's all wrapped up in, because the pro-sex feminist perspective alone makes me feel uncool, unhip about my needs, which are lusty but, necessarily, *not* casually sexual. There's got to be some middle ground, something between the zipless fuck and the return to modesty.

Conclusion

Feminists theorizing pussy pain and pleasure remain largely concealed in the microcosms of academic and activist communities, while a large number of women are left in black holes of sexual shame, dissatisfaction, and frustration: waitresses, bartenders, receptionists, hair stylists, artists, students, even the more successful small business owners—all of whom could give a shit about feminism, except *maybe* to wonder in passing how it relates to their lives. Feminism isn't contributing to new realities of pleasure, at least not for the working girl. Porn does, though, and it made a woman out of me when cultural norms, physical ailments, and even feminism desexualized me.

Part Three
Our Inner Men

Is there nothing in masculinity we should salvage?
    —Pat Califia, *Doing It for Daddy*

13 *The Importance of Being Lester*

LESLIE HEYWOOD

Her swordplay moved the world.
Those who beheld her, numerous as the hills,
Lost themselves in wonder.
Heaven and Earth swayed in resonance . . .
Swift as the Archer shooting the nine suns,
She was exquisite, like a sky-god
Behind a team of dragons, soaring.

—Tu Fu

The Gym Scene

Benchplay. Arcs of muscle swung through space. Bar resting on steel frame, waiting for the plates. Thick discs of iron, 45, 35, 25 pounds. Black rubber floor for dug-in feet. Human backs like bridges, the weight of the world in between. Humidity, liniment, sweat, grind in the joint, exhalation, shadows more than twice your size. With your broad back and small waist, you are under it, a monster, 225 pounds. Outweighed by a wide margin. Back arched, thighs tight. Draw air in through the nose until the chest fills. Feel it sitting there, patient as a mountain, but when it touches your breastplate, breath rushes from your lungs and up the weight flies, just wind. Arms of molten stone, magnificent, every movement smooth. Padding through the gym, shoulders relaxed and tight, barely registering the other bodies pumping, preening, irrelevant. This is the one place where you are not seething in smallness, bright hair and smiles, ferocious in your cage.

Women float around the edges, bright buzzing lights, distractions from the work of this place. But you are a woman, and you are part of the work.

Birth of Lester

I am a power lifter who is, at the moment, ranked eleventh in the country in my weight class for bench press. I train four days a week with a male power lifter, lifting thousands of pounds in a given session. I have a constant low-grade ache in my back and chest. My upper body, by most standards, is huge. I've been lifting since I was thirteen, but I didn't take it seriously—didn't test my own strength—until four years ago, when a training partner, Terrance, watched me bench press 135 and scoffed. "No question: You could do much more." Because I am female, at least provisionally, I'd always thought 135 pounds was "a lot of weight for a girl" and never tried to push beyond it. Terrance didn't see me as male or female, just someone who trained hard. Terrance happened to be right. In a single year, I added 50 pounds of weight to my benchpress, maxing out at 185. When Terrance left, I started training with Billy and Chris, and, soon after, Lester made his public debut.

It took me twenty years to become Lester. He was born the day I broke the two hundred pound barrier on the bench. Two hundred is one of those turning points that clearly separates one class of lifter from the next, and in the everyday world it separates the men from the boys, and, almost not worth saying, from the women. When I broke it, I went from being "strong for a girl" to indisputably "one of the guys." I sat myself down on the bench that day, flat on my back, pulling myself under the bar and feeling strong. I'd always faltered on this weight, lifting it only an inch or so off my chest, like some biological limitation I'd never transgress. But today was different, I could feel the bar, the weight on it, but there was the sensation of not feeling it, too. This time, there was no sticking. This time, the weight flew up like nothing at all, and as I racked it at the top, Billy and Chris roared with joy, jumping up in the air shouting "Lester! Lester! She's with the big dogs now!" Great grunting noises filled the room, animal pleasure and camaraderie. Everyone around us stared. Years of frustration dropped away. I soared.

It was a small thing, the shift from Leslie to Lester. A single bench press in a single gym, lost in the backwoods of an upstate New York town. It didn't change the world. It certainly added nothing to any organized political cause. But I felt inside something, part of something. An acceptance I'd never felt in any other place. This is who I was, and the people around me had seen and proclaimed it with great joy at high volume. The part of myself I'd always been encouraged to smother, feel ashamed of, cover up at all costs—my manhood—entered the legitimacy of public space.

My elation conflicts with most intellectual positions in feminist sport studies. What I was feeling would be cause for criticism, not celebration, among these intellects. This argument is most clearly summed up by Varda Burstyn in *The Rites of Men: Manhood, Politics, and the Culture of Sport.* "U.S. culture," she writes, "influenced by men's culture, is marked by an intense denigration of the 'feminine' and its associated qualities of softness, receptivity, cooperation, and compassion. Today's erotic athletic flesh is hard, muscled, tense, and mean. The unquestioning emulation of hyper-masculinity by women does not constitute 'androgyny' or 'gender neutrality,' but rather the triumph of hyper-masculinism."[1]

Lester is all about hyper-masculinity, and for this reason, Burstyn would not like him very much, and would perhaps think that pride in my "hard, muscled, mean" flesh is a tangible sign of my own antifeminism. She sees the recent success of women's competitive sports as indelibly marred by masculine values, and Lester is linked to precisely these values. Burstyn argues that "sport has acted as a political reservoir of antidemocratic and elitist values that coexist with, and have often overwhelmed egalitarian, cooperative, and democratic values."[2] She associates the former qualities with masculinity and men and the latter qualities with femininity and women. Since Lester falls into the former category but names a body that is biologically female, s/he can't be accounted for by this position, except as evidence (from Burstyn's perspective) of the way women blindly internalize "male" thinking.

Burstyn's bias marks a debate at least a century old between supporters of masculine competitive sport and supporters of feminine "participatory" sport, which de-emphasizes winning in favor of everyone-gets-a-chance-to-play egalitarianism. According to sports historian Susan Cahn, "several generations of professionals sought to protect the reputation and health of female athletes by devising separate, less physically taxing versions of women's sport. In effect educators created a respectable 'feminine' brand of athletics."[3] Yet such regressive essentialist positions were not the only positions posited in the first half of the twentieth century. There is a historical precedent for Lester. Cahn writes:

> [O]ver the course of the century, advocates of women's sport developed numerous and often competing strategies to cope with the dissonance between masculine sport and competitive womanhood. The boldest among them accepted the charge of masculinization but claimed its positive value. They contended that women's athleticism would indeed endow women with masculine attributes, but that these qualities would benefit women as well as men, contributing to female emancipation and eliminating needless sexual distinctions.[4]

As evidence that women can be part of a talented minority associated with competitive sport, Lester disproves stereotypes of female weakness and, more importantly, he disproves that men and women and the qualities associated with each can be broken into polarized categories. The critical tradition that Burstyn represents distrusts "eliminating needless sexual distinctions" because, in her terms, such an elimination would mean the celebration of traditionally masculine qualities like domination and strength over traditionally feminine qualities like cooperation.

There is little agreement, however, that women are or should be feminine, and a revaluation of the masculine within feminism is currently taking place within the younger generation that is sometimes dubbed (wrongly, I think) postfeminist. Forms of second wave feminism (like Burstyn's work) that condemn masculinity and extol the virtues of femininity will find a hostile audience in third wave feminists, for many of us highly value the masculine as well as the feminine parts of ourselves. In the words of Annalee Newitz et. al in the essay "Masculinity without Men," "each of us thinks of herself, to a certain extent, as male-identified, and each of us is resolutely feminist." They continue, "The idea that some women might want to assume certain 'masculine' traits or consider themselves as 'male-identified' does not suggest that women are becoming 'like men,' but rather that the relationship between gendered social roles and biological sex is more fluid than we have been taught to believe. . . . [N]either does such a shift automatically signal a regressive step for feminism."[5]

Is it a sign of political regression for feminism that in the months after his birth, "Lester" became both a term of endearment between us guys, and the code for everything that signified achievement and value? I can't see it that

286

way, because it established some unbreakable bonds. Billy is still my training partner. Five feet six, biceps the size of roast hams, works at a used car lot fixing trucks, polishing Trans Ams. On weekends in the fall he hunts. He gives me bottles of whiskey for Christmas. During the spring and summer, he's Nascar crazed, and often goes off for the races or has get-togethers at his trailer before the big races on T.V. He is one of my closest friends. He shows up every day we're set to train, religiously. I never doubt him. He's the first person I'd trust if I needed anything. It's been four years: We've seen each other through divorce, the tenure process, the death of his brother, the near death of his son. We've both got alcoholic fathers and explosive personalities, and we both see poetry in the skeletons of upstate New York winter trees. Except for that last part, he's the poster child for simple machismo, from the outside, anyway.

But machismo is a trait often misunderstood.

I'm macho—always have been, on some level. The gym is the only space I know where that's okay, so that's the only place I feel completely comfortable. It wouldn't be an exaggeration to say it is one of the few places I feel fully loved. I know—good feminist women and grrls aren't supposed to want to be men, or be like men. We're not supposed to identify with elitist, retro, bonehead ideologies of physical superiority, or with anything that claims one person is "better" than the next. We're supposed to affirm ourselves as women, all equal, and to redefine "woman" and "girl" to encompass value and strength. We're supposed to be creating "alternative femininities," but to keep seeing

ourselves fundamentally as women. I know already, and I
don't care. From earliest childhood, "woman," "feminine,"
and everything those words carry with them, have been a
foreign language, as remote from me as the countries I've
never visited. It's gotten me called a bitch. It's made a lot of
people not like me. It's made people suspicious of my politics. But let's face it, some of us *are* men, and we feel strangled and angry by the idea that everyone is essentially the
same. We do not identify as women. I'm tired of pretending that I do.

I don't care if we're het or hom or bi or trans, I don't
care to what extent we perform femme, some of us are born
with (*not* taking steroids) more testosterone than others,
and this, among many other factors, has concrete effects on
our bodies and personalities. That's not necessarily good,
not necessarily bad, it just *is*. Testosterone exists on a continuum. Whenever the media (or certain wings of feminism) want to evoke ineradicable biological gender difference, they write about testosterone as if only men have it.
But everybody's got it to one degree or another, and some
men have less of it than some women. It makes these
women more aggressive and competitive than we are supposed to be. We don't love peace. We are not P.C. With our
aggressively selfish insistence on living for ourselves, not
others, we are the horror figures in popular culture, the
crazed career woman of *Fatal Attraction*, the bloody
extremities of *G.I. Jane*.

So testosterone is one of the factors behind Lester. As is
an awareness of the cultural denigration of women and the

desire to be seen as *different*. And the fact that my build—short arms and legs, mesomorphic body type—is perfectly suited to power lifting. Behind Lester lies a contemporary consumerist desire to "play" with gender—to pick and choose between feminine and masculine characteristics and looks, to put them on at will, and to take them off. Twenty-some-odd years of intense athletic training joined with an internalization of American individualism to produce this male persona. Even the legacy of three decades of feminist activism made my man self possible. Lester, in fact, is all of me, the whole monstrous mess.

Nonetheless, my feminist friends were horrified by the birth of Lester. "Shouldn't you tell them [my training partners]," one friend said, "that calling you 'Lester' instead of 'Leslie' because you can bench a lot of weight implies that women are weak? Shouldn't you tell them that you can be strong and be a woman, too?"

Been there, read that.

But admit it or not (and a lot of the time, for strategic reasons, we don't admit it), there is now a whole demographic of us post-Title IX babies who have played sports our entire lives, suckling competitive individualism (a feminist bogeyman) like mother's milk, nourished by it in body and spirit. We want to be Lester, loom with his size and stature. Most writers on female athletes play down the competitive spirit that makes us want to do sports in the first place, emphasizing how female athletes are more motivated by "teamwork" and their relationships with each other. It's necessary PR in a culture that until very recently has seen the female athlete as a contradiction in terms, a freak of the nature. Teamwork's great. So is kicking ass. Why can we have one and not the other?

I train as one of the guys. With female-identified women, I'd have to make too many concessions, be self-effacing, as if it made no difference that I can bench hundreds of pounds more, or that there are women out there who can bench hundreds of pounds more than me. Call me male identified if you want, but I love being one of the guys because with them I don't feel the pressure to be a nice girl, little Miss Congeniality pretending she's the same as everyone else. I'm not the same as everybody else. I'm better—at least in this arena. Like it or not, feminist or not, men are still the only ones culturally sanctioned to say something so self-assured. But in the boy-space of our training group, bravado is a form of affection and playfulness: "I'm going to kick your ass today, you wuss." I am a good deal more comfortable with verbal sparring than the "you go first, no *you* go first" group-therapy style expected among women. The way the guys and I joke with each other and participate in constant one-upmanship is, paradoxically, a form of respect. Confident in ourselves and each other, we know a little ribbing and friendly competition poses no threat to anyone's sense of identity or self-worth.

I hear the voices of my critics already: subsuming a successful and strong woman under the category of "one of the guys" implies that women are not as good as, less than. Yet this phrase, first applied to me in a hometown newspaper story about me as a star track team member, fills me with joy. When, in a raucous mood at a Nascar party, Billy yells out in a drunken voice that "Lester is THE man, no doubt about it," I get those good-time goosebumps and a rush of heat across my chest. Because, goddamn it, he isn't saying *literally* that I am a man. He's saying he loves and respects me, that he sees every ounce of my worth. And if, as certain kinds of feminist formulas would have it, Billy's words reinforce the idea that only men have worth, so be it. I would posit an alternative way of hearing him say, "man," in which women can be *real men* (something many biological men aren't, at least not in the connotative sense of assertiveness and competence). You have to earn this term of value and honor. Belonging is no longer assumed or denied on the measly basis of what's between your legs. And maybe it would be more progressive if the term to designate such value were "you're the WOMAN!" but, as the song says, "If lovin you is wrong, I don't wanna be right." Call me "the man" any day. It has a nice ring.

Female masculinity has a long history with many valuable lessons for women in the present day: "[T]he history of American cowgirls suggests that . . . these women saw no particular contradiction in being heterosexual and, by some standards, masculine."[6] I see no particular contradiction in Lester, either. Even though he was officially born—publicly named—the moment when I overcame the physical barrier of benching two hundred, symbolically marking my passage from the land of the girly weights into the territory of real men, he has always been with me, the core of my determination, part of my expressions of anger and aggression. Like the all-American spirit with which his traits are linked, he was the part of me who believed in competing ferociously.

He was the part of me who believed in physical excellence with no artificial boundaries. Anyone raised to excel in intercollegiate Division I athletic culture or any other culture that emphasizes individual achievement (academia or corporate America for instance), for better and worse, will have their own versions of Lester. We—I—need to admit this fact and create some public endorsement for the complicated joys he brings, so that the part of ourselves we love and value most, what motivates us most, is publicly validated.

I still wonder to what extent Lester is an adaptive behavior to competitive environments and to what extent he is the hormone levels in my blood. I don't know to what extent he is a defense mechanism, warrior persona, a hardening to the warlike domestic environment in which I grew up. A hybrid self living in what Peggy Orenstein refers to as "a half-changed world." What will happen to him when and if I decide to have kids? Is childbearing—as it would be if we retain traditional definitions of gender—necessarily incompatible with female masculinity? Will there still be time and place for Lester, will I be able to preserve him, preserve myself? Is there anything in all this that might help other women in some way?

Finally, I don't care what his origin is, or whether he's acceptable to this or that form of social critique. In the often hollow world of gender theory, weight lifting grounds me, fills me up, gives me presence. In the small space of a gym in Binghamton, New York, my benchplay moves the world.

And Lester is the name of human longing.

A Cock of One's Own

Getting a Firm Grip on
Feminist Sexual Power

SARAH SMITH

> Silly Rabbit, Dicks are for Dykes.
> —Lynn Breedlove, lead singer of Tribe 8

I'LL NEVER FORGET Lynn's dick. Eight inches of shiny black rubber protruded from her unzipped pants, obscene and affrontive. Sexy. Lynn Breedlove is the lead singer of a lesbian punk band, Tribe 8, a group of women well-known for making spectacles of themselves by pushing the traditional boundaries of sex, gender, and self-presentation. The summer I officially "came out," I ventured to the Michigan Womyn's Music festival and witnessed my first Tribe 8 show. Despite the festival's long commitment to womyn-born, womyn-only space, I saw my first lesbian dick there—the real nasty, fuck-me-till-I-can't-take-it kind of cock. I was enamored. And I wasn't the only dyke swooning at Lynn's display. Screaming lyrics about trans/gender identity, being a fag hag, and cruising for girlies, she teased the young lesbians in the front rows with her dildo, pretending she would let them suck it, seductively stroking the realistic rubber (yes—veins and all) from base to head until the whole crowd creamed with delight.

Tribe 8 focuses frequently on uncomfortably controversial topics for song themes, but outrageous dildo play seems to be the band's trademark. Lynn invites audience members on stage to perform fellatio, and dildos are often dismembered in a carnivalesque chainsaw massacre. But this particular show was unique because Tribe 8 was not performing at the typical smokey pick up bar—this was Michigan! For over twenty years, the festival had been cherished as a safe space, free of all male influences, for women around the globe. Several groups of women protested Lynn's dildo because, as a representation of a penis, it reminded protesters of men's power to violate women. This strict group of separatists, set against the dykes gushing with delight and throwing their undergarments on stage, created a bizarre tension. Michigan—a "hotbed" of feminism—had come alive with an issue I had recently been grappling with privately. What does it mean when a dyke takes up with a dildo?

When I first came out as a lesbian I believed I should leave sex toys (particularly those in the shape of a penis) behind. The lesbian feminist texts I was reading at the time denounced penetration as a symbol of heterosexism and recommended recentering sex around the intense intimacy cultivated between two women. Lesbians enjoy simple touching and kissing. Orgasm follows organically from clitoral worship. The pleasure of vaginal penetration was revealed as myth. This discovery was hard for me to accept because the entire time I was male partnered, I played with vibrators and dildos during sex play. I wanted so badly to be a "real" lesbian that I resigned myself to throwing my pearly vibrator and favorite pink jelly dildo in the trash, my eye cast toward the emerald city of lesbian utopia. Step one in feminist-approved lesbian sex is ridding one's self of the sexual repertoire of the dick (in flesh or form).

Tribe 8 hit one of feminism's open wounds: the phallus. The problem is one of slippage, the slipperiness of words. *Phallus* and *penis* do not mean the same thing, but they are often treated as synonymous: "the imaginary symbol which represents male power—economic, social, political, and cultural as well as the sexual."[1] The penis has been the primary phallic symbol in so many different cultures throughout time, from Ancient Greece to early Christianity to modern times, that most people, including many feminists, assume the penis *is* the phallus, that is, that the penis is power personified.

Traditional psychiatry slips carelessly between the terms, linking them under the label of scientific objectivity and truth. "By making the penis the linchpin of human sexuality," Charlotte Ashton writes, "Freud created men as 'normal' and women as 'other,' thereby relegating femininity to an eternal second best in relation to the supremacy of masculinity as symbolized by the phallus."[2] Freud's theory of "penis envy" positions maleness at the center of power, indicating his own assumption that men possess the "superior" organ. Thus Freudian psychiatry denies women—as the sex without a penis/phallus—sexual autonomy and power. While other schools of psychiatry exist, none has permeated mass culture so thoroughly. It is against this backdrop of cultural sexism that the transgessive performance at the Michigan Womyn's Festival came to bear so much meaning for me. Seeing Lynn take hold of her "phallus" initiated my own process of dismantling stereotypes about men and phallic power, creating in me an extremely liberating new perspective on my own sexuality and sexual relationships in general. But many of my peers insisted that Tribe 8's dildo antics reinforced a woman-hating heterosexism by putting a cock in their fans' faces.

For decades, feminist theorists in radical and lesbian strands of feminism have problematized the penis and dildo in much the same way as the protesters at the Michigan festival. To these feminists, the words *penis* and *phallus* are one and the same; therefore, the penis, a relatively simple and fragile human organ, is invested with power. Because dildos are typically fashioned after the penis and are used for one of the same purposes—penetrating a woman's body—they are also considered a phallic tool, very powerful and potentially hurtful. Within this "antidildo feminist" perspective, women who use dildos become agents of male domination by imitating, and therefore celebrating, the penis.[3]

Antidildo feminists view penetration, with dick or dildo, as exploitive, male-identified, sexual behavior.

Andrea Dworkin is perhaps the most infamous feminist to have written against penetration. In her book *Intercourse*, a project dedicated entirely to the analysis of penetration, she states:

> The normal fuck by a normal man is taken to be an act of invasion and ownership undertaken in a mode of preda-tion: colonializing, forceful (manly) or nearly violent; the sexual act that by its nature makes her his.[4]

And further:

> Physically, the woman in intercourse is a space inhabited, a literal territory occupied literally: occupied even if there has been no resistance, no force; even if the occupied per-son said yes please, yes hurry, yes more.[5]

In this view, sexual penetration is both literally and theo-retically a system of dominating women's bodies. The penis, as phallus, is the primary cause of women's oppres-sion, since phallic power tacitly permits sexual violence against women and keeps women sexually and economi-cally dependent on men.

Housing men's phallic power in their penises is not merely a linguistic problem; it affects social policy and cul-tural belief systems. For example, the legal right to rape one's wife remains on the books in certain states and is still enforced, based on the historical treatment of women as a husband's property. The admissable defense used by mar-ital rapists—"She's my wife" (code for "I deserve pussy") —underlines the remaining ambiguity in American culture over women's human rights as separate individuals with physical integrity equal to men's. (You can be sure "I deserved ass" would not excuse the less visible phenomenon of male rape.) When sexual power is culturally located in an organ that only men have—as is the case in all of Western culture—the balance of power between the sexes is clearly tipped in men's favor.

On the other side of the dildo debate are the postmodern feminists and sex liberals who believe the dildo destabilizes the penis/phallus relationship. "Prodildo feminists," backed by a blossoming and decisively postmodern "sex-positive" ideology, believe dildos represent increasing complexity in female sexuality. Strapping one on permits women to embody phallic power, weakening the myth that the phallus can only be represented by the male sex organ. Prodildo feminists, like Tamsin Wilton and Carol Queen, even suggest that dildos are *more* phallic than penises; since penises

> come attached to male people and demonstrate a troublesome tendency to resist both the burden of phallic power (they may become soft and flaccid at the most inconvenient moments) and the imposition of disciplinary power (they are not easily controlled or directed by their "owner"), it is not hard to see that dildos may be perceived as superior.[6]

This is the defining distinction between the opposing camps of the feminist dildo wars. Antidildo feminists assume that dildo use "imitates" patriarchal heterosexual sex, a belief that paradoxically serves the egocentric penis by conceding it as the original phallus. Postmodern feminists and sex liberals do not believe men have the handsdown right to the phallus. Their prodildo discourse sees that the phallus is symbolized by, but not interchangeable with, the penis, and therefore examines how the penis is granted the institutional authority to represent phallic power and how that authority might be more equitably distributed. Dildo play is encouraged in this camp because it represents experimentations with power, challenging deeply ingrained gender role assumptions.

In fact, the dildo issue is not the only phallus-related problem over which the women of Michigan are at odds. The battle over whether to let male-to-female transsexuals onto the land has dragged on for years, and the exclusion of male children from the festival also marks a sore spot.

I for one was thrilled by the dissonance of lesbian dick, the titillating possibility of a female phallus. And judging by the dreamy, glazed look on the faces of my fellow Tribe 8 fans, I was far from alone.

The Dildo Debate

For Sheila Jeffreys, one of lesbian feminism's most prominent antidildo crusaders, dildos are perceived as part of the traditional heterosexual sex industry because "like the penis, they symbolize male power and the ability to violate women."[7] All women—lesbian, bisexual, heterosexual, and solo-sexual—are denounced as traitors if their desires include penetration.[8] Jeffreys believes this group of sexually diverse dildo users suffers from "heterosexual desire," characterized by an "eroticised power difference which originates in heterorelations but can also exist in same sex unions."[9]

This perspective is problematic. It means that when I penetrate my consensual lesbian partner with a dildo I am an agent of the heteropatriarchy—the double-agent dyke. Or when she penetrates me and I enjoy it, I am actually suffering false consciousness about my own sexual desires and responses. The antidildo feminists believe the only way I could possibly enjoy such an act is to have been brainwashed. Tamsin Wilton rightly complains that lesbians live their sex lives in the shadow of the "Lesbian Sex Police," a mostly mythical group that enforces the no-dildos standard.[10] She notes that, "[f]or lesbians, faced with a wider society which refuses to recognize our existence, or which is directly hostile, to lose the support of our local lesbian community can be devastating."[11]

If penetration with a dildo or a penis contributes to women's oppression, it follows logically that there must be a way to have sex that is "feminist." A laundry list of must-nots that would hold our libidos hostage: must not penetrate or be penetrated, must not "objectify" my partner by getting off on her body, must not be on top of my partner, must not role-play or talk dirty. What's left? Lesbian feminism's only suggestion for a radical feminist sex thus far has been Sheila Jeffrey's elusive concept of "homosexual desire," outlined in (the aptly named) *Anticlimax*. She calls for a "sexual desire and practice which eroticizes mutuality and equality," but gives no concrete suggestions for what a "sexy" equality might look like.[12] My partner and I tried to have "egalitarian" sex once to see if we were missing out on some quintessentially lesbian intimacy. We set up mood lighting, laid out massage oil, and tried to concentrate simply on the pleasure of being near each other's bodies to help us subdue that burning desire to fuck and be fucked. Every movement and position we tried—even simply caressing my partner's body—seemed to involve some type of power differential. The event was so calculated and restrictive, we soon turned to the more alluring popcorn-and-a-movie Friday night.

This dildo debate needs to listen to Davina Cooper: "[T]here is no simple freedom beyond power; we cannot ignore force relations through an illusory attempt to construct a power-free society."[13] The tension between self and other, that continual negotiation for power, is what drives society—and sparks passionate sex. Egalitarian sex, homosexual desire, fails to do so, at least in any concretely envisioned way, because it attempts to escape power relations. A completely power-free society does not exist; neither does power-free sex.

I'm not sure this is a bad thing.

Although the feminist sex wars produced valuable insights and theory, I believe the dispute has done more harm than good for women's everyday lives, alienating many women from feminism altogether.[14] To me, there is an obvious link between the declining interest in feminism among nonacademics and the increasing hostility of the feminist sex wars. Despite its lack of "egalitarian" models of sexuality, antidildo feminist theory thrives in the media. The man-hating lesbian is a familiar cultural stereotype. MacKinnon and Dworkin, well-known feminist names with best-selling books, get press coverage while prodildo feminists remain known primarily in feminist circles. Judith Butler and Tamsin Wilton are typically only read in women's studies classes; their messages of sexual plurality and symbolic shifts have not been absorbed into the mainstream.[15] Young heterosexual women do not identify with "antidildo feminists," young lesbians prefer Lynn's dick to sexual correctness, and, as Carol Smart notes, "the feminist old guard is left increasingly speaking to itself."[16]

The urgency to create models of female sexual agency—to make feminism relevant to women's lives—is one of the reasons I decided to enter the sex toy industry. Offering women the opportunity to shop for sex toys, to make their sexual desire primary, is an example of sex-positive feminism at work. It is necessary for feminism to encourage female sexual autonomy, and I believe postmodern (prodildo) feminism offers a practical solution for change through the reinterpretation of cultural symbols such as the phallus. In fact, the dildo may be the key we've been looking for to unlocking gender norms and expanding women's sexuality.

Power and Change

Antidildo feminists produce a feeling of strict boundaries and policing because they base their discourse on a simple binary dominance/submission model of power. They assume that there is always a clear division between who has power and who does not. The dominance/submission model of power does not account, however, for all the complexities involved in sexual relations, especially when plastic cocks enter the equation. When a reader wrote a letter complaining about the use of dildos in *On Our Backs* magazine, one editor responded, "try fucking a girl with a dildo before you knock the sensations involved: I've come just from the hip movements and the thrill of giving my baby a whirl."[17] Although the editor claimed a "dominant" role, she acted as the receiver of sexual pleasure even as she thrust her member into her girlfriend's cunt.[18] Using double dildos or masturbating with a dildo further unsettles the dominance/submission model. Double dildos put each member of the couple simultaneously in the dominant and submissive position. In this instance, there is no clear masculinized dominant position. Likewise, Wilton and Cherry Smyth both note that when a woman masturbates with a dildo she steps outside the male/female, active/passive framework.[19] During this sexual act she is both the penetrator and the penetrated, so there can be no question of losing sexual autonomy. In these cases, the "dildo is used in ways which utterly resist its interpretation as an agent of heterosexuality."[20] Women who are not sexually disenfranchised by fucking put a different face on the women's liberation movement, with an outrageousness, pleasure, and effrontery I find far more appealing, one I feel better about advocating to would-be feminists.

My female sex toy customers enjoy playing with dildos not only for sexual pleasure but also for the excitement of trying on various sexual personae. They are fascinated by the power dildos offer to undo expected gender relations and evoke the culturally erased female phallus. Far from enacting "penis envy," these women in no way see their dildos as inferior to men's equipment. On the contrary, many customers express feeling "equal" to their male partners as they share the aggressive pleasures of topping with their man.

And many of the dildos I sell perform actions that penises cannot. For example, the Rabbit Pearl vibrator includes a rotating shaft, beads that tumble to stimulate the G-spot, and a cute rabbit shaped branch to vibrate the clitoris. When I turn the Rabbit Pearl on, women customers light up and say, "Well my boyfriend certainly can't do *that!*" In moments like these, when the penis is reconceived as an inferior dildo, the power delegated to men as sole proprietors of the phallus is revealed as fiction, and the penis loses the definitional hold on social dominance. And as the "cuteness" factor of the rabbit pearl vibrator mixes penetration and solo-stimulation with girliness, the connection of female pleasure with veiny penises and penis look-alikes loosens ever more.

As Judith Butler has made clear in *Gender Trouble*, masculinity and femininity only *appear* to be coherent sets of sex-bound characteristics. In actuality, stable gender roles are created and reproduced through heteropatriarchal institutions like the family, the media, the new hype of evolutionary biologists selling scientific essentialism, and the old stand-by, government discrimination. Lesbians performing masculinity through dildos "expose the penis as itself, 'only' a representation or failed imitation of the phantasmatic phallus."[21] Dildos derail the repetition of the penis/phallus relationship in a truly "egalitarian" move: *Everyone* can have a dildo. (Suddenly I feel like holding hands with a bunch of people and singing, "I'd like to buy the world a *cock*. . . .")

The dildo's potential as a feminist tool is sometimes belittled because of the stereotype that only lesbians use dildos. Richardson, Jeffreys, and Wilton all call the recent female-friendly sex industry the "lesbian sex industry."[22] Yet my own experience and that of others who work in sex boutiques or research the field present a much different picture. While preparing a chapter on dildos for his book *Sexy Origins and Intimate Things*, Charles Panati found that the general consensus in the sex toy industry was that "Gay couples, with two real penises between them, are thought to be the biggest purchasers of dildos."[23] So although lesbians do buy sex toys, the sex toy business is by no means a "lesbian sex industry."

In fact, lesbians seem to be the least likely to explore or promote dildo play. My partner and I specifically targeted lesbian markets in advertising our business at the start. But many of our friends were so hung up on the political "meaning" of buying a sex toy and how the purchase would look in the eyes of their peers that few have come out to support us. Heterosexual women, on the other hand, embrace us and comprise the majority of our customers. Nationwide, heterosexual couples are perhaps the largest growing segment of sex toy purchasers. Carol Queen and Susie Bright, former workers at Good Vibrations, reveal that many of the people in the dildo harness aisle are male/female couples.[24] Bright says, "[t]his is what I call one of the biggest secrets of the last two decades: the popularity of anal sex has become outrageous . . . particularly with men who want their female lover to fuck them in the ass."[25] Fatale Film, a women-owned pornography production company, released a video called *Bend over Boyfriend* to address the growing group of heterosexual couples interested in penetration role reversals. The film was so successful that *Bend Over Boyfriend 2: Less Talkin', More Rockin'* has recently been released. The phenomenon of dildo play currently in vogue in these circles affirms a hard, assertive female sexuality as well as the culturally maligned permeable male body.

A large part of this mainstream entrance and acceptance of dildos results from sexual liberationist attempts to bring pleasure into the center of sex discourse. Sex liberationists, like Pat Califia and Susie Bright, believe doing "what feels good" is integral to a positive sexual self-image, and that restrictions on sexual desire only cause feelings of guilt and shame. Many sex liberationists encourage safe, consensual exploration of penetration—something notably missing in the traditional heterosexual education placed egregiously in fumbling adolescent hands in the back seats of parents' cars—in order for women to learn more about their bodies and sexual response. Dildos are thus a terrific tool for learning by oneself or with one's partner about *penetration without pain*, or, in fact, reconfiguring vaginal/penile intercourse as a "taking in" of the penis/dildo, prompted by the woman's pace of receptivity rather than the penis/dildo's degree of force. At Pleasure Parties (imagine a Tupperware party with sex toys), my partner and I give customers a genital anatomy lesson with a large plush puppet vulva. After covering the basics, we discuss a variety of sexual desire and response issues—the G-spot, penetration, and female ejaculation—encouraging women to know their bodies well and abandon sexual shame or self-subordination.

Our customers love this sex-ed session and often tell us they feel empowered by discussing sexuality openly. Many women are especially interested in learning about the "G-spot" and the potential for female ejaculation because these vagina-centered sexual possibilities remain invisible or inappropriate to much of the American population. My women customers ask for tips on how to integrate their chosen sex toy into the bedroom and openly express a desire to move beyond their prescribed sex role. They want to know what to say to their male lovers to avoid creating performance anxiety in them. In a dick-central culture, after all, men harbor feelings of inadequacy because the vulnerable and quirky penis cannot—and should not have to—achieve rock hard phallic authority at all times. It seems silly to have to say so, but the penis is only human, and should not be posited as the *be-all end-all* of sexual satisfaction. My argument is two-pronged: Sex is more than penile/vaginal penetration—and penetration is unnecessarily demonized or celebrated.

Conclusion: The Right Tool for the Job

I like to stand by the bed and pick out just the right dildo and harness from the toy box, arrange condoms and dams on the nightstand while my girlfriend lounges on the pillows fondling her clit, legs wide, silently watching my calculated moves. Once the dildo is snapped into place, I put my leather harness on slowly and seductively so she can savor my ritualistic transformation, and I can watch her get wet with anticipation. Then, when all the straps are tightened to fit perfectly around my hips, I like to look down at my dick and admire its firm, smooth erection. I feel so powerful in this moment, and so feminine.

Social change is slow, especially when the object is to alter such a powerful cultural concept as the phallus. Despite successful steps in this direction, many feminists are impatient:

> To suggest that we can effect social change through (queer) performances, however transgressive, provocative or challenging, would seem to assume, amongst other things, that such performances will have a revolutionary effect on (straight) audiences, rather than being interpreted as imitating and reproducing heterosexuality. . . . I am extremely skeptical of the extent to which "parodic replication" of heterosexual constructs such as, for instance, understanding the "lesbian cock," or chicks with dicks, as a parody of the phallus/penis, will challenge heterosexuality as a social institution.[26]

Yet evidence of the postmodern phallus, a phallus unlinked to biological sex, increases every day. Feminism must pay close attention to the methods that are working, instances where the phallus has changed, and be in tune with what women desire in sexual relations and need from the feminist movement. This requires something that, unfortunately, does not appear often in theory—an active, social connection with real women.

What happened after the Tribe 8 concert proves moving beyond the dildo impasse is possible. In the best collaborative spirit of feminism, concert-goers, protestors, and Tribe 8 themselves decided to "process" their issues with the phallus in an impromptu workshop. One workshop turned into several. The talks were so successful that Tribe 8 returned for the 1997, 1999, and 2000 festivals.

15   *Pearl Necklace*

The Politics of
Masturbation Fantasies

MERRI LISA JOHNSON

> My sexual semiotics differ from the mainstream. So
> what? I didn't join the feminist movement to live inside
> a Hallmark card.
> > —Pat Califia, "Feminism & Sadomasochism"

MY HEAD RESTS on the hard porcelain bottom of
the bathtub, hair swimming in two inches of tepid water.
Legs raised in a vee, I welcome the warmth from the faucet
thudding in between. Time is limited—I have to reach
orgasm before the water runs cold, which means I must
take a shortcut through my mind, taunt myself with lurid
scenes. Some are memories of past erotic trysts; some are
entirely made up. I collect images. With time each one
wears out and stops working, so I keep a wide range in my
repertoire at any given moment. On this day, I am searching almost frantically to get the right fantasy as the heat of
the water softens to lukewarm. This is my last chance to

finish here; otherwise I'll have to relocate to the bed and use my hands, which feels like defeat, adding to an already mounting frustration with my inability to come quickly or easily. When I was younger, fourteen, say, I would spend whole afternoons with my hands down my pants, watching soap operas with my Amway polarator (a massaging device that will always hold a special place in my heart), building incredible fires between my legs, culminating in several explosive orgasms that left me feeling scummy but sated. As an adult, I resent the time it takes to reach orgasm; I remember only vaguely what it was like, pre-intercourse, to give no thought to the final destination, enjoying stimulation for its own sake, where the universe hung suspended in one long, bleary unit of delight. Because I am not able to come fast enough, my sex partners often stop stimulating me before I come. Time is my enemy now. (Or is it my body colluding against me?)

The limits of the hot water heater reinforce those of the human tongue. So I am letting my mind fly recklessly this afternoon, like a bird caught inside a house, flapping against the ceiling until she stumbles across a way out. I soon discover a half-raised window of perversion that gets the job done. A woman lies beneath me, sucking my dick. I imagine telling her I won't come in her mouth. And then doing it anyway. (Yikes.) It is the sharp edge of inappropriateness that makes me come. I slow it down, savoring each stage: sucking, promising, coming. I play it over again. I pause on the moment between promising and coming, tasting the metallic edge before orgasm on the tongue of my skin. I hold it there—the image, the sensation, the story moving towards climax—I hold it there. I hold it there. I *hold* it therrrre. Hold. It. There.

And I come.

Taboo images often spring to mind when I masturbate, so it makes sense that the commitment I developed to feminism in graduate school would designate a new field of possibility for transgression. With my hand between my legs, I become feminism's enemy number one. Crude, forceful, selfish. I put my dick in her mouth and she does not like it.

Transgender masturbation fantasies—fantasies where I play the boy—strike me initially as unfeminist. Yet I am aware at the same time of a feminist dimension to this fantasy. When Germaine Greer urged a generation of feminists in the 70s, "Lady, love your cunt," and Nancy Friday collected women's masturbation fantasies in *My Secret Garden*, when Anne Koedt rejected what she called "the myth of the vaginal orgasm" in favor of centralizing the clitoris in female sexuality—these women laid the groundwork for a feminism that gives women permission to explore, discover, reveal, and celebrate what gets us off. No matter what.

But I want to do two things with this image at once: to acknowledge the way U.S. culture shapes my fantasies into scenes of dominating women, displacing my orgasm onto the male sex organ, and simultaneously to guard my right to fantasize freely, to come at whatever cost. What kind of feminism might I develop to resist the traditional dampers on female sexuality—the church, the family, the public school system, all of Western literature—as well as the progressive limits imposed by feminist consciousness? What to do when a movement for women's liberation constrains my own personal freedom, when feminism conflicts with itself?

Out of this grinding impasse, a third wave ambiguity arises. My title means to evoke the sedimentation of many layers comprising my erotico-political vision, as I negotiate *first*, a family upbringing that adorned my body in the trappings of nice, upper-middle-class femininity—"real" jewelry, modest hemlines, sensible Sunday-school shoes, crossed legs; *second*, the cultural upbringing that targeted my body with vicious, mocking rock lyrics, crude jokes, violent male-centered pornography, and a blow-up-doll vision of female sexuality as hollow and objectified; *third*, a feminist education that equips me to perceive family and culture as antagonistic to my sexuality; and, *fourth*, a masturbation fantasy that flies in the face of all three. In my fantasy, I tug at the pearl necklace clasped around my neck even as I aim one made of semen at the imaginary girl lying beneath me in the tub.

What does this fantasy mean? Upon first reading, it seems to replicate the sexual inequality my culture immerses me in from birth. Perhaps I am fighting the feeling of drowning in subordination by taking the boy position when I masturbate (appropriating, as well, the term "jerking off" to describe my solitary pleasures). Perhaps in fantasy I identify with the dominant, male role, siphoning off sexual pleasure from the penis, bootlegging jism from the

Man. ("It is all too easy," writes Lynne Segal, "to see why in fantasy women may choose male figures for erotic identification."[1]) It might seem that I am trading on existing inequalities, accepting female sexuality as passive and reinforcing this structure by taking a *me-tarzan-you-jane* approach to the women in my imagination. It's true that when I kiss women in real life I almost always take the dominant role, initiating the flirtation, making the first move, pressing her hard against the car seat, my thigh between her knees. Do I treat these *girlies* the same way men do? Do I use the material of their luscious bodies for the selfish satisfaction of my own raw urges?

Jean Grimshaw offers a range of answers to consider. She surveys the feminist debates over fantasies of domination and politically correct sexuality, offering a comfortably reconciled position, a theory that lets me off the hook (if I want off). In her essay, "Ethics, Fantasy and Self-Transformation," she lays out the various angles feminists have taken on the complicated fact "that women's sexual fantasies often involve various forms and elements of domination, submission, humiliation; even rape itself."[2] The liberal feminist position asserts simply that it's "a good thing that sexual desire and fantasy is freed as much as possible from structures of guilt, fear, shame and psychic distress." This group says women should "just learn to live with [their fantasies of domination and submission] and accept them" because "there is no necessary connection at all between fantasy and real life."[3] Quite an attractive stance for those of us who feel our fantasies are so terribly

bad, yet I fear it's one of those "too good to be true" trap
doors of intellectual self-deception, the Houdini function
of theory, getting oneself out of compromising erotic binds
through cheap chicanery.

Grimshaw paraphrases the opposition to this fantasy
free-for-all: "Those sexual liberals who argue that anything
goes in the matter of sexual desire and fantasy . . . have simply failed to respond to radical critiques of female subordination."[4] I can't argue with that. In fact, I feel dissatisfied
with the easy way out, the simpleton's insistence on wanting what I want. Grimshaw attributes the second position to
Sandra Bartky, author of *Femininity and Domination*, who
argues against "politically correct sexuality" as a concept
that is "bound to be judgmental, divisive, and coercively
alienating of those who seem to fall short of a (mythical)
ideal."[5] As Bartky, Grimshaw, and others assert, fantasy isn't
easy to change or disavow, even if one should want to do so.

Finally, Grimshaw's thesis suggests that my fantasy of
getting a blow job and shooting my load across a really nice
rack may not be what it seems: "Given the constant slippage of meaning, there is no way in which the 'real meaning' of a fantasy can simply be read off from a first account
of the narrative or scenario."[6] She points to the Freudian
psychology of dreams, which suggests that our unconscious mind dramatizes the conflicts and wishes we repress
or inadequately address in our conscious lives. This raises
some interesting possibilities for reading my masturbation
fantasy as something other than the misogynist assault it
first appears to be. Who is this girl I picture with my dick

in her mouth? Why do I take pleasure in tricking her into crossing her erotic boundaries? Why do I want her to go further than she wants to? To take more of me into her than she asks for? One theory of how dreams work says that every character or element of the dream represents an aspect of the dreamer. From this viewpoint, the object of my domination emerges more clearly. I begin to recognize her features. She is not an anonymous stand-in for women in general. She is me. She is the part of me that was trained in the "good girl" tradition of waiting for sex until marriage, of inhibition and modesty, alienation from one's body, shame for its carnal urges. She wears sea shell pink lipstick and matching nail color; she is given a set of pearls early on, training pearls, around the time when she begins to menstruate, along with other signs and lessons of ladyhood. In my fantasy, I am struggling with this girlie-girl in me, overwhelming her, pushing her limits down her throat.

The phraseology here reeks of rape culture. (God forbid a feminist should speak of forcing a woman to do anything, even if that "woman" is imaginary or symbolic of culturally conditioned female sexual passivity.) Grimshaw argues, however, that power is inevitable, "constitutive . . . of human eroticism," while acknowledging that it "can all too easily get overlaid . . . with more malign structures of gender, class or race-based forms of domination and exploitation." "The problem in thinking about sexuality, eroticism and power," she continues, "is how to give an account of these kinds of 'power' and 'submissiveness' which both recognizes their constitutive role but does not build into that constitutive role the sorts of power that come along with other forms of exploitation and domination."[7] The dynamics of power, from this theoretical perspective, do not necessarily entail traditional gender roles. Girls don't have to be on bottom, and—it seems so obvious as to hardly need stating—when girls are on bottom, we aren't necessarily replicating the rape culture.[8]

In *Outlaw Culture*, bell hooks comes right out and says in order to become the kind of feminist she wants to be, she must consciously change what turns her on: "[O]ne major obstacle preventing us from transforming rape culture is that heterosexual women have not unlearned a heterosexist-based 'eroticism' that constructs desire in such a way that many of us can only respond erotically to male behavior that has already been coded as masculine within the sexist framework."[9] (Being turned on by *Fight Club* would, I imagine, fit within this framework.) Her unmitigated argument and unflinching old-school feminist style, admirable in its clarity of vision but daunting in the discipline it would require, is worth quoting at length:

His was not the usual "dick-thing" masculinity that had aroused feelings of pleasure and danger in me for most of my erotic life. While I liked his alternative behavior, I felt a loss of control—the kind that we experience when we are no longer acting within the socialized framework of both acceptable and familiar heterosexual behavior. Then I asked myself whether aggressive emphasis on his desire, on his need for "the pussy" would have reassured me. It seemed to me, then, that I needed to rethink the nature of female heterosexual eroticism, particularly in relation to black culture. Critically interrogating my responses, I confronted the reality that despite all my years of opposing patriarchy, I had not fully questioned or transformed the structure of my desire. By allowing my erotic desire to still be determined to any extent by conventional sexist constructions, I was acting in complicity with patriarchal thinking. Resisting patriarchy ultimately meant that I had to reconstruct myself as a heterosexual, desiring subject in a manner that would make it possible for me to be fully aroused by male behavior that was not phallocentric. In basic terms, I had to learn how to be sexual with a man in a context where his pleasure and his hard-on is decentered and mutual pleasure is centered instead. That meant learning how to enjoy being with a male partner who could be sexual without viewing coitus as the ultimate expression of desire. Talking with women of varying of ages and ethnicities about this issue, I am more convinced than ever that women who engage in sexual acts with male partners must not only interrogate the nature of the masculinity we desire, we must also actively construct radically new ways to think and feel as desiring subjects.[10]

hooks is well-known for her frank speech about various cultural oppressions; in fact this quality is probably what many third wave feminists find so compelling about her work. She is cited by this group frequently, like the big sister who understands the world better than we do, whom we emulate but never completely match step for step.

In processing this idea of moving away from sex as a dick thing, I can only get so far before running into brick walls. I understand on an intellectual level that many women are conditioned to desire many things that are not good for us, but I balk at the idea of wrenching fantasy free of the power underpinnings that drive it, make it sing, zing with that mercurial membrane lining the big "O." I won't do it. I am not that feminist, not that kind of feminist, not down with the *cultural feminists* who "believe that the struggle against male supremacy begins with women exorcizing the male within us and maximizing our femaleness," not one of those "good" feminists, like Mary Daly, for instance, who proposes elective spinsterhood and a corresponding "Misterectomy."[11]

In contrast to their clear cut political separatism, my fantasy stands out as gender-impure, a sort of genderclasm, in that it isn't entirely "female" in the traditional meaning of the word. The visual narrative works as a wedge to pry open old ideas about gender and desire that remain relatively influential in pop culture: "Men crave power and orgasm, while women seek reciprocity and intimacy."[12] Against this essentialist paradigm, Alice Echols writes,

> Rather than develop a feminist understanding of sexual liberation, cultural feminists reject it as inherently antifeminist and instead endorse a sexual code which drastically circumscribes the sorts of sexual expressions considered acceptable. And, in demanding "respect," rather than challenging the terms upon which women are granted "respect," cultural feminists reinforce the distinction between the virgin and the whore.[13]

Perhaps the girl in my fantasy represents a femininity based on sexist definitions of respectability, and my dick in her mouth is me "challenging the terms on which women are granted respect." Even though my fantasy is not necessarily the coercive, masculine model of eroticism it seems, it might be, and that's okay too.

The nicey-nice persona of cultural feminists ruins much of Fiona Giles' collection, *Dick for a Day: What Would You Do if You Had One?*, as women pussy-foot around the obviously playful and politically incorrect tenor of the titular question. My answer comes without hesitation: I would get a blow job. A nasty one, and a little mean. I'd tangle my right hand in her dirty blonde hair and push a little too hard into her mouth. The women Giles interviewed are tame in comparison for the most part. Tricia Warden is the only one in *Dick for a Day* who really has balls. She shocks me, and I like it. In a fantasy of forceful oral sex, she writes:

> I pushed her head down. I tore her shirt off from behind. With a knife I found in the sink I cut off her bra straps and freed her tits. She shuddered when she felt the metal touch. The place was so quiet except for her moans and my heavy breathing. Bits of light meandered in as if to say we were in hell and paradise was just right outside. I bent her over at her waist and checked out her ass. It was Eden enough for me. She was my whore; my little sinning apple; my bitch; mine; mine; my ass; my pussy; my fuck box; my warm twitching toy.[14]

Good grief. That's terrible—and terribly sexy. A poet in the collection voices my second thought: "I knew / I was going / to fuck myself / first."[15] This form of feminist desire strikes me as particularly third wave, immodest and cocky, the wanting and taking, the little girl with the cereal saying *too much is how much I want*. Here, finally, is a reflection of the sheer fun my generation pursues in the performance of our erotic personas. The silliness, the impromptu acting out of our aggression toward the expected, or accepted. How I loved those nights at the strip club where I worked when "Barbie" would take the stage in her sardonic black vinyl suit and mouth the words to Prodigy's techno hit, "Smack My Bitch Up," while she danced—all two lines of it:

> Smack my *bitch* up.
> Change my *pitch* up.

What does Barbie mean when she says these words on the strip club stage? What do I mean when I mimic her? And then when I jokingly use the phrase as code for masturbation on the phone with my boyfriend? (Tee hee.)

Cross-gender identification does not diminish one's biological girlness, I am coming to see; it expresses playfulness rather than poor self-image. In fact, integrating the "masculine" parts of one's erotic identity may be a sign of good mental health despite a culture that would deem such thoughts perverse. I remember one particular Saturday afternoon in early adolescence, I lay on the couch and whipped myself into quite a state while watching a porno movie and "self-pleasuring," only to become suddenly snagged up in realizing I was masturbating *wrong*. I was thrusting where I should have been, what, bouncing backwards? I tried reversing the rhythm of my hips to match the porno girls, but I lost all momentum towards orgasm. Everything went awkward and self-conscious. I returned to the other way, the "boy" way as I now saw it. This was a source of concern. As long as I was alone, I supposed it didn't matter that I pushed rather than pulled, but eventually I would need to take this show on the road, and then what? I figured I better get the gender of my hips right before doing it with a guy. It didn't turn out to be a problem, though. I followed my lovers' leads flawlessly, passive and female.

Years and years later, a decade maybe, I find myself on another couch, the time not alone. My then boyfriend and I face each other, kiss and crawl all over each other, legs interlacing and all that wine setting things loose inside, where sobriety would have kept them still. We are grinding, but it's different from the dry fucking I remembered from high school where the boy pushes and pushes just like regular sex only through jeans. Instead, I feel the erotic lead pass back and forth between us, at certain moments losing all grip on the reality of who has what body part. When I try to talk about it afterwards, the awkwardness returns and I choke. I never realized how much fear I housed about being perceived as "masculine" in bed. But the times when I've had sex "like a boy"—in it to win it, having raucous fun, being as outrageously voracious as a person could possibly be—these rare times have been the best sexual experiences of my life.

In the preface to *Pomosexuals*, a collection of writings by and about the queerest of the queer, I stumble across a deeply pleasurable surprise of recognition—like running into a long-lost best friend on the opposite coast from where you knew her before. Imagine the look on my face when I read this passage: "You're a woman, born with all the medically-sanctioned grrl equipment, and you wanna jerk off with your own dick, but you don't want any kind of chemical or surgical intervention, you just wanna stroke your own cock and feel it."[16] Right *on*. I agree with Kate Bornstein about this fantasy:

> Me, I think that situations like those are exactly what we need to stretch our brains beyond the banal. I think that if we want to grow at all, spiritually, intellectually, individually or even as a race, however we want to grow, we need situations like these to tease our reluctant, recalcitrant, and (let's face it) lazy little selves into some growth.[17]

Like pressing regular straight guys to acknowledge that a woman can "fuck" another woman—with or without the aid of a dildo—just by doing "it" (whatever "it" is) to her, pressing against her, getting naked, making out, all the rest of what a person can do with, to, and for girl parts. Stretching our culturally compartmentalized brains beyond the "men fuck women" paradigm and the only slightly more progressive "women fuck men" inversion, this kind of mental exercise is good for getting everyone to see sexuality as the fluid thing that it is. To see fucking as wet clay. We are in it to the elbows.

Finally, the fantasy is also a product of my bisexuality. The scene, if you think about it, is sort of a threesome: me, the other girl, and my dick. Yet when asked, only a few years ago, "Are you bisexual?" I answered with a reflexive no, quickly correcting myself: I am attracted to both men and women, I have sex with men and with women, but I wouldn't call myself "bisexual." Hmm. I recognize this reluctant identification now as common among bisexuals, never feeling quite bi *enough*, thinking only equal attraction and equal sex with men and with women qualifies as "real" bisexuality.[18] Those feminist porn stars on the west coast who make sex-ed videos with their cohabitational male and female partners are the "real" bisexuals; I'll just sit in the back and sneak out early.

But what is the difference between being bisexual and "just" having sex with, or "just" being sexually attracted to men and women? Bisexuality is an idea as much as it is a practice, a way of seeing as much as a way of doing; bisexuality "is what escapes, what transgresses rules, breaks down categories, questions boundaries."[19] I lean towards being a heterosexual-identified bisexual woman: fucking men, fantasizing about women, and thus far primarily fucking women in the hetero-normative context of heterosexual couples, but bisexuality infuses my identity in small ways (sable lipstick, python boots, being attracted to the weird girl in *American Beauty* instead of the blonde cheerleader all the guys want to fuck) and in large ways as well, like recognizing how fine the line is between friendship, desire, and fucking, challenging neat divisions like het/homo, mind/body, intellect/erotic, friend/lover. It's just not that simple.

The first time I ever told my masturbation fantasy in public was at a party. I was more than a little tipsy and terribly attracted to this dark-haired graduate student with harsh red lipstick and matching sarcasm. We bonded. It was me, her, and a guy, all of us barely new acquaintances somehow talking about the most personal and multitextured parts of our psyches. My throat constricted as I told the shameful secret; my cheeks flushed hot in terror and excitement. I was risking something and my body felt this risk intensely. ("[W]e live terrified," as Amber Hollibaugh has written, "that other people will discover our secret sexual desires."[20]) When neither of them drew back in horror or got up and walked away, my muscles began to relax. Could it be possible? Could I have just revealed my most horrible self to strangers? Could they really have taken it in stride, like perversion is practically passé? With this brief, anonymous exchange, my fantasy was defused of its explosive shame. "The system of sexual hierarchy functions smoothly," after all, "only if sexual nonconformity is kept invisible."[21] Mikaya Heart gets it right when she says, "by talking openly about our sexuality, we can use it as a tool to bring us into community." In *When the Earth Moves: Women and Orgasm*, she writes,

> At the present time, sex is something that separates us from our communities. . . . I am suggesting that we talk about it in a real way—not just joking and laughing, not boasting, but saying what is real for us about sexual play: what works and what doesn't, what we fear as well as what we desire.[22]

I'm the absolute worst at making human connections in real life, but here, in writing, I am able to speak—forthright and raw—to forge connections with others and beckon them to follow with stories of their own intricate, unique "sex-prints."[23]

326

16 *Liquid Fire*

Female Ejaculation &
Fast Feminism

SHANNON BELL

For Gad Horowitz

Stood in line last night from 10:15 P.M. to 12:30 A.M. to get into the Pussy Palace. When men go to the baths they come in one by one; when women go, they come in groups, lining the street. The neighborhood johns kept cruising the butches and fems in line; it took two hours to reach the door. I amused myself by reading Freud's *Civilization and Its Discontents* for the next day's lecture in Psychology and Politics. The tale of the control of fire and the beginning of civilization particularly amused me as I ran my hand over the outline of the young butch's dick, immediately behind me in line.[1] Primitive man put fires out by urinating on the burning site. Woman, on the other hand, was the "natural" guardian of fire "because her anatomy made it impossible for her to yield to the temptation of this desire."[2] Then Freud makes a bizarre claim. He says that analytic experience shows a connection between ambition, fire, and urethra eroticism. I make a mental note to put out a butch's cigar from eight feet; I am ambitious.

The line is moving; I enter the Pussy Palace; the volunteer at the door hands me a kit: lube, condoms, and sex gloves; she skips the safe sex promo, "I'm sure you know the drill." She had been a student in my Sex and Intimacy class. I hear, as I walk through, that the pool and whirlpool are for socializing; the sex rooms are upstairs, and the S&M room is in the gym. I make a mental note to get flogged on the lifesteps, but that's another night and another tale. The pool seemed a good place to begin. I had a project: to fuck—actually, to make them fuck me, because I'm doing fem tonight, and the only position for a fem is to be "invaded, penetrated, split, occupied"—I'd digested my MacKinnon. While standing in line, I learned there was a shortage of fems; should be a fun night. I am every butch's dream—since I've done heterosexuality I have no problem crawling around on my knees sucking dick. (Your cock is in my mouth; that would make you in charge? I doubt it.)

I make it to the pool; a butch I've wanted for fifteen years walks over. She's muscular, extremely handsome, a talented leather craftsman, earning her living from crafting whips and leather sex tools for the North American girl market. "How are you doing, Shannon?" she inquires. I laugh, "Are you still into baby fems or have you graduated to older, more mature women?" I throw my long blonde hair back, stick my ass out, press my knees together in that famous Monroe pose. She replies, "I've always been into older women, maybe I'll see you later, Shannon." "I think I'd like to see you now." I drop my nose on her chest and run my tongue over her leather harness and skin down to her waist, undoing her tight leather boxer shorts; "in my hand I held her straight-risen sex."[3] I slowly roll a condom on with my hand and tongue and proceed to take her medium-sized member into my mouth; we do the appropriate cock-sucking discourse: "you taste so good," "you're so hard," "suck it bitch," "suck harder," "softer," "don't bite," "give it to me," "take me."

Spent on this, I turn around, offer her my crack from behind and say "Fuck me sir daddy and make it hard and good." There is a cheer from the pool; a hundred women are watching and yelling "fuck her," "make him work harder." "Want to do a homage to heterosexuality?" Sir Switch reflects for a moment. "Sure." Switch guides me to a lawn lounge chair, tosses me on my back, I raise my legs up, placing my red suede mule-clad feet with matching soul-fire toenail polish on both of her shoulders. I grab the paddle out of her sex belt and slap her ass with it as she drives into me again and again and again because repetition with a slight difference is the key to heterosexuality. From somewhere deep inside a low guttural howl-chant starts to rise, I hear monks chanting, my teeth are chattering, and there is an endless scream—come-cry-come-laugh—passing through me. We hit the piercing moment at the center

JANE SEXES IT UP

of orgasm—terror and wonder—she ejaculates hot sticky liquid fire out of her urethra, just below her cock. The pool voyeurs send up a wave of cheers, applause, cat calls, blessing us with laughter.

We untangle, disembark. Switch says, "Catch you later," and true to her word she does—three times. I follow the iron stairs leading from the pool outside to the inside chamber, and there encounter target number two, the butch lesbian playwright, filmmaker, bicycle courier I had propositioned two or three times over the years but no go. "Hi Shannon, what are you doing?" *You*, I thought, smiling with relish.

> I'm bare-arsed . . . "Let's fuck" . . . He was thickset, solidly built. [I] twined myself around him, fastened [my] mouth upon his, and with one hand scouted about in his underwear. It was a long heavy member [I] dragged through his fly. I eased his trousers down to his ankles.[4]

Then drop to my knees, roll a condom on his member with my hand and tongue and start to jerk and lick when a band of roving public whores joins us. The orgy begins; one pins Alex's head with her tits, another straddles Alex's chest and makes him suck her strap-on, I handle Alex's cock, snap a glove on my right hand, lube it and enter Alex's pussy. I'm sucking her dick and fisting her pussy; the beautiful fem has her perfect ass in my face as she runs her dick in and out of Alex's mouth. From behind Mistress de Sade raises my ass to her crotch and fucks me with her pussy lips. Switch snaps a flogging whip over my shoulders. "You slut, I can't even get my pants back on and you are fucking the next guy, you dirty pig, you're a sex pig!" She loves me, I can tell. Alex comes on my hand, contracting against my fist, and comes in my mouth, pushing his dick to the back of my throat; I remove my hand from his pussy; the glove is covered in blood. I lean over, brush past the fem's thigh whose dick is still in Alex's mouth and whisper in Alex's ear as I show him the glove: "You're a guy who covers all her bases." I leave the orgy and finally make it inside to the bar.

There I spot Tobaron, the intense, brilliant young Yeshiva girl (soon to be Yeshiva boy). I look her in the eye, "How do you feel about a Joe Orton bathroom sex scene? There is a community shower upstairs." We enter the square tiled shower room; I press my knees together Monroe style once more, the one daddy-girls and Yeshiva-boys like so much, raise my red lace mini-negligee and piss in the shower drain. Within seconds, Mistress P. comes by. "Hey, bitch, you pissing or ejaculating?" "Both/and," I reply. I am a *fast feminist philosopher*; it is most often both/and. I hand Tobaron the leather blindfold. "Put this on me, here's the flogger, do what you will." I lean face forward on the cold tile wall, my forehead resting on my bended left arm as if counting for hide-and-seek. Tobaron begins to strike my ass; on the third blow the roving community of public whores arrives from out of nowhere. Switch, their leader, grabs her whip and starts in on my ass. "You slut, daddy can't go away for a moment and you are at it again; daddy's going to teach you a lesson." Daddy has a beautiful accomplice mommy with him and she is mean.

She pins me against the shower wall. "Stop moving bitch and give daddy that ass," the vinyl and stiletto clad mommy demands. She continues: "You worthless, stupid, piece of shit." I call the scene for a second, turn to the voice of beautiful, cruel mommy and say "I can't take verbal abuse—it makes me want to kill." She laughs, "Neither can I." Mommy lets up. Daddy does the bad-little-girl routine. "I have a present for Daddy." Mommy takes the blindfold off, and I pull a very expensive, medium-sized, Cuban cigar out of my bag. "Fuck baby with this." We shift from Orton to Clinton just like that. Daddy outdoes the president bringing me to orgasm with the cigar. He lights it while still in my pussy. I try to draw in smoke with my pussy lips but I am a novice at this trick so no go. Daddy pulls the cigar out, bites the end off and draws in the fire repeatedly until the flame stabilizes. He holds his lighter several feet away from me, about three feet off the ground. Mommy says "Let's see you put out that fire." I raise my cunt, point my urethra, push out, and a "fountain of boiling water, heart-bursting furious tideflow"[5] dampens the flame.

Female ejaculation—the expulsion of sexual fluids from the female body, specifically the urethra—has been the object of medical and philosophical discourses since the early Greeks. Aristotle in the *Generation of Animals*, for example, connects female fluid with pleasure:

> Some think that the female contributes semen in coition
> because the pleasure she experiences is sometimes similar
> to that of the male, and also is attended by a liquid dis-
> charge. But this discharge is not seminal. . . . The amount
> of this discharge when it occurs, is sometimes on a differ-
> ent scale from the emission of semen and far exceeds it.[6]

Aristotle lived with the hetaira Herpyllis whom one con-
jectures taught him the secrets of liquid fire.[7] My research
reveals that the meanings ascribed to female ejaculation
over the course of Western history have varied consider-
ably, right up until its current invisibility. Female ejaculation has been framed in five ways: as fecundity, sexual
pleasure, social deviance, medical pathology, and a scientific problem.

Ejaculation is an incredibly powerful bodily experience;
it is, in addition, an incredibly powerful visual representation of the sexual female body. Revealing body fluid shooting with great velocity and force out of the female genitalia—out of the glands and ducts that surround the urethra, what is called the urethral sponge of the clitoris,
through the urethral opening—repositions the sexual
female body as powerful, active, and autonomous. The
lesbian pornographer and previous long-time editor/
publisher of *On Our Backs*, Fanny Fatale (Debi Sundahl)
suggests: "This is connectable to a broadening of women's
social and sexual roles."[8] With her, I say: "[T]he visual
image of female ejaculation relieves the phallus of its patriarchal burden. Female ejaculation is not spent. With stimulation one can ejaculate repeatedly and a woman in con-

trol of ejaculation may ejaculate enormous quantities, enough to put out fire. Males have to use urine."[9]

In *Making Sex*, Thomas Laqueur documents the displacement of the one-sex/one-flesh model of the human body that characterized the perceptions of philosophers, doctors, and scientists until replaced near the end of the seventeenth century by the modern two-sex/two-flesh model, which posits male and female as two distinct sexes. In the one-sex model, women and men had the same genitals; the woman's were inside the body and the man's outside. Female ejaculation is one route back to a potentially nonhierarchical one-sex/one-flesh model. In a past interview, I explored my own development toward this underrated, nearly invisible part of female sexuality:

SB: I always used to ask guys I slept with how to ejaculate.

BC: Why did you want to know?

SB: Because I figured that both male and female bodies could do it! Basically, men and women have the same anatomy—it's just that a woman's is internal. The spongy tissue on the top wall of the vagina goes into a full erection that links up with the clitoris. So inside, a woman gets a six to eight inch erection—the same as a penis, only inside. . . . Orgasm happens in two different directions. . . . [T]here are a lot more than two different kinds of orgasms, but there are two different directions: one when you're pulling in and one when you're pushing out. With ejaculations, you push out at the point when you feel you've had enough stimulation. You feel like you have to urinate, but it's not urine at all. You can push out and you can spray all over the place!

BC: Well, you certainly can! . . . How did you figure out the secret of the pushing down?

SB: I was trying everything. I was masturbating nonstop! My first ejaculation was in a [New York Forty-second Street hotel just before watching the famous porn star Ferron ejaculate close to late night sex TV entrepreneur Al Goldstein's face. Earlier in the day I had attended a workshop by one of the authors of *The G-Spot*.] She did not ejaculate herself, but she did know the important thing was to push out. The trick was to figure out when to push out and the amount of stimulation needed. I tried pushing out—endlessly! Finally I got one drop—and then I knew it was possible.[10]

The rest of the weekend I practiced. I sucked the cock of my Ginsberg/Genet bisexual lover. With my head between his legs, cock in mouth, right hand rubbing my clit and the external portion of my engorged urethra, I would start to burn and then push, burn and then push, burn real bad and then push real hard. Getting on the plane to return to Toronto, I could barely walk, my urethra was on fire, muscles contracted tight against a flame of water I had not yet learned how to shoot. G's cock was black and blue; every time I pushed I bit, but he supported me all the way for over fifteen years of pushing torrents of liquid fire out of my urethra. We took the varnish off floors in various apartments; we abandoned futton mattresses permanently drenched in girl-cum (until we discovered surgical sheets). I sprayed a large mirror as I sucked him, leaving the cum-streaked surface to remind all his fuck buddies and tricks they were playing in my territory. My internal erection would become so hard and large that G would have to remove his cock from my pussy while I sprayed a gushing flame of liquid in order for us to resume fucking. I would slide off his face, squat, and release burning hot fluid on the floor only to continue the ride. Sometimes perched on his face I would look over my shoulder to see puddles of female fluid scattered around our sexscape, tributaries overflowing one another, mapping our soul-fuck across the floor. On menstrual days when I pushed the fluid out of my glands and ducts, the pushing action would propel blood out of my pussy. Female cum and blood make pink pools in the body indentations on the bed; G's ass was often parked in a pink pond of cooling liquid fire when I returned to thrusting my member hard against his member—my member inside me, fucking his inside me. I did young boy, then I did girl, then sophisticated older woman; one thing remained constant: the sucking and spraying. Or really two things remained constant: sucking and spraying and my eternal gratitude/love for my companion in cum.

The expulsion of female fluids during sexual excitement was taken by many pre-enlightenment thinkers to be a normal and pleasurable part of female sexuality. The major controversy within the one-sex model was between one-seed and two-seed theories of generation: this centuries-long debate revolved around whether female fluids were or were not progenitive. Hippocrates and Galen were the most well known of those ancients who argued for the existence of female seed. Aristotle argued that the fluid was pleasurable and not progenitive. Western scholars and doctors throughout the Middle Ages remained faithful to Hippocrates' and Galen's notion of female sperm, which came to them through Arab medicine.

As the sameness of body gave way to differences between male and female bodies and semen became the property solely of the male body, the capacity of the female body to ejaculate, although still present and documented in medical writings and literature, was predominantly described as less than normal. In fact, in the nineteenth century female fluids were linked with disease. Alexander Skene, who in 1880 identified the two ducts inside the urethral opening, was concerned with the problem of draining the glands and ducts surrounding the female urethra when they became infected. The Skene glands and urethra became important to the medical profession as potential sites of venereal disease and infection, not as loci of pleasure.

The ejaculation of female fluids also came to be associated with a deviant sexual population and deviant sexual practice. In his study of sexual perversion, *Psychopathia Sexualis*, Richard von Krafft-Ebing identified female ejaculation as the pathology of a small subgroup within deviant sexualities. Under the heading "Congenital Sexual Inversion in Women," Krafft-Ebing discusses sexual contact among women; he contends:

> The intersexual gratification among . . . women seems to be reduced to kissing and embraces, which seems to satisfy those of weak sexual instinct, but produces in sexually neurasthenic females ejaculation.[11]

337

According to Krafft-Ebing ejaculation only occurs among women who suffer neurasthenia—body disturbances caused by weakness of the nervous system—contributing one among many historical examples of what might be called the medicalization of female sexuality. This pseudo-scientific approach linked girl spray with nervous disability.

The genealogy of female ejaculation has been one of discovery, disappearance, and rediscovery. As female ejaculation was being pathologized, a trace of female ejaculation surfaced in Victorian male pornographic discourse. *The Pearl* (a two-volume journal of Victorian short stories, poems, letters, and ballads) includes depictions of female ejaculation, interpreted by Steven Marcus in *The Other Victorians* as evidence of "the ubiquitous projection of the male sexual fantasy onto the female response—the female response being imagined as identical with the male . . . there is the usual accompanying fantasy that [women] ejaculate during orgasm."[12] Female ejaculation, according to Marcus's historical documentation, was relegated to the realm of men's fantasies.

Contemporary sexologists only began to address the phenomenon of female ejaculation in the late 1970s and 1980s. The big shift in representations of female sexuality began with Alice Kahn Ladas, Beverly Whipple, and John D. Perry in *The G-Spot*. This book popularized female ejaculation, yet did not explain how to do it, and it presented the female sexual organ as a whole, a unified organ, leaving behind the artificial division of the female genitalia into clitoris and vagina so popular with Freud, Masters and

Johnson, and Kinsey, all of whom pitted vaginal against clitoral orgasms, privileging one over the other. In an equally transformative reconsideration of women's sexuality, Josephine Sevely's *Eve's Secrets* sexualizes the urethra and emphasizes the simultaneous involvement of the clitoris, urethra, and vagina (the CUV) as a single integrated sexual organ. More than thirty prostatic glands and ducts are dispersed along the floor of the urethra located on the top wall of the vagina.

The female body, free from the limitations of the one-sex model which posited the female as an inversion of the male body, reveals physiological difference within anatomical symmetry. The female body can ejaculate fluid from thirty or more ducts and with stimulation can ejaculate repeatedly. It can ejaculate more fluid than the male body and can enjoy a plurality of genital pleasure sites: the clitoris, urethra, vagina, the vagina's entrance, the roof of the vagina, the bottom of the vagina, and the cervix. *A New View of a Woman's Body*, by the Federation of Feminist Women's Health Centers, redefines, in a brilliant political/sexual move, the urethral sponge as part of the clitoris; they have identified spongy tissue on the bottom wall and named it the perineal sponge of the clit. During sexual excitement this entire spongy body fills with prostatic fluid and other fluid that can be ejaculated.

Sexologists have spent quite a bit of time and effort analyzing the composition of female ejaculate to ensure that it is not urine. Samples have been collected in a number of laboratory settings.[13] Female ejaculatory fluid has been compared with urine and with male ejaculate. The fluid was chemically tested to determine whether it contained higher levels of glucose than urine does and whether or not prostatic acid phosphatase (PAP)—a major constituent of male semen, of prostatic origin, was present. The urea and creatinine levels of the fluid were tested against the levels in urine. The findings: the chemical content of female ejaculate is distinct from urine. Female ejaculate is higher in levels of prostatic acid phosphatase and lower in levels of urea and creatinine than urine; there is more fructose in ejaculate than in urine. Ejaculate changes in color, quantity, and odor during different phases of the menstrual cycle.

On my back, knees wide apart, I place the magic wand on my vulva area, just behind the clit, pressing hard on the urethra opening and the urethral erection that was beginning to show externally. I switch to being on my knees and snap the vibrant blue G-spot attachment onto the head of the magic wand; inside my pussy the hard plastic cock simulacrum vibrates on my top pussy wall. I rotate it, massaging different sensitive spots; the whole top wall of the pussy is sensitive, sometimes more so in different places. This seems to vary with the menstrual cycle; for example, just before bleeding I am more sensitive and produce more fluid closer to my pussy opening. I feel this burning, piercing heat. I contract my pussy muscles out and push. A flame of water erupts and lands in the catching bowl I have arranged on the floor four feet in front of me—about half a cup I estimate. I'd better do another one. This time, on my knees, legs wide apart, I use the center finger of my left hand to play with that spot just behind my clit and immediately in front of my urethra. With my right hand I press on my belly, squishing the fluid in my ducts that I can feel from the outside. I tilt my pussy forward; a piercing burning starts, and my pussy muscles contract. I press hard on a bulging duct, take a big breath, and push out as hard as I can; bull's-eye, I hit the collecting bowl once again, this time with about forty milliliters of fluid. Double bull's-eye: this time I orgasm; ejaculation and orgasm can go together, one can orgasm without ejaculating and ejaculate without orgasming; one can do both/and—bull's-eye. I pour the bowl's contents into a beaker, 180 milliliters, give or take. I pour what I can into a test tube, cap it, and set off to see my politically engaged, left-wing butch doctor at the neighborhood health clinic who agreed just this once to test my ejaculatory fluid. In order not to distract the lab he put both ejaculate and urine through as separate urine samples. Sure enough, my test replicated the sexology lab tests: ejaculate has a higher ph, more gravity, less urea, and less creatinine. However, the results also read: 3+ blood in the ejaculation sample (specimen 2) and a trace of blood in the urine sample (specimen 1). I was in the middle of my period, emitting a cocktail of cum, blood, and urine.

Freud, in his analysis of Dora, made a connection between Dora's hysterical symptoms and the secretion of female fluids:

The pride taken by some women in the appearance of their genitals is quite a special feature of vanity; and disorders of seeing one's genitals as provoking repugnance have an incredible power of humiliating women and lowering their self-esteem.... An abnormal secretion of the mucous membrane of the vagina is looked upon as a source of disgust.[14]

In "Some General Remarks on Hysterical Attacks," a short paper published in 1909, Freud discloses the source of masculine hysteria:

Speaking as a whole, hysterical attacks, like hysteria in general, revive a piece of sexual activity in women which existed during their childhood and at that time revealed an essentially masculine character. It can often be observed that girls who have shown a boyish nature and inclinations up to the years before puberty are precisely those who become hysterical from puberty onwards. In a whole number of cases the hysterical neurosis merely represents an excessive accentuation of the typical wave of repression, it allows the woman to emerge.[15]

Woman emerges when female masculinity is repressed, when the active girl is fully oedipalized into the feminine woman. The hysteric, marking incomplete oedipalization, is a figure of resistance. She resists through her body, which speaks through vision abnormalities, blindness, spasms or neurasthenia, sexual dysfunction, speech impediments, biting the tongue, nausea, rapid palpitations, multiple personalities, fugue states, absences and amnesia, hallucinations, temporary paralysis, thumb sucking, and the involuntary passing of urine. In an exquisite sexual encounter one can experience fourteen of the fifteen symptoms. It's best when strapped in a sling, legs cuffed to the chain suspensions, and a female daddy's full fist in your pussy as you contract and release your muscles and drench her pecks and forearm with liquid fire. If such a scene counts as sexual dysfunction, then all fifteen symptoms of hysteria are also features of active female sexuality. As Freud reasoned in his Postscript to his work on Dora, "The symptoms of the disease are nothing else than the patient's sexual activity."[16] While the hysteric resisted through her body, the post-hysteric resists through a public refusal to accept the female body as it has been constructed by societal authorities, and instead reconstructs her body from a subject position of agency.

The ejaculating female is an event-scene (a spectacular moment of the present that contains the promise of an altered state to come) of *fast feminism*. Fast feminism: a strategically lived (global/local) feminism of the now, a feminism that holds gender central, all the while realizing gender is slippery; a feminism that privileges the "masculine" female body, performed as fem or butch or any combination in between, in which master and hysteric (the flip side of master) merge into *one who knows and does*. Fast feminism is informed by postmodernism, but it differs from postmodern feminism in that the constituting features—gender as performative; no essential female or male self; the abandonment of grand referents and feminist ontology; the acknowledgement of multiple, complex, and contradictory subjectivities; the idea that philosophy is overshadowed by politics and lived as a realm of contestation, instability, and struggle; and ethics as a situated pragmatics—are taken as given. Fast feminism is concerned with *doing* theory; actions count.

Women's control over female ejaculation in order to ensure the greatest bodily pleasure has only recently entered public discourse. Since the late 1980s the ejaculating female has been speaking on her own behalf, presenting images and texts inside a fast feminist discourse.[17]

I regularly teach female ejaculation classes for women and men accompanied by women at Toronto's "Come as You Are," a women's sex store. Classes are available at women's sex stores in many North American urban spaces such as Boston, New York, San Francisco, Vancouver. I do seminars and workshops for university sex education centers, health professionals, Planned Parenthood associations, and family therapists.

The old knowledge that marked female ejaculation as the property of the hysterical woman, or the pornographic woman, or as a body to be scientifically investigated, is overturned by the ejaculating female herself, whom Freud pathologized as "involuntarily passing urine."

Sitting on the white cock simulacrum, I decide to dedicate the next shoot to my Mother. And with this dedication I return in my mind to my small child-self sitting in the back seat of the family's 1955 cream Dodge car, my pussy grinding into the car seat as I watched my Mother sitting in the front seat wondering what was going on in her body. My Mother with her fingers rubbing her belly on what I have come to recognize as woman's ejaculatory glands and ducts. These glands and ducts, at least thirty, are dispersed in the spongy tissue that surrounds the urethra on the top wall of the vagina. If you have big glands, like I do, and if you have very little flesh between the belly and the urethral sponge, you can feel [the ducts fill] on the outside of the body by pushing on your belly with your fingers. My Mother was telling my Father that her belly felt funny, hot and throbbing, and she was using that voice tone I have come to associate in myself with sexual frustration. As a six-year-old I made a mental note: Make sure this doesn't happen to me when I grow up. Make sure that I know the cause of the burning and throbbing. Make sure I know how to stop it. [A flame of water erupts]; I shoot [liquid fire] all over.

17 The Absolutely True & Queer Confessions of Boy Jane, Dick Lover

GEOFFREY SAUNDERS SCHRAMM

> He promises me that I'm as safe as houses
> As long as I remember who's wearing the trousers.
> —Depeche Mode, "Never Let Me Down"

AFTER A SOIREE not long ago, in the dim hour just before passing out in my living room, a dear girlfriend and I ventured into areas of discussion that remain off-limits in the light of sobriety, and eventually our ramblings culminated in a confession on my part, a kink I don't offer too freely: my sexual attraction to straight-acting and sometimes straight-identified masculine men. My drinking companion and newly elected confidante was taken aback, and for good reason. How could someone who repudiates male privilege simultaneously eroticize it in my lovers? How could I be into men who embody traits I intellectually abhor? My dirty little secret, this turn on, deviates slightly from the very visible gay and bi aesthetic, which consciously queers masculinity, revealing its artifice and revelling in its consequent undoing. The lion's share of scholarship on queer masculinities foregrounds the Nautilized body of urban white gay men as a site of gender parody. Muscles, however—straight, gay, or whatever—are not the meat of the matter when it comes to my fetish. In fact, the gym bunnies who lope around my former neighborhood of Dupont Circle interest me only on an intellectual level. I remain skeptical about assertions like David Halperin's that "[g]ay muscles do not signify power," yet I do see these cut, sinewy bodies and rigorous workout regimes as narratives of queer disillusion, a pining after boyhood notions of an ideal masculine body—impenetrable, forceful, absolute—that can never exist in the real world.[1]

I get off on what has been referred to as "male trouble"—the psychological dramas that unfold in the face of feminist critiques of male privilege.[2] Seeing men squirm when confronted with their systemic power makes me wet. I like to watch men react to uncomfortable positions within a conceptual system of gender roles they considered stable. There's just something about a gay man shoring up his masculinity right there in front of me. I am inside him, inside his psychic space, a destabilizing force, agitating from within. A product of growing up in the house of a stoic military officer and advocate of countless conservative causes, my desire reflects, perhaps, my father's daily constructions of nongay masculinity. While I distance myself from his reactionary masculinity, I nevertheless eroticize the rigid maleness he embodies.

First there was the rockabilly guy with whom I attended high school, only to date five years later in the sexually bizarre transitional year between college and graduate school. With his tattooed biceps, pomaded hair, motorcycle, and a healthy disrespect for the bourgeois standards at my middle-class core, he embodied everything that I wasn't (precisely why I liked him). I found myself aroused by the level of anger he displayed in scenes bordering on the psychotic. He once ended an argument by punching and kicking some anonymous person's car door with reckless abandon—a show of force shot through with vulnerability—the twisted logic of losing control as evidence of true love. Another time, as we waited at a red light he hopped out of my car and jumped on the hood, screaming obscenities at me. Unlike my father whose anger usually manifested passive-aggressively, I was secretly excited by these class-differentiated eruptions, for they revealed his willingness to be moved by emotion. I have only recently recognized the physical danger his rants posed for me. Eventually my fetishization of his white working-class masculinity drove a wedge between us and we broke up.

The last man with whom I sustained a long-term relationship appealed to my desire for a more subtle form of masculine anger. Obsessed with disciplinary figures like state troopers, he frequently demanded that we listen to a police scanner while fucking. His equally pathological preoccupation with Bryant Gumble notwithstanding (he used to carry a picture of the news anchor in his wallet), my lover and I would bicker over political issues for hours, followed by marathon fucking sessions of two hours or more (usually with him on top).

Raised in Fairfax County, a primarily white, upper-class echelon of social and fiscal conservatism in north Virginia, a recent graduate of the colonial William and Mary, my boyfriend acted decidedly and intentionally "straight." When pressed to explain this choice, he would launch into an invidious polemic against what he called *flambeaus* or effeminate gay men, biological male trannies (pre- and post-operative), and other men who make the conscious decision to cultivate femininity in any way. This all came as a big shock to me since, at the time, I presented myself as a club kid, often donning the now-infamous daisy dukes, complete with lace garters, hosiery (hairy legs and all), and chunky platform shoes (I was *so* early nineties). This getup deviated significantly from the normative white masculine heterosexuality my lover found so arousing. Yet there we were: me, bedecked in glitter and garters, ardent stigmaphile, Queer National, coming into leftist political consciousness; and him, the house DJ, controller of the beat, stigmaphobe and assimilationist, carefully *not* rocking the boat of mainstream liberal thought. After two months of fighting and fucking, we raised the stakes of our relationship. I threw out my little black book of fuckable former lovers, and he trashed his extensive collection of gay frat boy porn. We would be monogamous in body and mind.

Politically conscious queers, I felt certain, would not have endured this creepy replication of possessive heterosexuality and rigid gender roles, would have kicked this guy to the proverbial curb, emotional baggage in tow. Instead, I found myself sexually piqued by his pathologies, compelled by the erotic possibilities of fucking with law and order: the handcuffs, the hog-ties, the role playing. But looking back I see another aspect of this relationship that aroused me: the opportunity to witness, and to an extent experience, a degree of gay male masochism.

Our racial difference, as one manifestation of our sado-masochistic dynamics, is rich with material for queer analysis, given the racial fetishization practiced by gay men, both white and of color (which produced such pejoratives as "rice queen," "snow queen," "dairy queen," and "dinge queen"). My lover carefully avoided stereotypically black behavior, distancing himself from markings, habits, and beliefs associated with hoods or b-boys. He opted instead to follow the path of assimilation forged by Gumble. The racially homogeneous population of north Virginia was only too happy to support this disidentification with black culture. Black men who rejected the racist and classist black masculinity he represented were equated in his mind with the thieves and rapists populating the white racist imagination.

More crucially than race, however, gender figured centrally in our masochistic drama, resulting in a number of knock-down-drag-out fights—and some great sex. The relationship with my cop-fetishizing lover required me to address an issue every straight woman feminist eventually grapples with, an issue thirty years of feminism has not yet resolved: *how can I be fucking these dicks?* "Readings" of my desire surface and slam up against one another. Is my arousal by men's anger and pain a form of self-hatred? Do I eroticize their conventional masculinity as a way to cope with living in the persistently unequal and undemocratic culture of the United States? By desiring and valuing their behaviors, am I reinscribing the very male privilege I critique so earnestly? Or is there feminist value in eroticizing the theatrics of male dominance? Finally, what do my desires reveal about my own tenuous relationship to masculinity?

Arguing with my boyfriend about his desire to "pass" as heterosexual felt at the time like important feminist cultural work, one dick at a time, because it forced him to do the unspeakable in a heteronormative culture: pay attention to his own gender identity. Pushing my boyfriend to articulate his relationship to masculinity was a way of revealing to him the constructedness of all gender. The hard, glazed surface of masculinity within which he daily retreated began to crack under my relentless pressure, and he was often forced to "pull out" of our arguments when confronted with the logic of feminist critique. Each rejoinder tugged the loosening threads of masculinity, finally denuding his desperate defense mechanisms as gender fascism. The process forced him to consider how, despite his desire to "take it like a man," his gayness in a heteronormative culture will always undermine his status as a man, and this loss would be amplified by racial hierarchy.[3] Cultural conceptions of black male sexuality are shaped by racist fears and desires, positing the black man as ultimate penetrator—the big black dick threatening the white social body—and my lover's assimilative masculinity complied with this construct.

I now understand the sexual satisfaction I experienced after each argument with my boyfriend as a form of feminist sadism. Freud characterizes sadism as an inherently male phenomenon linked to the psychological "desire to subjugate," so I realize the notion of a feminist sadism is hard to swallow.[4] Linking feminism with sadism threatens to supplant the political goal of radical democracy with mere revenge fantasies. Freud's careful distinction between the use of sadism within "ordinary speech" and the kind he strictly labels as "a perversion" clarifies this diagnostic dilemma:

> In ordinary speech the connotation of sadism oscillates between, on the one hand, cases merely characterized by an active or violent attitude to the sexual object, and, on the other hand, cases in which satisfaction is entirely conditional on the humiliation and maltreatment of the object. Strictly speaking, it is only this last extreme instance which deserves to be described as a perversion.[5]

The sexual arousal I experienced by "humiliating" my boyfriend (my own sexual object)—dismissing his relation to the phallus and the power he benefited from it as a man—constitutes a clinical or perverse form of sadism. But here's the feminist twist: when I put men like him in their "place" as gay men, deploying a feminist critique of identity, I was showing him that there was literally no "place" for him in the culture to which he assimilated; that his relationship with dominant forms of masculinity could never be a place to call home. By reminding him of his desire to fuck and be fucked by other men, I urged him to see that the culture with which he identified erased the conditions under which he could exist, his possession of the revered dick always contradicted by having a penetrable asshole or "boy-pussy" that could be (and indeed was) fucked.[6] He, like other men and women who have intercourse with men, became estranged from masculinity and thus from power— whether he copped to it or not—through his penetrability; his desire and ability to take it like a "man" was undermined by the fact that he was taking it *from* another "man." By fighting with and fucking him, I forced his recognition of the feminist (figuratively as well as literally) within.

But, to turn the critical lens back on myself, I realized there was no place for me within heteronormative conceptions of masculinity, either. The clinical borders between sadism and masochism dissolve as I acknowledge that my pleasure in humiliating my lover was pleasure in humiliating myself as a gay man who identifies with the feminine. One of the painful truths of feminism is that no one, including a straight-identified man, gets to be *the man* once masculinity is exposed as an always imperfect relationship between the individual and the ideal. In other words, any articulation of postfeminism masculinity (not postfeminist) can only be masochistic in the context of "normative" society.[7] Even queers who articulate a parodic or performative relationship with masculinity are involved in some form of masochistic fantasy, struggling with its unstable meaning. Like gay bodybuilders, many gay men are mourning— despite our intellectual feminist consciousness—a masculine ideal that never was.

Here is where my family enters the fray. During my childhood, my father often accepted orders for overseas tours of duty to ensure advancement in the ranks, leaving my mother as the only consistent authority figure in our household. Consequently she modeled a (re)movable masculinity for me, straddling the attenuated line of gender difference as she imposed financial and disciplinary order upon the household. She performed a gender that could be both competent and emotional, openly missing my father—her husband, lover, and friend. His return, however, often produced border skirmishes between my parents. My mother wanted to continue running the household as usual, yet my father wanted to reassert the male privilege he learned from his parents and the United States military training. The conflict threatened the gender (dis)order my mother established for me.

My mother and I also shared a relationship some might describe as inappropriately close. As her confidante, I listened to her concerns, consoled her, and celebrated her many accomplishments. She treated me as an adult, consciously shedding the condescending attitude most parents adopt when dealing with their children. In response, I began to identify with her and with feminine culture. Rather than playing football with my brother and our neighborhood friends, I preferred tap dancing lessons, clarinet, and singing with our church choir—directed, not insignificantly, by my mother. My experience with masculine social activities was limited to sitting in left field, picking flowers, and making daisy chains.

This identification with the feminine was redoubled through my contentious relationship with my brother. As the older sibling, he did everything first, though seldom successfully. In fact, rather than living in his shadow, I learned from his mistakes so well he ended up living in mine. His close identification with the masculine realm further linked boy spaces in my mind with failure and second-best status. As he embraced normative masculinity, I responded by dismissing conventional maleness entirely.

By having fucked and been fucked by men, identifying with the feminine and placing within brackets my own relationship to normative masculinity, I inhabit my body as a daily disruption to dominant notions of gender. Crucially, though, my resistance to heterosexist culture is undermined by the eroticization of normative masculine behavior I am confessing here. By revealing this fetish for traditional masculinity, I hope only to carve new cultural space for feminists—hetero and queer—to wrestle with our most unspeakable desires, to bring the force of queer and feminist theory to bear on the concrete moments and practices in individual lives that dramatize the process of political consciousness settling through the layers of sexual desire. My confession is just one more voice in the growing chorus of radically disparate (his/her)stories.

The position I want to argue, as I look back over this catalogue of erotic conflicts—the rockabilly on my windshield, police scanner static as soundtrack to a violent fuck, Bryant Gumble in my boyfriend's wallet—is that, as feminists, we cannot act on our desires without carefully attending their repercussions on other people, ourselves, and American sexual culture. I join Gayle Rubin in recognizing that "[e]rotic chauvinism cannot be redeemed by tarting it up in Marxist drag, sophisticated constructivist theory, or retro psychobabble."[8] The third wave of feminists currently taking shape asks feminism to come back into our bedrooms, our kitchens, our closets, to help us understand our desires without dictating what they should be. For what we need from feminism is not a blueprint for a nonsexist bedroom, but a way of understanding the behaviors and relationships in our lives that are *still fucked up*, with faith that we all will eventually *get it* at—or, perhaps more appropriately, *in*—the end.

A number of people, knowingly or unknowingly, have had an incalculable impact upon both this essay and its author. I wish especially to thank Daniela Garofalo, Marilee Lindemann, Martha Nell Smith, and Lisa Johnson for the generous collegial and emotional support they offered as I struggled through the writing process. Nicole Louie can attest to every sordid detail, even though she might want to forget some of them. I thank her for standing by me. Finally, my family has been a constant source of support and inspiration, and they have generously allowed me to discuss private aspects of their lives in public forums, despite their own fears and concerns of exposure. To them I am grateful most of all.

Notes

Jane Hocus, Jane Focus

1. "Rape culture" is defined as "a complex of beliefs that encourages male sexual aggression and supports violence against women. It is a society where violence is seen as sexy and sexuality as violent. In a rape culture women perceive a continuum of threatened violence that ranges from sexual remarks to sexual touching to rape itself. A rape culture condones physical and emotional terrorism against women *as the norm.*" Emilie Buchwald, Pamela Fletcher, and Martha Roth, *Transforming a Rape Culture* (Minneapolis: Milkweed, 1993), vii.

2. I am borrowing from Andrea Dworkin's confrontational rhetoric in *Womanhating* to ally *Jane Sexes It Up* with a tradition of radical feminist social critique, claiming Dworkin as part of this tradition despite a pervasive ambivalence among third wavers toward her positions on sexual politics.

3. Elizabeth Kamarck Minnich's review essay on four antifeminism feminist books uses this term in its subtitle: "Feminist Attacks on

Feminism: Patriarchy's Prodigal Daughters." (Feminist Studies 24.1 [1998]: 159-75.) The truth is, it has been hard to resist the urge to announce that the girls of *Jane* are "today's truest and bravest feminists" (159). Maybe it's my American fetishization of progress and the "new," an angle Minnich argues is "compatible with those [values] of a conservative consumerist culture that exploits images of patriarchally sexualized and gendered fantasies of liberation," and worse, "reanimates patriarchal divisions of 'good girls' from bad feminists" by marketing "an upbeat feminism that promises women can have it all without troubling systemic changes" (166). Yet *Jane Sexes It Up* does resist this patriarchal booby trap, recognizing instead that no single side or position in feminism is all bad or all good; rather each is its own rhetorically and historically marked mix.

4. "The overemphasis on danger runs the risk of making speech about sexual pleasure taboo. Feminists are easily intimidated by the charge that their own pleasure is selfish, as in political rhetoric which suggests that no woman is entitled to talk about sexual pleasure while any woman remains in danger—that is—never." Carole Vance, ed., *Pleasure and Danger: Exploring Female Sexuality* 3rd ed. (London: Pandora, 1992), 6.

5. I refer here to the difference between Greer's early feminist writing ("Lady Love Your Cunt." [*The Madwoman's Underclothes: Essays and Other Occasional Writings* (New York: Atlantic Monthly, 1986), 74-77.] and her most recent [*The Whole Woman,* (New York: Knopf, 1999.)]. In the latter, Greer takes an irresponsibly dismissive tone toward young feminists, defining "post-post-feminism" as "ostentatious sluttishness and disorderly behavior" (9) and quoting Maureen Dowd's criticism of "bimbo feminism" (14). Greer fails to distinguish between Spice Girls and Riot Grrrls, lumping all young sexy things together as she takes aim: "A 'new feminism' that celebrates the right (i.e., duty) to be pretty in an array of floaty dresses and little suits put together for starvation wages by adolescent girls in Asian sweatshops is no feminism at all" (333). Her intended audience is clearly not the generation of girls she castigates, because her powerful critiques of global capitalism or penetration or the medical establishment or whatever

else will certainly be undermined by her sweeping generalizations about us; if she's wrong about this, we wonder, what else is she wrong about? She demotes my generation from wavedom—"The second wave of feminism, rather than having crashed on to the shore, is still far out to sea, slowly and inexorably gathering momentum" (343)—and I can live with that, being part of the second wave, but not as its frothy afterthought.

6. Dworkin's wry commentary often combines frank speech with a stinging humor, for which she is villified by many media-influenced young feminists, but I find much to like in her writing; in response to the simplistic labels applied to feminists debating sexual politics, for instance, she writes, "'Sex-negative' is the current secular *reductio ad absurdum* used to dismiss or discredit ideas, particularly political critiques, that might lead to detumescence." *Intercourse* (New York: Free Press, 1987), 48.

7. In an essay on being a porn consumer and feminist, Sallie Tisdale writes, "I have always just been trying to make peace with my abyssal self, my underworld." "Talk Dirty to Me," in *The Philosophy of Sex: Contemporary Readings*, ed. Alan Soble. 3rd ed. (Lanham: Rowman & Littlefield, 1997), 271-82, 281.

8. Vance, 108-11.

1. *Fuck You & Your Untouchable Face*

1. Celia Kitzinger and Sue Wilkinson, quoted in Lynne Segal, *Straight Sex: Rethinking the Politics of Pleasure* (Berkeley: University of California Press, 1994), 216.

2. The excerpt is taken from a song by Ani Difranco, "Untouchable Face," on *Dilate* (Righteous Babe Records, 1996). The "third wave" of feminism, for the purposes of this book, is situated at the intersection of queer theory, sex-positive feminism, and Generation X; with this definition in mind, I use "third wave" and "Gen-X" interchangeably in this chapter. The foundational links of this movement with Black feminism are addressed in more detail in other collections (see especially Leslie Heywood and Jennifer Drake's *Third Wave Agenda*). Because of

colonial histories of being stereotyped as hypersexual, the articulation of aggressive sexuality by women of color is particularly fraught with personal and cultural complications; however, I received several fascinating proposals on the subject that did not, I am sad to say, materialize into essays. I hope to see work in this area soon. I use "Gen X" to differentiate the third wave feminism forged by women of color in the early eighties from that of the many (primarily white) twenty- and thirtysomethings influenced and guided in the present moment by the writings of these women of color. I employ the term "Gen-X feminist" with reservation, however, recognizing that it places feminism in uncomfortable proximity with the commodification of political resistance (picture a baseball cap reading "No fear"), yet the term usefully specifies the historical context of *Jane Sexes It Up*. In fact, the idea of a generation is in some ways less useful than a historical era, as several contributors fall outside the actual generation's parameters, yet are strongly shaped by Gen-X culture, especially its sex positivism.

3. Kaye Gibbons, *A Virtuous Woman* (New York: Vintage, 1989), 20.

4. The original New Woman emerged in the late nineteenth century, early twentieth—the first wave of United States feminism—in the form of suffragettes and free love feminists.

5. The full quote is, "Perhaps the greatest gift we can give to another human being is detachment. Attachment, even that which imagines it is selfless, always lays some burden on the other person. How to learn to love in such a light, airy way that there is no burden?" May Sarton, *Journal of a Solitude* (New York: Norton, 1973), 201.

6. Elizabeth Wurtzel, *Bitch: In Praise of Difficult Women* (New York: Doubleday, 1998), 408.

7. Julie Burchill, quoted in Sue Wilkinson and Celia Kitzinger. *Heterosexuality: A Feminism & Psychology Reader* (London: Sage, 1993), 22.

8. John Stoltenberg, *Refusing to be a Man: Essays on Sex and Justice.* 2nd ed. (London: UCL, 2000), 10.

9. bell hooks, *Feminism Is for Everybody* (Boston: South End, 2000), 6. The Winter 2000 issue of *Bust* magazine, an alternative to

Cosmopolitan and its ilk, begins its issue-long look at the "F" word with a note from the editor assuring readers that feminism is easy, that "there are as many flavors of feminism as there are feminists" (4). While *Jane Sexes It Up* seeks to expand and attune feminism to the current cultural moment, we would not stretch it so far that it loses all elasticity, preserving the shape and snap of political force.

10. Karen Lehrman, "Feminism & the New Courtship," in *Cosmopolitan* 218.1 (1995): 186-91.

11. Andrea Dworkin, *Intercourse*. (New York: Free, 1987), 72.

12. Lehrman, 186-191.

13. Other *Cosmo* articles indicate a pattern of reassuring women they don't have to change themselves or the world, presenting an *I'm Okay, You're Okay* approach to politics: "Why It's Okay to Want a Man" appears in December 1997, for instance, and "The Backlash Myth" appears in August 1992.

14. Peggy Orenstein, *Flux: Women on Sex, Work, Love, Kids, and Life in a Half-Changed World* (New York: Doubleday, 2000), 25.

15. This letter is a slightly edited version of an email message I wrote to my long-term long-distance lover last summer. I have made minor changes from the original to incorporate some of the subsequent correspondence, as well as to elaborate and reorganize my ideas for the sake of clarity and succinctness.

16. Mikaya Heart, *When the Earth Moves: Women and Orgasm* (Berkeley: Celestial, 1998), 230-31.

17. Okay, so I edited in a poetic flourish. The phrase, "vestibule of the vagina," comes from *The American Heritage Dictionary*'s entry for *vulva*.

18. Reference to *Bend Over, Boyfriend*, a how-to video on anal eroticism, starring Carol Queen and her long-time lover, Robert.

19. Dworkin, *Intercourse*, 130-31.

20. Stoltenberg, *Refusing to Be a Man: Essays on Sex & Justice*, 97.

21. Jessica Baumgardner, "Dysfunction Junction: What's Your Function?" *Nerve.com* (December 2000), http://www.nerve.com/ Regulars/Editors/december00/main.asp. On a related note, Mikaya Heart, in *When the Earth Moves: Women and Orgasm*, reports from a

survey taken in 1993 "that only 29 percent of women regularly have an orgasm with a partner" (153). Despite Meg Ryan's best efforts at consciousness raising for the general movie-going public in her famous fake orgasm scene in the very popular *When Harry Met Sally*, the fact of widespread nonorgasmic sex in women's lives seems to garner minimal media coverage and even less concern in the privacy of monogamous heterosexual relationships; most men I know are astounded to the point of disbelief at the statistics cited above.

22. Judith Levine reflects on the issue of who can speak validly and authoritatively on the subject of heterosexual critique, noting that once "stripped of the social pedigree of Coupled Heterosexual," the feminist critic often loses her privileges of being listened to and possibly believed. "Single," she writes, "I was no longer dispassionately *discussing* man-hating. I might easily be accused of *practicing* it" (10).

23. *Intercourse*, 49.

24. Jennifer Baumgardner and Amy Richards, *Manifesta: Young Women, Feminism, and the Future* (New York: Farrar, Straus, Giroux, 2000), 245.

25. Ibid, 249.

26. As with *Fight Club*, Sublime's aesthetic resists simple feminist rejection as sexist. In the words of *Amazon.com* reviewer Steve Knopper, "There's more to this Long Beach, California trio's debut . . . than white suburban punks imitating Jamaican ska music. The band comes up with great songs . . . and surprisingly progressive lyrics that attack sexism and other social ills . . ." http://www.amazon.com/exec/obidos/ASIN/B0000020ZS/qid=999403837/sr=1-7/ref=sc_m_7/104-6621196-2115961

27. For a fascinating study of how culture produces certain stories to shape and constrain women's behavior, see Judith R. Walkowitz's *City of Dreadful Delight: Narratives of Sexual Danger in Late-Victorian London* (Women in Culture and Society Series. Ed. Catherine R. Stimpson. Chicago: University of Chicago Press, 1992.)

28. Michael Warner, *The Trouble with Normal: Sex, Politics, and the Ethics of Queer Life* (New York: Free, 1999), 18.

29. Ibid, 213.

30. Ibid, 215.

31. Carol Queen, "On Being a Female Submissive (and Doing What You Damn Well Please)," in *Real Live Nude Girl* (San Francisco: Cleis, 1997), 174-76, 175.

32. http://www.echonyc.com/~onissues/s96orgasm. html, World Wide Web 8/1/99.

33. *Intercourse*, 66.

34. Ibid, 125.

35. Caroline Ramazanoglu, "Love and the Politics of Heterosexuality," in *Heterosexuality: A Feminism & Psychology Reader*, eds. Sue Wilkinson and Celia Kitzinger (London: Sage, 1993. 59-61), 60.

36. This dilemma—whether to emphasize choice within one's given situation or to change the situation itself—constitutes a major thread of debate within feminism, what Lynn Chancer calls "the structure versus agency issue": "Should we concentrate on transforming institutionalized power structures with weighty influence, such as the state or the media? Or is it wiser to 'resist' as individual agents, trying to 'subvert' power through personal practices?" Chancer intelligently proposes the alternative option of "both transforming social institutions and asserting individual agency." *Reconcilable Differences: Confronting Beauty, Pornography, and the Future of Feminism* (Berkeley: University of California Press, 1998), 5.

37. *Straight Sex*, 260.

38. Rosalind Coward, *Female Desires: How They Are Sought, Bought & Packaged* (New York: Grove Weidenfeld, 1985), 131.

39. Carol Queen, "The Queer in Me," in *Real Live Nude Girl* (San Francisco: Cleis, 1997), 10-15, 15.

40. Eve Kosofsky Sedgwick, *A Dialogue on Love* (Boston: Beacon, 1999), 130.

41. This list is adapted loosely from chapters in Michael Bronski's *The Pleasure Principle: Sex, Backlash, and the Struggle for Gay Freedom* (New York: St. Martin's, 1998), Linda R. Hirschman and Jane

E. Larson's *Hard Bargains: The Politics of Sex* (Oxford: Oxford University Press, 1998), and Michael Warner's *The Trouble with Normal: Sex, Politics, and the Ethics of Queer Life* (New York: Free, 1999).

3. Sex Cuts

1. Jacque Lacan refers to this enjoyment of excess as *jouissance*.

2. This definition of the word *spill* comes from *Webster's New World College Dictionary*, ed. Victoria Neufeldt and David B. Guralnik, 3rd ed. (New York: Macmillan, 1996), 1291.

3. It is interesting to note that Leda's first name is actually spelled *Letta*, yet without thinking, I spelled it in a way that alludes to Yeats' "Leda and the Swan," revealing an association with the violence of rape.

4. Geoffrey Hartman, "Words and Wounds," in *Saving the Text* (Baltimore: Johns Hopkins University Press, 1985), 123.

5. Jean Clavreul, "The Perverse Couple," in *Returning to Freud: Clinical Psychoanalysis in the School of Lacan*, ed. and trans. Stuart Schneiderman (New Haven: Yale University Press, 1980). As we learn from Jean Clavreul, a Lacanian analyst who writes about the perverse structure, a child first becomes a desiring subject (that is, first enters language) when it realizes that the mother has no penis. Formerly, the child has not known that there is a difference between mother and father, thinking incorrectly that both are equipped with the same bodily accoutrements. The new discovery forces a reinterpretation, which situates the child as the one who did not know. Its new knowledge is thus lodged in a previous not-knowing: to wit, there is a before and an after, out of which come the concepts of past, present, and future. The past involves not knowing; the present involves both a wish to know and the subsequent discovery; and the future entails a relationship between these events or positions with respect to knowledge. The child must learn that someone else (father) knew more about the object of its desire (mother) than it did. This place of nonknowledge with

regard to sex and desire is the place at which the subject locates itself in the signifying chain, a place marked by the desire of the other. In the structure of perversion, however, this discovery of difference is rejected or disavowed. The child refuses to be the one who did not know, refuses to acknowledge that someone else had prior knowledge. What this means in more concrete terms is that the perverse subject refuses to recognize that the mother does not have a penis. By refusing to recognize this absence, the child may then avow its existence elsewhere, in some other part of the body or in some external object. The material object that represents or initiates this disavowal is the fetish.

6. Ibid., 215-33.

7. Lawrence Ferlinghetti, "A Coney Island of the Mind," in *The American Tradition in Literature*, ed. Sculley Bradley et. al., 5th ed., vol. 2 (New York: Random House, 1981), 1988-89.

8. Ibid, lines 13-15.

9. Jacques Lacan, *The Four Fundamental Concepts of Psycho-Analysis*, ed. Jacques-Alain Miller, trans. Alan Sheridan (New York: Norton, 1981), 165-66.

10. Roland Barthes, *The Pleasure of the Text*, trans. Richard Miller (New York: Hill and Wang, 1975), 47.

11. Georges Bataille, *Story of the Eye*, trans. Joachim Neugroschel (New York: Urizen, 1977), 6.

4. *I Learned from the Best*

1. Susan Brownmiller, *Femininity* (New York: Linden Press, 1984), 51.

2. Sandra Bartky, "Skin Deep: Femininity as a Disciplinary Regime," in *Daring to Be Good: Essays in Feminist Ethico-Politics*, eds. Bat-Ami Bar On and Ann Ferguson (New York: Routledge, 1998), 15-27, 17.

3. Leah Lilith Albrecht-Samarashinhaa, "Gender Warriors: An Interview with Amber Hollibaugh," in *Femme: Feminists, Lesbians & Bad Girls* (New York: Routledge, 1997), 210-22, 213.

4. Joan Nestle, "My Mother Liked to Fuck," in *A Restricted Country* (New York: Firebrand, 1987), 121.

5. Judith Roof, "1970s Lesbian Feminism Meets 1990s Butch-Femme," in *Butch-Femme: Inside Lesbian Gender* (London: Cassell, 1998), 27-35.

6. A note on spelling: British Guiana became Guyana after independence.

7. Joan Nestle, "The Femme Question," in *The Persistent Desire: A Femme-Butch Reader* (New York: Alyson, 1992), 138-46.

5. *Cutting, Craving, & the Self I Was Saving*

1. Armando Favazza, *Bodies Under Seige: Self Mutilation in Culture and Psychiatry* (Baltimore: Johns Hopkins University Press, 1987), xii-xiv.

2. Favazza, op. cit.; Jane Wegscheider Hyman, *Women Living with Self-Injury* (Philadelphia: Temply University Press, 1999); Marilee Strong, *A Bright Red Scream* (New York: Penguin, 1998); and Steven Levenkron, *Cutting: Understanding and Overcoming Self-Mutilation* (New York: Norton, 1998).

3. Caroline Kettlewell, *Skin Game: A Memoir* (New York: St. Martin's, 1999); Bob Flannigan, *Sick*, director Kirby Dick, coproducer Sheree Rose (New York: Avalanche Home Entertainment, 1997).

4. I do not mean to suggest that "getting out" is as easy as deciding to do it. This is not the case for many women, and it was not the case for me. The man abusing me did not come after me, nor did I try to confront his abuse through legal channels. The fact that I got away so easily sometimes makes me reluctant to call my experiences "abusive." My story is useful only if taken in context, not as a typical or even an atypical story of violence against women in general. My story is related to the stories of other women, but it is not another woman's story. Do not draw generalized conclusions from it.

5. I also enjoy reading novels, poems, theory, and pornography by women and men who have the same obsessions with their own exposed insides, with violence against themselves and others, and the

thin line between pleasure and pain. Something of the original relief maintains itself in the metaphor, the distant image, the staged, excessive scene. I am thinking of everything by Kathy Acker, some things by Sharon Olds and Ai, Toni Morrison's *Paradise*, Judith Butler and Kaja Silverman when I'm feeling cerebral, the more progressive S&M stuff and especially lesbian S&M—Pat Califia and SAMOIS—Jeanette Winterson, Georges Bataille.

6. Favazza, op. cit., 148.

6. *Of the Flesh Fancy*

1. Lisa Palac, *The Edge of the Bed: How Dirty Pictures Changed My Life* (Boston: Little, Brown, 1998), 135-42.

2. Jessica Benjamin, *The Bonds of Love: Psychoanalysis, Feminism and the Problems of Domination* (New York: Pantheon Books, 1998).

3. Sandra Bartky, *Femininity & Domination* (New York: Routledge, 1990).

4. Ibid.; and Carol Queen, *Pomosexuals* (San Francisco: Cleis Press, 1997).

5. Amber Hollibaugh.

6. Naomi Wolf, *Promiscuities: The Secret Struggle for Womanhood* (New York: Random House, 1997).

7. Lisa Palac, op. cit.

8. Carol Queen, *Real Live Nude Girl* (San Francisco: Cleiss Press, 1997), 170, 172.

7. *The Feminist Wife?*

1. Stacey D'Erasmo, "Single File: Why do the Sexy, Savvy New Heroines Want Nothing So Much as Rings on Their Fingers?" in *New York Times Magazine,* 29 August 1999, 13-14.

2. Jessica Benjamin, *The Bonds of Love: Psychoanalysis, Feminism and the Problems of Domination* (New York: Norton), 221.

3. Leslie Heywood and Jennifer Drake, eds., *Third Wave Agenda:*

Being Feminist, Doing Feminism (Minneapolis: University of Minnesota Press, 1997).

4. Anatasia Toufexis, "When The Ring Doesn't Fit . . . ," in *Psychology Today,* November/December 1996.

5. Ibid., 52.

6. Susan J. Wells, "What Happens if Harriet Makes More Money Than Ozzie?" in the *New York Times,* 1 August 1999, BU, 10.

7. Marcelle Clements, *The Improvised Woman: Single Women Reinventing Single Life* (New York: Pantheon Books, 1998).

8. Ibid., 21.

9. Ibid., 21.

10. Elizabeth Wurtzel, *Bitch: In Praise of Difficult Women* (New York: Henry Holt, 1997), 148.

11. Clements, op.cit.

12. Mark Caldwell, *A Short History of Rudeness: Manners, Morals, and Misbehavior in Modern America* (New York: Picador, 1999), 108.

13. bell hooks, *Wounds of Passion: A Writing Life* (New York: Henry Holt, 1997), 148.

8. *Stripping, Starving, & the Politics of Ambiguous Pleasure*

1. Over the past two decades of "sex wars" in feminism, there have been many different feminist positions offered in the theoretical analysis of sex work, and although I have addressed these debates in more depth elsewhere, I do not do so in this article. Further, while I discuss the concept of resistance here, I do not specifically focus on the many *overt* forms of political resistance taken up by sex workers: the multifaceted international sex workers' rights movement, sex worker involvement in community struggles over repressive laws and regulations, or the expressly political writings of self-identified (sometimes feminist) sex workers. I examine my resistant performances of gender as a stripper, then, as one small corner of the field of scholarship on sex worker activism.

2. Simone de Beauvoir (femininity as the adoption of an idealized identity), Joan Rivere (femininity as a defense against anxiety), Luce Irigaray (femininity as mimetic strategy), and Judith Butler (whose oft-cited concept of performativity has been extremely influential in reconceiving gender as an imitation of an ideal for which there is no "original," to name four major theorists of this philosophical concept.

3. Jane Ussher, *Fantasies of Femininity: Reframing the Boundaries of Sex* (New Brunswick: Rutgers University Press, 1992), 355.

4. Ibid, 356.

5. Ibid, 361.

6. Ibid, 363.

7. Ibid, 366.

8. Ibid, 367.

9. Vicki Funari, "Naked, Naughty, Nasty: Peep Show Reflections," in *Whores and Other Feminists*, ed. Jill Nagle (New York: Routledge, 1997), 19-35, 34.

10. Sex workers have been accepted by some theorists as "queers," whose work contests the heteronormative economy's mystification of exchanging money for sex in order to make marriage seem morally right rather than fiscally strategic.

11. Catherine Waggoner, "The Emancipatory Potential of Feminine Masquerade in Mary Kay Cosmetics," in *Text and Performance Quarterly* 17 (1997): 256-72, 263.

12. Eva Pendleton, "Love for Sale," in *Whores and Other Feminists*, ed. Jill Nagle (New York: Routledge, 1997), 73-82, 76.

13. Ibid, 79.

14. Jacqueline Zita, *Body Talk: Philsophical Reflections on Sex and Gender* (New York: Columbia University Press, 1998), 115-117.

15. Susan Bordo, *Unbearable Weight: Feminism, Western Culture, and the Body* (Berkeley: California University Press, 1993), 156.

16. Ibid, 159.

17. Ibid, 184.

18. Beverly Skeggs, *Formations of Class and Gender: Becoming Respectable* (Thousand Oaks: Sage, 1997), 8.

19. Ibid, 99.

20. Ibid, 100.

21. Ibid, 115.

22. Ibid, 102

23. Feminist theorist Teresa Ebert (*Ludic Feminism and After: Postmodernism, Desire and Labor in Late Capitalism*) has vehemently criticized feminists for focusing on issues like "'performing' and 'remetaphorizing' difference, for 'power feminism,' and for 'sexual-agency feminism.'" "Ludic" (playful) feminist theory, she believes, distances itself from issues of economics, labor, production, and exploitation. For Ebert, ludic feminism becomes, "in its *effects*, if not in its intentions," one in which "politics as collective action for emancipation is abandoned." While I appreciate Ebert's work, and despite the limitations I've explored in this section, I believe there is need for both kinds of analyses. (Ann Arbor: Michigan University Press, 1996).

24. Ussher, 372.

25. Merri Lisa Johnson, "Pole Work: Autoethnography of a Strip Club," in *Sexuality and Culture* (1999), 149-157, 155. I am drawn to Johnson's assertion: "What I have learned is that the work and fun and self-expression we dancers engage in is not about the men seated around the stage . . . We merely borrow men's eyes to complete the scene of our grand larceny, the thieving of new personas and a corner of cultural space in which to enact them" (156). We are never completely captured by their gaze.

26. Brooks, *The Centerfold Syndrome: How Men Can Overcome Objectification and Achieve Intimacy with Women* (San Francisco: Jossey Bass, 1995), 5.

27. Nagle, op. cit.

28. Johnson, op. cit.

9. *Co-Ed Call Girls*

1. Carol Queen, "Sex Radical Politics, Sex-Positive Feminist Thought, and Whore Stigma," in *Whores and Other Feminists,* ed. Jill Nagle (New York and London: Routledge, 1997), 133.

2. Ibid., 184.

Notes

3. In this paper, I use the words *whore, prostitute*, and *sex worker* interchangeably. This use reflects the work of many in the prostitutes' rights campaign, with whom I am aligned politically. *Sex worker* refers to any man or woman working in any part of the sex industry (pornographer, telephone operator, cybersex participant, prostitutes, erotic dancers). This blanket term insists on the labor involved in sexual service and is generally attributed to Carol Leigh and the 1987 publication *Sex Work. Whore*, a term traditionally used to insult and degrade all women, whether working as prostitutes or not, has been reclaimed and resignified by the prostitutes' rights movement in much the same way and for many of the reasons as, for example, the use of *queer* has within the gay and lesbian political movements. I generally refer to the Madison sex workers as *escorts* rather than *prostitutes* and *whores*; they identified themselves this way, and I don't want to give them labels they never used. I also tend to refer to the women as *girls*, this again reflects their use.

4. Andrea Dworkin, *Pornography: Men Possessing Women* (New York: Perigree Books, 1981), 203.

5. Wendy Chapkis, *Live Sex Acts: Women Performing Erotic Labor* (New York: Routledge, 1997), 26.

6. The theoretical underpinnings of this essay are drawn from both performativity and performance in everyday life models. *Performativity* has been used to describe the relations between individuals and society, and between individuals and other individuals. Judith Butler defines this kind of performativity as "not as a singular or deliberate 'act,' but rather, as the reiterative and citational practice by which discourse produces the effects that it names" (2). This use of performativity owes much to J.L. Austin's speech act theory. Austin claims there are two kinds of speech: constative speech is language that describes reality, that merely states something, and performative speech is language that performs an action, that calls a set of conditions into being. Further, for performative language to occur both parties must recognize that a set of conditions has been called into being. Performative language depends on the collective acceptance of the parties involved. Performance in everyday life, on the other hand, draws from the mod-

els of human interaction suggested by Erving Goffman in *The Presentation of Self in Everyday Life* (Garden City: Doubleday, Anchor Books, 1959). For Goffman and others who have developed his models, performance in everyday life refers to the social roles people adopt in order to influence others and convince them of their competence, trustworthiness, character, and purpose. In short, everyone engages in role-playing and performance in their interactions with others. Feminists have adopted performance and performativity models in order to call attention to the constructed nature of gender; for example, Riot Grrls zines such as *Bust* and *UpSlut* celebrate the accessories of girl culture, such as make-up, high heels, and lingerie while insisting on feminine power and autonomy.

7. Carol Leigh, "The Continuing Saga of Scarlot Harlot I," in *Sex Work: Writings by Women in the Sex Industry*. ed. Frederique Delacoste and Priscilla Alexander (Pittsburgh and San Francisco: Cleis Press, 1998), 34.

8. Kevin owns Exploits, Inc. I spoke with seven of his girls: Lesley, Kristeen, Ashlee, Amanda, Alex, Jodi, and Carrie. Darrell and Dwayne run Private Entertainment and allowed me to interview Cheri, their top booker. I spoke with Meshella, the owner of Luxuries, and Bonnie who runs a strip service. My sample is admittedly small; there are only a handful of agencies in Madison, and many girls refused to be interviewed. I conducted these interviews over the phone, in the escorts' homes, agency offices, and a local shopping mall. Because so many of the girls were worried about anonymity and privacy, I took very few notes during the interviews, and tape-recorded nothing. I wrote up the interviews from memory immediately after talking to the escorts and agency owners. Necessarily then, the conversations contained within this essay are reconstructed as well. All of the names of clients, sex workers, and agencies have been changed for considerations of privacy.

9. Goffman, *The Presentation of Self in Everyday Life*, 22-24.

10. Ibid., 112.

11. Margo St. James, "The Reclamation of Whores," in *Good Girls/Bad Girls: Feminists and Sex Trade Workers Face to Face*. ed. Laurie Bell (Toronto: Seal Press, 1987), 82.

12. Rebecca Walker, "Lusting for Freedom," in *Listen Up: Voices from the Next Feminist Generation.* ed. Barbara Findlen (Seattle: Seal Press, 1995), 94.

10. *The Plain-Clothes Whore*

1. Shannon Bell, *Reading, Writing, and Rewriting the Prostitute Body* (Indianapolis: Indiana University Press, 1994), 109.

2. Linda R. Hirschman and Jane E. Larson, *Hard Bargains: The Politics of Sex* (Oxford: Oxford University Press, 1998.)

3. I am indebted for this point to Merri Lisa Johnson's essay on being an academic feminist and a stripper. She writes, "The separation of sexuality and scholarship in both these places feels uncomfortable, and at times I think I cannot stand the incompatibility of my selves. But there is nowhere else to go. There is no place where my parts will fit seamlessly together" (153). "Pole Work: Autoethnography of a Strip Club," in *Sexuality & Culture* 2 (1998): 149-57.

11. *Autobiography of a Flea*

1. *The Autobiography of a Flea, told in a Hop, Skip, and Jump, and Recounting all his Experiences of Human and Superhuman Kind, both Male and Female; with his curious Connections, Backbitings and Tickling Touches; the whole scratched together for the delectation of the delicate, and for the Information of the Inquisitive, etc.* (1887, reprint; New York: Carol & Graf, 1983), 190-191.

2. *A Study of the Century: Sweet Seventeen, the True Story of a Daughter's Awful Whipping and its Delightful if Direful Consequences,* issued for the subscribers only (Paris: Charles Carrington, 1910), 35.

3. Ibid, 37.

4. Walter Kendrick, *The Secret Museum: Pornography in Modern Culture* (New York: Viking Press, 1987).

5. *The Vigilance Record* 5 (May 1902): 39.

6. Nicola Beisel, *Imperiled Innocents: Anthony Comstock and*

Family Reproduction in Victorian America (Princeton: Princeton University Press, 1997).

7. Joan Hoff, "Why Is There No History of Pornography?" in *For Adult Users Only: The Dilemma of Violent Pornography*, ed. Susan Guber and Joan Hoff (Bloomington: University of Indiana Press, 1989), 17-46.

8. Nadine Strossen, *Defending Pornography: Free Speech, Sex, and the Fight for Women's Rights* (New York: Scribner, 1995), 15.

9. Pat Califia, *Public Sex: The Culture of Radical Sex* (Pittsburgh: Cleis Press, 1994), 107.

10. Catherine A. MacKinnon, *Only Words* (Cambridge: Harvard University Press, 1993), 3.

11. Kate Ellis, Barbara O'Dare, and Abbey Tallmer, "Introduction" in *Caught Looking: Feminism, Pornography, & Censorship* (Seattle: The Red Comet Press, 1988), 6.

12. MacKinnon, op. cit.

12. *Vulvodynia*

1. Kegan Doyle and Danny Lancombe, "Porn Power: Sex, Violence, and the Meaning of Images in 1980's Feminism," in *"Bad Girls"/"Good Girls": Women, Sex, and Power in the Nineties*, eds. Nan Bauer and Donna Perry (New Brunswick: Rutgers University Press, 1996), 195-96.

2. Ibid, 198.

3. Nadine Strossen, *Defending Pornography* (New York: Scribner, 1995), 111, 161.

4. Sallie Tisdale, "Talk Dirty to Me," in *The Philosophy of Sex: Contemporary Readings*, ed. Alan Soble. 3rd ed. (Lanham: Rowman and Littlefield, 1997), 271-282, 279.

5. Andrea Dworkin, *Pornography: Men Possessing Women* (New York: Plume, 1989), 25.

6. Ellen Willis, "Feminism, Moralism, and Pornography," in *Powers of Desire: The Politics of Sexuality*, eds. Ann Snitow, Christine Stansell, and Sharon Thompson (New York: Monthly Review, 1983), 460-67, 464.

7. Ibid.

8. Lynn Segal, *Straight Sex: Rethinking the Politics of Pleasure* (London: Virago, 1994), 104.

13. *The Importance of Being Lester*

1. Varda Burstyn, *The Rites of Men: Manhood, Politics, and the Culture of Sport* (Toronto: University of Toronto Press, 1999), 267.

2. Ibid, xii.

3. Susan K. Cahn, *Coming on Strong: Gender and Sexuality in Twentieth Century Women's Sport* (Cambridge: Harvard University Press, 1994), 4.

4. Ibid, 4.

5. Annalee Newitz, et al, "Masculinity Without Men: Women Reconciling Feminism and Male Identification," in *Third Wave Agenda: Being Feminist, Doing Feminism*, eds. Leslie Heywood and Jennifer Drake (Minneapolis: University of Minnesota Press, 1997), 178.

6. Judith Halberstam, *Female Masculinity* (Durham and London: Duke University Press, 1998), 58.

14. *A Cock of One's Own*

1. Tamsin Wilton, *Finger Licking Good: The Ins and Outs of Lesbian Sex* (London: Cassell, 1995), 38.

2. Charlotte Ashton, "Getting Hold of the Phallus: 'Post-Lesbian' Power Negotiations," in *Assaults on Convention: Essays on Lesbian Transgressors*, eds. Nicola Godwin, Belinda Hollows, and Sheridan Nye (London: Cassell, 1996), 161.

3. Although the belief that dildos are inherently negative for women is most notably found in radical feminist and lesbian feminist theory, antidildo ideology can be found throughout the feminist continuum. Similarly, prodildo ideology is not necessarily restricted to postmodern feminism. I created the terms "antidildo feminist" and "prodildo feminist" in order to be as specific as possible, avoiding the problem-

atic "anti-sex"/"pro-sex" terminology that is typically used to describe the feminist sex wars (see Wilton's *Lesbian Studies*), and differentiating the dildo issue from other parts of this debate.

4. Andrea Dworkin, *Intercourse* (New York: Free, 1987), 63.

5. Ibid, 133.

6. Wilton, 200.

7. Sheila Jeffreys, *The Lesbian Heresy: A Feminist Perspective on the Sexual Revolution* (North Melbourne: Spinifex, 1993), 28.

8. "Solo-sexual" refers to women who do not engage in sex with others but do not define themselves as celibate because they engage in sexual play with themselves.

9. Jeffreys, 20.

10. Wilton, 7.

11. Ibid, 9.

12. Sheila Jeffreys, *Anti-Climax: A Feminist Perspective on the Sexual Revolution* (London: The Woman's Press, 1990), 313.

13. Davina Cooper, *Power in Struggle: Feminism, Sexuality, and the State* (New York: New York University Press, 1995), 126.

14. For example, lesbian feminism's critique of heterosexuality (see Adrienne Rich's essay on "Compulsory Heterosexuality") provides a clear analysis of heterosexuality as a social construction (rather than "natural" human inclination), but it does not offer any theories of how to change the institution of heterosexuality, nor does it account for the possibility of women who truly do desire a heterosexual relationship.

15. Wilton suggests that the popularity of antidildo ideology in the media alienates young women of all sexual orientations (*Finger Licking Good*, 1-3), a position affirmed by Carol Smart in *Theorizing Heterosexuality: Telling It Straight*, ed. Diane Richardson (Buckingham: Open University Press, 1996), 174-175.

16. Smart, 174.

17. *On Our Backs* is a lesbian sex magazine, featuring nude centerfolds, sex advice and tips, and erotic fiction. The magazine is very controversial in both lesbian and feminist communities. This letter appeared in the Dec/Jan issue of 1999, 6.

18. For a great analysis of power relations in sexuality, see Pat

Califia's "Feminism and Sadomasochism," in *Public Sex* (Pittsburgh: Cleis, 1994), where she explains how "dominant" does not necessarily correlate to "oppressive" and vice versa.

19. Wilton, *Finger Licking Good*, 201. Cherry Smyth, *Lesbians Talk Queer Notions* (London: Scarlet, 1992), 43.

20. Wilton, 201.

21. Colleen Lamos, "The Postmodern Lesbian Position: *On Our Backs*," in *The Lesbian Postmodern*. ed. Laura Doan (New York: Holt, Rinehart, & Winston, 1982), 95.

22. Diane Richardson, "Heterosexuality and Social Theory," *Theorizing Heterosexuality*, 7-9. Jeffreys, *The Lesbian Heresy*, 17-18. Wilton, *Finger-Licking Good*, 196-97.

23. Panati, 74.

24. Carol Queen, *Real Live Nude Girl: Chronicles of Sex-Positive Culture* (San Francisco: Cleis, 1997), 162. Susie Bright, "Interview," in *Angry Women* (San Francisco: Re/Search Publications, 1991), 216. Good Vibrations was the first feminist sex toy boutique, founded in 1977. It is located in San Francisco, California.

25. Ibid, 216.

26. Richardson, 8.

15. *Pearl Necklace*

1. Segal, Lynne, *Straight Sex: Rethinking the Politics of Pleasure* (London: Virago, 1994), 238.

2. Jean Grimshaw, "Ethics, Fantasy and Self-Transformation," in *The Philosophy of Sex: Contemporary Readings*, ed. Alan Soble. 3rd ed. (Lanham: Rowman & Littlefield, 1997. 175-88), 175.

3. Ibid, 176.

4. Ibid, 178.

5. Ibid, 179.

6. Ibid, 181.

7. Ibid, 182-183.

8. Emilie Buchwald, et al., define "rape culture" as "a complex set

of beliefs that encourages male sexual aggression and supports violence against women. It is a society where violence is seen as sexy and sexuality as violent. In a rape culture women perceive a continuum of threatened violence that ranges from sexual remarks to sexual touching to rape itself. A rape culture condones physical and emotional terrorism against women *as the norm*" (vii). *Transforming a Rape Culture*, eds. Emilie Buchwald, Pamela R. Fletcher, and Martha Roth (Minneapolis: Milkweed, 1993).

9. bell hooks, "Seduced by Violence No More," in *Outlaw Culture: Resisting Representations* (New York: Routledge, 1994), 109-13, 111.

10. Ibid, 112-13.

11. Alice Echols, "The Taming of the Id: Feminist Sexual Politics, 1968-83," in *Pleasure and Danger: Exploring Female Sexuality*, ed. Carole Vance (London: Pandora, 1992), 50-72, 53.

12. Ibid, 59.

13. Ibid, 64.

14. Tricia Warden, "Shhhhh," in *Dick for a Day: What Would You Do If You Had One?* ed. Fiona Giles (New York: Villard, 1997), 148.

15. Senator Sin, "1-800-YOR-DICK." (Giles 31-45), 35.

16. Kate Bornstein, "Queer Theory and Shopping: Dichotomy or Symbionts?" in *Pomosexuals: Challenging Assumptions About Gender and Sexuality*, eds. Carol Queen and Lawrence Schimel (San Francisco: Cleis, 1997), 13-17, 16.

17. Ibid, 16-17.

18. "I think many of us who take the label bisexual waver back and forth a great deal, wondering if indeed we are bisexual enough . . ." Elizabeth Reba Weise, "Bisexuality, *The Rocky Horror Picture Show*, and Me," in *Bi Any Other Name: Bisexual People Speak Out*, eds. Loraine Hutchins and Lani Kaahumanu (Los Angeles: Alyson, 1991), 134-39, 138.

19. Marjorie Garber, "Extracts from *Vice Versa: Bisexuality and the Eroticism of Everyday Life* (1995)," in *Bisexuality: A Critical Reader*, ed. Merl Storr (London: Routledge, 1999), 138-43, 141.

20. Amber Hollibaugh. "Desire for the Future: Radical Hope in

Passion and Pleasure," in *Pleasure and Danger: Exploring Female Sexuality,* ed. Carole Vance (Boston: Routledge, 1984), 401-10, 404.

21. Vance, 19.

22. Mikaya Heart, *When the Earth Moves: Women and Orgasm,* (Berkeley: Celestial Arts, 1998), 9.

23. Sandra Bartky takes the word "sex-print" from Ethel Specter Person, who defines it as "an individualized script that elicits erotic desire," an "individual's erotic signature." *Femininity and Domination* (New York: Routledge, 1990), 58.

16. *Liquid Fire*

1. Sigmund Freud, *Civilization and Its Discontents,* trans. James Strachey (New York: Norton, 1961), 42.

2. Ibid.

3. Georges Bataille, "Madame Edwarda," in *The Bataille Reader,* eds. Fred Botting and Scott Wilson (Oxford: Blackwell, 1997), 228.

4. Ibid, 234.

5. Ibid, 235.

6. Aristotle, "De Generation Animalium," in *The Complete Works of Aristotle,* trans. Arthur Platt, eds. J. A. Smith and W. D. Ross (Oxford: Claredon, 1912), paragraph 728a.

7. Paul Brandt, *Sexual Life in Ancient Greece,* trans. J. H. Freese (New York: Barnes & Noble, Inc., 1963), 398.

8. Shannon Bell, *Whore Carnival,* (Brooklyn: Autonomedia, 1995), 273.

9. Ibid, 273-74.

10. Barbara Carrellas, "Shannon Bell: Squirting with Shannon," in *Over* 40 (2000): 71-2.

11. Richard von Krafft-Ebing, *Psychopathia Sexualis,* trans. Franklin S. Klaf (New York: Stein & Day, 1965), 265.

12. Steven Marcus, *The Other Victorians: A Study of Sexuality and Pornography in Mid-Nineteenth Century England* (New York: Basic Books).

13. See *The Journal of Sex Research.*

14. Sigmund Freud, *Case Histories I "Dora" and "Little Hans,"* trans. Alix and James Strachey (Great Britain: Penguin, 1977), 121.

15. Sigmund Freud and Joseph Breur, *Studies on Hysteria,* trans. James & Alix Strachey (Great Britain: Penguin, 1983), 102.

16. Freud (1977), 156.

17. Here are various references that might be of interest: Film: Fatale Video, *Clips*; Kath Daymond, *Nice Girls Don't Do It*; Fatale Video, *How to Female Ejaculate*; Annie Sprinkle, *Sluts ad Goddesses Video Workshop*; House of Chicks (Dorrie Lane), *Magic of Female Ejaculation*. Audio: Canadian Broadcasting Corporation Naitonal Radio Program, "Ideas: One Sex or Two?" I do an audio-ejaculation—the listener hears the furious velocity of the spray leaving my urethra and the piercing twang of the flame of water arriving on a mirror surface. Print: I have published articles and pictures in a number of porn magazines for lesbians (*Rites, Bad Attitudes, Lickerish*) and for straight women (*Cupido, Spectator, Adam, Over Forty*), and I've written performative essays for two books of pop culture, *The Hysterical Male* and *Whore Carnival*. Debi Sundahl addressed a number of questions concerning female ejaculation in her regular *On Our Backs* advice column "Ask Fanny" throughout the early to mid-90s; Cathy Winks has written an excellent Good Vibrations Guide book, *The G-Spot*, and most recently, Rebecca Chalker, an original member of the Federation of Feminist Women's Health Centers, has written *the* definitive feminist book on the clitoris and female ejaculation, appropriately titled *The Clitoral Truth*.

17. *The Absolutely True & Queer Confessions of Boy Jane, Dick Lover*

1. Sigmund Freud, *Three Essays on the Theory of Sexuality*, trans. James Strachey (New York: Basic, 1962), 117.

2. See Constance Penley and Sharon Willis, eds. *Male Trouble* (Minneapolis: University of Minnesota Press, 1993).

3. This idiomatic expression refers to David Savran's *Taking It Like*

a Man: White Masculinity, Masochism, and Contemporary American Culture. Although I disagree with Savran's conclusion that queer theory offers "strictly individualistic" forms of resistance (239), I share his concern with the limits of queer resignification to deconstruct the gendered power hierarchy. (Princeton: Princeton University Press, 1998.)

4. Freud, *Three Essays*, 23.

5. Ibid, 24.

6. My reference to the anus as "boy-pussy" is not a product of my own fashioning, for the term exists within certain gay speech communities. Given, however, that women also have anuses, as Eve Sedgwick, *Tendencies* (Durham: Duke University Press, 1993), has pointed out within the context of queer theory, I can only wonder about this idiomatic expression and how it marks gay male bodies as having feminine apertures that beg for penetration while simultaneously problematizing the inherent threat or lack these apertures contain through the presence of the penis. (Durham: Duke University Press, 1993.)

7. Susan Faludi's *Stiffed: The Betrayal of the American Man* (New York: William & Morrow, 1999) offers a problematic examination of the "failure" of American masculinity, seeming to mourn men's loss of phallic authority; unlike her compelling best-seller, *Backlash*, *Stiffed* resists analysis of masculinity based on relationships of subordination and domination in favor of sympathetic documentation of men's perceived disempowerment within a bureaucratized post-Cold War America. Faludi absolves men of accountability for remaining locations of privilege and, further, she leaves blank the role feminism could play in reformulating masculinity as something other than sadistic or masochistic—beyond either *stiff* or *stiffed*.

8. Gayle S. Rubin, "Thinking Sex: Notes for a Radical Theory of the Politics of Sexuality" in *The Lesbian and Gay Studies Reader*, ed. Henry Abelove, Michèle Aina Barale, and David Halperin (New York: Routledge, 1993. 3-43), 32.

Bibliography

Alexander, Priscilla. "Prostitution: *Still* a Difficult Issue." *Sex Work: Writings by Women in the Sex Industry*. Ed. Frederique Delacoste and Priscilla Alexander. Pittsburgh and San Francisco: Cleis Press, 1998. 184-230.

Allison, Dorothy. *Bastard out of Carolina*. New York: Plume, 1983.

———, "Public Silence, Private Terror." *Pleasure and Danger: Exploring Female Sexuality*. Ed. Carole Vance. Boston: Routeledge, 1984. 103-14.

Aristotle. *The Complete Works of Aristotle*, eds. J. A. Smith & W. D. Ross. Oxford: The Claredin Press, 1912.

Austin, J. L. *How to Do Things with Words*. Cambridge: Harvard University Press, 1962.

Barry, Kathleen. *Female Sexual Slavery*. New York: Avon Books, 1979.

Barthes, Roland. *The Pleasure of the Text*, trans. Richard Miller. New York: Hill and Wang, 1975.

Bartky, Sandra Lee. *Femininity and Domination: Studies in the Phenomenology of Oppression*. New York: Routledge, 1990.

Bataille, Georges. *Story of the Eye*, trans. Joachim Neugroschel. New York: Urizen Books, 1977.

Baumgardner, Jennifer and Amy Richards. *Manifesta*. New York: Farrar, Straus and Giroux, 2000.

Baumgardner, Jessica. "Dysfunction Junction: What's Your Function?" *Nerve.com* (December 2000).

de Beauvoir, Simone. *The Second Sex*. New York: Vintage Books, 1989.

Bell, Laurie, ed. *Good Girls/Bad Girls: Feminists and Sex Trade Workers Face to Face*. Toronto: Seal Press, 1987.

Bell, Shannon. *Reading, Writing, and Rewriting the Prostitute Body*. Indianapolis: Indiana University Press, 1994.

———. *Whore Carnival*. Brooklyn: Automedia, 1995.

Benamou, Michel and Charles Caramello, eds. *Performance in Postmodern Culture*. Madison: Coda Press, Inc., 1977.

Benjamin, Jessica. *The Bonds of Love: Psychoanalysis, Feminism and the Problems of Domination*. New York: Pantheon Books, 1998.

Bordo, Susan. *The Male Body: A New Look at Men in Public and in Private*. New York: Farrar, Straus and Giroux, 1999.

———. *Unbearable Weight: Feminism, Western Culture, and the Body*. Berkeley: University of California Press, 1993.

Botting, Fred and Scott Wilson, eds. *The Bataille Reader*. Oxford: Blackwell Publishers, 1989.

Bradley, Sculley et. al., eds. *The American Tradition in Literature*, 5th ed., vol. 2. New York: Random House, 1981.

Brame, Dr. Gloria G. *Come Hither: A Commonsense Guide to Kinky Sex*. New York: Simon & Schuster, 2000.

Brown, Lyn Mikel. *Raising Their Voices: The Politics of Girls' Anger*. Cambridge: Harvard University Press, 1998.

Brown, Lyn Mikel, and Carol Gilligan. *Meeting at the Crossroads: Women's Psychology and Girls' Development*. Cambridge: Harvard University Press, 1992.

Brownmiller, Susan. *Femininity*. New York: Simon & Schuster, 1984.

Bibliography

Buchwald Emilie, Pamela Fletcher, and Martha Roth. *Transforming a Rape Culture*. Minneapolis: Milkweed, 1993.

Bullough, Vern and Bonnie Bullough. *Women and Prostitution: A Social History*. Buffalo: Prometheus Books, 1987.

Burstyn, Varda. *The Rites of Men: Manhood, Politics, and the Culture of Sport*. Toronto: University of Toronto Press, 1999.

Butler, Judith. *Bodies that Matter: On the Discursive Limits of "Sex."* New York: Routledge, 1993.

———. *Gender Trouble*. New York: Routledge, 1990.

Cahn, Susan K. *Coming on Strong: Gender and Sexuality in Twentieth Century Women's Sport*. Cambridge: Harvard University Press, 1994.

Caldwell, Mark. *A Short History of Rudeness: Manners, Morals, and Misbehavior in Modern America*. New York: Picador, 1999.

Califa, Pat. *Public Sex: The Culture of Radical Sex*. San Francisco: Cleis Press, 1994.

———. "Feminism & Sadomasochism." *Feminism & Sexuality: A Reader*. Eds. Stevi Jackson and Sue Scott. New York: Columbia University Press, 1996.

Chalker, Rebecca. *The Clitoral Truth: The Secret World at Your Fingertips*. New York: Seven Stories, 2000.

Chancer, Lynn. *Reconcilable Differences: Confronting Beauty, Pornography, and the Future of Feminism*. Berkeley: University of California Press, 1998.

Chapkis, Wendy. *Live Sex Acts: Women Performing Erotic Labor*. New York: Routledge, 1997.

Chesler, Phyllis. *Letters to a Young Feminist*. New York: Four Walls Eight Windows, 1999.

Clavreul, Jean. "The Perverse Couple." *Returning to Freud: Clinical Psychoanalysis in the School of Lacan*. Ed. and trans. Stuart Schneiderman. New Haven: Yale University Press, 1980.

Clements, Marcelle. *The Improvised Woman: Single Women Reinventing Single Life*. New York: W.W. Norton & Company, 1998.

Cooper, Davina. *Power in Struggle: Feminism, Sexuality, and the State.* New York: New York University Press, 1995.

Coward, Rosalind. *Female Desires: How They are Sought, Bought and Packaged.* New York: Grove Press, 1985.

Delacoste, Frederique and Priscilla Alexander, eds. *Sex Work: Writings by Women in the Sex Industry.* Pittsburgh: Cleis Press, 1998.

Dimen, Muriel. "Politially Correct? Politically Incorrect?" *Pleasure and Danger: Exploring Female Sexuality.* Ed. Carole Vance. Boston: Routledge, 1984. 138-48.

Doza, Christine. "Bloodlove." *Listen Up: Voices from the Next Feminist Generation.* Ed. Barbara Findlen. Seattle: Seal Press, 1995. 249-257.

Dworkin, Andrea. *Intercourse.* New York: Free Press, 1987.

———. *Pornography: Men Possessing Women.* New York: Perigree Books, 1981.

———. *Womanhating.* New York: Penguin, 1974.

Echols, Alice. "The Taming of the Id: Feminist Sexual Politics, 1968-83." *Pleasure and Danger: Exploring Female Sexuality.* Ed. Carole Vance. Boston: Routledge, 1984. 50-72.

Elias, James E., Vern.L. Bullough, Veronica Elias, and Gwen Brewer, eds. *Prostitution: On Whores, Hustlers, and Johns.* New York: Prometheus Books, 1998.

Faludi, Susan. *Stiffed: The Betrayal of the American Man.* New York: William Morrow & Company, 1999.

Favazza, Armando. *Bodies Under Siege: Self Mutilation in Culture and Psychiatry.* Baltimore: Johns Hopkins University Press, 1987.

Federation of Feminist Women's Heath Centers. *A New View of A Woman's Body.* West Hollywood, CA: Feminist Heath Press, 1991.

Feinberg, Leslie. *Transgender Nation: Making History from Joan of Arc to Dennis Rodman.* Boston: Beacon, 1996.

Findlen, Barbara, ed. *Listen Up: Voices from the Next Feminist Generation.* Seattle: Seal Press, 1995.

Foucault, Michel. *The History of Sexuality: An Introduction.* Vol. 1. New York: Vintage, 1978.

Bibliography

Freud, Sigmond. *Civilization and Its Discontents*. New York: Norton, 1989.

Friday, Nancy. *My Secret Garden*. New York: Pocket Books, 1998.

———. *Women on Top: How Real Life Has Changed Women's Fantasies*. New York: Pocket Books, 1993.

Funari, Vicki. "Naked, Naughty, Nasty: Peep Show Reflections." *Whores and Other Feminists*. Ed. Jill Nagle. New York: Routledge, 1997.

Gallop, Jane, ed. *Pedagogy: The Question of Impersonation*. Bloomington: Indiana University Press, 1995.

Garber, Marjorie. "Extracts from *Vice Versa: Bisexuality and the Eroticism of Everyday Life*." *Bisexuality: A Critical Reader*. Ed. Merl Storr. London: Routledge, 1999. 138-43.

Giles, Fiona, ed. *Dick For a Day: What Would You Do if You Had One?* New York: Villard Books, 1997.

Goffman, Erving. *The Presentation of Self in Everyday Life*. Garden City: Doubleday, Anchor Books, 1959.

Greer, Germaine. "Lady Love Your Cunt." *The Madwoman's Underclothes: Essays and Other Occasional Writings*. New York: Atlantic, 1986. 74-77.

———. *The Whole Woman*. New York: Doubleday, 1999.

Halberstam, Judith. *Female Masculinity*. Durham: Duke University Press, 1998.

Hancock, Emily. *The Girl Within*. New York: Dutton, 1989.

Harris, Anita. "Generation (Se)X." *Talking Up: Young Women's Take on Feminism*. Ed. Rosamund Else-Mitchell. Melbourne, Australia: Spinifex. 79-92.

Hartman, Geoffrey. *Saving the Text*. Baltimore: Johns Hopkins University Press, 1980.

Heart, Mikaya. *When the Earth Moves: Women and Orgasm*. New York: Celestial Arts, 1998.

Heilbrun, Carolyn. *Reinventing Womanhood*. New York: Norton, 1979.

———. *Writing a Woman's Life*. New York: Ballantine, 1988.

Heywood, Leslie and Jennifer Drake, eds. *Third Wave Agenda: Being*

Feminism, Doing Feminism. Minneapolis: University of Minnesota Press, 1997.

Hirschman, Linda R. and Jane E. Larson. *Hard Bargains: The Politics of Sex.* Oxford: Oxford University Press, 1998.

Hollibaugh, Amber. "Desire for the Future: Radical Hope in Passion and Pleasure." *Pleasure and Danger: Exploring Female Sexuality.* Ed. Carole Vance. Boston: Routeledge, 1984. 401-10.

hooks, bell. *Feminist Is for Everybody.* Boston: South End Press, 2000.

——. *Feminist Theory: From Margin to Center.* Boston: South End Press, 1984.

——. *Outlaw Culture.* New York: Routledge, 1994.

——. *Wounds of Passion: A Writing Life.* New York: Henry Holt, 1997.

Hyman, Jane Wegscheider. *Women Living with Self-Injury.* Philadelphia: Temple University Press, 1999.

Jackson, Stevi and Sue Scott, eds. *Feminism & Sexuality: A Reader.* New York: Columbia University Press, 1996.

Jeffreys, Sheila. *The Lesbian Heresy.* New York: Spinifex Press, 1994.

——. *Anticlimax.* London: Women's Press, 1990.

Karp, Marcelle and Debbie Stoller, eds. *The Bust Guide to the New Girl Order.* New York: Penguin Books, 1999.

Kettlewell, Caroline. *Skin Game: A Memoir.* New York: St. Martin's Press, 1999.

Kipnis, Laura. *Bound and Gagged: Pornography and the Politics of Fantasy in America.* New York: Grove Press, 1996.

——. *Ecstasy Unlimited: On Sex, Capital, Gender, and Aesthetics.* Minneapolis: University of Minnesota Press, 1993.

Kiss & Tell. *Her Tongue on My Theory: Images, Essays and Fantasies.* Vancouver: Press Gang Publishers, 1994.

Kristeva, Julia. *Powers of Horror.* New York: Columbia University Press, 1982.

Lacan, Jacques. *The Four Fundamental Concepts of Psycho-Analysis.* Ed. Jacques-Alain Miller and trans. Alan Sheridan. New York: W.W. Norton & Company, 1981.

Laclau, Ernesto, and Chantal Mouffe. *Hegemony and Socialist*

Bibliography

Strategy. London: Verso, 1985.

Ladas, Alice Kahn, Beverly Whipple and John D. Perry. *The G-Spot.* New York: Dell Publishing Company, 1983.

Laqueur, Thomas. *Making Sex: Body and Gender from the Greeks to Freud.* Cambridge: Harvard University Press, 1990.

Lehrman, Karen. "Feminism & the New Courtship." *Cosmopolitan* 218.1 (1995): 186-91.

Leigh, Carol. "The Continuing Saga of Scarlot Harlot I." *Sex Work: Writings by Women in the Sex Industry.* Ed. Frederique Delacoste and Priscilla Alexander. Pittsburgh and San Francisco: Cleis Press, 1998. 32-34.

Levenkron, Steven. *Cutting: Understanding and Overcoming Self-Mutilation.* New York: Norton, 1998.

Levine, Judith, ed. *My Enemy, My Love: Man-Hating and Ambivalence in Women's Lives.* New York: Doubleday, 1992.

Longman, Jere. *The Girls of Summer: The U.S. Women's Soccer Team and How it Changed the World.* New York: HarperCollins, 2000.

MacKinnon, Catherine. *Feminism Unmodified: Discourses on Life and Law.* Cambridge and London: Harvard University Press, 1987.

——. *Only Words.* Cambridge: Harvard University Press, 1996.

Maglin, Nan Bauer and Donna Perry. *"Bad Girls"/"Good Girls": Women, Sex & Power in the Nineties.* New Brunswick: Rutgers University Press, 1996.

Mandle, Joan D. *Can We Wear Our Pearls and Still Be Feminists?: Memoirs of a Campus Struggle.* Colombia: University of Missouri Press, 2000.

Marcus, Steven. *The Other Victorians: A Study of Sexuality and Pornography in Mid-Nineteenth Century England.* New York: Basic Books.

McDonald, Mary G., ed. *Reading Sport: Critical Essays on Power and Representation.* Boston: Northeastern University Press, 2000.

Millett, Kate. *Sexual Politics.* Garden City: Doubleday, 1970.

Minnich, Elizabeth Kamarck. "Feminist Attacks on Feminism: Patriarchy's Prodigal Daughter." *Feminist Studies* 24.1 (1998): 159-75.

Morrison, Toni. *Paradise.* New York: A.A. Knopf, 1998.

Muscio, Inga. *Cunt: A Declaration of Independence.* Seattle: Seal, 1998.

Nagle, Jill, ed. *Whores and Other Feminists.* New York: Routledge, 1997.

Nestle, Joan. "The Femme Question." *The Persistent Desire: A Femm-Butch Reader.* New York: Alyson, 1992. 138-46.

———. "My Mother Liked to Fuck." *A Restricted Country.* New York: Firebrand, 1987. 120-22.

Newitz, Annalee, et. al. "Masculinity Without Men: Women Reconciling Feminism and Male Identification." *Third Wave Agenda.* Eds. Leslie Heywood and Jennifer Drake. Minneapolis: University of Minnesota Press, 1997.

Orenstein, Peggy. *Flux: Women on Sex, Work, Love, Kids, and Life in a Half-Changed World.* New York: Doubleday, 2000.

Palac, Lisa. *The Edge of the Bed: How Dirty Pictures Changed My Life.* Boston: Little, Brown and Co., 1998.

Panati, Charles. *Sexy Origins and Intimate Things.* New York: Penguin, 1998.

Parker, Andrew and Eve Kosofsky Sedgwick, eds. *Performativity and Performance.* New York: Routledge, 1995.

Payne, Patricia. *Sex Tips from a Dominatrix.* New York: Regan Books, 1999.

Pendleton, Eva. "Love for Sale: Queering Heterosexuality." *Whores and Other Feminists.* Ed. Jill Nagle. New York: Routledge, 1997. 73-82.

Penley, Constance and Sharon Willis. *Male Trouble.* Minneapolis: University of Minnesota Press, 1993.

Pipher, Mary. *Reviving Ophelia: Saving the Selves of Adolescent Girls.* New York: Ballantine, 1994.

Platt, Arthur, trans., J.A. Smith, and W.D. Ross, eds. *The Complete Works of Aristotle.* Oxford: The Claredon Press, 1912.

Queen, Carol. *Pomosexuals.* San Francisco: Cleis Press, 1997.

———. *Real Live Nude Girl: Chronicles of Sex Positive Culture.* San Francisco: Cleis Press, 1997.

———. "Sex Radical Politics, Sex-Positive Feminist Thought, and Whore Stigma." *Whores and Other Feminists*. Ed. Jill Nagle. New York and London: Routledge, 1997. 125-135.

Ramazanogle, Caroline. "Love and the Politics of Heterosexuality." *Heterosexuality: A Feminism & Psychology Reader*. London: Sage, 1993.

Rhode, Deborah L. *Speaking of Sex: The Denial of Gender Inequality*. Cambridge: Harvard University Press, 1997.

Richardson, Diane. "Heterosexuality and Social Theory." *Theorizing Heterosexuality: Telling it Straight*. Ed. Diane Richardson. Buckingham: Open University Press, 1996. 161-177.

Roiphe, Katie. *The Morning After*. Boston: Little, Brown and Co., 1994.

Rubina, Gayle. "Thinking Sex: Notes for a Radical Theory of Politics of Sexuality." *Pleasure and Danger: Exploring Female Sexuality*. Boston: Routledge, 1984. 267-319.

Sarton, Mary. *Journal of Solitude*. New York: W.W. Norton, 1973.

Schneiderman, Stuart ed. and trans. *Returning to Freud: Clinical Psychoanalysis in the School of Lacan*. New Haven: Yale University Press, 1980.

Sedgwick, Eve Kosofsky. *A Dialogue on Love*. Boston: Beacon Press, 2000.

Segal, Lynne. *Straight Sex: Rethinking the Politics of Pleasure*. London: Virago, 1994.

Skeggs, Beverly. *Formations of Class and Gender: Becoming Respectable*. Thousand Oaks: Sage, 1997.

Snitow, Anne, Christine Stansell, and Sharon Thompson, eds. *Powers of Desire: The Politics of Sexuality*. New York: Monthly Review Press, 1983.

St. James, Margo. "The Reclamation of Whores." *Good Girls/Bad Girls: Feminists and Sex Trade Workers Face to Face*. Ed. Laurie Bell. Toronto: Seal Press, 1987. 81-87.

Stoltenberg, John. *Refusing to Be a Man: Essays on Sex and Justice*. Portland: Breitenbush Books, 1989.

Strong, Marilee. *A Bright Red Scream*. New York: Penguin Putnam, 1998.

Ussher, Jane. *Fantasies of Femininity: Reframing the Boundaries of Sex*. New Brunswick: Rutgers University Press, 1992.

Vance, Carole, ed. *Pleasure and Danger: Exploring Female Sexuality*. Boston: Routledge, 1984.

Von Krafft-Ebing, Richard. *Psychopathia Sexualis*. New York: Bloat Books, 1999.

Walker, Rebecca. "Lusting for Freedom." *Listen Up: Voices from the Next Feminist Generation*. Ed. Barbara Findlen. Seattle: Seal Press, 1995. 95-101.

———, ed. *To Be Real: Telling the Truth and Changing the Face of Feminism*. New York: Anchor Books, 1995.

Warner, Michael. *The Trouble with Normal: Sex, Politics, and the Ethics of Queer Life*. New York: Free, 1999.

Weise, Elizabeth Reba. "Bisexuality, *The Rocky Horror Picture Show*, and Me." *Bi Any Other Name: Bisexual People Speak Out*. Eds. Loraine Hutchins and Lani Kaahumanu. Los Angeles: Alyson, 1991. 134-39.

Willis, Ellen. *No More Nice Girls: Countercultural Essays*. Hanover: Wesleyan University Press, 1992.

Wilkinson, Sue and Celia Kitzinger. *Heterosexuality: A Feminism & Psychology Reader*. London: Sage, 1993.

Wolf, Naomi. *Promiscuities: The Secret Struggle for Womanhood*. New York: Random House, 1997.

Woodward, Kathleen, ed. *Theories of Contemporary Culture*. Bloomington: Indiana University Press, 1995.

Wurtzel, Elizabeth. *Bitch: In Praise of Difficult Women*. New York: Doubleday, 1998.

Zarrilli, Phillip, ed. *Acting [Re]Considered: Theories and Practices*. London: Routledge, 1994.

Zizek, Slavoj. *The Sublime Object of Ideology and Tarrying with the Negative*. New York: Verso, 1989.

Contributors

P A U L A   A U S T I N, born in Guyana, South America, came up in the subways of New York City; now thirty-three, she lives in Durham, North Carolina. For the last ten years, she has been a literacy teacher, trainer, and advocate. Currently, she works as the executive director of the North Carolina Lambda Youth Network—a lesbian, gay, bisexual, transgender youth organizing and leadership organization—and is pursuing a master's degree in education at North Central Carolina University. "I Learned from the Best" is a sort of sequel to her essay on femme lesbianism, which appeared ten years ago in *The Persistent Desire: a Femme-Butch Reader*.

S H A N N O N   B E L L is the author of *Reading, Writing and Rewriting the Prostitute Body* (1994), *Whore Carnival* (1995), and co-author of *Bad Attitudes on Trial* (1997). Her work continues to mix feminism, philosophy, and pornography in a form she calls *pornosophy* or *fast feminism*. A member of the Political Science Department at York University, Toronto, Canada, she teaches postmodern theory, classical political theory, psychoanalytic theory, and feminist theory.

CHRIS DALEY is pursuing her Ph.D. in twentieth century literature at the City University of New York Graduate Center. Her previous incarnations include Sunset Boulevard cocktail waitress, script doctor, and lingerie peddler. She lives in Brooklyn and is a founding member of the pub quiz champions the Filthy Whores. She has published fiction as well as criticism in various collections and online journals. Her most recent work focuses on the relationship of the body and technology in speculative fiction by women of color.

CAITLIN FISHER is an assistant professor of Fine Arts and Cultural Studies at York University, Toronto, Canada. Research interests include hypertext, feminist theory, and narratives about childhood. Her longstanding interest in integrating autobiographical and critical writing is finding an outlet these days in the Stern Writing Mistresses collective, based in Toronto, where she writes *all the time* about desire and girlhood.

KATHERINE FRANK received her doctorate in Cultural Anthropology from Duke University and teaches anthropology and feminist theory at the College of the Atlantic in Maine. Her research focuses on sexuality, gender, commodification, and fantasy, and she is currently completing a book based on an ethnographic investigation of male customers' use of strip clubs, titled *Private Dancers, Public Fantasies*. In addition to her academic publications and interests, she also writes short fiction.

JANE GALLOP teaches at the University of Wisconsin—Milwaukee. She is the author of a number of books including *Thinking Through the Body* and *Feminist Accused of Sexual Harassment*. She is currently completing *Anecdotal Theory* to be published in 2002 by Duke University Press.

Contributors

LESLIE HEYWOOD is an associate professor of English & Cultural Studies at the State University of New York, Binghamton. Her recent works include the memoir, *Pretty Good for a Girl: An Athlete's Story*, and the critical monograph, *Bodymakers: A Cultural Anatomy of Women's Bodybuilding*. Her next project, *Built to Win: The Rise of the Female Athlete as Cultural Icon*, is scheduled to be published in 2002. Nationally ranked eleventh in her weight class for the bench press, she has been powerlifting competitively for five years, and was recently elected a trustee to the Women's Sports Foundation.

KATINKA HOOIJER is head voluptuary of the group Feminists for Fornication and is also quite the talented waitress. She can persuade even the most virginal of sushi eaters to indulge in raw urchin eggs. Katinka attempts graduate school on a regular basis and pushes porn at the University of Wisconsin in Milwaukee where she teaches a course in feminist rhetoric and pornography. Burning vulvas are her not-so-secret obsession and she is working on an anthology of stories featuring flaming lips and fast cars. Send your hot rod sex stories to katinka@uwm.edu.

MERRI LISA JOHNSON teaches composition at the State University of West Georgia. Her work has appeared in *Women's Writing: A Literary Magazine By & For Women* (http://www.womenwriters.net), *Scarlet Letters: A Journal of Femmerotica* (http://www.scarletletters.com), *Moxie: A Magazine for Women Who Dare*, and, strangely enough, the *Henry James Review*. She will refrain from mentioning her *shih tzu* companion, Millie, since she explicitly outlawed references to pets in contributor bios.

KARI KESLER is a self-proclaimed third wave lesbian sex radical feminist, currently completing a master's degree in Women's Studies at Texas Woman's University. Her research interests include sexuality, queer studies, Latin American women's issues, and community organizing. She lives in Denton, Texas, but is planning to run quickly back to the safe haven of Seattle upon graduation.

JENNIFER LUTZENBERGER is a Ph.D. candidate at the State University of New York at Binghamton researching resistant literature and teaching methods. She is a member of the Methodologies for Resistant Negotiation Working group and a coeditor of the journal *Radical Teacher*. She is also a published poet, a martial artist, a knitter and seamstress of some renown, and a foul-mouthed hard-scrabble champion of justice and right.

BECKY MCLAUGHLIN is an assistant professor of English at the University of South Alabama, where she has taught courses on psychoanalysis and feminism, modern and contemporary poetry, world literature and postcolonial theory. She has written on perversion and paranoia in the works of Angela Carter; feminine jouissance and the gaze in the poetry of Amy Lowell; and fashion and fetishism in Restoration comedy. She is currently putting together a collection of essays, titled *Big Sex*, that explores how academic institutions as the big Other(s) shape and/or influence sexual identity and practices.

PATRICIA PAYETTE is completing her Ph.D. in English at Michigan State University. Her research focuses on the ways in which *Jane Eyre* influences the work of twentieth-century ethnic women writers. She currently lives in East Lansing, Michigan, with her husband Ed and her daughter Molly.

KIRSTEN PULLEN recieved her Ph.D. from the University of Wisconsin at Madison. Her dissertation, "Performing Prostitution: Agency and Discourse, Actresses and Whores," looks at significant moments in the discursive formation of the prostitute as actress. She has contributed a chapter to *Web.Studies: Rewiring Media Studies for the Digital Age* edited by David Gauntlett and published by Arnold Press. She gratefully acknowledges Jessica Berson, Josh Heuman, Lisa Johnson, Ann Linden, Jami Moss, and Lisa Yaszek, whose insightful comments significantly shaped this essay.

GEOFFREY SAUNDERS SCHRAMM is a doctoral candidate in English at the University of Maryland, College Park. In addition to completing his dissertation entitled "Man Enough: Male Same-Sex Desire and Fraternity in the American Renaissance," Schramm currently works as an editorial assistant for the *Classroom Electric: Dickinson, Whitman and American Culture*, a project member of the Dickinson Electronic Archives, and as a webmaster for the National Endowment for the Humanities' "My History Is America's History" project. While it has been almost two decades since he portrayed a member of the Von Trapp family (when he was madly in love with the boy who played his older brother), he still has a thing for clothing that resembles Austrian draperies.

L I S A Z . S I G E L received her Ph.D. in history from Carnegie Mellon University. She teaches history and gender studies at Millsaps College and Depaul University. Her book *Governing Pleasures: Pornography and Social Change in England,* 1815-1915 has recently been published by Rutgers University Press.

S A R A H S M I T H is a women's studies graduate student at Ohio State University. Research interests include gender representation, consumerism, and postmodern feminist theory. Along with her partner Deb, Ms. Smith owns and operates The Chrysalis, a sex-positive sex toy business out of Columbus Ohio (http://www.chrysalisonline.com), and is a member of Sexline Information, a local nonprofit organization dedicated to providing sexual health information and referrals.